Enjoy

MW00462264

Wiles of the Devil

2016

Neillo Russell

10/23/16

Psalm 37:23

Newton's Riddle
BOOK ONE

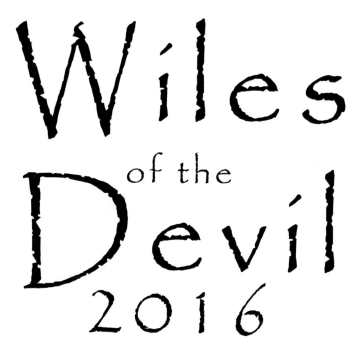

Wiles
of the
Devil
2016

SATAN'S 2016 PRESIDENTIAL ELECTION PLANS REVEALED!

NEILL G. RUSSELL
with Kelly Christenson

TATE PUBLISHING
AND ENTERPRISES, LLC

Wiles of the Devil 2016
Copyright © 2016 by Neill G. Russell. All rights reserved.

No part of this publication may be reproduced, stored in a retrieval system or transmitted in any way by any means, electronic, mechanical, photocopy, recording or otherwise without the prior permission of the author except as provided by USA copyright law.

This novel is a work of fiction. Names, descriptions, entities, and incidents included in the story are products of the author's imagination. Any resemblance to actual persons, events, and entities is entirely coincidental.

The opinions expressed by the author are not necessarily those of Tate Publishing, LLC.

Published by Tate Publishing & Enterprises, LLC
127 E. Trade Center Terrace | Mustang, Oklahoma 73064 USA
1.888.361.9473 | www.tatepublishing.com

Tate Publishing is committed to excellence in the publishing industry. The company reflects the philosophy established by the founders, based on Psalm 68:11,
"The Lord gave the word and great was the company of those who published it."

Book design copyright © 2016 by Tate Publishing, LLC. All rights reserved.
Cover design by Bill Francis Peralta
Interior design by Richell Balansag

Published in the United States of America

ISBN: 978-1-68301-479-9
Fiction / Religious
16.01.27

I dedicate this book to four uniquely gifted women, all of whom God has divinely placed in my life.

To the wife of my youth, Cindy
(October 26, 1954–November 16, 2009)

Your life was a living example of God's grace and unconditional love. I am anxiously anticipating that future moment when the last trumpet sounds and our bodies are raised incorruptible. What a phenomenal future we have in store, Cindy, serving God together once more in eternity, forever and ever!

To the wife of my present and future, Mary Ann

What a gift you are from God! Amid my darkest hours, He alone directed my path to a widowed neighbor across the street, a devoted companion who has brought meaning and joy back into my life. Together, we will serve the Lord into the future and show His love to all who cross our path.

To my divinely appointed ninety-four-year-old editor, Clarice (Kelly) Christenson

Needless to say, Kelly Girl, God is so smart! He foreknew from the beginning of time that I would need someone with your grounded grammatical skills. (Kelly was a teacher/librarian in Anchorage, Alaska, for over thirty years.) Through our united prayers, the Holy Spirit gave her guidance, direction, and discernment in assisting me in the completion of this important, monumental task.

To my beautiful eighty-two-year-old mother, Selma Russell

Mother, you gave me life, and for the past sixty-two years, your presence in my life has provided me a living example of God's gift of unconditional love! Thank you, Mom!

Foreword

Author Neill G. Russell has written another blockbuster book, precisely applicable to where we are in human history today.

With great skill and insight, Russell reveals behind-the-scenes activities of the dark spiritual forces opposing God's people and plan. These forces—actually demons—have personal names, and they are active in plotting and planning their opposition.

The centerpiece of this story is Israel, which is the centerpiece of history. Satan and his minions hate Israel and want to destroy that nation, thwarting God's plan for the return of our Messiah, Jesus. But God's people are aware of their evil and take bold action against it. This conflict is the climax of the book.

An intriguing aspect of this book is how the events described in it closely parallel current world conditions. You will be reading near-term history in advance.

Neill G. Russell does an amazing job in describing accurate, technical details in his narrative, aptly including military terminology and geopolitical matters.

The scenario described in the book is almost upon us. May we all be ready, and may God bless and protect us.

James Bramlett
Lt. Col., USAF (Ret.)
Former vice president of CBN Ministries

Prologue

"Put on the whole armor of God that you may be able to stand against the wiles of the devil."

~ Ephesians 6:11 (NKJV)

Most people wrestle their entire lives with the question of whether they have free will. Do they have control over their lives, or does life have a pre-ordained path already chosen for each individual? This very question was posed in one of my all-time favorite movies—Forrest Gump. The 1994 Academy Award winning movie begins with a nondescript white feather drifting through the opening sequence, ultimately landing at Forrest Gump's feet. While waiting for a city bus, he talks with others nearby. Without any explanation or dialogue, he picks up the feather and carefully places it in a Curious George book, which he puts into his briefcase. The feather is never mentioned, nor does it play any part in the entire two and a half hour movie until the very end.

At the end of the movie, many years have passed since the day Forrest Gump first encountered the drifting feather. While waiting for the school bus with his young son, Forrest reopens the same Curious George book, which held the compressed feather so many years. Exposed to the wind, the feather catches a breeze and takes flight, gently drifting up into the air as it continues once again on its hapless journey through space and time. This final scene resonated a reflective statement Forrest Gump had made when he pondered life's big questions at his wife's gravesite.

"I don't know if we each have a destiny, or if we're all just floating around accidental-like on a breeze."

Allow me to introduce myself. I am Joveniel, an angel, a created spiritual being sent to earth on a specific assignment by the Lord Most High. You may think it strange that angels watch human movies, but we do. Little do humans realize, or even comprehend, the clandestine roles we spiritual entities play in their lives and surroundings. Humans are totally unaware that there is an unseen world at work all around them—an active spiritual dimension existing just beyond the range of a mortal's limited senses. We spirits are eternal beings and, as such, are not constrained by the natural world's limits of space, energy, matter or time. Unless God authorizes angels to do otherwise, our roles are to remain subtle and totally imperceptible to a mortal's finite intellect.

At the moment of birth, humans are assigned spirits. One is a ministering angel, who is charged by the Creator to protect a human along a predestined path leading toward a successful fulfillment of God's plan for his or her life in this world, and eternal salvation in the next. The other is a spiritual malefactor appointed by Satan, also known as the devil—the adversary of God. These grotesque demonic apparitions are equipped by the powers of Hell with an arsenal of lies and deceit intended to lead their deceived humans down a path of destruction that culminates in death and everlasting separation from God.

What humans fail to realize is that the spoken Word of God activates ministering angels into action. This fact is clearly stated in chapter one, verse 14 of the Book of Hebrews: "Are they not all ministering spirits, sent forth to minister for them who shall be heirs for salvation?" Only when our assigned human gives sound to the promises found in God's Word can we act. For this reason, we listen very carefully to what our assigned humans say. We are also very aware that our roles are limited to assist only those who have been spiritually marked by God as heirs unto salvation. It is only by the wisdom of God's divine choice that humans are to be solely responsible for the consequences of their own self-willed decisions and, ultimately, their own destinies.

Though the story you are about to read has the appearance of fiction, let me assure you, it is not. No other book allows its readers to peer into the reality of an active spiritual realm where angels and demons clandestinely interact in the lives of their assigned humans. You will soon realize that characters and accounts recorded in this book are just as real to you as the actual people and events that you assign to them. And though my specific assignment will not be revealed until later in this story, nevertheless, I have been charged by the Lord Most High with the awesome task of exposing to this spiritually deceived world the wiles of the devil.

Tuesday, July 27th, 2004
11:09 p.m. Eastern Time
The Democratic National Convention
The Fleet Center Arena
Boston, Massachusetts

Two minutes before the speech of a lifetime he stood unaccompanied, separated from the crowd beyond by a thick blue curtain. After conducting a whirlwind of morning interviews, his voice had weakened, but that was not his main concern. It was not even the thought of standing alone in front of all those people and TV cameras that bothered him. For the past two days, one prevailing challenge troubled Rashid Jabbar Harris more than any other. *Would I be able to take my 25-minute prepared speech and say everything I want to say to the world in the required time limit of 17 minutes?* Campaign staffers had encouraged Harris to highlight his "fresh voice" in the speech. He wrote a first draft, exploiting his life story to cast himself as the ultimate Washington outsider—the grandson of a goat herder, the son of a domestic servant. He added "I was a skinny kid with a long funny name."

11

Harris steadied himself one final time while Senator Mike Corbin of Illinois, the chosen moderator for the 2004 Democratic National Convention, introduced him as the convention's keynote speaker. Then he stepped onstage. He approached the lectern a virtual nobody in the world of national politics, unproven, never having held a federal office. This Illinois state senator, who four years earlier had been unable to obtain a floor pass to the Los Angeles Democratic Convention, walked out to see over 7,000 people crammed onto the floor of Boston's Fleet Center Arena, all waving blue signs imprinted with his name. Rashid Jabbar Harris responded to the cheers of the standing only crowd by raising his right hand in a triumphant entry. He shook Corbin's hand, and then hugged him. Corbin walked to the side of the stage and stood next to Harris' elated wife, Micalyn. Corbin then looked back over his shoulder, as if hesitant to leave Harris alone.

Intently watching these same proceedings from the high vantage point of the upper balcony, located directly behind the arena stage were two towering giants. Unseen by mortal eyes, Yahriel, the taller of two observers, was a bronze-skinned being dressed in a brilliant white garment held securely at his waist by a golden belt. The other, Muriel, was garbed as a mighty warrior. A highly polished golden breastplate protected his muscular torso and a golden belt girded his waist with an attached golden sword suspended against his burley thighs.

Archangels, both of the highest heavenly order, Yahriel was charged by His Creator with the title of Prince of Prophetic Wisdom and Worldly Affairs. He had full knowledge of the present national and international earthly affairs and how they're aligned with our Lord's prophetic plans. Yahriel's angels are stationed in every nation, every capitol, and every city on earth.

Even by angelic standards, Muriel was exceedingly handsome. He was cropped with curly brown hair, his complexion dark olive, his eyes a velvet brown, his lips cupid-shaped, and he bore a strong, chiseled chin. Known also by those under his command as the Prince of God's Truth, Muriel was charged by his Creator to make sure that the Lord's

Truth was preached and communicated throughout the world in these End Times.

Looking down at the boisterous crowd, Yahriel commented, "It never ceases to amaze me how easily deceived these mortals are."

"Especially this group of deceived mortals," Muriel responded with a somber nod. "I've listen carefully to their speeches and looked deeply within their hearts. For the majority, they've made no room for God in their lives. They only trust in themselves." Muriel continued, "These are the very ones identified in God's Word as double-minded doubters, lacking wisdom, unstable in all that they do."

"By rejecting God's Truth," Yahriel asserted, "little do they know that every word they speak and every decision they make is corrupted by their own self-serving agendas for power, greed and control."

The two archangels were not the only supernatural beings present at tonight's convention. Mingled among the unsuspecting mortals gathered on the arena floor were scores of grotesque apparitions of all shapes and hierarchical sizes. Some appeared almost reptilian in stature with clawed appendages and bodies covered from head to toe with scaly yellowish skin. Still others retained much of their former angelic appearance. Distinguished only by their yellowish skin tone and bright yellow eyes, these high-ranking demonic princes were assigned the specific task of nurturing and fashioning their assigned human hosts for leadership roles of great influence. They all joined in unison with the deafening roar of thousands of unsuspecting humans standing to introduce a virtually unknown to the world's political stage, Satan's human of choice to lead America to its ultimate demise, Rashid Jabbar Harris.

Harris: "Thank you so much. Thank you."
(APPLAUSE)
"Thank you. Thank you so much. Thank you so much."
(APPLAUSE)
"Thank you, Mike Corbin." Harris turned one last time to his left to acknowledge the moderator for the 2004 Democratic National Convention. "You make us all proud." Then facing his

worldwide audience, the state senator from Illinois opened his keynote speech to another rousing applause.

"On behalf of the great state of Illinois…

(APPLAUSE)

… crossroads of a nation, land of Lincoln, let me express my deep gratitude for the privilege of addressing this convention. This is a significant honor for me because, let's face it, my presence on this stage is somewhat unlikely. My father was a foreign student, born and raised in a small village in Kenya. He grew up herding goats, went to school in a tin- roof shack, and his father, my grandfather, was a cook, a domestic servant to the British. But my grandfather had loftier dreams for his son. Through hard work and perseverance, my father received a scholarship to study in a magical place—America, a place that was a beacon of freedom and opportunity to many who had come before him.

(APPLAUSE)

"While studying here, my father met my mother. She was born in a town on the other side of the world in a state called Kansas.

(APPLAUSE)

"Her father worked on oilrigs and farms through most of the depression. The day after Pearl Harbor, my grandfather signed up for duty, joined Patton's army, and marched across Europe. Back home my grandmother raised a baby while working on a bomber assembly line. After the war, they studied under the GI Bill, bought a house through FHA, and later moved all the way to Hawaii in search of opportunity.

(APPLAUSE)

"They had big dreams for their daughter, a common dream born of two continents. My parents shared not only an improbable love; they shared an abiding faith in the possibilities of this nation. They gave me an Arabic name, Rashid Jabbar, meaning, "guided by Almighty God," believing that in a tolerant America, your name was no barrier to success."

(APPLAUSE)

"They imagined that I would go to the best schools in the land, even though they weren't rich, because in a generous America you don't have to be rich to achieve your potential. They are both gone now, and yet I know that, on this night, they are looking down on me with great pride. I stand here today, grateful for the diversity of my heritage, aware that my parents' dream lives on in my two precious daughters. I stand here knowing that my story is a part of a larger American story, that I owe a debt to all who came before me, and that in no other country on Earth would my story even be possible."

"I must commend Zagam," Muriel commented, staring at the gloating demonic prince who accompanied his assigned human host, Rashid Jabbar Harris, onto center stage.

"Indeed," Yahriel nodded in response. "It appears that his prodigy is ready."

"Groomed to perfection," Muriel scoffed. "Harris appears as a bright, articulate and genial fellow, who can energetically promote the leftist ideals of healing the racial and partisan divides that exist in America today."

"I also see that Zagam has invited some of his associates here as well. Look at them gloating." Yahriel directed his angelic companion's attention to the eleven demonic princes standing in various privileged locations throughout the capacity-filled arena.

One by one, Yahriel, the archangel endowed by his Creator with exceptional wisdom and foreknowledge of worldly affairs, presented Muriel with an orderly progression of Harris's formative guides, both human and demon alike. "It has taken over forty-three years, but each has played an intricate role in crafting Rashid Jabbar Harris's character into a person who espouses the same radical leftist ideals as his godless mentors."

"What about him?" Muriel questioned, directing his companion's attention to a particularly handsome demonic prince standing near the far right end of the stage.

"A very good place for us to start,"Yahriel acknowledged. "His name is Harborym and his specialty is saturating the lives of his assigned human hosts with the lying virtues of liberalism and communism. In 1942, Zagam assigned Harborym to be the sole mentor to a young girl born in the state of Kansas with the unusual name of Stanley Ann Morris. Zagam selected Morris because her parents, Stanley and Kathleen Morris, were a perfect match for Zagam's plan, a plan to have America's first black president nurtured in a household where liberal and communistic ideals were readily accepted."

"What about Harris's father? What role did he play in his son's life?"

"Good question! Harborym made sure that Rashid Jabbar Harris would never have just one father figure in his life, but several."

"Several?" Muriel questioned with a puzzled look. "Interesting. Please continue."

"According to his official birth records, Rashid Jabbar Harris was born in Hawaii on August 4ᵗʰ, 1961, the son of a foreign exchange student, a Kenyan national named Rashid Jabbar Isweire, and a seventeen year old American mother named Stanley Ann Morris."

"So Isweire was Harris's biological father?"

"No, Stanley Ann Morris was already pregnant by another black whose name was Franklin Harris at the time of her marriage to Isweire in February of 1962. When the child was one year old, Rashid Jabbar Isweire Sr. left his family in Hawaii to pursue a Ph.D. in economics at Harvard University, and never saw his son again."

Muriel looked puzzled. "So Stanley Ann Morris married Franklin Harris?"

"No," Yahriel replied with a smile. "Stanley Ann divorced Isweire in 1962 and started dating another foreign exchange student from Indonesia named Kolo Kalapebo, who she met while taking classes at the University of Hawaii. After obtaining her degree in the field of anthropology from the University of Hawaii in 1967, Stanley Ann Morris married Kolo Kalapebo and along with her then six-year-old son, Rashid, whose name was later changed to Rashid Kalapebo, moved to her husband's homeland of Indonesia."

"And Harborym went along with them to Indonesia?"

"That was all part of Zagam's plan. He arranged for Stanley Ann Morris to meet and marry the Indonesian, Kolo Kalapebo. It was Zagam's scheme all along for young Rashid to be fully immersed in the Indonesian culture. For the next two years, while living with his parents in the outskirts of the capital city of Jakarta, Harborym filled young Rashid's mind with visions of a world in which the white western nations became prosperous by oppressing and exploiting the non-white, non-western nations."

"Okay," but when did Rashid's last name get changed to Harris?"

"I believe the answer to your question, Muriel, is presently standing just opposite of us," Yahriel replied, pointing his finger at a lone dark skinned demon waving at him from the adjacent side of the upper balcony.

"Who is he?"

"His name is Daeva, known as the demonic prince of false gods and false doctrines." He was specifically assigned by Zagam to mentor Rashid throughout his impressionable adolescent years starting at the age of ten when his mother sent him back to Hawaii to reside with his grandparents. It was then that Rashid's grandfather introduced him to a black man named Franklin Harris, who had a long career of anti-American, anti-white propaganda that included a stint as a member of the Communist Party. Harris was Rashid's mentor on race throughout his adolescent years, until Rashid left for college."

"So when did Rashid finally find out that Harris was his real biological father?"

"Again, it's all part of Zagam's plan. In the spring of 1971, a discouraged Stanley Ann Kalapebo left her husband, Kolo, behind in Indonesia and returned to Hawaii. She enrolled in a graduate program at the University of Hawaii to study cultural anthropology of the Indonesian people. That same year she filed for divorce against her husband Kolo and married Franklin Mitchell Harris, the father of her son, Rashid."

"Are any of Harris's parents and grandparents still alive?"

"Unfortunately, no. Like most of the deceived mortals in this arena, they made their decision long ago to live their lives apart from God's saving grace and accept the lies of the devil."

"Who were the rest of Harris mentors? Are they seated here today?"

"Some are, like Harris's hate-filled racist pastor, Jeremiah Wilson, seated in the front row along with his left winged political associate, the Reverend Jesse Jarrett," Yahriel acknowledged, "but most are probably at home watching Harris's speech on TV along with the rest of the world."

"Then who are the other eight demonic princes gathered here today?"

"You can really ask a lot of questions, Muriel. They are some of Zagam's best skilled princes selected to radicalize humans throughout their entire educational experiences and political careers."

For the next few minutes, Yahriel directed his companion's attention to the sequential mission of each of Rashid Jabbar Harris's human and demonic mentors starting first with his college professors who were prominently seated nearest their star pupil in the first and second rows.

"The progression of Harris's left-winger mentors continued as he went through Occidental College, Columbia University and the Harvard Law School. These included Professor John Dury, a well-known communist activist on the campus of Occidental College, professor Edward Sayer at Columbia, a spokesman for Palestinian terrorists, and professor Darrell Belt at the Harvard Law School, an advocate of the "critical race theory", a radical position that Harris fully embraces to this very day. When Harris started his political career by running for state office in Illinois, his campaign began with a fundraiser in the home of Jack Ayers, who had been a domestic terrorist who planted bombs in public places, including the Pentagon."

"I have one final question," Muriel stated. "Where did Rashid Jabbar Harris get the funding to not only put him through college and law school, but to place him on this stage below us?"

"Zagam!" Yahriel replied. "See that demonic prince standing in center aisle beside that well-dressed man?"

Muriel nodded in affirmation.

"That man's name is Vernon Garnett. His demonic mentor's name is Allahzad. Working together, they arranged for the Saudi prince Alaweed bin Talal, the 19ᵗʰ wealthiest man in the world, to totally fund not only Harris's entire education, but his political career as well.

"For what reason?" Muriel queried.

"To provide the funding to advance the Arab's main agenda in the United States of America," Yahriel replied.

"And what are the Arab's agenda?"

"To spread Islam to the ends of the earth."

Chapter One

"Be sober–be vigilant; because your adversary the devil walks about like a roaring lion, seeking whom he may devour."

~1 Peter 5: 8 (NKJV)

Twelve Years Later
Friday, October 26th, 2016
2:10 p.m.
Trinity Mills Christian Academy
Trinity Mills, Texas

At first glance, all appeared quite normal at the campus of Trinity Mills Christian Academy. Inside the sprawling brick structure, its front entrance adorned with a large stained-glass mosaic cross, sat 1,400 anxious middle through high school aged students, all awaiting the familiar tone of the dismissal bell announcing the start of a long awaited three-day weekend. Like any other typical day at this time, a dozen or so yellow school buses, all with motors running, lined the front parking lot only a short distance away from the school's main entrance. Scattered throughout the adjacent side parking lots were scores of anxious parents, some standing outside parked cars conversing with one another; others were waiting patiently inside their vehicles until 2:15 p.m., the exact moment when the daily adolescent assault on the school's parking lot would commence.

But just beyond the range of human perception, the scene at Trinity Mills Christian Academy was anything but normal. Countless scores of massive sword drawn warriors, some standing as tall as twelve feet, were strategically stationed throughout the large campus in assigned groups of seven. With only moments remaining before the dismissal bell sounded, their warrior leader, Kiel, known also by his legion army as the Demon Slayer, raised his massive hand and commanded time to stop. With human time temporarily placed on supernatural hold, Kiel gave his final directive to his warriors.

"I order each one of you to do one last, thorough search of your assigned area before I release the children."

Kiel's commanding voice, just beyond the detectable limits of human hearing, was loud enough to be heard by every single warrior positioned both inside and outside the large human complex.

Upon their leader's command, the teams of warriors, moving with lightning speed and fluid agility, sprang into immediate action. Their final mission was to seek out, find, and destroy tiny demons, some no larger than a spider, that may have concealed themselves in some of the most inconspicuous places possible to hide—inside student book bags, the underside of student desks, inside and under bathroom toilets and urinals—any place imaginable that could possibly conceal a creature, so imperceptibly minute that only those endowed with supersensitive abilities could possibly detect their presence.

This would make the warrior's fourth and final thorough search and destroy mission of the day. Arriving on campus unexpectedly just before the first lunch bell had sounded at 11 a.m., Kiel's warriors immediately assumed their assigned positions. Their plan of attack was facilitated by the fact that a team of seven angelic sentinels had already been assigned to provide an angelic hedge of protection around the entire 158 acre campus since it was first dedicated back in 1967. This team of seven was intimately familiar with every square foot of the Trinity Mills Christian Academy's campus. Their ever- present vigilance over the years had successfully kept any midlevel demonic activity from entering their school—the types of typical demonic behaviors such as *fighting, drugs, cursing, teen pregnancy,* and the blatant display of disrespect for authority that caused daily havoc in similar-sized public school campuses. It had been the low-ranking demons that had been a problem, not only at Trinity Mills Christian Academy, but also in other private Christian schools throughout the land. Due to their minuscule sizes, some no larger than a tiny bug, these highly elusive demons for the most part had gone totally undetected until their presence was made known by the overt problems they might have caused. These savvy little demons had devised a whole host of clever schemes to freely infiltrate the angels' protective barrier. Demons of infirmity had the easiest access. On any given day, scores of children, already infected at home by an entire host of demonic-related illnesses such as colds and flu, entered the campus, bringing with them totally undetected demons. Other low-ranking demons such as lying spirits, demons of envy and deceit, evaded the ever-watchful eyes of assigned sentinel angels by concealing themselves in children's book bags and jacket pockets.

Kiel's first raid of the day was highly successful, routing out and destroying well over a thousand carefully concealed demons. Those evil spirits were no match for the massive warrior angels in Kiel's army. Once discovered by an angel's keen eyesight, the tiny demons are instantly doomed to a stinging pierce from the warrior's razor sharp sword. All that remains of a demon's former presence after the lightning-fast swipe is a tiny puff of reddish brown smoke and the distinct stench of burning sulfur.

One by one, Kiel's team commanders began reporting in: "All is clear in the receiving area." "All is clear in the middle school." "All is clear in the high school." "All is clear in the cafeteria." "All is clear on the outside campus." Before lowering his mighty hand, Kiel turned his attention to Aniel, the commander of his own team of angelic warriors. "All is clear, Demon Slayer," declared Kiel's personal and most trusted comrade.

Kiel nodded in affirmation. Kiel was, as with all his fellow angelic warriors, a towering giant. A head topped by wavy golden brown hair

23

offset his handsome, well-formed, olive-toned face. Standing every bit of fifteen feet above the ground, he wore only a highly polished golden breastplate of protection over his brawny chest. A golden belt, supporting a blindingly golden sword, girded his sleek waist, and a brief white skirt covered his massive loins. While his angelic legions were busily conducting their final mission searching for more concealed demons, their leader bent down low to look at his human charge, a 16-year old human female named Sydni Graham, who was seated among her fellow human classmates in their 11th grade biology class.

All was now ready. Kiel lowered his hand, allowing human time to follow its naturally set course. The bell rang, announcing the end of another week of school.

The students emerged from the biology classrooom, and as soon as Sydni Graham steppped out into the crowded hall, an ecstatic group of nearly a dozen cheering classmates surrounded her.

"Sydni, girl, I can't believe it!" screamed a teary-eyed Becca Sowder. "You're going to be leaving us and moving into the White House!"

Sydni raised her hands above her head, attempting to quell her friend's over-exuberant emotions. "Girls, please!" she admonished with a smile. "I don't want you guys getting your hopes up too high just yet. The elections are still two weeks away, and as we all know, anything can happen by then!"

"Listen to me, Miss Sydni Graham," interjected Ashley Price in a strong Texas accent. "When it comes to predicting elections, my daddy's never wrong, and he said your father is a shoo-in to be the next President of the United States of America."

"That's right, Sydni," cut in Jocelyn Scott. "I've been on the Internet all day long, and let me tell you, missy, every single poll—Gallup, Neilson, Fox—you name it, has your dad on top by at least five percentage points over both Devoe and Berry. Get used to it, babe—come January, your new address is going to be 1600 Pennsylvania Ave, Washington D.C., and as your best friend, I expect a White House visitor's pass with my name and picture printed right on the front."

"What am I going to do with you guys?" Sydni laughed, throwing up both hands as a gesture of surrender.

Within mere minutes of the sounding of the dismissal bell, the Christian Academy's hallways and classrooms had emptied. Most of the students and teachers had already vacated the building, anxious to get an early start on their long weekend, the exception being student athletes remaining after school for practice and a group of about dozen girls standing in the hallway adjacent to the school's biology classroom.

"Sydni!" whispered Sarah Lawrence, attempting to redirect her friend's attention to point out a solitary figure standing alone at the end of the long empty hallway. "Don't look now, but I think your guardian angel is growing impatient."

"If heaven has angels that look like him, I am ready to go right now!" jokingly swooned 12th grader, Cara Brown.

"He is such a dream!" raved Ashley Price.

"Forget it ladies; Jerry is already taken. He's married to Sheila, and they have three kids: Tommy's 6, Ryan's 4 and Erika was 22 months old this past Wednesday," Sydni methodically announced to her awestruck friends. By now, they had all redirected their full attention in the direction of the handsome Secret Service agent assigned to protect Sydni Graham and standing about twenty feet away. "And by the stern look on his face, I think this would be a good time to say our goodbyes."

Before leaving, every girl in the circle of friends gave Sydni Graham, the celebrity amongst them, a big hug of support.

Friday, October 26th, 2016
2:35 p.m.
Trinity Mills Christian Academy
Trinity Mills, Texas

As the humans departed the building, each one going his separate way, two mighty angelic warriors carefully watched as Sydni Graham and the Secret Service agent assigned to protect her approached a dark gray vehicle with dark tinted windows parked immediately in front of the school.

"Is everything taken care of?" Kiel asked his trusted companion standing to his right.

"Completely!" Aniel declared. "Upon your orders, two teams of our best warriors have gone on ahead of us. Once the Grahams arrive home shortly after three o'clock today, we will have four teams of our warriors protecting their house, plus over a dozen human Secret Service agents as well."

Over the eons, Aniel had fought many a battle alongside fearless Kiel, but this time, standing almost shoulder-to-shoulder, he could sense an unexplained tension emulating out from his commanding general.

"What is it that is bothering you, Demon Slayer?"

Kiel glanced briefly at his friend before returning his full attention to the humans now entering the parked vehicle.

"You know me too well, Aniel," Kiel admitted. "Even though we have taken every necessary precaution, my intuition keeps telling me 'it's not enough.' I can just sense we've missed something, but what? We both know there is no way that Satan is going to allow a true believer to become President of the United States."

Jocelyn Scott's earlier comments about the national polling statistics proved to be absolutely correct. Every newspaper across the United States, from the local *Trinity Mills Review* to *USA Today*, had posted similar headlines printed boldly across the tops of their front pages: GRAHAM BY 5! With only two weeks remaining before the general presidential elections, the long shot, third-party candidate, Eliot Graham, born and raised in the small Dallas suburb of Trinity Mills, had just surpassed his two political rivals for the most powerful position on Earth…the President of the United States of America.

The local newspaper quotes in the *Trinity Mills Review* said it all:

"Wake me up; I must be dreaming."

"This could not be happening in Trinity Mills."

"The Almighty has spoken! Graham is God's man to lead America back to its destined course of being the world's number one military, financial, and most importantly, moral superpower."

Nowhere was the jubilation over the recent turn of events more evident than in the 1,500-member congregation of the Trinity Mills Baptist Church, the very church Eliot Graham presided over until he stepped down as pastor in the late 1980s. It was at that time that Dr. Graham decided to give up his pastoral reins in order to focus his full attention on a ministry he personally founded some ten years prior. His new ministry is now the most listened-to conservative radio broadcast in America, *American Values Hour.* Reaching an estimated twenty million listeners daily via 900 licensed radio outlets, Eliot Graham has dedicated every single program over the past thirty years to nurturing and defending family values and protecting what he views as the moral fabric of America.

Friday, October 26th, 2016
2:40 p.m.
Interstate 35 East
Trinity Mills, Texas

For sixteen-year-old Sydni Graham, the youngest of Eliot and Rosemary Graham's seven children, the fifteen-minute daily commute from Trinity Mills Christian Academy to the family's ten-acre estate built along the southern shores of Lake Lewisville was a time to escape from the strange new world that was rapidly closing in on her.

"And how is your day going so far?" inquired the driver of the Crown Victoria.

"Same ole', same ole', I guess," replied the totally disinterested backseat passenger, fumbling through her small Coach purse to locate the all-important lifeline of all teenagers, her cell phone.

"I just got word from the big boss," Agent Sterns announced. "Your parents' flight landed about an hour ago at DFW (Dallas-Fort Worth). Now, given the time of day, traffic and all, I wouldn't be a bit surprised that they may have already beaten us home."

"That's nice," commented Sydni in a nonchalant tone of voice.

"Don't you miss your parents?" the secret service agent inquired with a voice of concern. "I know your grandma's been taking good care of you, but your parents have been gone for over two weeks now on the campaign trail. Come on Sydni, I bet you miss them just a little bit by now?"

"Who said I didn't miss them?" Sydni Graham snapped back. "Let me tell you what, Jerry Sterns, I love my parents. My mom and dad are the best parents I could ever want."

"Then, tell me Miss Sydni," Sterns interjected, "why am I sensing all this tension all of a sudden?"

"If I tell you, you've got to swear to me, Jerry, this is just between you and me," Sydni demanded.

"I promise," agreed Agent Sterns, raising his right hand symbolically above the steering wheel as an act of gaining her confidence. "I hereby swear an oath, on my flawless record as a secret service agent for the United States government that whatever you tell me will not go beyond this car."

"Ok, I was born and raised in Trinity Mills. All of my friends and relatives live here. I don't want to leave Trinity Mills." Sydni confessed, with tears streaming her face. "Up until now, I never dreamed my dad had any chance of winning this election, but now...."

"I thought as much," Stern smiled in relief, looking back in his rear view mirror to give the teary-eyed teenager a reassuring wink. "Miss Sydni Graham, it's my professional opinion, and I've been doing this job for over 15 years now, that you'll make a great first daughter. And besides, your popularity among the teenage boys all across America is going to skyrocket to the moon and back!"

"I definitely know my father is not going to be in favor of that!" Sydni responded with a smile.

"You're such a hot b..... You make my thighs twitch. Every time I see your body, you make my eyes stitch...

"What the heck was that?" reeled a shocked Agent Sterns in response to the obscene blaring music pulsating outward from behind the driver's seat. "That sounds like Gangster Rap Crap Music to me!"

"It's just Jocelyn!" Sydni affirmed, instantly recognizing the digital name displayed on her cell phone. "Please, Jerry, don't tell my parents about the ring tone! Promise, I will change it back to its original sound before they get home."

"As long as you change it before we get home, your secret is totally safe with me." Jerry laughed, returning his full attention to the road ahead. "Go ahead and talk to your friend. We'll be home in about five minutes or so."

"Jocelyn, girl, what's the word?"

"You've got it!" Jocelyn quietly announced.

"When did you do it?" Sydni asked, toning her voice down to a whisper.

"Just a few minutes ago," Jocelyn proudly replied. "While you were hugging everybody in sight, I was able to sneak it into your book bag."

"Are you absolutely sure no one saw you do it?"

"Syd, honey, I purposely stood there until no one was looking. Then I made my move. You can keep it until after the elections. Just get it back to me sometime before Thanksgiving. I promised Becca she can read it after you were finished with it."

"Jocelyn Scott, you're such a good friend," Sydni affirmed, while at the same time carefully removing what appeared to be a rather thick bounded book from the confines of her book bag. The book had depicted on its cover what appeared to be two cuffed hands holding and extending outward a red ripened apple. "I can't wait to read this book!" Sydni excitedly whispered into her phone's receiver. "The cover says it all! It's as if I'm being enticed to bite into the forbidden fruit. It's just like you told me. The fruit represents Bella and her blood is forbidden to Edward. I think it is so cool to fall in love with a vampire. You know, Jocie, my parents would ground me forever if they knew I was reading this book!"

"Believe me, girlfriend, I know exactly where you're coming from." Jocelyn sighed in agreement. "It is so hard sometimes living the goodie-two-shoes life of a Christian teenager."

"Amen, my sister, I totally agree." Sydni quickly followed. "Boy, do I ever agree."

"Sydni, honey, just do what I did. Hide that book in a place where your parents would never think of looking."

"And I know just the place to hide it," Sydni whispered with devilish grin.

Kiel and Aniel were totally oblivious to the human's conversation going on inside the car. From their vantage point, sitting high on top the car's roof, their only concern was guarding the human occupants they were charged with protecting from external demonic attacks. But unbeknownst to their keen angelic senses, a potent enemy had already infiltrated their seemingly impenetrable barrier. Concealed within the confines of the female human's book bag, ingeniously embedded within the paper thin pages of a seemingly innocent romantic vampire novel, was planted a potent agent of death. So exceedingly powerful was the poison that this hideous spirit possessed, that one bite from its venomous fangs would cause its intended victim to suffer the most horrible and debilitating effects of an irreversible death.

Friday, October 26th, 2016
2:55 p.m.
Exit 12 Lake Park Road
15 miles North of Trinity Mills, Texas

"We're now rounding the bend for the home stretch, Miss Sydni," Agent Sterns announced in his best Texas accent, exiting the Crown Victoria off the interstate onto Lake Park Road. Glancing into his rearview mirror, the secret service agent smiled, noting his backseat passenger was too absorbed in text-messaging her numerous friends to respond to his comment. Before long, the government owned car turned onto Mockingbird Drive, a long narrow road lined on each side with weeping willow trees.

It was just about this time Agent Sterns received a very disturbing call.

"Uh oh!" Agent Sterns said with a voice of concern. "Don't look now, Miss Sydni, but we have visitors!"

To the dismay of both passenger and driver alike, Agent Sterns' mention of visitors was a gross understatement. The scene outside their vehicle windows appeared more reminiscent of a major protest held in a large city, not along some backcountry road in nowhere Texas. Literally hundreds of angry people, holding up banners and signs, lined both sides of the road that ended at a gated cul-de-sac protected by over a dozen Dallas County police.

"Who are all those people?"

"From my past experience with these matters, I believe you would call them protesters," replied Agent Sterns.

"Protesting what?"

"Well," Agent Sterns again glanced back at his backseat passenger and smiled, "Going by the statements written on their signs, I don't think these people agree with your dad's political policies."

"Look carefully around." Kiel instructed from his high rooftop *vantage point. "Anyone out there you know?"*

"Over to your far right, Demon Slayer." Aniel replied, his eyes firmly fixed on the familiar face of a mid-level demon standing beside a human female holding up the sign stating 'Texans for Gay Marriage'. "Do you see him? He's giving us both the finger."

"How can I miss the scarred face of my old friend Balazad," Kiel commented with an affirming smile. "It was the edge of my sword that sliced that scar into his scaly scalp. Now where is his slime-covered sidekick, Klezo?"

"Demon Slayer, I do see Klezo! Do you see the bearded humans holding up the large banner stating 'Protect a Woman's Right to Choose, Americans for Safe Abortions.' "

"No," Kiel stated, his eyes firmly fixed in another direction. Something else had captured the warrior's keen attention, something very dark and sinister standing off along the distant fence that paralleled the road.

"Amducious," Kiel announced in a low, seething voice.

"I, too, see him, Demon Slayer," Aniel affirmed.

Except for a pair of black, bat-like wings jutting out from his massive back shoulders, the lone demonic prince appeared strikingly angelic. Standing over twelve feet tall, his jet-black hair flowed freely over his muscular broad shoulders as he attempted to keep pace along the fence line with the slowly moving car. His true demonic identity was easily revealed by the combination of his distinctively yellowish-black skin, a high protruding brow, and a deep-set pair of piercing yellow eyes. The arch demon stopped his advance at the junction where the long wooden fence and the gated cul-de-sac met. As the dark gray vehicle with the two angelic warriors sitting on its roof passed by his stationary position, Amducious boldly proclaimed:

"Take every measure you feel necessary to protect the humans inside that house, but I promise you this, great and mighty Kiel. Eliot Graham will never become President of the United States of America. Never!"

The demon prince continued shouting obscenities, mocking the vehicle's angelic escorts as they entered the guarded confines of the

Graham estate behind the closing metal gate. Once the gate closed, scores of sword drawn warriors assumed their assigned positions along the entire perimeter of the ten-acre lakefront estate, making absolutely sure Amducious' bold claims would never come to fruition.

Friday, October 26th, 2016
3:05 p.m.
The Graham Estate
Along the southern banks of Lake Lewisville
15 miles North of Trinity Mills, Texas

With the closing of the front gates, a contingency of over two-dozen Secret Service agents immediately went into action, assuming their assigned roles protecting Eliot Graham's immediate family members now gathered safely inside the manor house estate.

Before parking the Crown Victoria in a designated makeshift lot of at least a dozen similar government-owned cars located in the back of the three-story brick manor house, Agent Sterns stopped directly in front of the Grahams' double hung entrance doors, which were graced on each side by two large white pillar supports, to allow his lone passenger to exit the vehicle.

Sydni Graham entered the foyer to her family's home to a very familiar sight, her entire family once again gathered under the same roof, where they had all grown up.

"Mommy, Daddy!"

"Sydni girl!" cheerfully acknowledged a balding, middle-aged gentleman, extending opened arms for an anticipated big hug. "We've missed you so much!"

Also with arms opened wide and standing alongside her husband of thirty-seven years, was Eliot Graham's best friend in the entire world and the mother of their seven children, Rosemary.

"I've missed you guys so much!" the perky teenager openly cried as the threesome embraced each other in a tight circle of love.

"Looks like Grams has been feeding you very well." Eliot Graham jokingly commented, stepping back and observing his dark-eyed, dark-haired beauty, a living picture image of his wife when they were first married so long ago.

"Oh, Daddy," Sydni smiled, wiping the tears from her eyes.

By now, all seven of Graham's children and their respective family members had gathered in the family's foyer. Their eldest, Mary Elizabeth, 34, was married and the mother of twin 10-year-old boys. Eliot, Jr., 32, was married and pastor of a non-denominational full gospel church located just outside of Cleveland, Tennessee, the father of three boys and two girls. Aaron, 31, was a successful Dallas trial lawyer and presently his father's chief campaign manager, married and the father of two beautiful little girls. William, 28, the head technical engineer for the *American Values Hour*, was married and the father of a cute Down's syndrome baby girl. Nicole, 26, nicknamed Nikki, was the program director for *AVH (American Values Hour)*, had been married just one year and was presently four months pregnant with her first child. Jonathan, 22, was a recent graduate from his father and mother's alma mater, Dallas Theological Seminary, and finally, Sydni Briana, 16, was the youngest member of the Graham clan, and only child still living at home.

With his entire family present and standing around him -seven children, two sons-in law, three daughters-in-law, ten grandchildren, with one on the way—Eliot Graham signaled with his hands for everyone to gather in for a big announcement. "OK everybody, before getting all comfortable and sitting down at the dining room table to eat the wonderful meal Grams and our church's fabulous kitchen staff have all prepared for us, your mom and I have a really big announcement to make."

On cue, as they have done so many times before, the entire Graham clan spread out, holding each other's hands tightly in a closed circle of prayer.

"*Dear Heavenly Father,*" Graham began, "*from the very beginning, when all those present in this room took full advantage of my benevolent personality and purposely manipulated my good nature, literally wrenching my arm to its fullest backward extent in order get me to cry uncle to their crazy idea of me, running for President of the United States...*"

Graham paused momentarily to allow the snickering to stop before continuing.

"*Father, your Word says, 'With You, all things are possible.' But Father, I must admit, before You and the people standing here whom I love most; never in my wildest dreams could I have imagined this to be possible; to stand here and say, with all humility, that with only two weeks remaining before the general elections, you have honored me, of all people, as the front runner for that most powerful human office on Earth. Father, in order for me to carry out this daunting task, I need your total help and I need it now! Lord, as the father of this family under the Lordship of your Son, Jesus Christ, I ask for your continued direction for our individual lives during the last two weeks of this vital campaign. More importantly, Lord, supply each one of us with your supernatural wisdom to make decisions that we, as faulty humans, are not capable of making on our own.*"

Though Graham's appeal to God was truly sincere, his fervent prayer lacked the one key provision guaranteed to safeguard his entire family for these two last weeks before the election. If only Eliot Graham had prayed the prayer of faith to petition the very throne room of God for divine protection, no demon in hell could ever gain access to either him or his family members. After briefly stopping to remove the heartfelt tears streaming down his face, Graham finished his prayer.

"*I ask this all in Jesus' precious name.*"

And everyone present said, *"Amen."*

"Now," Graham smiled, turning his full attention in the direction of the women standing to his immediate left. "I have asked your mom to propose to all of you the really big question."

"Thanks a lot, Mr. Wimp," Rosemary playfully responded, affectionately providing her retreating husband a mild love tap on his shoulder. "And they want him to be president. Go figure!"

Everybody standing in the large circle chuckled.

"Seriously, now," their mom continued. "Your father and I want all of you guys to prayerfully consider this request. We've talked this over and the way we see it, with only two weeks remaining before the elections, we believe now is a good time for the entire family to join us on the last leg of this campaign."

"What about missing school?" Sydni interrupted with a voice of concern. "I'll be starting the new quarter on Monday. I couldn't possibly make up that much missed work!"

"That's already been taken care of," responded Rosemary Graham with her best reassuring motherly voice. "I talked with your principal, Mr. Lilley, on Wednesday and explained the entire situation. He has since contacted all your teachers and they have agreed to assign you special projects that will more than make up for the work you will be missing in class while you're gone."

"So Miss Sydni, start packing up all your pretty clothes." Eliot Graham interjected with his own homegrown Texas accent. "Starting Monday, missy, you'll be heading out with old mom and dad on the campaign trail."

Friday, October 26th, 2016
9:55 p.m.
The Graham Estate
Along the southern banks of Lake Lewisville
15 miles North of Trinity Mills, Texas

Ask any member of the Graham family this question: what are the two most important virtues to living life on Earth, and this would be their unequivocal answer: *'You must love the Lord your God with all your heart, all your soul, all your strength, and all your mind. And you must also, 'Love your neighbor as yourself.'* Upon this single verse of Scripture, recorded in the tenth chapter of Luke's Gospel, Eliot and Rosemary Graham built the foundation of their life together and raised each of their seven children.

After spending an enjoyable evening once again as family, sharing both old and new stories at the dinner table, while playing four intense rounds of UNO, the Grahams decided it was time to retire to their individual bedrooms, with grandchildren and spouses sleeping on anything comfortably available, such as sofas and fluffy sleeping bags.

After spending at least ten additional minutes making their rounds, going room to room delivering kisses and hugs, Eliot and Rosemary Graham finally retired to their large master bedroom, located in the far upstairs corner of their six-thousand-square-foot manor house estate.

Walking over to his wife's side of the large king-sized bed, Graham bent down low, as if to give his wife a goodnight kiss, but instead, offered her an apologetic smile with this comment, "Rosie, give me about ten more minutes. I promised Phil Hanson I would call him today to finalize everything for next week's big agenda."

"All right," she smiled, "but remember, big shot, promise me you'll be in this bed in exactly ten minutes."

"Start the timer, now!" Graham conceded, giving his wife a conciliatory kiss on her forehead before exiting their bedroom for his private downstairs office den.

Deciding to wait up ten additional minutes until her husband's return, Rosemary Graham reached over to her adjacent nightstand to pick up a book she had already started reading.

As he paced the upstairs hallway, checking and double-checking to make absolutely sure no enemy had infiltrated his protected borders, a strong sense of cautious urgency still plagued Kiel's internal being. Even with an entire legion of angelic warriors strategically positioned both inside and outside the human dwelling, Amducious' words kept resonating throughout his mind.

"Take every measure you feel necessary to protect the humans inside that house, but I promise you this, great and mighty Kiel. Eliot Graham will never become President of the United States of America. Never!"

Even now, ingenuously concealed within the bound trappings of a seemingly innocent romantic vampire novel, its attendance unknown to any other being within the darkened recesses of the Graham house, a tiny demon senses its timing to act is now. In a moment's flash, a set of three unperceivable spindle-thin fingers project outward from Sydni Graham's book bag. Even before a second of time is displayed on the digital face of a nearby alarm clock, two infinitely small yellow eyes jet out from the book bag's cloth cover, intently scanning Sydni Graham's bedroom for the company of another supernatural being. Finding none, a grotesque apparition, closely resembling the biological cross between a winged bat and a slimy frog confidently emerges from the internal confines of the bag. No larger than a common housefly, the hideous creature instantly takes flight, quietly making its initial landing just under the inch-high gap of the closed bedroom door.

Sensing no time to spare, it hastily makes its move toward a solitary beam of light projecting outward from a bedroom door approximately twenty feet down the darkened upstairs hallway.

"*Perfect!*" *The tiny demon proudly applauded itself as it stood alone under the threshold of the Graham's bedroom door. "Just as we planned. No one here to stop us! Graham's wife's angelic guard left his post to follow Graham. Praise be to Lord Satan!"*

Without a moment's hesitation, the tiny demon took flight, delivering its deadly thrust at the female human sitting about fifteen feet away in an upright position on the bed. The force of its tremendous impact was such that Rosemary Graham's entire body lurched forward, as if she was struck directly in her midriff by the hammering force of an invisible hand.

"Oh, God!" She cried out in intense agony.

That single groan was just enough warning needed to audibly capture the attention of two warriors strategically positioned at opposite ends of the upstairs hallway. With no time to spare, the angels converged on the Grahams' bedroom. Joveniel, being closest, was the first to arrive. What he found upon his arrival was a doubled over Rosemary Graham, both hands pressed firmly against her abdomen as if she were instinctively directing the warrior's attention to the source of her intense pain. Sensing no time to waste, Joveniel immediately inserted his face directly against Rosemary Graham's painful abdomen.

"What is it, Joveniel?" asked his concerned angelic comrade, Zorriel, standing only feet away.

"We're too late!" Zorriel's distraught companion declared. With the precision skill of a trained surgeon, Joveniel inserted his right hand into the woman's abdomen and carefully removed the hissing culprit that had firmly attached itself to Rosemary Graham's liver.

By now, Joveniel and Zorriel were not alone in the master bedroom. Five other warriors, including Kiel, stood silently beside the bed, too stunned to speak.

Careful not to become a victim himself from the bite of the demon's lethal fangs, Joveniel stretched out fully the heinous little creature's inch-and-a-half wingspan to confirm its true identity.

Before slicing the tiny spirit in half with the razor-tipped edge of his golden sword, Kiel confirmed what every angel present in the room already knew.

"A demon of cancer."

As he had promised, Eliot Graham returned to his bedroom with a little over two minutes to spare.

"Rosie, I'm back!" he whispered, standing outside the partially opened master bathroom's door. "Rosie, is everything all right in there?" a concerned Graham asked again, careful not to raise his voice and awaken his sleeping children in the adjacent bedrooms.

"Eliot, come in here and make sure you shut the door behind you," projected a troubling request from inside the bathroom.

Eliot Graham opened the door to his master bath to a shocking scene he would never forget.

"My God, Rosie, what's wrong?" demanded her horrified husband.

"Eliot, I think you need to call 911, now!" a helpless Rosie Graham declared as she continued projecting streams of what appeared to be vomit, mixed with fresh red blood, all over the bathroom's ceramic tile.

Saturday, October 27th, 2016
5:53 a.m.
Texas Health Presbyterian Hospital
8200 Walnut Hill Lane
Dallas, Texas

From the moment the first ambulance arrived at the Graham estate, shortly after 10:30 pm last night, until this morning, few members of the Graham family, with the exception of the youngest grandchildren, had any measurable sleep. Amazingly enough, up until now, everyone involved, including the family members, the EMTs called to the scene, and the entire emergency center staff at Texas Health Presbyterian Hospital had managed to keep a tight lid on alerting the press and media that anything was medically wrong with Rosemary Graham. But before the sun would make its appearance this morning along the eastern Texas horizon, the entire world would know the status of Eliot Graham's wife's condition.

Due to the immense political implications of the situation, the hospital staff decided it would be in the best interest of everybody involved to keep the Graham family in a secluded area of the hospital until something definitive could be revealed.

"Daddy, why do you think we haven't heard anything yet?"

"Nikki," an exhausted Graham replied in his calming fatherly voice. "You all remember what Dr. Fisher told us last night when we first arrived. It's going to take some time to run all the tests and get all the results back before they can tell us what's wrong with Mom."

No sooner had Eliot Graham finished answering his daughter's question then the door to the hospital's main conference room opened wide and several somber-faced doctors walked inside.

"Hello everyone. My name is Doctor Sal Goldstein. I am in charge of all surgical procedures performed here at Presbyterian Hospital. Please allow me the privilege of introducing the other doctors who will be directly involved with Mrs. Graham's case."

Dr. Goldstein wasted little time introducing each doctor and the related area of expertise. Each doctor cordially stepped forward as his or her name was called.

"On my far left is Dr. Richard Halpern, our hospital's chief gastroenterologist. To Dr. Halpern's immediate right is his talented associate, Dr. Leslie Jamison. Dr. Jamison is our hospital's chief liver specialist. On my far right is Dr. Muriel Sinclair, the head of our radiology and oncology department, and standing to his left, on my immediate right, is Dr. Lowell Smith, our chief oncology surgeon."

Dr. Goldstein led the family in a brief applause of appreciation for the team of highly trained specialists taking time to join him so early in the morning.

"Before we begin answering your many questions," Dr. Goldstein continued, "let me reassure all of you, Mrs. Graham is now resting comfortably in a private room and you will all be able to see her shortly. We are now prepared to answer any and all questions you might have about Mrs. Graham's present condition and her future treatments."

The first hand to be raised was Eliot Graham's.

"Yes, doctors," Graham stood, briefly clearing his voice before proceeding.

Never in his entire life, not as the pastor of a large church, as the host of the nation's most listened-to radio broadcast, or as candidate for the office of President of the United States of America, had he faced asking such a daunting question as the one he was about to propose.

"I represent all of my family members and I have two major questions to ask. First, what specifically is wrong with my wife, and second, most importantly, how do you intend to fix it?"

"Dr. Graham," Dr. Goldstein responded, "we are prepared to fully answer both of your questions. I will ask Dr. Jamison to answer your first question."

"Dr. Graham," Dr. Jamison said as she stepped forward, displaying a brief, but solemn smile, "all the results from a full battery of tests run on Mrs. Graham, including a full body PET Scan, a CAT Scan, a three dimensional MRI, and a conclusive liver biopsy, all point to one single diagnosis. Mrs. Graham has Cholangiocarcinoma, an extremely rare cancerous tumor that is presently covering over 80% of her liver."

"Well, then tell me this, doctors," Graham asked in a forced, trembling voice, "What can be medically done to cure it?"

"I'll ask Dr. Sinclair to answer that question," Dr. Goldstein responded.

"Unfortunately, Dr. Graham, very little." the oncology specialist conceded. "Your wife has been diagnosed with what we, in the medical profession, call 'the cancer from hell.' It is totally unresponsive to both chemo and radiation treatments. The only treatment available that has any track record of previous success when dealing with Cholangiocarcinoma, is resecting it completely."

"Resecting it, Dr. Sinclair?"

"Yes, Dr. Graham, remove the cancerous tumor completely."

"Then that's what we'll do!" Graham declared.

"I'm afraid it's not that easy, Dr. Graham." Dr. Smith interjected. "Fortunately for some, the liver is one of the few internal organs that regenerates. Perhaps if your wife's liver were 30%, or maybe as high as 50% affected, I might consider surgically removing the tumor, but Dr. Graham, 80% of your wife's liver is already compromised with tumor. No one in the history of mankind has ever had 80% their liver removed and survived."

"Then doctors," Mary Beth, the oldest of Graham's seven children asked, "what medical options does our mother have left?"

Dr. Halpern stepped forward to answer Mary Beth's question. "After carefully studying all of your mother's test results, in our professional opinions, we each sadly concur, there are no medical options available for Mrs. Graham at this time."

"You have no idea how hard this is for us to share this truly disturbing information," interjected Dr. Goldstein, "but believe me when I say, our hearts go out to each and every one of you, and I can promise you this. We, at Presbyterian Hospital, will do everything possible to keep Mrs. Graham comfortable and pain free. With our help, and a possibly a little luck from above, she may just live to see Christmas."

With that last chilling statement, the five doctors departed the large conference room, closing the door behind them, leaving in their wake a roomful of dispirited family members.

"It's over with," mumbled Eliot Graham. His muffled voice was just loud enough for his youngest son, Jonathan, sitting beside him, to hear.

"What's over with, Dad?"

"Everything," his crushed father replied.

"Don't say that. Nothing's over with, Dad!" Jonathan stated firmly. "We're all believers. God is on our side and Mom is going to be fine!"

"It's all my fault!" Graham declared with tears streaming down his face. Standing, he summoned his entire family over to give him support.

"You guys know your mom is more important to me than anything else in the world!" Graham acknowledged, wiping his tear-drenched face with his right shirtsleeve.

Turning his full attention toward his second oldest son, Aaron, the manager of his presidential campaign, Graham announced loud enough for those present in the room to also hear. "I made up my mind and I am not going back on it! Aaron, I want you to call a press conference for 10 a.m. this morning. Forget the election. Your mother needs me now more than ever before. As of this moment, I am officially withdrawing my name from the race for President of the United States of America, so help me God!"

Chapter Two

Where have you come from?" the LORD asked Satan. And Satan answered the LORD, "I have been patrolling the earth, watching everything that's going on."

~Job 1:7 (NLT)

Three years earlier
Monday, February 11th, 2013
4:27 p.m.
MOI International Airport
Mombasa, Kenya

"Ladies and gentleman," a voice with a heavy French accent came over the plane's intercom, "as Captain of Air France Flight 005, I would like to welcome you to Mombasa, Kenya. Please make sure you have removed all luggage and personal belongings from the overhead compartments before exiting, and thank you once again for choosing to fly Air France."

The Air France jet soon came to a complete halt, stopping on the hot tarmac surface just meters away from Kenya's MOI International Airport's main terminal. For the lone American passenger seated in the back recesses of a nearly empty plane, this ended his grueling ten thousand mile, three-stop journey that started well over twenty-four hours ago.

If anyone can pull this off, Turner, it's you! The burly framed, fiery red-haired young American journalist took a brief moment longer to relax in his seat and reflect on the immensity of his mind-boggling African assignment.

Turner Lucas grew up, a confident person, who was willing to take on any challenge. Always the fearless competitor, he captained both his school's football and lacrosse teams to state championships. That was one of the main reasons his boss, Sarah Lynch, founder, editor and CEO of the world's number one-ranked conservative website, World Truth Daily, asked her top investigative reporter to go to Africa on this secretive mission. However, before joining the handful of passengers making their way toward the plane's front exit door, this veteran Army Special Ops officer, serving his country in both Iraq and Afghanistan, sat back in his seat, staring in silent awe at the glistening moisture clearly visible on the backside of his hand after wiping his forehead.

From the moment he boarded his first transatlantic connection out of Washington D.C.'s Dulles International Airport, Turner Lucas, a man who prided himself as never being a stranger to danger, sensed an unexplainable source of uneasiness which had accompanied him during the entire 16-hour flight. *Good thing nobody's here to see this one,* he thought to himself. Before standing up, Lucas removed all vestiges of perspiration from his hands and forehead with a clean paper napkin he took out of his top shirt pocket.

Still, as the reporter arose to his feet, a sudden alarm went off from deep within his psyche as if he were being watched—the same type of internal warning he had experienced many times prior when searching out Taliban soldiers concealed behind the rocky crags of the Afghanistan mountains. Standing center aisle, the former Special Ops officer proceeded to do a quick, but thorough search throughout the entire back section of the plane. Content that he was quite alone, Lucas reached up to remove the remaining travel bags exposed in the opened overhead storage compartment. With bags in hand, the American reporter proceeded down the long empty aisle toward the front of the plane.

Little did he know that the source of his unexplained restlessness was walking down the same center aisle just three steps behind.

Turner Lucas was confronted once again by the stark reality that he was about to enter the non-convenient realm of a third world nation.

"Well, we're not in Kansas anymore," he smiled as he stood at the plane's open door. Absent from his view was the convenient jet-way that bridged the gap between the plane's door and the air-conditioned terminal at the other end. In its place, he was greeted at the open door by the intense scorching rays of a late afternoon tropical sun.

"Bring it on, baby!"

With bags in hand, Lucas promptly walked down the inclined flight of steps, temporarily placed against the plane's hot metal fuselage. Acting with total disregard for the oppressive heat, Lucas walked with vigor across the sun-baked tarmac toward the welcoming terminal doors only meters away.

Before entering the one story antiquated building that served as Mombasa's only airport terminal for the past sixty years, Turner Lucas dropped his traveling bags to his side and spun around facing an empty Air France jet. For the second time in five minutes, profuse sweat began streaming down his brow. With every single nerve fiber screaming out, *you're being followed*, the former Special Ops officer, turned Internet reporter, shouted with total disregard for anyone within the range of his voice, "Who **are** you? I'm warning you, you inexplicable idiot, show yourself now and stop following me. Have I made myself clear?" In every direction he turned, near and far, nothing, nobody. Not even a baggage handler could be seen, just a handful of empty parked jets baking on a sun-scorched tarmac.

Get a grip on yourself, Stupid! There's nobody there! For the first time in his entire life Turner Lucas stood in a state of shock, gripped by an emotion that up until now was totally foreign to his trained psyche.

"Screw it!" Lucas defiantly declared, picking up his bags from the blacktopped surface below. "Whatever's going on here, this assignment is far too important for me to allow anything, including my mind, to play tricks on me."

Turner Lucas entered the airport terminal through a gate door designated for Air France passengers only. Following just three steps behind, totally imperceptible for even the exceptional mortal senses of Lucas to detect, a towering olive-skinned giant walked while holding a golden two-edged sword. Protectively garbed with a golden breastplate covering a brilliant white linen robe pulled tight along his waist by a golden belt, his massive twelve-foot frame instantly transformed to the dimensions of a normal sized man in order to allow his immortal body mass to pass easily under the same eight-foot high terminal door opening as the humans. Once safely inside the air-conditioned building, constructed with fifteen-foot high ceilings, the angelic warrior's body supernaturally transformed to its original size as he continued following closely behind his assigned human charge, World Truth Daily reporter, Turner Lucas.

Once inside the building, Lucas followed the instructions he had memorized. With a glance, he immediately spotted his first destination, the men's room directly opposite the Air France ticket counter. Once inside, he had been instructed to locate the third bathroom stall, enter it, and close the door. Further instructions, as to what to do next, were to be handwritten on the stalls inside door.

Unfortunately, when Lucas arrived inside the designated bathroom, he discovered the third stall door locked and occupied. After what seemed like an eternity of standing patiently outside listening to the annoying drips of a leaky faucet, the toilet inside stall three finally flushed and out came a rather tall, slender black man, smiling from ear to ear. With a newspaper folded under his left arm, the dark-skinned African extended his right hand in the direction of a hesitant Turner Lucas.

"You may shake it, Mr. Lucas! I assure you, my hands are clean! I was simply sitting inside the stall this whole time awaiting your arrival."

With his buttock firmly pressed against the porcelain rim of the dripping, brown- stained bathroom sink, Turner Lucas slowly extended his hand to the smiling black man standing directly in front of the third bathroom stall.

"Just a formality if you don't mind, Mr. Lucas," the African commented, this time exchanging his grin for a cordial smile. "Before we continue, may I see some form of identification?"

"Absolutely," Lucas released his grip on the man's hand in order to secure his official WTD press corps badge concealed under his loose-fitting khaki green shirt.

"Excellent, Mr. Lucas! My first name is Macaria, which in my native Kenyan language means "seeker." For now, that is the only name I prefer to be called. I am the person who contacted you last month and arranged this entire three-day visit to our country. Like yourself, Mr. Lucas, I seek truth and that is why I believe God has ordained our paths to cross. If you would be so kind, Mr. Turner Lucas, please follow me and I will lead you to the source of truth that you have come all this way to find."

Exiting the airport bathroom, three beings, two humans accompanied by their massive angelic protector, walked the entire length of the long central aisle leading toward MOI airport's front entrance lobby. Only now, two other spirits joined their ranks, clandestinely concealing their shadowy existence from detection behind a host of common objects that lined the terminal's central aisle such as chairs and framed pictures along the entire length of the wall.

Stopping briefly at the front entrance lobby, Macaria removed his cell phone from its leather belt holster and proceeded to contact his driver, who was parked on the street just outside the terminal's main lobby doors. Following closely, Turner Lucas exited the building, then stopped at the yellow painted curb where a very expensive burgundy Lexus was parked. Its windows were tinted dark, preventing any outside spectator from looking in.

"Nice car," Turner acknowledged, as Macaria proceeded to graciously open the vehicle's front passenger door.

"I would be honored, Mr. Lucas, since you are our guest in Kenya, please sit in the front seat beside my personal driver, Jimiyu."

The moment Turner Lucas sat in his seat, two hands from the backseat gripped Lucas's forehead, forcing his head backward against the seat's headrest.

"Please, Mr. Lucas. I assure you, in no way will you be harmed." *Was this a female voice?* "Please follow my every word and do not struggle. You must be blindfolded and remain that way until we reach our destination. I hope you understand, Mr. Lucas. It must be done this way to protect the lives of our people. If word gets out about their true identity and where they live, their lives would be in constant danger by those who want to silence the truth that they, and they alone have in their possession. Agreed, Mr. Lucas?"

"Agreed!" Turner Lucas affirmed as the hands of the person seated directly in back of him finished securing the blindfold around the American's entire face.

"Welcome to Kenya, Mr. Lucas," Macaria proudly proclaimed as he entered the backseat of the vehicle, sitting directly in back of the driver. "It will take us less than an hour to arrive at our first destination, Mr. Lucas. Just sit back, close your eyes, and enjoy the ride."

"And who is the charming lady sitting in back of me who was nice enough to tighten my blindfold?"

A chorus of spontaneous laughter erupted from the backseat of the car immediately following Lucas's question. "Mr. Lucas, I would like to introduce you to my two oldest daughters,

Akinyi, meaning born early in the morning, and Dalila, meaning gentleness in her soul."

"That would be my very strong sister, Dalila, Mr. Lucas," giggled the sister who had first greeted the American when he entered the vehicle.

"Dalila, I hate to tell you this, but going by first impressions, you don't live up to your name."

Once again everyone in the car laughed.

Regaining his composure, Macaria reached forward, gently tapping his driver on the shoulder. "Alright, Jimiyu, I believe it is time." Nothing more needed to be said. The diligent driver, Macaria's trusted employee and loyal friend, knew the great importance of today's task. First, after glancing in his rearview mirror, Jimiyu shifted the luxury vehicle into forward gear, and they were off to their first destination, Malindi, a beautiful coastal city located 65 kilometers due north of Mombasa.

As the burgundy colored Lexus drove away from MOI airport's front entrance, a sixth passenger, totally imperceptible to the mortal senses of the car's five human occupants, sat atop the vehicle's roof, utilizing every one of his supernatural abilities to detect the slightest signs of danger.

Parked also within four blocks from the airport's main entrance, the human occupants of two other vehicles, separated by two city blocks, patiently awaited their assigned quarry, a burgundy colored Lexus now heading up the same street in their direction.

"Here they come!" the driver of a late model dark blue Honda Accord said as he held his cell phone to his ear. "They'll be passing us in three, two, one...they are now past our location."

"Good, I see them coming now in my mirror," the driver of a black Range Rover responded. "You two stay a safe distance in back of them. I'll pull out now and remain at least three to five car lengths in front. We will our introductions known to our American visitor and his African guests when we pass by the deserted Swahili outpost located 25 kilometers outside of the city limits along the coastal highway."

A usual trip leaving Mombasa airport and traveling northward along Kenya's coastal highway to the Malindi takes no more than an hour, but on this particular journey, time would soon prove irrelevant.

"Mr. Lucas, we will be arriving at our first destination in approximately twenty-five minutes," Macaria announced. "Perhaps I can offer you something to drink? We have a variety of chilled soft drinks, or perhaps you prefer mountain spring water?"

"No thanks, Macaria, I can wait until we arrive."

"Mr. Lucas, I believe this may be an appropriate time to discuss some of the details of our first destination."

"Go ahead, Macaria, being blindfolded at the moment, I'm all ears." Lucas jokingly agreed.

"Only a temporary inconvenience, I assure you, Mr. Lucas," Macaria smiled as he continued. "As you may recall, Mr. Lucas, when I first contacted World Truth Daily over a month ago, I made mention to your boss, Sarah Lynch, that I am an avid reader of the conservative website where are you presently employed. I also made mention to Ms. Lynch that I truly admired the journalistic scholarship and integrity of the articles you have written; however, that is not the only reason you are sitting here blindfolded in the front seat of this rented car."

Macaria paused momentarily, allowing the blindfolded American reporter a brief moment longer to reflect on his comments before continuing. "Mr. Lucas, you may, or you may not believe what I am about to tell you. The only reason we are sitting here at this moment in time is because the Holy Spirit of God directed me to contact you."

"Macaria, you're telling me that God arranged this meeting?" Lucas chuckled in a tone of disbelief.

"Precisely, Mr. Lucas," Macaria smiled. "As I mentioned moments ago, whether or not you accept or reject this fact is totally irrelevant to me. The important issue is that God has chosen you, Turner Lucas, a gifted reporter for the world's number one conservative website, to announce the truth to the entire world."

"And that truth is?"

"That the current President of the United States is no more an American citizen than I am! My sister, Malandi, the first person I've arranged for you to meet, will verify that fact for you first hand. You see, Mr. Lucas, Malandi was the labor room nurse on duty at Mombasa's Coast General Hospital on August 4th, 1961 when a white, fifteen-year-old American female, whose husband was registered as a Kenyan national, was rushed to the hospital in full labor, giving birth later to a mixed-race, baby boy named Rashid Jabbar Isweire. Today that same little baby boy is known throughout the entire world as Rashid Jabbar Harris, the current illegally elected President of the United States of America."

Bang.....Zing !

"What was that?"

"I believe that was the sound of gunfire, Mr. Lucas! I also believe there is a strong possibility that we are being fired upon by the car in back of us."

"What in Sam's Hill is wrong with you, man? Being shot at is not what I call a minor inconvenience!"

"I assure you, Mr. Lucas, being shot at is by no means a minor inconvenience, especially when my daughters are in the car. As I said before, God has ordained this meeting and to those who fully trust Him, He promised that His angels would protect us in all our ways."

Without giving it a second thought, Lucas immediately removed his blindfold. From the vantage point of his passenger side mirror, the American reporter could clearly see what appeared to be a late model Honda Accord rapidly approaching from behind. Bang! ....Zing! ....Again and again, the high-pitched sound of bullets were either striking or ricocheting off the car's metal surface. "God better send us an entire squadron of His angels, ASAP! Don't look now but those nuts in the SUV in front of us are also shooting at us!"

Without saying another word, Macaria immediately closed his eyes and began praying: "Dear Heavenly Father, I trust in You and Your Word alone to get us through this attack of the enemy. According to Your word in John Chapter 15 verse 7, *"If I abide in you, and your Words abide in me, then I can ask what I desire, and it shall be done for me."* Father God, in the mighty name of Jesus, Your Holy Son, I now declare Your Word over this entire situation. I hereby declare this vehicle and all the occupants therein to be divinely protected according to Your Word found in Psalm 91. *"That he who dwells in the secret place of the Most High shall abide under the shadow of the Almighty. I will say of the* Lord, *"He is my refuge and my fortress; My God, in Him I will trust. Surely He shall deliver you from the snare of the fowler and from the perilous pestilence. He shall cover you with His feathers, and under His wings you shall take refuge; His truth shall be your shield and buckler. You shall not be afraid of the terror by night, nor the arrow that flies by day, nor of the pestilence that walks in darkness, nor of the destruction that lays waste at noonday. A thousand may fall at your side, and ten thousand at your right hand; but it shall not come near you. Only with your eyes shall you look, and see the reward of the wicked. Because you have made the* Lord, *who is my refuge, even the Most High, your dwelling place, no evil shall befall you, nor shall any plague come near your dwelling; For He shall give His angels charge over you, To keep you in all your ways."* Now, dear Heavenly Father, according to the authority of your Word in the mighty name of Jesus, deliver us from evil!"

Right after Macaria prayed *'deliver us from evil,'* a cloud of dense translucent fog appeared out of nowhere, engulfing their entire vehicle and the surrounding coastal highway, as well. Also, at that very moment, the drivers of both the Honda Accord and the Range Rover slammed on their brakes, their individual cars screeching to a complete halt in the middle of the very same coastal highway. The four human occupants immediately exited their respective vehicles, walking about the highway in a state of awestruck disbelief. Where once a burgundy colored Lexus was present, now there was a car length void between their Honda Accord and the Range Rover SUV. To their utter shock, it appeared as if some unseen hand had reached down from the cloudless skies above, instantly snatching the Lexus they were pursuing right out of their midst. *Also, standing in the middle of the coastal highway were beings of another sort. Having temporally deserted their human hosts, four infuriated mid-level demonic spirits were walking aimlessly about, each one shaking its scaly-clawed fists toward heaven, blaspheming the Holy Name of God the Father and His Son, Jesus Christ.*

One month later
Monday, March 11ᵗʰ, 2013
10 a.m. Central Standard Time
American Values Hour Studios
Trinity Mills, Texas

All available seats in the American Values Hour studio auditorium were filled with anxious visitors, many of whom had traveled from far and wide to witness first-hand a live recording of America's top-rated conservative radio broadcast. On a raised stage only feet away from the live audience, three gentlemen are sitting in a soundproof broadcast booth, patiently awaiting the start of today's show. Staring above her head at a digital clock ticking off the seconds, program director Nikki Graham Fisher holds up her right hand motioning to her team of five technicians that today's hour-long show is about to start. "On my signal, ready? Five, four, three, two, one…" she points to the technician to the far left of the large control panel. With a quick point of her index finger, the familiar introductory music begins playing in the background and the show is underway.

Within the glass-enclosed broadcast booth, a clean-cut, youthful gentleman, perhaps in his mid-thirties, speaks: "Welcome to Monday's edition of the American Values Hour, America's one stop shop for everything family. I'm Mike Hampe, along with AVH's Founder and President, Dr. Eliot Graham. Today, we would like to give a hearty Texas welcome to our very special guest, Turner Lucas! Mr. Lucas is not only an award-winning investigative reporter for the web's number one-ranked source of conservative news, World Truth Daily, he also served our country, both in Iraq and Afghanistan as a decorated army special operations officer."

"Wow, a special OPS Army Officer," an impressed Graham exclaimed as he extended a welcoming handshake to the gentleman seated between himself and his co-host Hampe.

"Yes, Sir, I'm proud to have served."

"Mr. Lucas," Graham continued, "I don't have to tell you how much I have looked forward to having you on today's show. You, sir, have been the talk of all America since your article was first published right after Christmas on the WTD website. You have not only stirred up a literal hornet's nest in Washington, D.C., but you, sir, have single handedly caused a political tidal wave to rise up that may indeed strike the very steps of the White House."

"Believe me, Dr Graham, I've had lots of help along the way," Lucas responded with a smile.

"According to your article entitled, *Is there an illegal alien living in the White House?*, published on December 27th on World Truth Daily's Website, you, James Turner Lucas, allege that you have in your possession conclusive documents and other evidence obtained from first hand living sources that President Harris was, in fact, not born in the United States of America on August 4, 1961, but in a hospital in Mombasa, Kenya. Also, you go one step further in your article alleging that President Harris may have intentionally perjured himself by knowingly covering up this gross constitutional breach in order to win the presidency. In your article, you site specific names of high-ranking government officials, and also, names of several influential private sector supporters, who you allege knowingly conspired to both fund and conceal the fact that President Harris was not born in America as he alleges, but in Mombasa, Kenya. You also state that all President Harris has to do to end this controversy once and for all is to show the American public an official copy of his birth certificate. I must tell you, Mr. Lucas, your article reads like an explosive plot to a well-written fictional thriller."

"Unfortunately, Dr. Graham, every word stated in that article is true, and I am here today to bear witness to that fact."

"Before we get into the specific details of what you claimed to have discovered about the president's actual place of birth while on a recent trip to Kenya, Africa, what I personally found even more fascinating is the strange account you recorded in your background story about being rescued from certain death by an angel sent by God. Mr. Lucas, could you please share that story with our audience here and with the millions of folks listening in at home?"

"Dr. Graham, I've done at least two dozen TV and radio interviews over the past few weeks. You, sir, have been the first person to ask me to retell that story." Lucas quickly wiped a visible tear from the corner of his right eye. "I would be truly honored to share that story with your audience."

"This is the first time we've actually met face-to-face, Mr. Lucas," interjected Graham's perceptive co-host, Mike Hampe, "but I'm getting the impression that you have really been touched by that entire experience."

"More than you'll ever know, Mr. Hampe," Lucas confessed, hanging his head low in shame. Looking up, he continued. "You see, I grew up believing only in my own abilities to get me through any situation that life threw my way. I really didn't trust people and I definitely didn't trust God. In fact, even though I was raised Catholic and attended parochial school twelve years, I can now honestly say, I never believed God existed. Not, at least, until three weeks ago."

"Tell us about the story, Turner. Let the whole world know exactly what happened three weeks ago to change your heart about God."

Closing his eyes, Lucas sat back in the cushioned studio chair and began recalling the life-changing events that took place in his life that late afternoon along Kenya's main coastal highway.

"Thank you, Dr. Graham. You know, it all happened so fast, it was almost like a dream. A man, I'll call him Mark, just to protect his real identity, and three other Kenyan nationals, picked me up at Mombasa's MOI airport and drove me up along the East African coast to meet my first contact, a former nurse who claimed to have witnessed the actual birth of a baby boy named Rashid Jabbar Isweire. The baby's last name was later changed to Harris when his stepfather at the time, Mohammed Kareem Harris, legally adopted him three years later. I almost forgot, my Kenyan host, Mark, had blindfolded me for security purposes the moment we left the airport. About a half hour past the airport, somewhere along the coastal highway, I heard what sounded like gunfire coming from the car behind us. I immediately removed my blindfold and gave my full attention to the car's side view mirror. It was then that I spotted what appeared to be an older model Honda Accord directly in back of us with some guy hanging out the window firing a handgun. The next thing I can recall, the SUV traveling in front of us slows down, its back window opens and danother guy in that car starts firing at us. I'm telling everyone that I've been involved in so many dangerous situations over my lifetime—ambushes and cross-fires like you would never believe, but at that moment, there was no doubt in my mind whatsoever that we were toast! We were definitely caught in a well-planned out crossfire with absolutely no means of escape. No doubt about it! Bullets were literally flying off the hood, penetrating into the trunk. Shards and slivers of broken windshield glass were flying in every conceivable direction, but miraculously, no one inside the car was hurt, not even a tiny scratch."

"In one word, Lucas, how would you describe what happened next?"

"That's easy, Dr Graham," Lucas smiled. "Miraculous! There is no other word in the English dictionary that could describe what happened next. Just when I thought it was all over, out of nowhere this dense layer of fog totally encompassed, not only our car, but the surrounding highway as well. From that moment on, until we arrived at our first destination, we had zero visibility."

"Did your driver have to pull over?"

"He didn't have to," Lucas chuckled. "If you weren't there, yourself, this part's really hard to explain, but even though you couldn't see anything on either side of the car, the road in front of us had some sort of perpetual light shining on it, as if it were sent there to guide us along our way."

"How did you feel during this time, Turner?"

"Funny thing that you should ask that question, Dr. Graham." Lucas smiled. "The very moment the fog engulfed the car, the first words out of my mouth were, *Sweet Mary, Mother of God, what in God's name is going on here?* Next, I remember shutting my mouth for a second, thinking I had actually died. It was at that moment that fear gripped my entire being and I actually started repenting of every single sin I could remember doing. I even asked God to forgive me for setting the old Rylan barn on fire when I was eight years old. I later confessed to the police, after all my childhood friends had admitted to doing it, and I was later given fifty hours of community service."

Everyone, inside and outside the soundproof broadcast glass enclosure, laughed.

"Well, how long were you guys traveling in the fog?" a curious Mike Hampe asked.

"That's also a funny thing," Lucas chucked. "I have to admit, I've yet to figure that one out. We later determined that it would have taken us at least another twenty minutes before we reached our first destination; with God as my witness, within moments of the fog arriving, we were already there."

"What?" both host and co-host exclaimed.

"I'm not done yet!" the giddy Internet reporter declared. "Not only were we at the exact location we were driving to when the fog lifted, there were absolutely no signs of broken glass or bullet holes visible on the entire car. In fact, when we pulled up to the nurse's house that late Wednesday afternoon, that burgundy colored Lexus was in showroom condition, both inside and out."

"What?" Graham exclaimed, at the same time lifting his hands up high, praising God.

"God is my witness, Dr. Graham," a tearful Lucas admitted, "before the events of that day, I wouldn't have believed it myself."

"Turner Lucas, I believe your last statement says it all," Eliot Graham declared.

"Amen, to that!" Graham's teary-eyed co-host, Mike Hampe, agreed.

Chapter Three

He (the devil) was a murderer from the beginning, and does not stand in the truth, because there is no truth found in him. When he speaks a lie, he speaks from his own resources, for he is a liar and the father of lies.

~John 8: 44 (NKJV)

Two years later
Friday, April 10th, 2015
8:09 a.m. Pacific Standard Time
North Exhibit Hall D
Moscone Center
San Francisco, California

In the natural world, a dozen or so human technicians were scurrying about the Moscone Center's Hall D, the largest convention hall in the City of San Francisco, doing last minute audio/video checks before the start of the Progressive Democrats of America Convention, scheduled to begin promptly at noon. In this same cavernous chamber, completely obscured to the humans' limited senses, another convention was just about to conclude. In attendance at this clandestine assembly, which had begun sometime during the wee hours of the morning, were demonic princes and mid-level demonic beings of the highest hierarchical rankings.

Demonic rankings on earth are based entirely upon the demon's heavenly status before their fall. As archangels in their former state, demonic princes are the highest order of demons. Except for their yellowish skin and their distinctly bright yellow eyes, demonic princes retain much of their former angelic appearance. On the other hand, mid-level demons, former warrior angels, are more reptilian in appearance with winged bodies covered with scaly yellowish black skin and a grotesquely fashioned snakelike head.

Familiar spirits, former guardian angels at this hellish gathering, displayed characteristic bouts of gross unruliness. They are one ranking below the midlevel demons. Referred to as chimeras, because of their half-human, half-animal appearance, familiar spirits have the innate ability to change into any form at will. Known by their honed deceptive crafts as lying spirits, religious spirits, and spirits of pride, jealousy, lust, greed or envy, familiar spirits have been charged by their master Satan with the ultimate task of destroying the lives of their assigned human hosts. Because these demonic beings are fewer in number than their angelic counterparts, familiar spirits are sometimes charged with overseeing more than one unsaved human in the same household.

Also noticeably missing were the myriad of grossly deformed aberrations at the bottom of the demonic hierarchy, the hideous spirits of infirmity—former ministering angelic spirits that have, since the fall, been transformed into minuscule, frog-like slimy creatures that cause the majority of mankind's sicknesses and diseases.

An ominous hush, accompanied by a noticeable chill, permeated every inch of this great hall, constructed by humans to exemplify their own worldly achievements. Every demon present sat fixated on the edge of his seat, proudly looking up at their commander, the Arch Demon Amducious, known also as the "Destroyer," who stood solo on the raised center stage platform above them. "As we conclude this part of our meeting, I want to state again that I am proud to be in the company of such a distinguished gathering of princes, rulers of America's great states, cities, counties, boroughs, and townships. You have left your important responsibilities temporarily to be here this morning in San Francisco, a great bastion of progressive human thought. Let me remind each of you once more of your charge. We are gathered for one solitary purpose—to achieve our unified goal to its ultimate conclusion—the utter and complete destruction of the United States of America.

This morning you have each received your new assignment—to guide, nurture, and direct the political agenda of each human from your individual assigned post here at the Convention of the Progressive Democrats of America. Once you leave this convention and return with your human, treat your assigned human with the utmost respect. Not only are these stupid humans unwittingly supporting our stated agenda for a fallen America with a dark future, but they are also unknowingly supporting our ultimate cause, to thwart God's prophetic plan for Christ's return."

Since the beginning of time, Satan and his millions of demons have been acutely aware of the one major guiding force behind all of their motives and plans, their ultimate fate. Putting off the inevitable by attempting to alter the events of God's prophetic time clock has always been their game plan. Every demonic plan has only one motive in mind, "how does this plan further my cause of avoiding God's judgment in hell at the end of time?" As the seconds on God's prophetic clock tick off even louder, Satan and his evil cohorts plan a final scheme in a desperate attempt to ward off the inevitable—spending the rest of their miserable eternal lives in the Lake of Fire.

"Before we depart, I want every last one of you back here before noon," the arch demon strongly admonished. "I also want each of you to focus your full attention on this familiar human face." With a slight gesture from the arch demon's clawed left hand, a picture of a partially balding middle aged human male's face instantly illuminated the five sets of screens suspended overhead, causing a spontaneous outbreak of hisses, boos, hoots, and jeers throughout the large auditorium. "Anyone ever see this face before?" the arch demon mockingly asked, attempting to deliberately stir up even more animosity toward Graham's hated image. "Behold, the man, Eliot Graham – born in Trinity Mills, Texas on July 16, 1950!" Amducious methodically proclaimed this in *the same tone of voice he used when speaking through the Roman, Pontus Pilate, two thousand years earlier.*

"Just give the orders, Destroyer! I'll kill him, now!" an agitated midlevel demon shrieked as he jumped up and down along the auditorium's back wall.

"Who said anything about killing such a fine, outstanding human as Eliot Graham?" Amducious commented with a conniving grin. "And besides, our demons have already tried to kill Dr. Graham several times without success. You can't come within a hundred yards of either Graham or any of his family members. Supposedly, there is a team of b-stard warriors assigned to all of them wherever they go."

"What are you saying, Destroyer?" a thoroughly confused demonic prince asked as he bobbed impatiently up and down from his second row seat. "This human, Graham, has done more damage exposing our hidden agenda than any other human alive today!"

"True!" Amducious agreed as he displayed a devious grin. "Absolutely true! For almost thirty-years this big-mouthed conservative has used our airwaves to single-handedly convince his core based, dim-witted, Bible thumping, backwoods idiots into believing that our efforts to legalize abortion and provide government based affordable healthcare coverage for all are financially draining on the United States economy. Eliminating over fifty million Americans, who would otherwise be paying into the Social Security System coffers, has put a major financial drain on the system. But more importantly, just think how many potential doctors, teachers, and praise Satan, preachers have been aborted since the passing of Roe versus Wade in 1973 in the name of one my favorite catchphrases, 'a woman's right to choose.'"

The arch demon stopped momentarily and proceeded to walk forward toward the edge of the large raised platform. "Killing Graham is not the answer!" the massive demon declared with a thunderous voice, lifting his clenched left fist high as his thousands of his attentive subordinates looked on. "What I suggest we do with Dr. Eliot Graham might shock the yellow scales right off your backs, but I believe this plan will work!"

To demonstrate his superior will over this vast assembly of unruly spirits, the cunning arch demon purposely unfurled his daunting twenty-five foot wingspan that covered nearly half the distance across the entire stage. Amducius proceeded to raise his muscular left arm high above his head. By the simple supernatural act of clicking his clawed fingers together, an audible human conversation was instantly heard throughout the great chamber. With over two thousand of his demonic cohorts attuned to a specific human radio frequency, transmitted from a location halfway across America, the intimidating arch demon bellowed his final warning. "Until I say otherwise, I command each of you to sit here and listen to every word spoken on Eliot Graham's current radiobroadcast. Graham is presently exploiting the lies about evolution from a filthy mouthed Jew named Ezra Schroeder. If anyone is caught twitching a single muscle during this time, you will answer directly to me. Now shut up and listen!"

Friday, April 10th, 2015
10:09 a.m. Central Time
American Values Hour Studios
Trinity Mills, Texas

"Dr. Schroeder, before we get started," interjected the show's host, Dr. Eliot Graham, "will you define for our listeners what is meant by Intelligent Design?"

Dr. Ezra Schroeder, a retired MIT mathematics professor, a noted Bible scholar, and an expert on the life of Sir Isaac Newton, had been invited to be the guest on today's broadcast of the American Values Hour to share both his and Newton's views on the hot-button issue, Evolution vs. Intelligent Design. With introductions completed, Dr. Schroeder responded to Graham's first question.

"Yes, Dr. Graham," Schroeder agreed as he held up a picture of a skyscraper for the audience to see. I view Intelligent Design this way, Dr. Graham. Just as a building like this skyscraper requires a builder, creation demands a creator. And as any outstanding design points to a gifted designer, our awesome universe points to the glory of an awesome Creator."

Pausing for a brief moment, Schroeder opened his Bible to a place he had already book-marked and read: "Genesis 1:1 says: *'In the beginning God created the heavens and the earth.'* The book of Romans Chapter 1, verses 20 through 22 states: *'For since the creation of the world, God's invisible attributes are clearly seen, being understood by the things that are made, even His eternal power and Godhead, so that they are without excuse. Although they knew God, they did not glorify Him as God, nor were thankful, but became futile in their thoughts, and their foolish hearts were darkened. Professing to be wise, they became as fools.'"*

When he had finished reading, Schroeder closed his Bible and stated, "In other words, Dr. Graham, no matter where you search throughout this vast universe, the undeniable imprint of our Creator's handiwork is evident, revealing to the open-minded observer His power and wisdom, His majesty and His care for every single detail. Psalm 90 verse 2 says: *'Before the mountains were brought forth, before You had formed the earth and the heavens, even from everlasting to everlasting, You are God.'* Isaac Newton said it best: "The fact that we have a universe tells us that we need a Creator."

"Alright, Dr. Schroeder, but people are going to say 'fine, God made the universe, but who made God?'"

"Excellent point Dr. Graham! However, it seems that Isaac Newton didn't have a problem with that. Newton's answer was quite simple: *'God is eternal; God doesn't have a beginning and therefore doesn't require a cause.'"*

"Well, that may be a little hard for some to grasp," Schroeder continued, "but there is nothing irrational about having an eternal being. There is something irrational about something popping into existence from nothing, because according to Newton, that violates causality."

"I'm not quite sure I'm following you, Dr. Schroeder," Graham admitted as he looked at his equally confused co-host for help.

"Can't help you, boss!" Mike Hampe shrugged. "He lost me on the term 'causality'!"

"All right, I'll try my best to simplify the problem," Schroeder conceded with a smile. "Look at it this way. Science has taught us a lot about what makes up the universe, mass and energy. Both matter and energy are eternal, or God is eternal. You can't have both being eternal. Like the proverbial scenario which came first, the chicken or the egg, Newton rationalized that given the choice between which of the two had to be eternal, God, or matter and energy, Newton chose God as the eternal creator of the universe."

"OK!" Graham affirmed, carefully monitoring the time remaining on the overhead clock. "I believe we've established a scientific explanation for God's eternal existence, but what about providing our listeners with rock solid scientific evidence that God is responsible for designing the universe?"

"I have just what the doctor ordered!" Schroeder declared with the youthful enthusiasm of a schoolboy. Holding a large poster of what appeared to be the familiar double helix shape of a DNA molecule, Schroeder continued, "Dr. Graham, consider for a moment the design ingenuity behind large complex structures like this DNA molecule. DNA contains the blueprint for all life and is by far the densest information storage mechanism known in the universe.

"In the universe, Dr. Schroeder?"

"In the universe, Dr. Graham!" affirmed. "For example, the amount of information stored on a pinhead sized volume of DNA would fill a stack of books five hundred times higher than the distance from here to the moon."

"Five hundred times higher?"

"From here to the moon, Dr. Graham! The program code and design of such an incredible system indicates—no, let me rephrase that—the program code and design of such an incredible system cries out the fact of an extremely intelligent designer. DNA is a massive, powerful information storage system. Let me put it this way: the DNA that makes up our genes is actually like books of highly technical information written by an encoded language system."

"And isn't that what you do for a living, Dr. Schroeder, decipher coded information?"

"Good point, Dr. Graham. That is exactly what NSA pays me to do!" Schroeder laughed, "and as a scientist who deals solely with coded information, I can say unequivocally that language, especially coded language, comes from a source of intelligence."

"Dr. Schroeder," Graham again interjected, "is it safe for me to say that matter and energy cannot give rise to a code?"

"Precisely, Dr. Graham," Schroeder wholeheartedly agreed. "A sophisticated coded language, such as DNA, comes only by means of an intelligent designer. We all begin as a single cell the size of a period at the end of a sentence. Now let me ask your listeners to think about this question. How does that cell know how to build an entire body, with over one hundred trillion cells in it, all differentiated into thousands of different kinds? Each cell is so complex, containing nano-chemical machinery beyond our human comprehension of how it works. And encoded within each cell's nucleus is an instruction manual on how to build and operate every part of this incredible body. It is a three-dimensional molecule that is self-replicating. Each molecule comes preprogrammed to make an exact duplicate of itself quickly and efficiently."

"Preprogrammed!" declared an astonished Graham.

"And one thing further, which should really blow your mind, Dr. Graham. The DNA molecule has its very own built-in repair shop for fixing errors."

"No way!"

"Absolutely!" declared Schroeder with a brimming smile. "The DNA molecule is so well designed that it can actually detect and correct replication errors."

"How does it do that?"

"OK, Dr. Graham," an equally excited Schroeder proclaimed, "the answer to your question is a little technical, so everyone listen to this very carefully."

While Eliot Graham displayed a colorful detailed poster of a twisted DNA molecule for the audience, Ezra Schroeder went on to explain how a DNA molecule comes preprogrammed to actually fix itself. "The DNA molecule comes equipped with a special protein called editorial type enzymes that go up and down the DNA molecule looking for and making repairs on a minute by minute, second by second, basis. Just as an editor reads a newspaper or a book looking for mistakes, there are these special enzymes that go up and down the DNA molecule, repairing the mistakes in ways that are unbelievably complex."

"Why aren't they teaching these scientific truths in our public schools?" a stymied Eliot Graham demanded.

"To paraphrase the same biblical quote I made earlier at the start of the program, Dr. Graham, if you present these same scientific facts to any rationally thinking individual, he can reach only one conclusion: God is the Creator! Mankind has always known the truth, but he refuses to accept it."

"Dr. Schroeder, in your professional opinion as an MIT-trained scientist, when it comes to the teaching of the origins of life, are our federal and state governments mandating that our public school children be taught a lie?"

"Unfortunately, my answer is yes." Schroeder shook his head in agreement to Graham's poignant question. "It is the same lie that was started over two hundred years ago by a man named Erasmus Darwin."

"Wait a minute Dr. Schroeder, I thought his first name was Charles!"

"Everyone thinks that, Dr. Graham!" Schroeder chuckled, then continued, "Erasmus was Charles Darwin's grandfather. It was he, Erasmus Darwin, not Charles, who came up with the concept of macroevolution."

"Macroevolution?" Graham asked. "I'm not quite sure I understand what that means, Dr. Schroeder. Could you explain that term for our listeners?"

"Simply put, Dr. Graham, given slime and time, species will evolve into other species."

"Slime and time—I never quite heard evolution expressed that that way before, but it makes sense."

"Listen carefully as I read the words to a poem penned in 1802 by Charles Darwin's grandfather, Erasmus, entitled *The Temple of Nature*." Ezra Schroeder proceeded to open his best-selling book to a previously marked page and read aloud the words of a little-known poem:

> '*Organic life beneath the shoreless waves; Was born and nurs'd in ocean's pearly caves; First forms minute, unseen by spheric glass, move on the mud, or pierce the watery mass; These, as successive generations bloom, New powers acquire and larger limbs assume; Whence countless groups of vegetation spring, And breathing realms of fin and feet and wing.*'

Closing the book, Schroeder proceeded with his argument that challenged the established scientific tenets preached over the past one hundred years from every secular high school and college science classroom. "A hundred years after his grandfather wrote this poem, Charles at 22, signed up for a four-year voyage aboard the HMS Beagle as a naturalist. What drove Darwin to take such a long journey was his passion to prove his grandfather's big idea correct—that life on earth had evolved over millions of years from lower forms to higher forms."

"Dr. Schroeder, did Charles Darwin find any solid scientific evidence supporting macroevolution?"

"No, Dr. Graham," Schroeder calmly replied. "What Darwin found, instead, is what scientists like to call microevolution, or, as we, who believe in an intelligent design, call, 'Mediated Design'—that life was created with the genetic potential to adapt for survival. Where Darwin believed that species developed from one animal into a different species, Mediated Design says the Creator imprinted within the DNA of each living thing the genetic potential to produce variations within a species."

"No evidence supporting macroevolution?" Eliot Graham once more asked.

"Dr. Graham, as a scientist, I am not opposed to the idea that animals change. I would love to see some evidence that macroevolution really does happen. We can talk about it happening—a fish growing legs, coming out of the sea as a new species, and yet, where is the evidence that it happened? The idea that life forms change into new kinds of species is ludicrous, and there is absolutely no scientific evidence to say otherwise."

Drawing from both his ageless enthusiasm and his vast storehouse of knowledge, Dr. Ezra Schroeder was able to verbally craft such an abstract concept as Intelligent Design into a logical argument of how a Creator was clearly behind the design of everything in the universe. "The Bible states clearly that all living things are separated into "kinds" instead of species. For example, there is a lot of room in the 'dog kind.' Great Danes, cocker spaniels and poodles are all diverse, but they are also all dogs. The fossil record is constantly emphasizing there is no intermediate missing link between kinds."

"So, in other words, Dr. Schroeder, we have never found a half-dog, half-cat." Mike Hampe commented.

"Never!" Schroeder declared, shaking his head in agreement with the co-host's statement. Turning next to the show's host, Schroeder made one last closing comment. "Dr. Graham, if it's all right with you, I would like to give your listeners one final example of Intelligent Design."

Receiving an affirming nod from the show's host, Schroeder proceeded to display a picture of what appeared to be a spiny-skinned reptile, basking along a barren rocky shoreline. "For well over a century, the scientific community has made the Galapagos Island marine iguana, a salt-spitting lizard inhabiting these archipelagoes, its poster child in support of macroevolution. What we really find here is a lizard, remarkably similar to the green tree iguana found on the South America mainland, created with a specific genetic program that has allowed this unique creature to adapt a way of removing excess salt from its system when feeding in a restricted environment where sea plants happen to be more abundant than land plants."

"And Dr. Schroeder, you say this Galapagos Island marine iguana has been used by evolutionists as their prime example supporting evolution?"

"The marine iguana along with Darwin's highly touted Galapagos Island finches, which, Dr. Graham, like breeds of dogs, are all different genetic variations of a common finch."

The moment Schroeder ended his statement, program director, Nikki Graham Fisher, signaled to those seated inside the enclosed broadcast booth that it was time to take the first call. With precision timing, Graham responded to his daughter's gesture with a quick thumbs up and, in classic fashion, blasted into his microphone a hard-hitting transitional statement sure to fire up his listeners.

"I'm not sure how our listeners are receiving this information, but I, for one, am literally fuming at our government for forcing entire generations of American kids to accept as truth this big fat lie of evolution. Let's go to our first call."

"Dr. Graham, our first caller is Quincy from Dayton, Ohio."

"Hi, Quincy, welcome to AVH. Quincy, let me start off by asking if you have any kids living at home?"

"Yes Dr. Graham, my wife, Brenda, and I have been blessed with three great kids: two girls and a boy, ages 17, 14 and 12."

"And Quincy, may I ask if your children attend public or private schools?"

"Unfortunately, Dr. Graham, on our salaries, we have no other choice but to send our three kids to the local public schools."

"So then, Quincy, after listening to our discussion on intelligent design versus the theory of evolution, how do you, as a parent, feel about your children being forced to learn the lie of evolution, and let me also add, all funded by your hard-earned taxes?"

"Dr. Graham, before I answer your question, I have a burning question that's been on my mind for some time now to ask you. Next time around, why don't you consider running for president and put an end to all this nonsense that we both know is destroying America?"

Graham sat completely stymied by the caller's unusual comeback. For the first time in his long career as a hard-hitting conservative broadcaster, Eliot Graham could not find the words to respond to a caller's question.

"Thanks, Quincy," interjected Graham's quick thinking co-host, Mike Hampe. "We'll be right back to answer Quincy's question and take more calls after we take a station break."

The scheduled three-minute station break gave Graham the time needed to collect his scattered thoughts. "God bless you, Mike. I feel like such an idiot. I can't believe I let myself be broadsided like that by such a ridiculous question."

"Eliot, if you don't mind me saying, Mike interrupted, "I personally think it was a fair question. Your listeners look up to you as their leader."

"The Lord knows this country needs some good leadership right now," Ezra Schroeder exclaimed. "Before coming here this morning I just heard Fox News report that another senator had called it quits."

"I heard it, too!" Hampe agreed. "Mitch Byler from Nebraska resigned his Senate seat out of sheer disgust over what he said was a dysfunctional political system riddled with brain-dead partisanship and not enough progress—too much narrow ideology, as he called it, and not enough practical problem-solving."

"Eliot," Schroeder smiled, placing a reassuring hand on Graham's shoulder, "I have to agree with Quincy. You would make one heck of a good president."

"Guys, no way! It's not going to happen! And besides, last time I checked my bank account, I don't think I have an extra 150 million dollars on hand to run an effective presidential campaign."

"But what if you did?" Hampe questioned.

"I don't, and I won't!" was Graham's firm response. "Have I made myself clear?"

Mike Hampe looked up at the overhead digital clock and smiled. *Saved by the bell,* he thought to himself, going by his boss's intense stare that this would be a good time to change the subject. "OK, station break's over!"

"Good!" Graham firmly stated, his eyes now fixed on his daughter Nikki's right hand, a signal to start the final segment of today's show.

"Dad, we lost Quincy during the break," Nikki broke in holding up a paper displaying the first name and location of the next caller.

"Next, we'd like to welcome Judy from Charlotte, North Carolina. Hi, Judy! A hearty Texas welcome to you from all of us on AVH! And what is your comment or question for Dr. Graham and his guest, Dr. Ezra Schroeder, today?"

"Hi, everybody!" a bubbly voice announced over the studio's speaker system. "I'd like to follow up on the comment the last caller made about Dr. Graham seriously considering running for president next time around."

Everyone in the studio smiled at the dramatic turn of events. No one would have guessed at the start of the hour-long show that a serious discussion of an Intelligent Designer could switch so easily to a conversation about presidential politics. Even

Graham sat back in his seat, gesturing with his hands raised high above his head a motion of voluntary surrender. As strange as it seemed, for the next fifteen minutes or so, a total of seven callers reiterated the same exact message: that the government of the United States was broken and only a man with Dr. Eliot Graham's God-given insight and leadership skills could possibly fix it and return America back to what its founding fathers had originally envisioned, *One Nation Under God.*

What the humans in the studio could not have possibly perceived was the fact that each of the previous human callers was prodded to contact the American Values Hour studio, and coached on the exact words their assigned familiar spirits wanted them to say.

With only four minutes remaining before the close of the show, co-host Hampe looked directly into his boss's eyes with a very strange look. "Dr Graham, we have a very interesting caller on the line who says he wants to make you an offer you won't be able to refuse."

"Don't tell me he's the Godfather!"

"Close!" Hampe stated emphatically, trying his best to maintain his straight-faced composure.

Friday, April 10th, 2015
11:56 a.m. Eastern Standard Time
Open World Institude
500 West 50th Street
Suite 50
New York, New York

On the top floor in the executive suite of the Open World Institute Building, located in downtown Manhattan, a human male sat, his aging seventy-nine year old frame hidden behind an oversized computer monitor positioned in the center of a lavishly decorated mahogany office desk. The human seated behind the computer monitor was no ordinary company executive. He was George Kaufman, best known as the founder and chairman of the Open World Institute, a network of foundations that promote, among other things, the creation of open, democratic societies based upon the rule of law, market economies, transparent and accountable governance, freedom of the press, and respect for human rights.

The vision of Mr. Kaufman's Open World Institute is a society based on the recognition that nobody has a monopoly on the truth, that different people have different views and interests, and that there is a need for institutions to protect the rights of all people to allow them to live together in peace.

Without Kaufman feeling the slightest tinge of pain, two clawed hands plunged deep within the billionaire's skull, allowing Kaufman's assigned familiar spirit, Kamozad, complete access to his human host's every thought.

"Mr. Kaufman, sir, we are ready whenever you are," a hospitable voice projected over the conference-line speakers.

"Yes, Mr. Hampe, I am ready," Kaufman answered, his words carefully scripted by an unseen presence positioned directly behind his plush leather-backed chair.

"Folks," Mike Hampe announced proudly, "we here at the AVH studios are truly honored to accept today's final call from a very special listener in New York City, the world-renowned global financier and philanthropist, Mr. George Kaufman."

"Dr. Graham, I know we have never spoken to one another personally before today, but I have often listened to your show, and I, too, am a great admirer of yours."

"Mr. Kaufman, it is a great honor to have one of America's most generous philanthropists as a caller on our show today."

"The honor is all mine, Dr Graham, and as your last caller this morning, I promise to make my comments brief. Although, I must admit, we do not always see eye to eye on all the issues, Dr. Graham, you are, in my opinion, an honest, caring man with a good heart. As I have been listening to your broadcast today, it is clearly evident, by the passionate response of your previous callers, that they view you, as do I, an American who loves his country and wants to see it restored once more to its former greatness. On this next point I believe you and I will both agree. Politicians, from both sides of the aisle, have aimlessly depleted most of America's wealth, placing our great country on the brink of financial ruin, and that needs to stop now!"

"Mr. Kaufman, I applaud you for correctly pointing the finger of blame at the true cause of our country's dire financial situation," Graham respectful affirmed. "I also believe it is imperative that we act now to bring jobs back to America and turn this economy around!"

"Dr. Graham, if you say yes, I am willing to financially back you on a successful third party run for the office of President of the United States of America."

For the second time in one single program, Eliot Graham sat speechless. After a brief pause, he responded to the billionaire's astonishing offer. "Mr. Kaufman, I'm not sure how to respond to such an offer. I am sure you can appreciate that making a decision of this magnitude and importance requires much thought and discussion, and in my case, fervent prayer."

"Dr Graham, I would not expect anything less of you. I am sure you would like to discuss such an important matter with your entire family. And, in the meantime, I will be looking forward with great anticipation to receiving your answer."

Chapter Four

And the devil said to Him (Jesus), "All this authority I will give You, and their glory; for *this* has been delivered to me, and I give it to whomever I wish.

*~Luke 4:6 (*NKJV*)*

Friday, April 10th, 2015
8:59 a.m. Pacific Standard Time
North Exhibit Hall D
Moscone Center
San Francisco, California

Except for a cluster of rowdy mid-level demons, segregated purposely in the far back recesses of the large auditorium, the vast majority of the two thousand-plus demonic spirits packed into the Moscone Center's large convention hall had remained remarkably attentive during the entire human radio conversation. Being spirits, their keen senses were supernaturally adapted to receive undetectable frequencies that were far beyond mortal human perception.

"Dr. Schroeder and Dr. Graham, to say the least, it has been a very different program today!" Both guest and host smiled, shaking their heads in agreement with co-host Hampe's observations.

"Mike, upon that note of agreement, will you do me the honor of closing today's broadcast?"

"It will be my pleasure, Dr. Graham," Hampe replied, displaying a wide smile of relief. "Folks, before we close today, I'd like to mention to our listeners that we are offering signed copies of Dr. Ezra Schroeder's best-selling book, *Newton's Riddle*, for a donation of twenty dollars or more, checks payable to AVH. You can place your order by either calling us directly at our Trinity Mills office, or by going online at our AVH website. Dr. Eliot Graham and I would like to welcome you back again tomorrow for another exciting presentation of the America Values Hour, America's one-stop shop for everything family."

As the human radio transmission came to its logical conclusion, Amducious, the Destroyer, positioned himself at the edge of the convention hall's large center stage to make his closing remarks. "I commend each of you for being so attentive! Are any of you out there smart enough to figure out what my plans might be for Dr. Eliot Graham?"

To the arch demon's astonishment, a reply immediately followed his verbal challenge from somewhere in the midst of the surrounding demon ranks. "You are planning to use the same exact strategy you employed back in the early 90's to get Bill Clinton elected president, but this time, Destroyer, instead of having an idiot like Ross Perot as the third party presidential candidate to siphon the votes off of the Republican candidate, you will use Eliot Graham!"

"I know that voice!" Amducious declared with a devious grin. The arch demon turned, focusing his deep-set golden eyes on a particularly repulsive demon sitting in the last seat at the end of the front aisle. "Zagam, come right up here on this stage and let me take a good look at your ugly face."

Amducious was not exaggerating in describing Zagam's facial attributes. In fact, even by demon standards, Zagam's entire exterior form was downright repulsive. Instead of hair, his head was crowned with thousands of knobby horn-like projections that joined at the base of his skull in a line of crested yellowish-brown ridges that continued down the length of his spine. Zagam's body was even more grotesque, covered by sagging layers of reptilian skin from his scaly yellowish brown head all the way to the tips of his blackened clawed toes. What Zagam lacked in outward appearance, this cunning malformed ogre more than made up for with his inherent abilities to deceive both mortal and spirit alike. It was this specific innate gift of deceit that won Zagam notice, when in 1947, Amducious, Satan's assigned demonic arch demon lord over America, asked this demon prince of deception to employ the same subtle, but highly effective tactics on America that he had used to destroy the Roman Empire.

Zagam's plan to destroy America was both brilliant and quite simple: Make Americans the richest and most prosperous people on earth and, at the same time, deceive the American populous by counterfeiting the word 'need' for Zagam's favorite word, 'greed.' Zagam's plan was to let Americans drown in their own wealth by opening the floodgates of easy credit, and drown they did! Before the 1950's, except for the purchase of a house, Americans would pay only for things they could afford like the necessities of life. Introducing them to easy credit was like placing a bunch of children in a room full of candy. Need turned instantly to greed. One television wasn't enough. Americans wanted one in every room. They were no longer satisfied with an old reliable car. They wanted the same expensive gas-guzzler that the rich people down the street drove. It didn't take long before every American over the age of eighteen was the proud owner of a wallet full of credit cards. The credit card gave Americans a false security, one, which allowed them to purchase things they could never afford. They became addicted to spending more than they could ever afford to pay back. Their expensive high-mortgaged homes were literally stacked full of things and gadgets that simply collected dust. Thanks to Zagam's ingenuity, today's Americans have everything their greedy hearts could ever desire, but they dwell in constant misery because of accumulated debt.

On a much larger scale, Zagam focused his secondary plan of attack on corporate America. Back in the early 1950s, American corporations required the advanced skills of the American worker to make their vastly superior products. During the next two decades, America was the leading exporter of everything from cars to shoes. That all changed when their need turned to greed. Millions of Zagam's specialized *demons rolled up their blue- collar and white- collar sleeves, and went to work tempting union bosses to strike for higher salaries. Corporate executives dreamed of larger mansions, sportier cars, and longer, more expensive corporate vacations. American workers began demanding higher wages to pay for what they owed on their credit cards, and American corporate bosses demanded higher profit margins to pay for their expensive corporate lifestyles. American companies have since pulled up their corporate stakes and migrated to those areas of the world where labor was cheap and profits were high. The end result; today American workers no longer have high-paying jobs, and the vast majorities are buried under mountains of unpaid debt.*

In a matter of mere moments, a scaly imp no taller in stature than an average-sized human mortal joined the massive arch demon, Amducious, on the stage. "Zagam, my old friend," the massive arch demon acknowledged as he extended his left clawed hand downward to grasp the scaly left appendage of his dwarfed subordinate in an act of camaraderie, "I am truly honored to have such an astute prince as you in my presence."

"The honor is all mine, Destroyer," Zagam bowed while replying in a gravely voice.

"Zagam, the platform is all yours," Amducious conceded, stepping aside, allowing his dwarfed subordinate to address his fellow demonic hordes. "Tell us once again what you were saying earlier about my strategy to use Eliot Graham as a third party presidential candidate."

"As I said before, Destroyer, Ross Perot was an idiot; Eliot Graham is not!"

Taking a calculated risk, Zagam turned his attention away from the audience toward his towering commander. The hideous demon lifted his sagging jowls just high enough to boldly state, "Destroyer, even with your brilliant plan to have the billionaire Kaufman financially back Graham as a third party presidential candidate, what makes you so sure that Graham, an intelligent human, would even consider sacrificing his ethical standards on the altar of political aspirations?"

"Zagam, for Satan's sake, Eliot Graham is not Jesus Christ!" an infuriated Amducious thundered. "You call yourself the 'master of deceit'! You should know better than any prince in this room that Graham is human, and as such, he is weak and can be manipulated!"

Appearing totally unperturbed by Amducious' fiery response, Zagam asked the incensed arch demon another audacious question, "Then may I be so bold as to ask you, Destroyer, have you found a way of persuading Graham to run as a third party candidate for president?"

"Yes!" Amducious replied definitively with his typical devious sneer. Looking at the thousands of yellow eyes staring back up at him, the massive demon continued, "Eliot Graham will be the next third party candidate for President of the United States. All of you here will be happy to know that our good friends in China and Iran will help make this fact a reality!"

A spontaneous outburst of cheering hoots and hollers thundered throughout the large hall following their commander's announcement that both the Chinese and the Iranians would assist their cause in prompting a reluctant Graham in his decision to run for president. Allowing the revelry to continue a moment longer, both Amducious and his much shorter assistant, Zaham, stood, gawking proudly from their raised vantage point over the rowdy spectacle below. They were each fully aware that the present venting of built-up energies was long overdue for a room jam-packed with restless demons.

"If there are no more questions," their commander's bone-piercing voice announced loudly in an attempt to return order and stability to the large hall, " listen carefully to my every word."

Over the eons, by not showing favoritism and consistently honoring acts of devotion to their cause, Amducious was by far the demons' most respected commander. Within moments of his command, his loyal hordes of two thousand strong had quietly returned to their seats.

"The humans attending the Progressive Democrats of America Convention will be arriving here as early as 11 a.m.," Amducious stated as he concluded the morning's meeting. "I want each and every one of you back in this hall one hour before your assigned human arrives. Is that clear?"

"Yes, Destroyer!" two thousand voices thundered.

"All stand!" Amducious ordered with a sneer.

Upon the arch demon's command, all of his demonic subordinates stood, raising a clinched left fist high above to give homage to their lord and master.

"Praise be to Satan, this meeting is adjourned!"

"Praise be to Satan!" over two thousand voices thundered in unison.

As the demonic hordes quickly made their exit from the large convention hall, Amducious turned once again to Zagam and commented, "It was good that you didn't show an outward offense to my earlier outburst."

"No offense taken, Destroyer," Zagam responded with a grin.

"Good!" Amducious exclaimed in a prideful sneer. "I now have your next assignment."

"With all due respect, Destroyer," Zagam said in a visibly shaken voice as he peered upward at the towering arch demon through his squinty yellow eyes, "I have no time right now to take on a new task. Not with the American economy on the brink of collapse!"

"I have already taken care of your concerns," Amducious replied with a prideful smirk. "For now, your associate, Pyro, is more than capable of finishing off the American economy until you have accomplished your new mission."

"What exactly is my new mission, Destroyer?"

"I believe you already know."

"Eliot Graham!" the dwarfed demon intuitively replied.

"Don't disappoint me, Zagam!"

Friday, April 10th, 2015
12 o'clock noon Eastern Standard Time
Washington, D.C.
The Cabinet Room
West Wing of the White House

Strategically positioned along the fenced perimeter of the White House grounds, an entire legion of sword-drawn warrior angels remained stationed at the exact post assigned to them after the British army sacked the White House during the War of 1812. From that time until the present, the guardian warriors were charged, not only with the protection of the president and the human inhabitants within the White House, but more importantly, to deny access to unwelcome spiritual intruders, namely demonic spirits. On any given day, until their human hosts exited through the heavily guarded White House gate, scores of familiar spirits assigned to the White House staff, and other invited human inhabitants, had to wait patiently outside the fence, just as any member of the uninvited human public.

The seven women and ten men, who made up the president's cabinet, along with the Vice President, found themselves sitting around the Cabinet Room's long cherry wood table patiently awaiting the arrival of their boss. The entire presidential cabinet was summoned by the president to meet in the West Wing, but this time, the usual domestic matters were not part of the agenda. At the president's request, intentional changes had also been made to the secretarial seating order for this meeting. Both the Energy Secretary and the Vice President, who usually flanked the president in previous meetings, were moved to opposite ends of the table and replaced by Treasury Secretary Robert Byler, now seated to the president's left, and the Secretary of State, Andrea Jacobs, to his right. Also, Secretary of Defense, Jonathan Bates, was now seated directly across the table from the president. At exactly noon, all members of the cabinet stood and clapped as the pesident made his entrance into the room.

"Good morning, everyone," President Harris announced curtly as he entered the long narrow room. Then he walked over to a chair left vacant at the center of the long table. The president smiled briefly as he turned to face the entire group and commented, "I want to thank all of you for coming on such short notice. You may be seated."

Everyone in the room sensed a degree of tension in both the president's voice and in his demeanor as if some great burden had been suddenly placed on his shoulders.

"Folks," a clearly distraught President Harris began as he made direct eye contact with each of his seventeen cabinet members, "I don't have to tell you that these are truly difficult times." The president sighed as he continued, "The reason I have called you together is that we have a potentially serious crisis on our hands, all centering on recent actions taken by the government of China. First, I will brief you on the general nature of this crisis, and then, I will turn the specifics over to our resident experts—Andrea Jacobs, Jonathan Bates, and Bob Byler, who have already been thoroughly briefed."

President Rashid Jabbar Harris, America's first elected black president, wasted no time updating his handpicked presidential cabinet on one of the most serious situations he had faced so far in his three year tenure as Commander in Chief of the United States.

"At approximately 9:17 a.m. Eastern Time this morning, I received a phone call from the President of Taiwan, Chen Shui-bian, stating that a full scaled military attack on his island nation from the mainland's Peoples' Republic of China was an imminent possibility. Within minutes of receiving this urgent call, the Pentagon, plus the intelligence agencies from Japan, Australia and Great Britain, quickly confirmed President Shui-bian's suspicions. Both ground intelligence and satellite analysis corroborate that a fleet of over thirteen of China's most advanced Russian bought destroyers have left China's naval port cities of Ningpo, and China's southern most naval port of Zhanjiang, accompanied by tank landing ships which feature a large helicopter flight deck and a docking area for up to four aircraft cushion landing crafts. According to this latest Pentagon and Defense Department analysis, everything appears to point to a possible military assault by the Peoples' Republic of China on Taiwan and its surrounding islands."

"President Harris, have we made contact yet with the Chinese Premier Wen Jiabao and his government?" the Secretary of Labor, Jerome Wallace, asked.

"Mr. Wallace, I've been on the phone for the past hour with both our Chinese ambassador Lee Myung-bak, and the Chinese Premier, trying everything within my power to avert what I foresee as a potential catastrophe of immeasurable proportions."

"And, Mr. President, what did Premier Jiabao have to say?"

Sitting almost diagonally across the cherry wood table, President Harris stared his long-time friend directly in the eyes and responded with his own chilling statement. "Jerome, I pray that what I am about to tell you, and everyone else here, never comes to fruition. All indications appear that the Chinese government has made a horribly wrong decision this morning. It is my belief that the Beijing government has every intention to remove, by military means they feel necessary, the present democratically elected government of Taiwan and attempt to replace it with their own form of provincial government, controlled solely by their central government in Beijing."

A state of near pandemonium followed the president's statement. This room had seen its share of daunting predicaments over its two hundred-year history, and now this?

"Mr. President, what specific actions is the United States going to take to avert such a catastrophe from happening?" the perplexed labor secretary demanded.

This time, instead of answering the labor secretary's question directly, the president deferred it to his Secretary of State, Andrea Jacobs, seated to his immediate right.

"I will attempt to answer Secretary Wallace's question," the Secretary of State, Andrea Jacobs, said in a calm, reassuring tone. Rising, she raised her arms in an attempt to quell the fears of her fellow secretaries. "Let me just state that never in my wildest dreams would I have ever contemplated a moment like this happening. For the past several months now, my State Department staff and I, along with Treasury Secretary Robert Byler's staff, have combined efforts to reduce tensions with the Beijing government over debt concerns and inequitable trade practices. Up until now, everything appeared to be on track for resolving some of our key trade issues and more importantly, repaying the Chinese some of our borrowed debt."

"Then what in the world happened?" Education Secretary Neil Addison asked.

"I'll tell everyone here what's happening, plain and simple!" Secretary of Commerce, James McFarland exclaimed. "We've all been duped by the Chinese government."

"I'm afraid Secretary McFarland's frank assessment of this situation may be closer to the truth than we'd like to believe," Secretary Jacobs admitted candidly. "As of this morning, the Beijing government has made it perfectly clear that as of now, all trade negotiations are off the table. They have also been very explicit in stating that the United States is to stop meddling in their government's internal affairs over Taiwan, or consider the risk of having the Chinese government call our loan."

"What?" Secretary of Veterans Affairs, Bill Nicholson, cried. "Have the Chinese completely lost their freaking minds?"

"According to our way of reasoning, I would say, yes," Treasury Secretary Robert Byler replied. "If the United States were to stop buying Chinese goods altogether, the Chinese government would not only be risking massive unempoyment and civil unrest, but the price of every cheap item China sells would go straight through the economic roof like a puff of smoke."

"Don't they even care about the dire economic effects this will have on their own people?" Secretary Nicholson asked.

"Secretary Nicholson, there's an old saying: 'He who pays the piper calls the tune,'" the secretary of treasury calmly stated. "I believe what we are witnessing here is nothing less than the Chinese declaring themselves to be the world's newest superpower. The way the Chinese see it, regardless of the short-term effects on their economy and people, this is an economic risk they are presently willing to take."

Turning his full attention toward his fellow secretaries, Treasury Secretary Byler went on to methodically list possible reasons for the Chinese government's apparent lapse toward insanity: "Even though everyone here is explicitly aware of our present economic predicament as far as our relationship with China is concerned, let me present these stark facts. Unlike the United States, China is an export economy with national debt of zero. We, on the other hand, have to import almost everything we use, and we in the United States, presently have a national debt of over 16 trillion dollars—growing by the astonishing rate of over four billion dollars a day. China owes us nothing. Over the past three decades, the United States has borrowed more than one trillion dollars from the Chinese, which makes China the largest holder of US Treasuries."

The Treasury Secretary paused momentarily looking at a room full of somber blank stares.

"To summarize," Byler said in closing, "I believe The Peoples' Republic of China has decided to take a calculated risk. It is my firm belief that China plans to use our substantial U.S. debt as a persuasive leveraging tool in its quest to overthrow the democratically elected Taiwanese government—thus in effect, making the United States lie helplessly prostrate before the Chinese dragon without a shot ever being fired."

The president calmly interjected, "Folks, I'm afraid our hands are tied on this one. The Chinese Premier has made it clear to me in no uncertain terms that if the United States attempts to intervene militarily, China would take immediate economic measures to punish us by dumping all of our treasury bonds."

"Mr. President!" the visibly shaken Secretary of Labor, Jerome Wallace, exclaimed, "I can't believe I am actually hearing you say that the United States of America is selling out one of our long-time friends and allies by giving into economic blackmail!"

"All of you can think what you want, but as President of the United States, I am first and foremost responsible for the citizens of this country. Let me remind everyone here. Over ten percent of our citizens are presently unemployed. If China were to follow through with their threat to unload our treasury bonds, that number would instantly skyrocket to over twenty-five percent. That would be an unprecedented catastrophe that would far outweigh any thought of our intervening between the Chinese and their claim to sovereignty over Taiwan. I cannot and I will not allow the United States' economy to suffer that kind of irrefutable damage!"

Friday, April 10th, 2015
12:15 p.m. Pacific Standard Time
North Exhibit Hall D
Moscone Center
San Francisco, California

They arrived by the thousands at the front entrance doors to San Francisco's largest convention center, a diverse procession of people from every state in the union, all excited to be part of a two-day convention that would highlight keynote speakers, who would exemplify their brand of liberal-leaning political ideals. As the enthusiastic conventioneers filed into Moscone Center's two thousand seat capacity North Exhibit Hall D, they were greeted by a party-like atmosphere, complete with ear-piercing rock and roll music, and five strategically hung video monitors all displaying the same repeating digital message:

The Progressive Democrats of America Convention
Welcomes all of you to the Moscone Center

"We believe that the greatest need of our nation is to redirect the resources of our government from destruction to creation, from war to peace, from military spending to social spending, from sickness to health, from selfish desires to universal needs. The future of humanity and our planet are at stake."

Already seated on the raised center stage, Progressive Democrat party organizers and their invited keynote speakers readied themselves for the start of what they hoped would be a productive two-day event that would set the political stage for selection of a presidential candidate, who would best represent their political ideals.

With few minutes remaining before actress-turned-political activist, Kate Kennedy (also the Board Chairperson and Founder of the Progressive Democrats of America), takes center stage to announce the start of the convention, two angelic giants, dressed for battle in full warrior armor, made an unwelcome entrance into the capacity filled hall through an opened back exit door. The mere presence of these uninvited intruders sparked an outburst of spontaneous rage from the demon hordes clandestinely dispersed throughout this great hall. So intense was the resonance of boos, hisses, and hollers that it produced an ear-piercing high-pitched electrical feedback throughout the convention hall's elaborate human sound system. The intruder's presence also captured the attention of several high-ranking demonic princes, standing adjacent to the human mortals seated on the stage.

"We have party crashers!" Amducious announced, his bright yellow eyes intently fixed on the two massive forms positioned less than fifty meters away at the beginning of the wide center aisle.

"Who in hell invited them?" Dolzar, the demonic prince assigned to oversee the entire convention, demanded.

"There's nothing they can do," Amducious replied in a tone of evil disdain. "Anyway, the vast majority of the humans here have already sold their despicable souls completely over to Satan. Those b-stards can stay if they behave themselves."

Even with the numeric odds vastly in his favor, the demonic arch prince knew from past encounters that he and his demonic hordes were no match for the superior abilities of his angelic rivals. As the massive giants proceeded to walk shoulder-to-shoulder down the center aisle toward the front center stage, scores of terrified demonic imps abandoned their assigned human hosts, safely distancing themselves away from the warriors' blazing swift swords. Stopping at the base of the stage, Kiel, the warrior on the right, raised his blazing gold sword high above his head and commanded human time be placed on hold. Faster than a split moment, all movement and motion, every minute detail of human activity, came to an abrupt halt throughout the great hall. Incensed by the angelic intrusion, Amducious left the side of his frozen-in-time human host, Kate Kennedy, and reluctantly proceeded to walk toward the edge of the stage to encounter his angelic counterpart.

"Yahriel, prince of prophetic wisdom and worldly affairs, you are definitely not welcome here and neither is your b-stard bodyguard, Kiel."

"Thank you, Amducious, for such a warm, heartfelt welcome, and for allowing Kiel and myself to stay for the remainder of this week-long charade." Yahriel responded with a subtle smile. Yahriel is an Archangel, fully knowledgeable of the present national and international earthly affairs and how they're aligned with our Lord's prophetic plans. He has assigned angels to be stationed in every nation, every capital, and every city on earth.

With his sword-drawn angelic companion, Kiel, standing firmly entrenched at his immediate right, the Archangel Yahriel looked up and began to boldly mock the arch demonic prince standing directly above him at the edge of the stage.

"If I haven't told you this before, Destroyer," Yahriel began with a smile, "there was a time in the far distant past that even I thought you had a few sparks of intelligence, but, once again, you've proven me wrong. You just keep on making the same stupid mistakes over and over again."

"Up your ass!" he defiant arch demon commented, extending his left clawed middle finger high above his head as he walked away from his angelic antagonist.

Before Amducious could take another step away from the edge of the stage, he was prevented from doing so by a searing sharp pain piercing his right temple.

"Going somewhere?" Kiel, asked as he extended the razor sharp tip of his golden sword against the arch demon's head.

"You have no authority at this time to destroy me and you know it, Kiel," Amducious boldly challenged. "If you push that blade any further, you will taste Satan's fury long before I meet God's wrath in the Lake of Fire."

Kiel smiled as he lowered his sword. Nothing would give this warrior angel more pleasure than to bring his nemesis' immortal existence to a premature end, but until Michael, the chief archangel *and commander of all angelic beings, gives the final order, Amducious and all arch demons must be allowed to exist.*

By now, Archangel Yahriel also took flight, joining both his demonic adversary and his angelic companion on the raised stage floor.

"You can't possibly be as stupid as the rest of those demons you lord over," taunted the Archangel. "American voters are much smarter than you think. After three torturous years of high unemployment with no end in sight, they are sick and tired of living under a liberal administration whose failed socialist policies have placed their beloved country on the brink of moral and financial ruin. They are totally fed up with a government system that wants nothing more than to tax their hard-earned money and control every aspect of their lives. Open your big yellow eyes, Amducious, and see the wasted fruits of your labor. Americans no longer want your godless form of Marxist liberalism. They can see clearly that the biggest fear liberal politicians have is that people they serve might be able to live their lives on their own without the assistance of government."

Yahriel paused with his verbal assault momentarily, and stared into the yellow face of his grinning rival.

"If you have finished boring me with your worthless speeches, could we get on with this convention?" a yawning demon prince countered mockingly. "Just stay far enough out of my way and I'll pretend the two of you aren't even here."

Yahriel accepted the terms of his demonic rival by motioning his angelic companion, Kiel, to lower his sword, thus returning human time to its natural state.

With human time restored, Amducious returned to his earlier position, standing directly in back of his chosen human host, Kate Kennedy. Looking up at an overhead screen suspended above the stage, the arch demon smiles. With only seconds left before the one p.m. start time, Amducious, the Destroyer, plunges his clawed hand deep within Kate Kennedy's torso. It was now exactly one p.m., time for the long-awaited announcement:

94

"Ladies and gentlemen, as Chairperson and Founder of the Progressive Democrats of America, I am honored to welcome each of you to the great city of San Francisco and to the Moscone Center. Today marks the beginning of a week-long historic event that will showcase our nation's future leaders ! These leaders all share the same progressive vision – a vision that will transform America into the model nation it was called to be. This will be a nation, whose charter will exemplify peace by converting military spending to social justice, a nation that will replace its past selfish desires to meet its future universal needs of not only its diverse citizenry, but more importantly, its entire global community and the planet we all call home."

Saturday, April 11th, 2015
8 p.m. Pacific Standard Time
Progressive Democrats of America Convention
North Exhibit Hall D
Moscone Center
San Francisco, California

After two days of sitting through hours of long-winded speeches touting the Progressive Democrats' past accomplishments in the areas of health care, gay rights, liberal courtroom decisions and immigration reform, the two-thousand-plus capacity crowd was more than ready to hear tonight's final keynote speaker, the progressive's champion of social rights and the outspoken former United States Attorney General, Analise Devoe. For months she has been crisscrossing the country, promoting her new best-selling book, *Made in America,* and accepting numerous television and radio interviews at every stop along the way. However, until today, Analise Devoe has refused to answer the number one question everyone in America wants answered, 'Will you run?'

With all eyes and cameras focused on center stage, Kate Kennedy, the convention chairperson, stood up to introduce the person everyone in America was waiting to hear. As Kate Kennedy took the microphone, the entire chamber erupted into a chorus. Thousands of voices shouted in unison the first name of the person they had traveled from far and wide to see. For several minutes Kennedy stood idly by, allowing the crowd's unified mantra to eventually wane, but to her surprise, the thunderous chants of "Analise! —, Analise!" became louder and more intensified. The scene within Moscone Center's Hall D was instantly transformed from a mere political assembly of like-minded people to that of a presidential nomination event complete with hundreds of red, white and blue signs and banners waving, displaying two simple, but powerful words, 'Go, Devoe!" Kate Kennedy, as with everyone else gathered either in this great hall or at home watching on their televisions, realized only too well that America was at a pivotal crossroads in its history and it needed a leader now, more than ever, to redirect and restore its path back to greatness.

The Democrats, with a very unpopular Democratic President Rashid Jabbar Harris still in office for one more year, also knew more than any other time in their tumultuous political history, that they needed a new message and a strong leader to deliver if they were to keep control of the White House. The question was not if Analise Devoe would be that leader. After watching her serve tirelessly for two terms as the nation's top legal authority, everyone in America, both her political foes and allies alike, knew she possessed leadership qualities to lead America. Would she commit tonight? That question was about to be answered. Deciding for time's sake that it was more prudent to forgo her formal introduction, Kate Kennedy turned around and signaled an attractive middle-aged brunette at the far end of a row of over a dozen VIPs and other dignitaries on the stage in the back. When Analise Devoe joined the convention's host at the center stage microphone, both locked arms around shoulders. When they waved their free hands at the two thousand supporters, pandemonium exploded! After a minute or two, Kate Kennedy turned and gave her popular keynote speaker a final embrace before returning to her seat among her fellow progressives.

As she had demonstrated so many times in the past, either standing before Congress or the Nation's Supreme Court, this seasoned lawyer took immediate charge of the seemingly out-of-control situation. She raised her right hand high for all to see and attempted to quiet the boisterous crowd. Then, the nation's former Attorney General boldly proclaimed one word everybody wanted to hear, "JOBS!" She continued shouting that same word over and over again until the only sound heard was her own. With compete attention focused on her every word, the skillful attorney began building her case.

"As the proverbial saying goes," she began, "I have some good news and some bad news to share with you. Which would you all prefer to have first?"

"The good news!"

"Well," Devoe said with a smile, "the good news is, 'we Democrats' are now in charge of this country, and 'we' have a plan that will place all Americans back to work in high-paying jobs."

The entire hall was in an uproar again. Had she had stopped there, Analise Devoe knew that everyone present would have been satisfied with her message: jobs, high paying, blue and white-collar American jobs. This was her message, plain and simple. Millions had already read her book, *Made in America*, a well-thought-out, detailed plan on how to implement all of America's resources to elevate the United States' standing, once more, to the number-one economic superpower on earth.

"Folks, it has already been stated over and over again in these past three days, Progressive Democrats have won tremendous political social strides over the past three years of the Harris administration. For the first time in our nation's history, health care is a right for every American, and all Americans are

97

presently covered by a health insurance policy tailor-made to suit their needs."

Everyone rose, giving the speaker a standing ovation.

"For the first time in our nation's history, gay marriage is legally accepted in fifteen of our states including in our nation's capitol, Washington D.C."

Once again, a rousing standing ovation followed the speaker's comments.

"But folks," Devoe continued as she raised both hands above to regain order, "as you know, I stand by my word, and I will not stop fighting against this travesty of social injustice until every gay couple throughout America can freely express their love for one another with all the legal benefits and titles they so rightly deserve."

Applause

"Allow me to quickly state one other progressive legal achievement during the Harris administration. Abortion is not only safe and legal, but it is a woman's choice to choose her own reproductive rights in all fifty states. And, now it is close to being fully funded as a healthcare benefit for all Americans!"

Applause

"Another major achievement accomplished during the Harris administration was passing last year's Immigration Reform Act. As of now, millions of productive, hardworking individuals, who have come to our shores seeking a better tomorrow for themselves and their families, have been granted the full rights and benefits of American citizens."

Another rousing applause

After expounding once more all of the progressives' hard-fought social achievements, Analise Devoe abruptly changed the subject and stated some facts that no progressive had been brave enough to mention during the two days of hyped up speeches. Accessing the hall's overhead digital monitors, Devoe signaled her team of off-stage technicians to project an image no one present wanted to see.

"Now, my friends, this is the bad news!"

The very moment the ominous words were projected on the overhead digital display, an eerie silence permeated every square inch of the great hall. Projected on each of the five highly visible screens in bold red numbers below the words Present National Debt was an amount totaling $17.3 trillion dollars.

The brazen Attorney General paused momentarily to give those in mental denial time to fully absorb the enormity of such a number.

"This astronomical number in bold red print shows not only leftovers from the previous administration, it is our doing as well!" she unashamedly proclaimed. "Please keep in mind, this number does not include the money owed by states, corporations, or individuals, nor does it include the money owed to Social Security beneficiaries in the future. With figures from the last quarter just in, the US payment deficit is running at an annual rate of one and one half trillion dollars, requiring the United States Treasury to borrow nearly $4 billion a day from the rest of the world—mainly from China, Japan, and other Asian nations— just to finance it. With our current population hovering slightly under 335,000,000, in order to pay off our national debt today, each citizen would have to shell out over 48 thousand dollars."

Attorney General Devoe paused once again to let out a brief sigh.

"That, my friends, is the bad news and in my opinion, it doesn't get much worse. This millstone of public debt is literally choking the life out of our country, and if we don't make drastic changes right here and now, the United States of America will be completely bankrupt within as little as five short years from now. I believe the American people were well aware of this problem when they cast their vote back in November of last year, removing every congressional incumbent from office. They are the ones now who are looking to us to bring needed changes to fruition."

At that point, Analise Devoe paused her speech, just long enough to muster enough courage to make her next statement.

"If you are all feeling a bit depressed right now, folks, I am right there with you." Devoe once again scanned her audience before continuing, "Even though all of the warnings were shouting out at us, no one heeded the call. It is now, with a heavy heart, that I stand here today in this great hall to say that America is no longer at a crossroad. Opportunities to solve and resolve the economic problems plaguing our great country during the past several administrations have, for the most part, been totally ignored and now we must face the following grim realities. I personally decided to start my speech tonight by first presenting America's real enemy, the mountain of accumulated debt that has been and continues to literally choke the life out of our great country.

"I planned to end my own speech tonight with this final point. The plan I described in my book, *Made in America*, is not to waste four years chipping away at this mountain of accrued debt; my plan for America is to cast that mountain into the sea forever. I, for one, am sick of watching the evening news and asking the same questions I believe most Americans are asking themselves. How could we have been so passive – to simply sit back and allow America to get into such a mess? My fellow Americans, as I said over and over again during the past several months, America needs jobs. My plan would bring high-paying jobs back to the American workers, jobs with security and real benefits that would be there for the next generation of Americans, and for generations to come. I stand here before you with no hidden agenda. I have no affiliation with any special interest group. America is my special interest and now I plan to deliver! This is as good a place as any to stop and make the announcement that all of you have been waiting for me to say."

The savvy lawyer's timing for this all-important statement was impeccable. Whether they loved her, or hated her, whether they agreed with her politics or not, everyone in America watching this televised broadcast was anxiously waiting the next words that were about to be spoken from Analise DeVoe's lips.

"Yes!"

Nothing more needed to be said. That one simple word of affirmation said it all. Pandemonium over Devoe's announcement spread like wild fire, not only throughout the four walls of the Moscone Center's North Exhibit Hall D, but also, at the speed of light, instantly transmitted to every satellite linked media source and broadcast by television, smart phones, Ipad and android tablets, and the Internet throughout the world. In a mere matter of microseconds, literally billions of earthlings on all seven continents were aware of Analise Devoe's decision to run for the President of the United States of America. Meanwhile, at Moscone Center, every available security guard employed throughout the mega complex was called upon to not only bring a sense of order to North Exhibit Hall D, but also to form a secure human barrier of protection around the person at the center of all the excitement, Analise Devoe.

Saturday, April 11th, 2015
10 p.m. Central Standard Time
The Graham Estate
Along the southern banks of Lake Lewisville
15 miles North of Trinity Mills, Texas

Over a thousand miles away from this scene of euphoric jubilation in San Francisco, a subtle, but just as far-reaching decision in its implications on future national politics, was about to be made. It was here, within the quiet confines of a lakefront Texas estate, that eight members of the Graham family, minus the oldest son and daughter, Eliot, Jr. and Mary Beth were gathered. Every eye was fixed on a large television screen, and they watched in silent awe as ecstatic members of the Progressive Democrats of America danced about center stage, hugging and celebrating the fact that one of their chosen had just decided to carry their liberal torch into the future.

As Aaron Graham positioned himself on a wing backed chair only a foot away from the large dark brown leather couch where his father and mother were sitting, he asked, "What are you thinking, Dad?"

"Truth?" a smiling Eliot Graham responded with a smile. "Personally speaking, Analise DeVoe is a very charming person, and I believe she is sincerely true to her convictions, but as President of the United States, she would be worse than Harris by a factor of a thousand!"

"How so, Dad?" Graham's youngest son, Jonathan, abruptly inquired. "You've read her book! You even admitted to her during your face-to-face interview last month that you agreed with her jobs plan."

"What's wrong with you guys?" a clearly confused Graham asked as he looked around the large room at his equally perplexed loved ones. "My strong feelings about Analise DeVoe have absolutely nothing to do with her jobs plan. The woman is an outright atheist, and she makes no bones about it! In the eight years she served as Attorney General she did more to strip God out of American society than any other single person."

"You're really fired up, aren't you, Dad?" Graham's youngest child, Sydni, declared as she sat with her sister, Nikki, on an adjacent leather loveseat.

"You bet I'm fired up!" He got up and began walking around the large family room.

"Does that mean you're going to accept Kaufman's generous offer and run against her?" Graham's personal lawyer and second oldest son, Aaron, joked.

"Look, you guys know me better than that." With remote in hand, Eliot Graham promptly proceeded to switch off the television and turned to face his puzzled family members. "As I have said a thousand times, I will never sell out my soul to the devil and run for any public office!" He made a fist with his right hand and pounded it into his left hand to affirm his conviction.

Exhibiting the same degree of exuberant passion he would muster daily on his radio program, Graham pointed his index finger in the direction of his second oldest daughter, Nicole. "Nikki, who do we have on Monday's lineup?"

"Dad, we have your good friend, David Lorton, the Founder and President of the American Heritage Foundation. He's scheduled for both Monday and Tuesday's show."

"Alright, Nikki, call David right now and cancel him for both shows."

"What?" Nikki responded with a baffled look. "Dad, we've already paid for David's entire roundtrip plane fare and also for his two-day lodging expenses."

"You're right, Nikki! Scratch that idea." Graham admitted his mistake, and walked toward the far side of the room to gather his thoughts.

"Eliot!" his wife Rosemary interjected. "Will you please stop pacing back and forth for just a second and let us in on what you're thinking?"

"Absolutely!" the family patriarch conceded with a smile, stopping long enough to answer the confused stares of his surrounding family members. "Guys, I want each of you to think about this. Who worked hand-in-hand with Analise DeVoe over the past eight years, attempting to strip away almost every vestige of God's influence from American society?"

"Dad, that would be your old arch nemesis, the Executive Director of Americans for the Separation of Church and State, Harry Flynn!" William replied as he sat quietly by himself on the family room rocking chair.

"None other!" his exuberant father acknowledged. Graham then turned his full attention once more to his daughter and AVH program director, Nicole.

"Nikki, I know it's late, but see if you can get Harry Flynn on the phone. Ask him if he's available to link up with us live over the phone from his Washington office for both Monday and Tuesday's broadcast. I can't think of a better way of exposing both Analise DeVoe's true nature and her direct involvement in America's current moral and economic downfall than to have the number one expert on America's foundational Judeo-Christian heritage, David Lorton, going toe-to toe, or head to head with Devoe's side-kick in crime, the devil incarnate himself, Harry Flynn!"

"Makes sense to me, Dad," Nikki Graham responded with an affirming nod, "but can't this wait until tomorrow? It's after eleven o'clock on the East Coast."

"Honey, don't you know the devil never sleeps!" Graham jokingly stated. "And knowing Harry as well as I, this is one night he'll be out celebrating this victory until the wee hours of the morning."

Before reclaiming his time-honored position sitting on the family couch beside his wife, Rosemary, Graham stood before seven of his closest family members and made a passionate declaration that he would live to regret. "Starting this Monday, I will use every resource available to make sure Analise DeVoe will never sit behind the presidential desk in the Oval Office, so help me God!"

The exact moment Eliot Graham finished making this final definitive statement, a familiar ring tone sounded from across the room.

"It's Nancy," William announced with a smile as he proceeded to withdraw his cell phone from the hidden confines of his inside jacket pocket. "I bet you any money she's calling to tell me it's time to come home."

"Hi Honey! I'm coming home, right now!" the boyish-faced husband answered happily with a roomful of smiling faces looking on. Only moments later, William's cheery expression changed to darkened gloom.

"William, what's wrong?" his mother asked with a voice of concern.

"Quick!" William frantically shouted, pointing his finger in the direction of the television remote control resting on the coffee table. "Someone, turn on the TV, now!"

All eyes in the Graham family room were once again fixed on the large centrally located television. Gone from its digital display was the scene of the euphoric Progressive Democrats hugging and congratulating one another, replaced by what appeared to be an unusual scene of somber-faced reporters packed into the White House Press Briefing Room. Within moments of turning on the television, an equally solemn President Rashid Harris stepped up to the centrally positioned presidential podium and declared this bone-chilling statement before the fretful stares of the White House Press Corp reporters and the entire world:

"As of fifteen minutes ago, at approximately 10:44   p.m. Eastern Standard Time, Kim Jiabao, the Chinese Premier of the Peoples' Republic of China declared that a state of war now exists between his nation and the independent island nation of Taiwan."

Chapter Five

"For Satan himself transforms himself into an angel of light"

~2 Corinthians 11:14 (NKJV)

Saturday, April 11ᵗʰ, 2015
11 p.m. Eastern Standard Time
Hunter Mountain Ski Resort Lodge
Hunter, New York

If silence had a voice, its tone at the moment would have been deafening to hundreds of Robert Berry supporters gathered at this evening's gala fundraising event held at Hunter Mountain Ski Resort Lodge. Everyone had gathered at this spectacular snowcapped mountaintop resort located deep within the grandeur of New York State's famous Catskill Mountains for one purpose only—to garnish financial support for the former New York Governor's bid to become the next Republican nominee for President of the United States. A party-like atmosphere, complete with toasting, drinking, cheering, and laughter, had prevailed all evening throughout this capacity filled banquet hall, but now, no one was partying or laughing. Expressionless faces gazed with blank stares; eyes stared in shock at the large video display screen in the front of the room. It was only moments ago that everyone in the room watched the same screen in horror as President Rashid Harris announced that the People's Republic of China had declared a state of war between their massive Asian country and the tiny Pacific island nation, Taiwan, located two hundred miles off the Chinese coastline. Seated at the front banquet table adjacent to the podium with a microphone, a youthful faced man turned toward the strikingly well groomed, gray-haired gentleman seated to his immediate right and whispered, "Grif, if you have any suggestions at the moment, I'm all ears."

"Bob, look me in the eye," Governor Berry's no nonsense, straightforward campaign manager, Griffin Gunson, demanded. "You've got to trust me on this one. The Chinese are only bluffing!"

"What makes you so sure of that?"

"According to everything I studied, and believe me, Bob, I'm really up on this one, the Chinese have only two things going in their favor right now—a strong economy and countless ground troops. Where it really counts, their naval and air force capabilities in the China Sea can't touch us. Our vastly superior military strength in that region has been, and still is, second to none."

"If what you say is true, why are the Chinese threatening us now?"

"Plain and simple, Bob—it's timing. It's all about timing." Gunson flatly stated.

"Go on, Grif; I'm listening."

"Think about it, Bob. Over the past two years, Beijing simply sat back to watch these crazy rogue nations like Iran and North Korea line up, threaten the security of the world, receive a slap on the wrist, a sanction or two, and in the end, they get everything they demanded. Now, the Chinese feel it's their turn to step up to the plate and demand what they've wanted all along—for America to hand them Taiwan on a silver platter. They are more willing to take the risk now, having Harris, a weak-assed socialist liberal in office, than waiting two years to deal with a hard-lined conservative like you as a president who won't put up with any of their b.s."

"As always, Grif, you've nailed it!" Berry commented, rewarding his campaign manager with a broad smile and a firm pat on the

107

back. "That's the reason I chose you as my campaign manager, and two years from now, you'll be my top presidential advisor."

With that said, an assured Bob Berry boldly stepped up to the microphone and addressed his dazed supporters. "My friends, everyone—please look up here," he calmly asserted. Berry paused briefly, allowing everyone, including a dozen or so stunned servers holding their food trays in hand, time to sit down and listen.

"I know exactly how you're feeling right now. Like all of you, when I first heard President Harris announce over the monitor that China had threatened to invade Taiwan, I had the same gut wrenching reaction as each of you. At first, I, too, was shocked, stunned, and fearful but not anymore. Three years ago, when I first ran against the then Senator Harris for president, I saw this coming. This is exactly what you get when you place a progressive appeaser in the office of president of the most powerful nation on earth. I shouted it from the rooftops back then, but no one cared to listen. You mark my words, friends, they'll be listening now! With your support, come next November, the entire world will know once more that America is a country where people support freedom, liberty, free enterprise, and democratic principles for all the world's people and, if you elect me president, I will never allow America to be bullied into submission by either Islamic radicals or Communist thugs."

Nothing more needed to be said. Everyone gathered inside the mountaintop resort's huge banquet hall stood and applauded the man who was not only determined to be the Republican nominee for the highest elected office in the land, but also, the president of that nation, as well.

Not everyone standing at that moment within the banquet hall was human. In fact, in another cheering section, over a dozen mid-level demons, were lined up, standing directly in back of their assigned human charges at the front VIP table. But, unlike the humans, they were assigned to deceive and manipulate this motley contingent of demonic beings, cheering their own established leader on, the demonic prince specifically assigned by Satan himself to oversee the complete destruction of America.

"Everything seems to be going as planned," the massive yellow-skinned giant standing directly in back of the human, Griffin Gunson, boasted.

"Lord Satan should be well pleased by our efforts, Destroyer," a distinctly feminine-toned voice emanated from within the confines of its assigned human host, Griffin Gunson.

"You have my permission to come out of the human and show yourself," the towering arch demon commanded.

"Lord Amducious, this might take a moment," the voice commented from inside the human. "I've not been outside this pathetic rotting body for over twenty mortal years."

The first body part to protrude from the back of Griffin Gunson's torso appeared to be the feathered head of an eagle, complete with a sharply hooked beak. Following the head, a bizarre-looking four-footed winged creature emerged. Its body was a clawed four-legged lion, but its feathered wings and head were that of an eagle. "Praise Satan, what a relief this is!" The overjoyed demonic apparition cried as it immediately stepped to the side. Then it stretched its long legs, each leg tipped with an entire set of razor-sharp clawed talons. Proudly it unfurled its extensive sixteen-foot wingspan.

"Lord Amducious, before you say anything further, just listen to my plea," implored the winged chimera, a griffin. "I've been confined inside Gunson's body every day now since he was sixteen years old, and pledged his life to Satan at a Motley Crue concert."

Turning its attention toward the dozen or so gawking mid-level demons now gathered in a tightly huddled pack to the right of their assigned human hosts, the Griffin (the same demonic title as its human host's forename) looked at its commander and made one final plea.

"Destroyer, I will go anywhere and do anything you say, but I beg you, assign one of them to take my place. Please, Destroyer, don't order me back in that pathetic body!"

Amducious smiled before reaffirming what the chimera already knew. "Griffin, you knew full well what my answer to your pathetic *plea would be even before you asked. Before releasing you from Gunson's body, your assignment must be carried to the very last detail. As you know, I, myself, selected you for this task for one simple reason—nothing hates humans more than a griffin. Let me remind you once again, Griffin, of your specific charge. You will continue existing inside Griffin Gunson's body until the day that you not only destroyed his life, but also, that human bast-rd, Robert Berry, and the entire Republican Party he represents, as well."*

In an astonishing show of ambivalence, Amducious reached his scaly hand out and proceeded to stroke his claws through the feathery scalp of his choice chimera's head.

"Now, Griffin, before you return to Gunson's body to carry out the remainder of your mission, you have my permission to take the next five mortal minutes of time to freely expand your wings and fly above the skies of this resort."

Totally blown away by its commander's rare act of kindness, the winged demon graciously bowed to the floor and declared, "Destroyer, I will not disappoint you."

"Good! Your loyalty will be rewarded," the arch demon commented as he, too, proceeded to crouch his massive frame low enough in order to wrap his scaly yellow arm securely around the demon's feather neck. Looking directly into the Griffin's eyes, Amducious made his final request known, "Before I allow you to set flight, Griffin, where is she?"

Using its superb supernatural senses, the demonic apparition focused its eagle eyesight on a woman standing and applauding with a group of four other humans at the first table at their immediate left. "You can't miss her, Destroyer. She is the big-breasted brunette wearing the seductively revealing red blouse."

"How has her training been going thus far?" Amducious asked with a devious sneer.

"She's coming along, Destroyer." The eagle-headed demon responded in a distinctly sensual female tone. "Gunson and I have personally spent many quality hours preparing her ourselves." The Griffin paused momentarily, allowing its long slithery black tongue to capture a

small flow of saliva escaping from its beak. "When the time is right, Destroyer," the Griffin continued, "we will personally introduce her to Robert Berry."

"Excellent!" the boastful arch demon proclaimed. "I couldn't have picked a more qualified human hater than yourself. Now, take flight, but remember this, you are to return to Gunson's body in exactly five mortal minutes."

As Amducious proceeded to release his tight grip from around the griffin's neck and return to an erect standing position, he made one last charge. "And Griffin, stay far away from any horses."

"No promises on that request, Lord Destroyer, but I will definitely try."

Following the standing ovation, Robert Berry graciously thanked everyone present for coming out and supporting his efforts to seek, for the second time in three years, the Republican nomination for the office of President of the United States. With his wife of twenty-seven years, Liz, standing at the front podium by his side, Berry bid everyone good night and retired to his executive suite hotel room. Not long after Berry's departure, the remainder of those gathered in the large banquet hall decided also to follow the governor's lead, leaving behind in their wake a small cleaning crew and a handful of Berry supporters taking their good old time exiting the building.

"Wow!" exclaimed Griffin Gunson, one of two still remaining at the front reserved VIP table. "I should be feeling dead tired right now, but I feel better than I've felt in years. It's as if some monster weight has just been lifted off my entire body."

"Let me know, Grif, whatever that is you've been drinking," Sam Price joked, his finger pointed down at the half-filled glass of clear liquid still remaining on the table. "I'll order some of that myself."

"That's it, Sam," a relaxed Gunson replied, proceeding to slouch into his chair with his hands folded behind his head. "Other than this half-filled glass of water here, I haven't had anything else to drink all night."

"Uh oh," warned Price, both eyes fixated on a very attractive young woman seated at a vacant table no more than twenty feet away to the left of the front table.

"Don't look now, Prince Charming, but I believe Snow White over at that first table is trying to get your attention."

"I see her," a beleaguered Gunson commented, struggling to open his right eye. "Do me a favor, Sam. Be a good friend. Go over there and keep her occupied while I slip out the back."

"What are you talking about?" Gunson's confused administrative assistant asked. "You're going to go and leave your hot chick with me? Where do I tell her you're going?"

Give her the old standard line." Gunson looked up and smiled. "Tell her I had a headache all of a sudden."

"Earth to Griffin Gunson," Price leaned over and whispered into his boss's ear. "Hello, Griffin, is anyone home in there?"

"I'm still here, Sam." Gunson affirmed with a grin.

"Grif, are you absolutely sure nobody came by and spiked that water in your glass, because, man, you're acting really strange at the moment."

No sooner had Sam Price finished his comments than Gunson burst forth into a spontaneous bout of laughter.

"Old buddy, boss of mine." Price chuckled as he too proceeded to sit back. "I was right all along. Somebody spiked your drink big time!"

Gunson continued to laugh uncontrollably. "Sam, be the man and take her back to her room!"

Shaking his head, a thoroughly confused Sam Price got up and proceeded to walk over toward the only other person, beside the hotel employees, still remaining in the banquet hall. With hands folded behind his back, Price stopped just short of her table and sheepishly introduced himself. "Sheila? Hi, I'm Sam Price, Grif's administrative assistant. You may not remember me, but we met briefly last month in Phoenix at that huge Berry fundraiser."

"I remember you," the eye-catching brunette responded with a girlish giggle. "You're that quirky nerdy guy who got me the tickets to the Carrie Underwood concert."

As she stood, Price's eyes once again became fixated, not only on her attractive external beauty, but this time, he zeroed straight in on her immodestly exposed midriff.

She might have all the right body parts going for her, but her brain is definitely missing some vital functions, Price chuckled to himself.

"Oh, I hope you don't take me calling you 'nerdy', personal, Sam," continued the ditzy female, again with a giggle. "I think you're really kind-of cute, in a nerdy kind of way."

Just beyond the senses of the few humans now remaining in the almost empty banquet hall, true to its word, the winged Griffin returns to the exact position it had vacated, not a mortal second under or over its agreed time. "Thank you, Destroyer, for allowing me this brief respite of freedom. Respectfully, the grateful chimera bowed before its demonic arch commander.

"Griffin, if you successfully carry out your mission, this momentary freedom you just experienced will be yours for much longer than a respite. And Griffin, before you return to Gunson's body, answer me this: Why is it that I sense the strong smell of horse blood in the air?"

"I tried, Destroyer, I really tried!"

"Woo! Do you smell that?" Sheila declared, immediately curling her nose up in response to a strange repugnant odor in the air.

"I may be mistaken, but it smells a lot like horse," Sam Price replied, reacting in turn to the stench by holding his own nose.

"I'll take her back to her room!"

"Grif!" a stunned Sam Price declared, staring in disbelief at the strikingly handsome, gray-haired gentleman standing directly in back of him. "I thought you said you had a headache?"

"It's passed!" Gunson calmly declared as he proceeded to walk over, pick up and kiss the hand of the big-breasted beautiful brunette wearing the revealing red blouse.

"Hi Griffy," Sheila responded in her best flirtatious voice. "Are you ready to party some more?"

"Baby, I'm ready when you are," Gunson replied with his own seductive smile, pulling her body close to his. "Let's go back to the room and party all night long!"

Saturday, April 11, 2015
8:54 p.m. Eastern Standard Time
Fox Broadcasting News Headquarters
6th Avenue West Rockefeller Center
New York, New York

With only minutes remaining before the close of her hour-long primetime news broadcast, Fox News anchor, Vanessa Lewis introduced her final news segment with a stern warning to viewers with children. "Folks, before we end tonight's edition of the 8 o'clock News Hour, we, at Fox News want to caution our viewers that our final news story contains graphically disturbing images and details. If you have young children in the room, please be advised, the following story contains very disturbing graphic details."

The moment those final words were uttered, the veteran newscaster visibly grimaced, facing away from the fixed broadcast monitor placed directly in front of her. Now appearing on the screen, a TV reporter stood in front of what appeared to be a large, well-maintained barn. Moving the microphone toward his mouth, the reporter, his facial expressions appearing both grim and solemn, began describing the gruesome events that took place at this seemingly tranquil location a little less than a week ago.

"Five days ago, Fox Cable News first reported a very disturbing story coming from the usually serene backdrop of New York's beautiful snow covered Catskill Mountains. As was first reported here on Fox News, sixteen thoroughbred racing stallions were found dead and grossly dismembered at the Hudson Valley Horse farm, located three miles south of the popular Catskill resort village of Hunter Mountain. After an intensive weeklong investigation by forensic experts, called in from all over the country, state and local police report that they still have no leads as to who could have committed such a despicable act. Everyone here agrees that this deed goes far beyond the suspicions of animal cruelty. According to the police report, sixteen registered thoroughbred horses were discovered dead, literally torn to shreds, early last Saturday morning in their individual stalls. Worst of all, a mixture of mangled and dismembered body parts were found scattered throughout the blood-drenched interior of this large well-maintained stable."

With the disturbing visual images still fresh in his mind, the reporter paused momentarily, gathering his emotions before continuing. "Without any hardcore evidence, the police can only speculate at this time that possibly members of a cult performed this despicable act as some sort of bizarre satanic ritual. We here at Fox will let our viewers know as soon as any further information is made available. Reporting from the Hudson Valley Horse Farm, three miles south of Hunter, New York, this has been Jason Jerald speaking. I'll now return you to Vanessa Lewis, live, in our New York studios."

"Thank you, Jason for that disturbing live report," Lewis returned to the screen, forcing a smile in an attempt to put a positive spin on the end of what turned out to be a very difficult broadcast. "And that brings another edition of Fox's 8 o'clock News Hour to a close." With her daily assigned duties all but over, the dark-skinned beauty smiles into the camera and proceeds to verbally pass her proverbial network torch to the next scheduled Fox Cable News commentator, Keenan McShea.

"We now switch to our upstairs studio where the nation's most watched cable news program, *Politically Most Wanted*, hosted by author, syndicated columnist, and political commentator, Keenan McShea, is just about to get under way. Don't change your station, for Fox's *Politically Most Wanted* is next."

Saturday, April 11th, 2015
9:00 p.m. Eastern Standard Time
Fox Broadcasting News Headquarters
Studio Three
6th Avenue West Rockefeller Center
New York, New York

With the vivid images of mutilated horses still fresh in everyone's mind, Keenan McShea's laser-sharp mind had to think fast to use this unsettling story to his advantage. The moment the show's introductory music stopped, the host of Fox's primetime political news broadcast went right into action.

"Good evening America and welcome to another edition of *Politically Most Wanted*. I'm your host Keenan McShea, and once again, welcome to, if I may steal a line from one of tonight's *Most Wanted* guests, 'America's one-stop shop for everything political.'

In the world of politics, when it comes to Keenan McShea, he's either loved or hated; there are no political in-betweens. This slightly balding, fifty-two year old son of Irish immigrants has been a regular fixture in the ever-changing landscape of TV broadcast news for over two decades, but it wasn't until the last round of presidential elections that his popular persona as a staunch champion of conservative politics launched him into the top hot seat of primetime cable news. With the fiery look of Irish determination radiating from his piercing blue eyes, McShea proceeded to set the stage for tonight's show.

"To say that that last news segment viewed on the 8 o'clock News Hour was unsettling is a gross understatement, to say the least. But America, I want all of you watching right now, at this very moment, to delete those vivid images of butchered helpless animals in your mind. Remove from your mind right now our nation's present ten percent plus unemployment rate. Erase our government's out-of-control spending spree in your mind. With our present national debt rapidly approaching 18 trillion dollars, America has become the most indebted nation in the history of mankind. Put out of your minds the fact that our nation's long-held top status as the world's number one economic superpower has been recently replaced by China. For a moment put out of your mind the fact that our nation's tragic decline in secondary public education has plunged from number one in the world twenty years ago to 18 out of 36 nations, according to the latest survey published in USA Today. Teachers back then were valued in the classroom; today they are assaulted. Put out of your minds for a moment that mental illness, autism, ADHD, pregnancy, suicide, sexually transmitted diseases and drug and alcohol abuse among America's youth are presently at an all-time high. Put out of your minds that forty years ago, one in five marriages ended in divorce. Today, it is 1 out of 2. At the same time, single parented families in America have increased by over 350%.

McShea briefly paused, allowing his audience a moment to absorb the gross volume of negative statistics before continuing. "Folks, what in God's name has happened to our beloved country?" McShea paused, raising the palms of his hands up as an expression of not only his frustration, but also, the frustration of millions of viewers watching in homes all across America.

"We, at PMW, have invited three very special Americans, who all claim they not only have answers to our nation's present woes, but also, workable solutions to get America back on track. As Ronald Reagan so aptly called it, 'a shining city placed on a hill.' Our first guest needs no introduction. For the past twenty years or so, he's been known throughout our land as the icon of the airwaves, the most listened to conservative talk-radio host in

America, broadcasting to us live from Trinity Mills, Texas, Dr. Eliot Graham. Along with Dr. Graham, we have also invited on the *Politically Most Wanted*, the cofounders of the American Values Party, Sean and Lindsay Wiggins."

Transcending vast distances from Texas to Minnesota, through the magic of digital technology, three familiar faces instantly appeared on screens across America. "Guys, welcome to *Politically Most Wanted*," McShea greeted. "I'll start by asking Dr. Eliot Graham that same plaguing question I just posed to all America. Being that you are a former Baptist minister, I'll rephrase my question, "Dr. Eliot Graham, "*What has happened to our beloved country?*"

"Keenan, as I tell my listeners daily, the answer to America's woes can be simply summed up by the old expression, 'If you don't give, you don't get.'"

"Dr. Graham, I'm sure your radio listeners understand that expression, but can you enlighten the two or three out there in America who probably don't listen to talk-radio anymore?"

Eliot Graham smiled. He knew better than most that radio's heyday as America's choice for entertainment and information had long past, but for those Americans forty years and older, he was still considered a media icon. Now was his opportunity to speak to a younger generation of Americans—those nurtured, a digital age of smart phone technology, ultra high-definition television, and high speed Internet. With the FOX studio cameras focused directly on him, the man personified by millions of his faithful followers as the conservative voice of America, began sharing his heart.

"I want everyone listening to my voice to stop whatever it is you are doing and hear what I have to say. With the exception of the academic and political elite, I believe most Americans are reasonably aware of the fact that our nation was founded on Godly, biblical principles. Our government and the very words of our Founding Fathers were framed on the premise that all men are created equal, that they are endowed by their Creator, God, with certain unalienable rights, and that among these are life, liberty and the pursuit of happiness. This concept of rights being unalienable is thus dependent upon belief in God as the giver of all these rights. This is the basis and the soundness of Jefferson's statement in his 1796 letter to John Adams, which I will now quote, "If ever the morals of a people could be made the basis of their own government it is our case." Simply put, if America refuses to give God the moral respect He is due, then God, the Giver of America's unalienable rights, will have no other choice but to remove these same rights from America. That, in a nutshell, Keenan, is what I meant by my statement, "If you don't give, you don't get."

"Powerful statement, Dr. Graham!" McShea affirmed with a nod.

The host of *Politically Most Wanted* momentarily shifted his attention from Graham toward the two individuals seated on the right side of the split-screen television monitor.

"Sean and Lindsay Wiggins, Cofounders of the American Values Party, welcome once again to *Politically Most Wanted*," McShea said. "As American citizens, who are deeply disturbed by the current trend of America's downward spiral, do you two accept Dr. Graham's basic premise that simply by abandoning God's moral standards, America has gotten itself into the big huge mess we find ourselves in today?"

"If it's all right with my husband," Lindsay Wiggins interjected, "I'd like to answer that question."

"By all means," the show's host nodded.

"Both Sean and I whole-heartedly agree with Dr. Graham's summation as to the root cause of most, if not all, of America's vast problems. Our nation has abandoned God's moral standards, which were explicitly established within our Constitution by our Founding Fathers. The very reason we are sitting here tonight discussing this issue with you, Keenan, is that we believe, along with the millions of other Americans, who fully support the American Values Party ideals, that unless we act now, America, as we once knew her, will be lost forever. Our strength," Lindsay Wiggins continued, "is in morals and values. Almost all Americans know that they're accountable to a God in heaven so, more than anything, they want to be self-governing individuals who police themselves. They don't need the tyranny of the state to do that."

Sean interrupted. "Honey, ccould I cut in right now? I'd like to also bring to light one eclipsing issue America faces, the most politically charged moral issue of our day, that according to the annals of recorded history, will either make or break a country."

"Let me guess," McShea interjected. "You wouldn't be talking about the gay marriage issue, would you?"

"Absolutely, there is no other moral issue out there that has the political potential to topple this country and right now, as we speak, the Harris Administration is doing everything in its power to literally ramrod this family destroying issue through the courts."

With precious airtime of the essence, McShea turned once again to Eliot Graham to ask his one last poignant question. "Dr. Graham, in your estimation, unless we have a constitutional amendment with at least thirty-eight states in full support of a measure to make the Marriage Defense Act, passed by the Clinton Administration, the law of the land, what will happen to America?"

"Keenan, I will state two facts: first and foremost, by a vast majority, in every single state, no exception, the American public does not support gay marriage in any way, shape, or form. I am not a prophet, and I've never claimed to be one, but if the liberal court system continues passing this against the will of the people, it will end up, in my opinion, the proverbial final straw that broke the back of America."

"OK, guys, we need some answers and we need them now!" the clever Fox host proposed.

"Mr. McShea," Sean Wiggins added, "with all America listening right now, I have a proposal to make."

"Go right ahead, Sean," McShea acknowledged, "You've got America's full attention."

"As far as I see it, there is only one solution on our plate at the moment to keep America from literally plunging head-first into the same moral abyss as nations in the past. It is now time for all Americans, regardless of their party affiliation, to come together in unity under one strong leader, draw a clear line in the sand, and shout this message out loud and clear, "No longer will we, the American people, allow a small minority of socialist progressives to dictate to the vast majority of freedom loving, God-fearing Americans, the Godless mandates of destruction and division. No longer can we, the people of America, allow the world to view our once strong and God-fearing country as decadent and soft, crippled by political correctness, confused and guilt ridden, without backbone or pride. We, in the American Values Party, hold fast to following our God-given unalienable rights, that according to the Constitution of the United States of America and the moral code of God Almighty, all men are created equal, that they are endowed by their Creator, God, with certain unalienable rights, that among these are life, liberty and the pursuit of happiness, and in addition, the sanctity of human life beginning at conception, traditional marriage, religious freedom, and the expression of all beliefs."

"So, would your party support the former New York Governor Robert Berry's run for president on the Republican ticket?"

"Absolutely not!" Lindsay Wiggins responded. "Governor Berry supports our proposed job's bill package and a strong national defense, but when it comes to social issues, he flip-flops back and forth. As far as our party is concerned, on the real issues of substance, the sanctity of human life and supporting traditional marriage, Berry is no different than that self-declared atheist on the Democratic ticket, Analise DeVoe."

"Then who do the two of you deem qualified to be the leader of your party?" probed the savvy political commentator.

"As far as Lindsay and I are concerned, there is only one person in all America right now, who meets all of the qualifications we deem necessary for the job."

"Incidentally," interjected Lindsay Wiggins, "according to all the latest polls, this person has also been selected by the vast majority of Americans as the most honest, trustworthy American living today."

With a calculated smile already present on his face, Keenan Wiggins, asked the very question that everyone sitting back watching the primetime political newscast had been patiently awaiting, "And who is this person that you believe to be the only leader presently qualified to pull America out of its present quandary of dismal despair?"

"Funny that you should ask, Mr. McShea! As we speak, the very person I'm talking about is located in his Trinity Mills radio studio, and is presently being seen by every single Fox viewer across America. He is sitting directly opposite Sean and me on their Fox television monitor holding both hands against his blushing face."

"Keenan McShea, Lindsay and Sean Wiggens" an ardently perturbed Graham declared, "I want to thank you for the compliment, but as I have made it clear to virtually everyone who asks in interview after interview, I have absolutely no political aspirations for seeking any form of public office what-so-ever, and I am not going to obligate myself to something that I have neither intentions or desire to commit to now, or anytime in the future."

"And that is the very reason why you, Dr. Eliot Graham, should now seriously consider running for president." McShea fired back. "Everyone in America knows the type of person you are. Your honesty and burning passion to restore America's greatness would never allow your principles to be tainted or compromised as hundreds of others have done once they crossed over inside the Washington Beltway."

"Once again," Graham reiterated his point, but this time with a forced smile. "As long as God continues supplying me with the air to breathe, I will continue doing my part in my quest to return America back to its former greatness using solely the medium of the free airwaves to make my voice of reason heard. And with that said, Mr. McShea, I have no further comment."

Keenan McShea smiled as he momentarily sat back in his chair shaking his head as a rare expression of defeat. If anyone had any further doubt at the moment about Eliot Graham's political intentions, the conservative radio talk show host had just made it explicitly clear; look for someone else beside Eliot Graham to fill those presidential shoes. Better than anyone, McShea knew he had taken a calculated risk prompting Graham to commit on air to run for president.

With the door to further discussions on a possible Graham run for the presidency closed, the host of Fox's *Politically Most Wanted* proceeded to cordially thank his initial three guests for participating on tonight's show and proceeded to introduce the next guest in his primetime lineup, Republican Senate Majority leader, Nancy Sperry.

Two angelic giants, standing in the background, completely unnoticed by the limited senses of the dozen or so humans assigned to the Politically Most Wanted technical crew, turned to each other and smiled.

"An adamant human, that Eliot Graham," the angel on the right commented.

"As humans go, I quite agree," Yahriel affirmed.

By all angelic accounts, Yahriel was well qualified to make such a statement. For what seemed like eons, he, alone, was assigned by His Creator the angelic prince of prophetic wisdom and worldly affairs. Though he didn't know the day or hour of Christ's return to earth, this massive, twelve foot tall archangel was endowed with full knowledge of the present national and international earthly affairs and how they're aligned with the Lord's prophetic plans. Yahriel's angels were stationed in every nation, every capitol, and every city on earth.

Standing at Yahriel's left was Muriel, prince of Truth and Powers of the Air. Murial was charged with making absolutely sure that the Lord's Truth was preached to humans throughout the world, utilizing all means of human communication available for this task. This directive was firmly established in God's Word, and Murial and his angelic hosts had been charged with fulfilling this vital mission.

"What makes you so sure he will agree to run for president," Yahriel's angelic counterpart inquired. "As you, yourself, heard from Graham's own lips, he denies the possibility exists."

"Very soon now, dramatic events will take place in America that will leave Eliot Graham no other option, but to step into the political arena he so deplores, and make those changes for his beloved country that only someone of his untainted character can make."

Chapter Six

"The day is near when I, the LORD, will judge the godless nations! As you have done to Israel, so it will be done to you. All your evil deeds will fall back on your own heads.

~ Obadiah 1:15 (NIT)

Tuesday, April 14th, 2015
8:15 am EST
White House Oval Office
Washington, D.C.

A smile came to Joyce Jordan's face as she sat behind her office desk diligently preparing for the busy day ahead. For the first time in weeks, she could hear a faint, but familiar tune coming from just beyond the closed-door only a few steps away from her office desk. Inside the adjacent room, her boss of ten years, President Rashid Harris, was once again cheerfully whistling the melody to his favorite childhood song, *I'd Like to Teach the World To Sing in Perfect Harmony.* In fact, Ms. Jordan had overheard President Harris say on many a private occasion, *"If I only had the authority, I'd swap the National Anthem in a heartbeat for something less parochial like my favorite song, 'Teach the World To Sing.' I might even salute it. Our present anthem, with its bombs bursting in air, conveys a war-like message. You know, that sort of thing really bothers me."*

"Joy has returned to the White House," Ms. Jordan said to herself, shaking her head with a chuckle.

"Good morning, young lady," a familiar voice said in greeting. Two gentlemen entered the private office, using it as a gateway entrance to the president's famous Oval Office. Even though she held the official title of Secretary to the President of the United States, it was this man, Pacer Maddox, the White House Chief of Staff that Joyce Jordan, as well as every other staff member employed at the White House, had to answer to.

"Oh, good morning, gentlemen!" the president's secretary smiled in greeting, displaying her bright beautiful teeth. "You both look exceptionally chipper this morning."

"Good news always makes for a good day, Ms. Jordan," an overly exuberant Pacer Maddox replied.

"I can tell right now that this is going to be a very good morning," beamed Leslie Hughes, the Presidential Press Secretary. "Is the boss in?"

"Mr. Hughes, the answer to your question is yes. He arrived about ten minutes ago," the attractive, slightly overweight secretary replied. "I'm sure the president will be equally thrilled to see the two of you this morning. I'll let him know you're both here."

The exciting news that everyone was talking about this morning was well overdue, especially for the beleaguered first-term president. After months of being literally bombarded daily by a constant barrage of negative reports: low ratings, high unemployment, neglecting immigration reform, passing a very unpopular healthcare bill, accusations by political opponents of squandering billions in taxpayer borrowed stimulus dollars on frivolous partisan causes, and finally, some good news, some very good news!

"Mr. President, may I be the first to congratulate you?" an elated Pacer Maddox, the first man to enter the world famous oval-shaped room, asked. A thin man in his mid-forties, crowned by brown hair highlighted with tinges of gray, Patrick "Pacer" Maddox was by far President Harris' closest longtime friend and confidante. His nickname was well-deserved. It was coined over a decade ago when he served the city of Chicago as a savvy attorney. Back then, the term 'pacer' meant master magician, one who could literally tweak whatever law he was dealing with to make it legally fit into any situation. Today, as far as having the ultimate power to tweak the affairs within the White House, he is the second most powerful man on earth.

"I'm not going to lie to you guys; I was really sweating this one!" admitted this man of a mixed-raced origin. He reclined in a relaxed position behind the presidential desk.

"As were we, Mr. President," Leslie Hughes added. He was known by his fellow colleagues in the press corps as "the enforcer" because of his well-deserved aggressive rapid-response methods for countering disinformation tactics from opponents.

After serving over six years behind the Oval Office desk, the vast majority of Americans still viewed Rashid Harris as an enigma. Some saw Harris as high-minded, principled and legalistic. Others called him their Messiah, America's Savior. To these ardent supporters, Rashid Harris remained, as always, the brilliant leader with a magnetic personality, an exceptional speaker, gifted with oratory skills that could do verbal gymnastics with any word within the English dictionary—twisting the meaning of each word's letters in any form he so desired.

But to those who vehemently opposed him, they looked beyond Harris' calm smiling exterior and seductive words. They viewed him as a shrewd man whose contradictory personality imparted words in their senses such as cold, manipulative, divisive. There were some who viewed the president as a Marxist communist, hell-bent on transforming America's free market capitalistic society into some form of European socialism. To others, President Rashid Jabbar Harris was a closet Muslim, secretly plotting to subvert all vestiges of America's Judeo-

Christian religious past, and replacing it with the scariest of all scenarios for any Western World society, Islamic Sharia law.

"Our negotiating team did it!" Harris proclaimed proudly, raising his clenched left fist triumphantly in victory above his head. "As long as the Taiwanese government follows through with their end of the bargain, Beijing has agreed to completely withdraw all their warships from the East China Sea and stop all further aggression against Taiwan.

"Mr. President, is there any chance that Taiwan might renege on the deal?"

"I wouldn't worry too much about it, Leslie," Maddox calmly responded. "In principle, it's exactly the same deal The People's Republic of China offered Hong Kong when the British handed the city over to Beijing back in 1997. China will still allow Taiwan a form of self-government as long as Taiwan gives the appearance of recognizing The People's Republic's right to sovereignty over their island.

"The news only gets better, Mr. President," the Press Secretary interjected with a beaming smile. "I also have some good news on the economic front."

"Bring it on, Les!" the smiling president coaxed.

"Well, Mr. President, not only is Wall Street reacting positively this morning to the good news, the January unemployment numbers have just come in and they are showing a drop of two full percentage points from December's figures."

"Excellent! Excellent! Excellent!" the clearly elated president declared. Acting very un-presidential, Rashid Harris pushed his office chair aside and clapped his hands vigorously, stopping briefly to slap a high-five on the raised hands of his two thoroughly amazed secretaries. With a boyish grin on his face, the giddy president placed both hands upon the shoulders of his subordinates and openly confided, "Guys, I have to admit, I've been waiting a long time to hear this kind of good news and this, my friends, is what I call a true adrenaline rush. I could not have asked for any better news leading into tomorrow's speech at the U.N. when I will ask for full U.N. support in passing the Middle East Nuclear Non-Proliferation Treaty."

With all the honesty and candor he could muster, the president looked at both men and said, "You two mark my words—after tomorrow's U.N. vote, everything from then on, will be going in our favor!"

Tuesday, April 14th, 2015
10:10 am EST,
United Nations Headquarters
New York, New York

Since the moment they were first cast out of Heaven, every demonic being, including Satan, himself, has had one solitary, motivating thought in their demented evil minds: "How does this plan further my cause of avoiding God's eternal judgment into the Lake of Fire? Knowing that this could very well be his last big opportunity to alter the events of God's prophetic time clock, Satan, king of demons, the adversary of God, was taking no chances.

Like some hellish scene from your worst nightmare, thousands of scaly winged, yellowish-black skinned demons—from every conceivable rank, size and shape imaginable—began descending from the skies above one of New York City's most famous landmarks, the United Nations Headquarters, built downtown along Manhattan's East River waterfront. Countless multitudes of free-flying demons, along with thousands of their earthbound counterparts, were arriving on the grounds of this completely autonomous riverfront estate. The human hosts were oblivious to the clawed hands within their torsos.

This was the moment Satan had long awaited. Denied access to the president by a continuous entourage of angelic protection, the UN complex was the one place on earth where he had total right of entry. As the official god of this world, the premise of this eighteen-acre site was solely contrived by Satan's own devious inspiration, a humanistic enclave, set aside for not only mankind's free access, but also for his own personal sanctuary, a literal demons' "country club" with no angels permitted anywhere on the premises.

After a month-long conference, which ended yesterday, the192-member representative body of the United Nations General Assembly was about to vote on a non-binding resolution calling for every Middle Eastern state to move forward on a 1995 proposal for declaring a total nuclear-free Mideast. The reason Satan, and every other demon destined to hell, was so interested in this particular resolution being passed was simple. Once passed, it would put extreme international pressure on Israel, the land God, Himself, promised to Abraham's descendants through the line of Isaac. For the very first time since God's prophetic covenant people, Israel, became a Nation in 1948 after their two thousand year Diaspora, the devil conceived a plan to expose Israel's strategic primary secret that both protected and sustained the tiny Jewish State's survival in the midst of its surrounding Muslim enemies for the past fifty years. Using the guise of Iran's hostile nuclear intentions, the entire deceived world was about to blindly cast its votes, not on the façade of a nuclear free Middle East, but on the Satanically contrived plan of a Muslim only Middle East, free of the Jewish State of Israel.

A moment after Dr. Ali Abdussalam Treki, the elected President of the sixty-fourth session of the United Nations General Assembly, finished his introductory remarks and stepped away from the podium, a dead-silence, comparable only to that found inside the walls of a funeral home at midnight, permeated the colossal 1800-seat, capacity filled auditorium. All eyes, both mortal and immortal, were focused on the centrally located front platform as two beings, one mortal, one not, approached the podium.

A spectacle, only perceptible to the thousands of squinty yellow eyes staring at the front podium, and standing directly in back of the mortal, Rashid Harris, was a towering three-headed apparition with two pairs of scaled covered wings protruding from its muscular shoulders. The head on the left, topped with raven black hair and ruby red eyes, spoke horrendous blasphemies in harmonic rhythms against both God and man. At the same time, the head on the right, identical in every detail to the head on the left, but with emerald green eyes, sang arrogant melodious praises to itself. The head in the center was the exception. Cropped with golden hair and sapphire blue eyes, the center head had retained all of its former beauty and splendor. Satan was now standing center stage, directly in back of the mortal he had personally groomed from the moment Rashid Jabbar Harris was born in a Kenyan hospital so long ago. How else could this extremely articulate man, with a mixed-race heritage and almost no record of his past, obtain a life, literally launched from the ranks of a local political activist, and five years later, before reaching the age of fifty, end up being the President of the United States? There is no other explanation.

With both opposite heads now silent, the center head began to speak in a cold, cruel voice. "Speak, mortal man, my words of divine truth. Speak, mortal, man only my words of truth that will bring the façade of everlasting true peace to all those who hear your voice."

Even before his lips had the chance to form the first syllable of the first word of his prepared speech, the razor-sharp talons of Satan's clawed hands pierced deeply within the human's torso, giving the Lord of the demons complete access to every fiber and nerve cell that composed Rashid Jabbar Harris's mortal body.

Directing the movement of the human's head toward the two mortals seated in back of the podium on an elevated platform directly under a large motif displaying the UN symbol, Satan commenced his speech. "Good morning, Mr. Secretary General, fellow delegates, ladies and gentlemen. It is my humble honor to address you for the 6th time in the capacity of President of the United States."

Taking the lead from the 1,800 human mortals, a thunderous applause uniquely composed of claps, hoots and hollers followed Satan's opening statement. Every demon, whether seated, standing, or hanging from the ceiling in the cavernous auditorium, was ecstatic.

"I am truly humbled by the responsibility the American people have placed upon me, mindful of the enormous challenges of our moment in history, and determined to act boldly and collectively on behalf of justice and prosperity at home and abroad. I took the office at a time when many around the world had come to view America with skepticism and distrust. Part of this was due to misperceptions and misinformation about my country. Part of it was due to the opposition of specific polices set up by my predecessors on certain critical issues in which America had acted unilaterally, without regard for the interests of others. This led to anti-Americanism, and I firmly believe that this concept will be erased due to my efforts here today. I stand before this world governing body, on behalf of the American people, who elected me to represent their best efforts, and humbly apologize to those nations and people groups, who may have been offended by either my country's past actions or inaction."

Once again, the demonic audience gave their leader a rounding, thunderous applause. After spending several more minutes mesmerizing the senses of every mortal within range of his host human's voice, Satan got right to his point. "It is my deeply held belief that more than at any other point in human history, the interest of nations and people must be shared. We must not allow external forces to divide us any longer when it comes to the religious convictions that we hold in our hearts. We truly live in a dangerous age where weapons of mass destruction can be used in the name of religion to destroy the good that mankind has brought upon this planet we call home. With this in mind, we must look beyond our religious differences and forge new bonds of trust among peoples and nations. The nuclear technology we harness from the atom to light our path to peace, can also forever darken it. The nuclear energy we use today can sustain our planet's future and also, destroy it."

Another thunderous applause, both mortal and demonic.

"Today, the UN will vote on setting the stage for removing these so-called weapons of mass destruction from an area of the world where access to such weapons could literally ignite a worldwide fuse to bring an abrupt end to mankind's journey on planet earth. I stand here today, before this body of world leaders representing the Western world, the Eastern and Asian world, and the great continent of Africa, my ancestral home. I call on our world leaders everywhere to finally put aside all the differences and the issues that divide us as one people, one world. Now is the time to re-launch negotiations—without precondition—that address the permanent-status issues that divides the Israelis and the Palestinians—borders, refugees, and Jerusalem." Satan poignantly declared everything through the calm demeanor of his mortal host, Rashid Harris.

Once more, a thunderous applause, both mortal and demons.

"Our goal is clear—two states living side by side in peace and security—the Jewish state of Israel, safe and secure within the borders that defined its existence before 1967, and a viable, independent Palestinian state with all the territory that has been illegally occupied since 1967.

"I also charge Israel to recognize the dangers of an escalating nuclear arms race in the Middle East, and sign the treaty today, placing all of their nuclear facilities under the auspices and inspection of the International Atomic Energy Agency. I am elated to announce that after two years of intense negotiations with the international community and the Islamic Republic of Iran, we have achieved a detailed arrangement that permanently prohibits Iran from obtaining a nuclear weapon. It cuts off all of Iran's pathways to a bomb. It contains the most comprehensive inspection and verification regime ever negotiated to monitor a nuclear program. In return, the United States and it world allies have agreed to lift all economic sanctions against Iran including the immediate release of between 40 and 50 million barrels of oil that Iran has in storage since sanction were first imposed.

"Now, when I ran for president eight years ago as a candidate who had opposed the decision to go to war in Iraq, I said that America didn't just have to end that war. We had to end the mindset that got us there in the first place. I will end with this simple, but profound statement: Our future will be forged by our deeds, not our speeches. It will take persistent action by all. That is why I am humbly making this one last plea on behalf of, not only my two children who are seated in the audience, but for all children around the world. Pass the proposed Middle East Nuclear Non-Proliferation Treaty! Only by doing this can we guarantee all children of the world a better and safer tomorrow."

Wednesday, April 15th, 2015
1:12 pm CST
GP's Devil's Tower
50 miles off the Louisiana Coast
Gulf of Mexico

Today was supposed to be the day Dr. Larry Bailey, Gulf Petroleum's chief engineer in charge of offshore operations, pictured himself literally standing on top of the world. After all, he had just sacrificed almost three and half years of his life, spending almost 1,200 grueling laborious days sweating and toiling to complete his lifetime dream, an engineering marvel in every sense of the word. Christened Devil's Tower, at a drilled depth of 35,253 feet (10,750 meters), Bailey's project would be the deepest drilled oil well to ever penetrate the earth's crust.

The celebration was just about ready to begin. In addition to Dr. Bailey's entire crew of one hundred and eight men and women, all working under various assigned titles such as geologist, operation coordinator, driller, roughneck, roustabout, and derrickhands, two company helicopters just departed Devil's Tower, leaving behind eighteen of Gulf Petroleum's top executives, including company president, Colin Jeffrey. One hundred and twenty-six people in all, gathered on the massive deck of this floating semi-submersible offshore drilling platform for one purpose, to be present when the first barrel of oil was pumped to the surface from the world's deepest drilled oil well. With buckets of chilled champagne waiting in the background, Bailey and his team of eleven engineers, made their final preparations, lowering the final cement seal down the mile length umbilical cable to the ocean bottom, capping off the world's deepest oil well. If everything would go as planned, in a mere matter of minutes, Devil's Tower would be officially be declared fully operational.

With two submersed robot cameras serving as remote eyes, the team of engineers operating on the surface was able to witness the massive circular cement seal being lowered in place. Seasoned engineers, all were confidant that the combined effects of the final cement seal, and the pressure of the surrounding seawater, would bring all petroleum seeping out around the umbilical cable to a complete stop.

"OK, everybody," cautioned the head project engineer. "Cross your fingers tight. I'm going to start the pumps. In a matter of minutes, we should have our first barrel of oil."

Larry Bailey didn't have to say another word. The horrified look on his face said it all.

"Do you see what I see?" Ginny Wagner, the chief geologist, exclaimed. "There's more fluid coming out than going in! What the in the world is going on?"

"The immense pressure down there should have already secured any petroleum seeping out around the final cement seal," a shocked Bailey acknowledged. "It isn't working."

"I don't believe it!" Frank Langley, project engineer, declared. "Something's wrong, really wrong!"

Wednesday, April 15th, 2015
12:12 p.m. EST
United Nations Headquarters
New York, New York

President Harris walked away from the podium, confident that the words he had just spoken had reached his intended targets: those fifty or so undecided UN delegates who were about to cast their votes for his proposed Middle East Nuclear Non-Proliferation Treaty and to lift all economic sanctions against Iran. Even though General Assembly resolutions are non-binding on member states, any resolution vote passed with at least a two-thirds delegate majority would carry considerable political pressure. But before the final votes were cast, one final speaker stepped to to the front podium to address the UN general assembly.

'Ladies and gentleman," Israeli Prime Minister, Yacov Ben Yizri, opened his speech to the capacity filled UN auditorium with a smile and a cordial nod, "I bring you greetings from Jerusalem, the city in which the Jewish people's hopes and prayers for peace for all of humanity have echoed throughout the ages. Thirty-one years ago, as Israel's ambassador to the United Nations, I stood at this podium for the first time. I spoke that day against a resolution sponsored by Iran to expel Israel from the United Nations. Then, as now, the UN was obsessively hostile towards Israel, the one true democracy in the Middle East. Then, as now, some sought to deny the one and only Jewish state a place among the nations. I ended that first speech by saying: Gentlemen, check your fanaticism at the door. More than three decades later, as the Prime Minister of Israel, I am again privileged to speak from this podium. And for me, that privilege has always come with a moral responsibility to speak the truth. So after three days of listening to world leaders praise the nuclear deal with Iran, I begin my speech today by saying: Ladies and Gentlemen, check your enthusiasm at the door. You see, this deal doesn't make peace more likely. By fueling Iran's aggressions with billions of dollars in sanctions relief, it makes war more likely. Just look at what Iran has done in the last six months alone, since President Harris announced the framework of this bad agreement just six months ago. Iran boosted its supply of devastating weapons to Syria. Iran sent more soldiers of its Revolutionary Guard into Syria. Iran sent thousands of Afghani and Pakistani Shi'ite fighters to Syria. Iran did all this to prop up the Syrian president's brutal regime. Iran also shipped tons of weapons and ammunitions to the Houthi rebels in Yemen, including another shipment just two days ago. Iran threatened to topple Jordan. Iran's proxy Hezbollah smuggled into Lebanon SA-22 missiles to down our planes, and Yakhont cruise missiles to sink our ships. Iran supplied Hezbollah with precision-guided surface-to-surface missiles and attack drones so it could accurately hit any target in Israel. Iran supplied Hezbollah with precision-guided surface-to-surface missiles and attack drones so it can accurately hit any target in Israel. I repeat: Iran's been doing all of this, everything that I've just described, just in the last six months, when it was trying to convince the world to remove the sanctions. In 2013 President Rouhani began his so-called charm offensive here at the UN. Two years later, Iran is executing more political prisoners, escalating its regional aggression, and rapidly expanding its unprecedented global terror network throughout the world. You know they say, actions speak louder than words. But unfortunately in Iran's case, the words speak as loud as the actions.

Ladies and gentlemen, it's not easy to oppose something that is embraced by the greatest powers in the world. Israel is working closely with our Arab peace partners to address our common security challenges from Iran and also the security challenges from ISIS and from other regional militant groups. I know that some well-intentioned people seated in this room sincerely believe that this deal is the best way to block Iran's path to the bomb. But one of history's most important yet least learned lessons is this:

The best intentions don't prevent the worst outcomes. Ladies and gentlemen, I have long said that the greatest danger facing our world is the coupling of militant Islam with nuclear weapons. The vast majority of Israelis believe that this nuclear deal with Iran is a very bad deal. And what makes matters even worse is that we see a world celebrating this bad deal, rushing to embrace and do business with a regime openly committed to our destruction."

Yacov Ben Yizri ended his speech to the 192 UN delegates seated before him with a positive request.

"Israel is civilization's front line in the battle against barbarism. So here's a novel idea for the United Nations: Instead of continuing the shameful routine of bashing Israel, stand with Israel. Stand with Israel as we check the fanaticism at our door. Stand with Israel as we prevent that fanaticism from reaching your door. Ladies and gentlemen, stand with Israel because Israel is not just defending itself. More than ever, Israel is defending you!"

After an hour-long recess, all 192 UN delegates returned to cast their votes. Resolutions are adopted by a recorded 'yea' or 'nay' vote, which clearly identifies the stand that each council member takes on the issue under discussion.

Seated in the auditorium's reserved front row with his wife, Micalyn, and twin twelve-year-old daughters, Dianna, and, Deyonna, President Rashid Harris smiled broadly as each "yes" vote was cast. After all the verbal votes were counted, the non-binding resolution, the Middle East Nuclear Non-Proliferation Treaty, passed with 142 votes in favor, and 11 no votes, including both Israel and Iran, whose delegates vehemently opposed the vote, and 39 abstentions, including France and Spain.

As the multitude slowly made its way toward the exit doors of the General Assembly's auditorium, President Harris remained behind, savoring, a moment longer, his hard-fought victory. Little did he, or anyone else, realize that this historic vote marked much more than an initial step of ridding the volatile Middle East from weapons of mass destruction. What the President blindly neglected to see was that for the very first time, America, the country he now headed, had voted against Israel on a U.N. resolution—whether binding, or non-binding, it didn't matter. Little did Rashid Jabbar Harris foresee the unfathomable harm he had brought upon the very nation he was sworn to protect. Rashid Harris, like so many of his presidential predecessors before him, had failed to recognize that God is in complete control of the affairs of man, and more importantly, that God had sworn an oath to not only protect Israel, but to severely punish any nation, or people, who would come against the Covenant Nation that He affectionately calls the Apple of His Eye.

Wednesday, April 20th
1:15 pm CST
GP's Devil's Tower
50 miles off the Louisiana Coast
Gulf of Mexico

"Shut off the pump for the sheen test!" Larry Bailey shouted to the engineer manning the well's switch.

The sheen test Dr. Bailey alluded to was an EPA-mandated step intended to spot free-floating oil to the surface. With no pump running, the well flow should have completely stopped, but it didn't. To the horror of the eleven engineers, streams of oily fluid kept rising toward the surface, and sensors indicated that the pressure inside the umbilical drill pipe was increasing exponentially.

By now, the scene on the outside deck had completely digressed from one of jubilant celebration to total chaos. Rig workers and GP executives alike were running toward the large platform's edge to witness a spectacle never seen before by human eyes. What they saw next could only be described as a surreal scene from the pits of hell. Where mere minutes prior, a panoramic scene of aqua blue surface waters surrounding the entire oil platform had existed, now, in an instant, the seascape transformed into a boiling brown brew of percolating oily mud welling up from the ultra-deep depths of the Gulf's bottom.

As his gauges continued to record an escalating pressure spike, Bailey shouted out in desperation, "Release the blowout preventer!"

On April 20th, 2010 at about 1:25 P.M CST, a massive bubble of highly flammable methane gas exploded one mile below GP's Devil Tower, skyrocketing hellish flames of burning oil 240 feet into the air above the rig. At the time, one hundred and twenty six people were on board the Devil Tower rig. Eleven were killed and 17 injured. Oil began gushing from the mangled wellhead at a tremendous rate, and an ecological disaster of unimaginable proportions was about to take place. Within minutes, planes above saw a five-mile long slick of greasy oil moving away from the burning oilrig in the direction of the ecologically fragile Louisiana coastline. Within twenty-four hours, the Devil's Tower oilrig, valued at more than $560 million, sank 5,000 feet (1,525 meters) to the bottom of the Gulf of Mexico.

At the exact same moment the U.N. General Assembly passed the non-binding, Middle East Nuclear Non-Proliferation Treaty, the greatest manmade disaster this world has ever known took place 50 miles off the Louisiana coastline. In all, eleven Gulf Petroleum workers were killed, seventeen were injured, and more than three million gallons of crude oil per day had been discharged into the Gulf of Mexico every single day.

Chapter Seven

The seed (God's Word) that fell on the hard path represents those who hear the message (the Truth), but then Satan comes at once and takes it away from them.

~Mark 4:15 (NLT)

Author's Note: The wiles of the devil are more than just subtle. His endless schemes are always meticulously concealed within the confines of elaborate plans for one purpose only: to defeat and destroy his targeted enemy, man. Few places are the wiles of the devil more carefully cloaked from the eyes of unsuspecting man than within the shadowy realm of politics. One such political ploy used effectively by the devil is buried deep within the very foundation of America's constitution and the selection of its president.

The right to vote is intended to be a singular privilege of citizenship, but the 1787 Constitutional Convention rejected allowing the people to directly elect their president. The delegates chose our Electoral College system instead under which 538 electoral votes distributed amongst the states determine the presidential victor. The Electoral College awards one elector for each U.S. Senator, thus 100 of the total, and D.C. gets three electors pursuant to the 23rd Amendment. Those electoral numbers are unaffected by the size of the noncitizen population. The same cannot be said for the remaining 435, more than 80 percent of the total, which represents the members elected to the House. The distribution of these 435 seats is not static; they are adjusted every ten years to reflect the population changes found in the census. That reallocation math is based on the numbers of persons in each state, as the formulation in the 14th Amendment states. When this language was inserted into the U.S. Constitution, the concept of an "illegal immigrant," as the term is defined today, had no meaning. Thus, the census counts illegal immigrants and other noncitizens equally with citizens. Since the census is used to determine the number of House seats apportioned to each state, those states with large populations of illegal immigrants and other noncitizens gain extra seats in the House at the expense of states with fewer such "whole number of persons."

Taking full advantage of the electoral votes awarded to those states with the largest increase of illegal immigrants, Satan has masterfully crafted a cunning plan to assure that not only his person of choice is elected President of the United States in 2016, but something even more devious. With Muslim immigrants streaming into the United States from the war torn regions of the Middle East like Syria and Iraq at a rate of 100,000 per year, the devil's contrived religion of choice, Islam, is now given free reign to spread its poisonous tentacles of Sharia Law throughout the Judeo-Christian void now present in today's America society. Even more frightening, the U.S. lacks the capability to properly screen out terrorists and terrorist sympathizers from their ranks. According to FBI Director, James Comey, in les than two years, ISIS has gone from a terror start-up overseas to what Comey calls a "chaotic spider web" in the US, with young Muslim men being radicalized in Illinois and the 49 other states.

Monday, May 20th, 2015
11:15 a.m.
Hamas Headquarters
Damascus, Syria

The long laborious taxicab ride that traversed steep city hillsides, marked by a confusing network of winding streets and narrow byways, had finally ended. The two weary travelers from afar had finally arrived at their appointed destination, Damascus, Syria's Hamas headquarters. After paying the fare in Syrian pounds, the two Americans, one male, one female, exited the taxi and began to walk up a steep set of stairways leading to what appeared to be an ordinary gated apartment complex built into a steep rocky hillside. Before entering the complex's main gated entrance, the Americans were met by two fully masked, armed security guards. As one of the black hooded guards stood by with his M-16 assault rifle lowered in the direction of the strangers, the other, not only checked the foreigners' passports and credentials, but he did a thorough search of their bags, temporarily confiscating cell phones and other electronic devices that could possibly be used as a means of transmitting or recording conversations. Next, the two travelers were ushered down a long hallway corridor that ended at a spacious and comfortable meeting room. As the two Americans entered the room, a large motif on the background wall caught their immediate attention. Across its top border, written in sprawling Arabic letters, was the organization's famous logo: *Harakat al-Muqawamah al-Islamiyya*, known by its popular acronymic name, Hamas. Below its grand title, inscribed in both Arabic and English, was its mission statement for all to see:

To contribute in the effort of liberating all of Palestine and restoring the rights of the Palestinian people under the sacred Islamic teachings of the Holy Quran, the Sunna (traditions) of Prophet Mohammad (peace and blessings of Allah be upon him) and the traditions of Muslim rulers and scholars noted for their piety and dedication throughout the world.

Once inside the room, the two Americans were met by three well-groomed, bearded gentlemen of Arab descent, all dressed in dark business suits with opened white collars. The oldest of the three, a distinguished looking bald man with a white beard, wearing glasses, extended the customary Syrian hand of welcome toward his American visitors.

"Mr. Khan, Ms. Raul, my name is Dr. Ahmad Yassin. I am our organization's head linguistics interpreter. On behalf of our Deputy Chairman, Dr. Musa Abu Marzook, standing to your left, and our organization's leader, Khaled Mishal, standing to your right, the Muslim Brotherhood and Islamic Resistance Movement, known affectionately throughout the world as Hamas, welcomes you both to our beautiful capital city of Damascus, also recognized as the world's oldest inhabited city."

The moment the two Americans entered the large brightly lit room, another visitor from across the Atlantic arrived, but not to a similar welcoming party. *Instead, he entered a room where five totally oblivious humans stood. The room was dimly lit and filled, wall-to-wall, with hideous winged, scale-covered yellowish black demonic beings from every imaginable hierarchical ranking. Like a proud father watching his children take their first steps forward, the demonic visitor from the shores of America traveled halfway around the world for one purpose only—to witness for himself the beginnings of his contrived scheme to bring total anarchy back to the land, the charge to destroy, an order given by Satan, himself.*

"Welcome Abdul Khan and Valerie Raul to Damascus, Syria," Amducious, the boastful demonic prince known throughout the spirit world as the Destroyer, sneered. "Whether you two know it or not, you've been selected by me for a very important task. Today will mark the beginning of the most important mission of your futile mortal lives, a mission that will not only change the American political landscape forever, but more importantly, help usher in America's second and final civil war."

"Destroyer, welcome to the Middle East!" announced a familiar voice from among the din of repulsive demonic chatter. "Shut up, you filthy b-st—ds" thundered a soul-piercing admonition from the mouth of their leader, Allazad, known also as the Persian Prince. This twelve foot high, scaly-skinned demonic aberration was assigned dominion by Satan himself over the entire ancient Persian Empire, extending from the blue water shores of the Mediterranean on its western border

to the East where the Himalayan Mountains joined the jungles of the Indian subcontinent. Once silence was firmly established, the massive black-scaled demon formally greeted his American guest with both demon princes exchanging traditional left-armed, closed fisted salutes.

"Praise to be Satan!" Allahzad, his closed fisted claw held high above his black scaly crown, proclaimed.

"Praise be to Satan!" Amducious returned with his typical devious sneer. "I assume by your smile that all details are in order?"

"If you are referring to the funding you requested from the Saudis," Allahzah paused mid-sentence, toying with his American equal. "The answer is yes." Allahzad finally relinquished his reply.

"Don't ever do that to me again, you scaly-skinned reprobate!" Amducious responded with a threatening yellow-eyed glare.

Allahzad smiled, unimpressed by his counterpart's brief display of annoyance.

"Given your tight time constraints, and everything else you demanded," sneered the Demonic Prince of Persia, "it was no small task gathering one hundred million dollars in American currency, but every last penny that you asked for, Destroyer, is in this room. It will soon be transferred to the American humans in small denominations of American currency that can never be traced back to its source."

"I hope you have richly rewarded each and every one of your Saudi demons for fulfilling such a vital mission to our cause?"

"You don't have to worry about my Saudi demons being rewarded." Allahzad smiled. "As long as Sharia remains the law of the land, my demons' devious minds will be totally preoccupied conjuring up all kinds of torment for the millions of oppressed Saudi women who live there, all with the full blessing of the Saudi government."

"To that end, I'm jealous of you, Allahzad," the American demon admitted, again displaying his devious sneer. "You've had over a thousand years to poison the minds of each and every Middle Eastern Arab boy and man to the blissful virtues of treating their women like dogs."

"Sorry, Destroyer, but according to my calculations, even though you've made positive progress converging the Muslim populations in inconspicuous places like Dearborn, Michigan, America's time is just about up."

"So we are gathered here today to witness the beginning of America's inevitable demise," Amducious reflected with a subtle grin. With small talk and formal introductions out of the way, the American demon turned to his Persian counterpart and demanded, "Get your ugly b-stards in line. The Hamas leaders are preparing to talk."

Allahzad regained control over his hyped-up, hodge-podge of demonic personalities by thundering a highly effective direct command, "Shut up right now, or you will be in Hell long before you anticipated!"

With literally hundreds of pairs of squinty yellow eyes focused on the five mortals in the room, Dr. Ahmad Yassin, the Hamas interpreter, continued to speak.

"Mr. Khan, Ms. Raul, we sent out our communiqué, and now, for time's sake, we will discuss the important matters that have brought the two of you to our Syrian Hamas headquarters, after dinner."

"Thank you, Dr. Yassin," a respectful Abdul Khan responded, "I am Abdul Khan, religious advisor to President Harris. Ms. Valerie Raul heads the president's Advisory Council on Faith-Based and Neighborhood Partnerships. On behalf of the United States government and President Rashid Harris, mere words cannot express what a great honor it is for Ms. Raul and me to have been selected to be here in the presence of your people's great representative leaders, Deputy Chairman, Dr. Musa Abu Marzook, and world leader of Hamas, Khaled Mishal.

As Dr. Yassin proceeded to translate Abdul Khan's words into Arabic, the two Muslim leaders standing adjacent to their translator responded in turn by passively accepting the American's welcoming gesture with nodding smiles.

"Our cooks have prepared a delicious mid-day meal in your honor. I believe that in America you would say a mouth-watering sampling of Syrian delicacies." Dr. Yassin pointed to a light-colored wraparound tan leather couch surrounding a serving table, and continued, "Ms. Raul and Mr. Khan, if you two would be so kind, please be seated against the wall so we can all face each other while we eat and discuss the matters that are most important to our great people."

As soon as the four men and one woman were comfortably seated at the centrally placed dining table, a host of chefs and servers descended with an array of appetizers, which included hummus, eggplant and yogurt dip, a variety of green and black olives with pits, and tomato or hot sauce. In addition, there were appetizers—grape leaves stuffed with rice and lamb and makdous, tiny, tangy eggplants marinated, and stuffed with walnuts and a variety of chopped raw vegetables.

"Umm, this is so delicious!" Valerie Raul commented, as she continued to sample all of the Syrian delicacies.

"I am so glad you are enjoying it, Ms. Raul," Dr. Yassin replied with a smile.

Deciding for time sake to forego the customary dinner salad, the chefs brought out the main course instead, which consisted of grilled skewers of chicken or lamb in the form of kabobs. As an added delicacy, a bowl of fatah, ground meat mixed with browned almonds and parsley, was served over a soupy bed of hummus and a drizzle of olive oil. There was also freshly baked bread for dipping, and all was placed within easy reach of the five diners.

After dinner, a basket of baklava, a doughnut-like dessert soaked in honey was placed on the table. "Please, Ms. Raul, try a baklava. It is one of our country's favorite desserts."

"Dr. Yassin, I'll take your word on that," the dark haired young American woman of Lebanese decent said. "Everything here has been so wonderful, but I'm afraid I overdid it! There is absolutely no room in my poor stomach for another bite of your delicious food."

"Good! Well, I think it is as good a time as any for all of us to begin discussing the important matters that have brought us together today. Our people's Deputy Chairman, Dr. Musa Abu Marzook, will talk first, and I will translate for you."

"Mr. Khan and Ms. Raul, as Deputy Chairman for the Islamic Resistance Movement, I welcome you to our modest Syrian headquarters. It is imperative to our organization's leader, Khaled Mishal, and me that the vision, clearly stated on our organization's charter, be fulfilled with no more time wasted. As we sit here today, the rights of our Palestinian people are still being subjugated under the illegal oppressive dominion of the Jewish swine the world calls Israel. We, the leaders of the Muslim Brotherhood and the Islamic Resistance Movement, will do everything in our power to rid every square centimeter of Palestinian land of this devil-sent tyrannical blight. We will do everything in our power to liberate Palestine once and for all, and restore the rights of our people to rule all of Palestine from its Lebanese and Syrian borders to the north, to its Jordanian borders to the east, and to its Egyptian borders to the south. Now, you will hear from our people's great leader.

"Absolutely!" Abdul Khan replied.

Allahzad smiled broadly, knowing his time to address the two mortals from America had finally come. With his claw-like hands buried deep within the Hamas leader's torso, the demon Prince of Persia began to speak through his human host— the same kind of mesmerizing message given less than a century earlier through another human vessel named Adolf Hitler.

"I also welcome our visitors from America and I send back with you my warmest greetings and sincere expressions of friendship to your great president, Rashid Harris. It is solely on the continuation of that friendship that we are meeting here today. There has never been an American president so willing to forego the support of the Jewish American swine in order to right a historical wrong, and support the causes of the oppressed

Palestinian people. That is why I will do everything in my power to make sure that Harris' democratic successor in two years will be elected President of the United States."

Allahzad stopped long enough to allow the Hamas leader to nod, sending a subtle signal to his interpreter, Yassin, to momentarily stop talking and to send a short digital text to someone standing just outside the meeting room. In less than a minute's time, two armed human guards, accompanied by a host of mid-level demons, arrived in the room.

"Excellent," Allahzad commented, once again speaking through his human host, Khaled Mishal. "Place it over here on the table."

Not saying a word, one of the two hooded guards, surrounded on each side by a gleeful horde of clapping mid-level demons, placed what appeared to be a rather inconspicuous black leather briefcase on the cleared serving table.

"Behold!" Allahzad boasted, as he displayed his own distinct prideful sneer. "This is what you have traveled all this way to Syria to see and to take back to America."

With the turn of a small metal key, the top cover of the black briefcase popped open, displaying to the awestruck onlookers, both mortal and/ or otherwise, an amazing sight never seen before by anyone present in the room.

"One hundred million dollars!" the prideful Prince of Persia declared arrogantly. "Every penny of it is in some form of legal variation of American currency, all donated to our great cause by the generous support of our mutual friends in Saudi Arabia!"

The mortal American travelers stood by, utterly amazed at the sight of so much American money so tightly packed into such a small enclosed space.

"Before you leave here today," Allahzad admonished through the voice of his unsuspecting human host, "along with this money you are to take back this stern warning: The Muslim Brotherhood expects every single one of our American friends to strictly adhere to our previous agreement—that every cent of this donated money will be

spent wisely according to our agreed plan, the plan that will assure that Analise Devoe will be the first elected woman President of the United States. Is that completely understood?"

"Absolutely!" Abdul Khan replied.

"I also give you my word, Mr. Mishal," Valerie Raul passionately continued, "as a loyal member of your noble cause to liberate your Palestinian people, I will personally make sure your request is conveyed. I swear by my allegiance as a pledged member of the society for worldwide peace, it will be taken care of!"

"Rest assured, Allahzad," Amducious, the Destroyer, smirked, "my brainless American mortals will faithfully carry out their cause. The money they will take back with them will ensure that the atheist, Analise Devoe, will replace Rasid Jabbar Harris in the White House in 2016"

Monday, May 25ᵗʰ, 2015
7:00 a.m.
47ᵗʰ Annual Convention of the
American Muslim Brotherhood Society (AMBS)
Rosemont Convention Center
Rosemont, Illinois

At first glance, this annual gathering of American Muslims looked no different than any other large convention held at this large arena located just five minutes from Chicago's O'Hare International Airport and 20 minutes from downtown Chicago. Except for the fact that every woman present had either her head covered by a colorful scarf called a hijaab, or the majority of her face and body concealed under a loose fitting cloth garment called a burqa, this weekend conference, which ends at sundown, had all the earmarks of any well-organized large convention. Dozens of attractive bazaar booths were setup throughout the arena's main lobby, displaying an endless variety of traditional Muslim foods, art exhibits, and live entertainment, while in the adjacent 4,400-seat capacity Rosemont Theater, national politicians and renowned Muslim speakers from around the world, discussed contemporary topics relevant only to American Muslims.

To the vast majority of the over 35,000 Muslims who had gathered at the Rosemont Convention Center, this two day conference represented nothing more than a joyful time of coming together with other fellow American Muslim believers to celebrate the uniqueness of their ancient heritage and faith. Just beyond the range of human perception, another, less benign conference, was coming to a close. With less than a mortal hour remaining before thousands of their assigned human hosts descended upon the Rosemont Theater, the invited keynote speaker of this clandestine conference made his closing remarks. "Before your assigned humans arrive, let us all shout aloud our battle cry."

With thousands of squinty yellow-eyes looking on, Allahzad, the Prince of Persia, the invited keynote speaker, ended this counterfeit conference from hell by quoting from one of his favorite verses in the Koran, Surah 9:30, a verse that he, himself, had uttered some 1,400 years prior directly into the mind of Mohammad. "The last hour will not come before the Muslims fight the Jews and the Muslims kill them, so that Jews will hide behind stones and trees and the stone and the trees will say, O Muslim, O servant of God, there is a Jew behind me; come and kill him."

The demonic Prince of Persia reiterated one final charge to his demonic hordes before leaving center stage. "Allow this verse to resonate deeply within your spirits, over and over again. If we eliminate the Jews, God's prophetic plan will never happen, and Satan will rule both earth and mankind forever! Praise, Satan!"

"Praise Satan! Praise Satan! Praise Satan!" Over a thousand demonic voices chanted in unison as they lifted their clawed left fists high above their scaly yellowish black heads.

"As you leave here today, each of you has a responsibility to saturate the mind of your assigned human host, not only with the vital importance of this verse, but also, as I have stated over and over again, you must make absolutely sure that your host Muslim family

blends in perfectly with their American surroundings. With that said, I want absolutely no negative publicity posted what-so-ever about American Muslims in the media. That means there will be no charges of polygamy filed against any married American Muslim man. Is that clear?" Allazhad thundered.

"Yes, Prince of Persia!" A thousand voices replied.

"That means no Muslim man will perform honor killings of their helpless wives or daughters, or be charged with raping little Muslim girls in a forced marriage while they are living on American soil. Is that clear?" Allazhad admonished in a bellowing voice.

"Yes, Prince of Persia!"

Standing at the very edge of the large theater's stage, the Persian demonic prince looked over the massive auditorium filled to capacity with fidgety hordes of hyperactive demons and closed the conference with this strong statement of admonition. "Before calling this conference to an end, I want to repeat my specific charge to each of you one last time. When you leave here with your assigned Muslim host family, you are charged with this very specific task. You are to do everything within the range of your power to make sure your assigned American Muslim family, especially its head male, is abundantly blessed, and receives favor in every aspect of their lives. This means favor at work, favor at school, favor with friends, favor with neighbors, but most importantly, favor in fertility. As we have successfully done throughout the Middle East and most of Europe, I want the American Muslim male and female assigned to you to outbreed every single race and ethnicity in America. When I return in the near future, I want to see a strong Muslim influence firmly established in every borough, town, city, and state in America. I want to see American Muslims at the forefront of power in all local, county and state governments. I want Muslims as American educators, doctors, lawyers, and especially politicians. You are responsible to deliver the message of Islam. Islam America is not to be equal to any other faith. It must become dominant. The Koran must replace the Bible as the highest scriptural authority in America, and Islam as the only accepted religion on earth."

"Is that clear?" Allazah thundered one last time.

"Yes, Prince of Persia!"

"Only then can we shout our favorite all-time Muslim word to the world, Sharia! Praise be to Satan!"

Praise be to Satan!" A thousand voices thundered back.

Monday, May 25th, 2015
9:00 a.m.
47th Annual Convention of the
American Muslim Brotherhood Society (AMBS)
Rosemont Convention Center
Rosemont, Illinois

Deception raised its veiled head early on this final day of the 47th Annual Convention of the American Muslim Brotherhood Society. Within the capacity filled Rosemont Theater, all eyes focused on a dozen or more prominent Muslim speakers sitting center stage in a prearranged speaking order. The AMBS convention's announcer came over the theater's loudspeaker system, "Ladies and gentlemen, we apologize for the inconvenience, but I must bring everyone's attention to a minor change in the order of this morning's speakers. Our first scheduled speaker, Mr. Omar Syeed, the cofounder of the American Muslim Brotherhood Society, will speak tonight at the end of the conference instead of this morning. In his place, please give a warm welcome to our first speaker this morning, nationally recognized Christian pastor and best-selling author, Rick Woolzy."

Aside from some initial disapproving boos, Omar Syeed's scheme seemed to be working just as he had planned. At first, only a handful of disgruntled convention attendees applauded as the well-known preacher walked out on the stage. As Woolzy began his conciliatory speech in his well-crafted pacifying words—apologizing for all the Christian atrocities against Muslims during the Crusades, he quickly captured the attention of his Islamic listeners, reversing their initial boos into a fervor of rousing applause. Energized by the crowd's newfound listening enthusiasm, Woolzy appeased his attentive audience even further by comparing similarities of their Muslim god, Allah, with the Christian God, Jesus. Appeasement aside, Omar Syeed selected Woolzy to be the conference's "token" Christian speaker for two other reasons: first, and most obvious, was public image. Syeed was savvy to the ways of the American media. Having such a respected Christian leader as Rick Woolzy speak at this all-Muslim event made, if for no other reason, good PR sense. But the reason for switching time slots with Woolzy was purely an act of intentional deception. Just before the start of the morning's proceedings, Syeed was notified that a very important package, he had been anxiously awaiting, would be delivered shortly by two couriers from Washington D.C., and more than anything else, Syeed wanted to be there to unwrap it the moment it arrived.

Monday, May 25ᵗʰ, 2015
9:43 a.m.
An Undisclosed Conference Room
Rosemont Convention Center
Rosemont, Illinois

Two humans, each concealing under their sports jackets holstered 9 mm weapons, were posted just outside a conference room. Unknown to the two mortals standing outside the locked door, an additional dozen or so scaly-skinned winged sentinels were also present in their midst, each one dangling a doubled edged razor-tipped sword from their clawed left hands. Just inside the highly protected room, five other mortals stood around a large table greeting one another with traditional Muslim embraces. What was about to be exposed at this secret assembly went far beyond even the most radically conceived topics discussed in any open forum during this entire Muslim convention. Truly sinister in its scope, the singular purpose of this meeting was to work out the minuscule details of a meticulously contrived scheme, so mind bogglingly and complex in its implications that most would say, in light of the insurmountable security obstacles involved, it would be all but impossible to accomplish.

With formal greetings over, Mr. Syeed graciously instructed his two guests from Washington D.C., Abdul Khan, President Rashid Harris' appointed faith-based religion Czar, and his silent, athletically framed traveling associate, known simply as Jamal, be seated directly across the large conference room table from where he and two of his AMBS associates were seated. Before his presidential appointment, Khan was the founder and executive director of the Chicago-based interfaith program called Youth Core. Its premise was to promote multicultural pluralism by teaming people with different faiths on community service projects.

"How was your trip from Washington, Mr. Khan?" a smiling Omar Syeed questioned.

"Much shorter, I assure you, Mr. Syeed, than last week's round-trip flight to Damascus and back." Khan replied, as he shook his head back and forth in an expression of relief.

Syeed smiled broadly. If anyone sitting at that long table was relieved, it was Omar Syeed. That black leather briefcase resting on the conference room table only an arm's length away finally gave him the peace of mind he had longed for. At last his long awaited plan was about to become a reality.

"I understand, Mr. Khan, that you have in your possession a rather substantial deposit to be transferred into our accounts," Abu Hafiz, Mr. Syeed's financial advisor, commented.

"Absolutely," Khan affirmed as he proceeded to unlock the black leather-bound briefcase that had been secured by an inconspicuous, thin metal, foot long chain to a bracelet secured around his right wrist.

155

All eyes in the room widened as Abdul Khan opened the black leather briefcase to expose more money than anyone in that securely protected room had ever seen.

"I requested the money be delivered here by means of the cash and carry method," Omar Syeed proudly boasted. "It's the only way to ensure anonymity."

"This is a substantial investment made by my superiors," Khan stated boldly. "When I return to Washington, I will assure them that this money will get the job done on the exact timeline we had agreed upon."

"Well, first of all, Mr. Khan," Syeed responded with a smile. He appeared unperturbed by the bluntness of the question, "As I said, this entire plan is almost 100% full proof. No one will ever be able to trace a single penny of this back to you or me or anyone else for that matter."

With that said, a strange chill suddenly permeated every corner of the room as Omar Syeed stood and stared intently into the eyes of Abdul Khan.

"You go back and tell my friend, Mr. Pacer Maddox, that every cent of this money will be invested exactly as we agreed," Syeed said in a well-composed, assertive tone.

"You tell Pacer Maddox from me that I fully understand his concern," the demonic Persian Prince, Allahzad, said. His two clawed hands controlled every thought and word that spewed from Omar Syeed's lips. "But we still agree that refocusing America's hatred away from AMBS onto The American Values Party remains our primary goal. Tomorrow, when you arrive in Washington, tell Mr. Maddox that I personally will assure him that come this 4th of July, America will begin celebrating the end of the American Values Party."

With that said, Syeed turned to his second AMBS associate, Tariq Quadri, seated on his right. Following his boss's lead, Quadri smiled as he placed a large manila folder on the table beside the open briefcase filled with money.

"This is what your $100 million dollars buys you, Mr. Khan," the demon prince of Persia, Allahzad, sneered as he stood directly in back of Omar Syeed, guiding the mortal's hand to open the manila folder, from which he removed what appeared to be the first of three large 8 x 11 inch colored photos.

Holding up a picture of what appeared to be a young American Marine fully dressed in uniform, Syeed looked at the confused Khan and said with a smile, "First, I'd like you to meet Sergeant Major Brad Daniel Kassel from Dearborn, Michigan." He paused briefly before continuing. "I know what you are thinking right now, Mr. Khan. In your mind, you are saying to yourself, 'how does this picture of an apple-pie faced, all-American marine help you to purchase your $100 million dollar prize?' Does September 11th, 2001, mean anything to you Mr. Khan? It does to Sergeant Major Kassel." Syeed grinned. "That was the day that Sergeant Major Kassel's first cousin, Brittany Kassel, went to work at the U.S. World Trade Center in New York City never to returned home again."

Khan's confused stare intensified as Syeed continued. "Does November 5th, 2009 mean anything to you, Mr. Khan? It does to Sergeant Major Kassel," Syeed repeated with an evil grin. "That was the day his older brother, Army Lieutenant Michael Kassel, along with 12 other U.S. Army personnel, was shot dead at Fort Hood, Texas, by a deranged Muslim, who happened to be a U.S. Army Major named Nidal Malik Hasan."

Syeed stopped once more, staring intensely at Abdul Khan

"Does Dearborn, Michigan mean anything to you, Mr. Khan? It does to Sergeant Major Kassel," taunted the demon controlled Syeed. "You see, Mr. Khan, Dearborn is not only the hometown of Henry Ford and the headquarters of the Ford Motor Company, it is also Sergeant Major Brad Kassel's hometown where his father, Joseph Kassel, is presently, not only losing his job of 27 years managing a once productive car dealership, but quite possibly, losing the family home to foreclosure as well. Coincidentally,

Dearborn, Michigan has the second-highest Muslim population outside of the Middle East."

"Mr. Syeed!" interjected an impatient Khan. "You've firmly established the fact that Sergeant Kassel has probable cause to be hostile toward Muslims, but you haven't shown me anything yet that's worth handing over this large sum of money."

"Be patient," Syeed/Allahzad sneered with a confident grin as he placed the next photograph over the top of the first. "Meet Samuel Tucker, a full-fledged white supremacy racist from the bayou swamps of Louisiana. It seems Mr. Tucker here lost his life-long job as a shrimper due to the effects of the Gulf oil spill, and now he puts full blame for the entire oily mess squarely on President Harris' shoulders. Not only that, until we got to him, this good old red-neck boy had been shooting off his mouth about how he was going do the country a big favor and shoot our Muslim-loving, n-ger president, as he so aptly refers to President Harris, 'right between his evil black communist eyes.'"

Everyone, including Abdul Khan, blushed, embarrassed by Syeed's poor imitation of the racist's hateful remarks. Little did they realize that it was the demon Allahzad, not Syeed, quoting those detestable bigoted comments.

"Oh, I almost forgot to tell you the best part of all!" Syeed recalled with grin, "Our Mr. Samuel Tucker, pictured here, is a full-fledged, card-carrying member of the American Values Party."

"And whose face is on this last photo?"

"That is a picture of our own man, Mr. Khan," Syeed replied. "Habeeb Quadri, alias Jeremy Landers, the true master of disguise. Habeeb Quadri is not only the catalyst of this entire operation, he will make absolutely sure that every single penny of your $100 million dollar investment will pay off in the big dividends that we are all confidently counting on."

Chapter Eight

"He who sins is of the devil, for the devil has sinned from the beginning. For this purpose the Son of God was manifested, that He might destroy the works of the devil."

~1 John 3:8 (NKJV)

From the Author:

Before continuing our story, we need to fully understand the ramifications of one of Satan's greatest tools of deception, the philosophy of our day, humanism. It has been said that humanism is simply defined as a philosophical statement that declares that the end of all being is the happiness of man. In other words, the reason for being is simply man's happiness. This lie, straight from the pits of hell, is diametrically opposed to the Gospel. According to the tenets of humanism, salvation has nothing to do with the redemptive act of a personal God. A humanist's definition of salvation is simply a matter of getting all the happiness you can out of life. The philosopher, John Dewey was the first to introduce humanism into American public schools back in the early twentieth century. Dewey was able to persuade educators that there were absolutely no moral standards; that the end of public education was simply to allow the child to express himself and expand on what he is, and find happiness in being what he wants to become. By misinterpreting the intent of Thomas Jefferson's wall of separation between church and state, our government has given legal license to educational humanists to sanitize all vestiges of God, Jesus, the Bible, the Ten Commandments, and prayer from public schools across America. The final end product of this devilish ploy is to produce a self-absorbed individual, accountable only to himself or herself, totally free to live his or her life without the limiting constraints of a sovereign Holy God. To quote a powerful statement made by the deceased pastor, Paris Reidhead, in his famous sermon, "Ten Shekels and a Shirt", *"Humanism is the most deadly and disastrous of all the philosophical stenches that's crept up through the grating placed over the pit of Hell."*

When the school bells ring and our first classes begin this fall, teachers, not only at my school, but in many other schools across the United States, will now be required to not only post their lesson's specific outcome on the front board, but also include, as part of our daily lesson, a 'one world citizen' component, an environmental 'earth' component, and an 'open minded thinking' component that requires the student learner to 'think out of the box', and no longer accept narrow-minded philosophical standards such as absolute truth. No longer are American students required to stand every morning and pledge their loyalty and allegiance to their nation's flag. No longer are American students encouraged to think in terms of absolute moral standards when it comes to guiding their lives or anyone else's. Instead, American public schools preach daily the secular virtues of pragmatism, multiculturalism, and humanism, now widely espoused in the new national curriculm named Common Core. Beginning this fall in a public school near you, the minds of our impressionable American children—from kindergarten through high school and beyond—will once again be at the mercy of Satan's select team of progressive humanists. The ways of the devil are subtle and to the spiritually blind, totally imperceptible.

Saturday, June 7th, 2015
American Values Party Rally
National Mall
Washington D.C.

Whether twittered over the Internet or digitally beamed into American homes nationwide over cable and satellite dishes, the word was out and everyone, everywhere could sense it. Not since the summer of 1963, when civil rights leader, Dr. Martin Luther King Jr., stood on the steps of the Lincoln Memorial and gave his "I have a dream" speech, has Washington D.C. seen this many concerned Americans pouring across its beltway borders. For a city that has seen its share of large protest rallies, this could be the day that breaks all records. As far as the eye could see, in every direction—from Constitution and Pennsylvania Avenues on the north, First Street on the east, Independence and Maryland Avenues on the south, and 14th Street on the west—throngs of people from every corner of America were seen exiting city metro buses and subways. Unlike the marches of the 1960's, these people were, for the most part, white; some were families with young children, but most appeared to be middle-aged and older. The vast majority were holding American flags in their hands and displaying homemade signs with slogans such as "Take America Back" or "Harris-care Makes Me Sick!" Millions of overly concerned grassroots activists from all reaches of American society were now converging on the grassy lawn of the National Mall for one singular purpose, one singular voice, and one singular theme, "Restore America Now!"

Taken altogether, the personal issues that prompted so many concerned Americans to attend this morning's American Values Party "Restore America Now!" rally, were grossly overwhelming. With gay marriage legislation poised to become the law of the land, a sweeping national health-care plan soon to take effect, continued government overspending, budget busting taxes inundating struggling families from all directions, and an annual U.S. National debt much larger than the gross income of over half the world's population, there was ample for these concerned Americans to protest at today's rally.

As scores of enthusiastic AVP staffers scurried about making last-minute preparations to the main stage—set up within feet of the US Capitol steps, a young couple stopped in front of one of the several mega screen displays, along the almost two mile length of the National Mall, to claim their temporary five-by-five foot domain for the rally.

"Brad, what's bothering you? You haven't said more than two words since we got off the metro."

"Helen, we went through this back at the parking lot," Kassel commented in a barely audible voice. With his attractive brunette girlfriend of six months standing at his side, the casually dressed Marine sergeant removed what appeared to be a folded, reddish-colored blanket from his backpack.

Passively watching as Kassel meticulously unfolded and spread the wool spun covering with the Marine Corps symbol at its center over the grassy surface below, Helen explained, "Brad, honey, I'm just concerned about you. That's all."

"God, Helen, how can you stand here on the National Mall of all places, with the Washington Monument right in back of us, and not feel what I'm feeling right now?" A perplexed Kassel sat down on the ground. "Our President, the leader of our Nation, the very man I am sworn to protect with my life, has taken sides with our blood-sucking enemies! Doesn't that affect you?"

"Brad, as I told you this morning when we met at the Metro Station parking lot, I am completely appalled that President Harris came out yesterday in support of building an Islamic Mosque only blocks away from Ground Zero, but I refuse to allow this one man's bad judgment to have any affect on my joy and peace."

"Helen, you didn't have Islamic crazies flying an airplane into the World Trade Center to kill your first cousin. You didn't have an American-born Muslim radical gun down your older brother, along with twelve others, at a secure Army base. Your dad still has a job, Helen, and your family still has a home. Mine doesn't! My dad lost his job of twenty-seven years, and their house is going into foreclosure!"

Before continuing, Kassel stopped momentarily to wipe away the tears from his eyes.

"Haven't you read about it, Helen? It's been on the news and all over the Internet. Muslims refuse to play by American rules or recognize our laws. They abide only by one law and that law is Islamic Sharia law! In my hometown of Dearborn, Michigan, Muslim thugs are enforcing Sharia law on non-Muslims. Right here in the USA! Helen, unless we stand up now and fight back, it's going to get much worse."

With a sincere look of compassion in her eyes, Helen McAllister turned to her boyfriend. "Brad, I know you've heard me say this a million times, but because I care about you, I'm going to tell you again."

"Helen!" Kassel interrupted, "I'm begging you, Honey! Please, please don't start with your Jesus crap right now. I've heard enough about how important it is for me to forgive and love my enemy—how hating Muslims only hurts me and not them."

Without saying another word, Helen McAllister closed her eyes and lowered her head.

"Helen, what are you doing?" Kassel asked in an irritated tone.

"Be quiet, Brad!" Helen replied. "I'm praying for you!"

Kassel looked up at his immovable girlfriend and smiled. "Helen, look. I'm sorry for the way I'm acting! I apologize and promise to change the subject, but please, Hon, at least for now, no more preaching or praying. Is that a deal?"

Keeping her head bowed, his girlfriend opened one eye and nodded in agreement.

Still smiling, Sergeant Kassel proceeded to reach up and affectionately secure his girlfriend's left hand in his. "Helen, I've got a great idea. Let's just sit here on this comfortable blanket for the next couple of hours, along with the millions of other like-minded conservative Americans. We can peacefully protest what this rotten, stinking, liberal, communist loving......"

"Brad, you promised!" Helen protested as she begrudgingly knelt on the blanket beside her boyfriend.

"...as I said," Kassel smiled, folding his hands behind his head before lying back on the blanket. "...a loving government will protect the individual rights of the American citizens."

Saturday, June 7th, 2015
9:42 A.M.
American Values Party Rally
National Mall
Washington D.C.

With the U.S. Capitol Building as a backdrop, all the excitement was focused around a handful of human mortals readying themselves on a raised stage. Little did these spiritually deceived, totally naive mortals realize, that even before the first human speaker would step up to the microphone and utter a single word, a diabolical plan straight from the pits of hell had already been conceived. Satan and his hierarchy of demonic aberrations would never allow these compassionate members of the American Values Party to achieve their ultimate goal—to restore the former greatness of their beloved America.

Unlike past American Values Party rallies, where only a trickle of conservative media outlets like Fox Cable News Network came out to give supportive coverage, today was an exception. With only minutes remaining before the start of today's "Restore America Now!" rally, over a dozen or more highly visible nationally known news anchors, liberal and otherwise, were strategically positioning themselves in front of their respective network's satellite-link cameras.

With close to two million people gathered in back, two other spectators sat on the National Mall's grassy surface, gloating at their well-earned prize. Arriving shortly before sunrise, they sat, no more than an arm's length away from the American Values Party's raised platform stage.

"Sam, I'm going to be leaving you now," Charlie Rich, alias Buck Jameson, said. A man of several identities added, "You ready, man?"

"Charlie, dontcha know, man, I was born ready for this moment!" Sam Tucker, a toothless, unemployed shrimper from Louisiana, grinned. "You just make sure, Charlie Rich, that your friends come through with their end of the bargain."

"Sam, you should know me well enough by now! Charlie Rich always keeps his word!"

Patting Tucker on his back, the sandy haired, green-eyed Rich got up and asked, "Hey, didn't I already hand-deliver you twenty-five thousand bucks just yesterday?" Pausing momentarily, Rich, his true name, Habeeb Quadri, looked down at the toothless grin of this self-professing white bigot and calmly stated, "This is the last time we'll ever meet face-to-face. Remember, Sam, after today, your fame begins. Every law enforcement officer around America—FBI, CIA, state police—is going to be watching your ass. As I promised, next week at this time, I will have someone else meet with your friend, Cheyanne Rogers, just across the border in Mississippi. At the designated time and location, she will personally hand-deliver the second cash installment of $500,000."

Pausing just quick enough to pat Tucker on the shoulder, Charlie Rich (Habeeb Quadri) continued, "You lucky red-neck, son of the Devil, all you have to do to earn your money is stand up here today and deliver a speech of your own choosing! Now, tell me how easy is that?"

"Piece of cake, Charlie!" boasted the toothless Tucker. "You and everyone else in America will soon be watching my brilliant acting debut on tonight's evening news. Hey, what about my next cash installment of $10,000,000?"

"As we agreed, it will once again be hand-delivered to Miss Rogers on July 5th, the day after you shoot and kill the President of United States of America."

Standing directly in back of Samuel Tucker, with its razor-sharp talons buried inside Tucker's torso, the midlevel demon, Kielon, boastfully declared through its naïve human host this final bone-chilling statement, "Charlie Rich, I swear to you in the presence of God, Almighty, that half-white, half-black interloper, Rashid Harris, is already as good as dead."

Saturday, June 7th, 2015
10:00 A.M.
American Values Party Rally
National Mall
Washington D.C.

With loud speakers, plus six mega screens strategically placed equidistant along the entire length of the rally's two-mile course, over two million spectators were able to both hear and see everything taking place on the American Values Party's stage platform, constructed within feet of the steps leading up to the U.S. Capitol Building.

At exactly 10 A.M., the announcement was made over the loud speakers that everyone had been long awaiting, "Will everyone now please stand for the singing of our great nation's National Anthem."

With a full military color guard standing in the background, a lone Marine painstakingly wheeled her battered body forward toward the center stage microphone. Severely injured by the detonation of a buried roadside bomb while serving her country in Iraq, she locked her wheelchair in position and held high a small American flag. With her right hand pressed firmly against her chest, this legless young Marine began to sing a song that had been sung many times before, but never with such passion and raw emotion. Not only did she sing the first verse of her nation's Anthem, she sang the words to all three verses, words that millions had never heard past the familiar first verse. As the valiant Marine's voice began to strain, a combined chorus of over two million fellow citizens looked up at a large digital screen and joined with her to complete the Anthem's fourth and final verses. According to unofficial estimates supplied by the Office of Homeland Security and the Emergency Management Agency, never before in America's history had so many like-minded Americans gathered in one place to sing the words of a song that spoke so clearly of the long forgotten message of their beloved country's national heritage.

'O! thus be it over, when freemen shall stand between their loved home and the war's desolation!

Blest with victory and peace, may the heav'n rescued land praise the Power that hath made and preserved us a nation.

Then conquer we must, when our cause it is just, and this be our motto: "In God is our trust."

And the Star-Spangled Banner in triumph shall wave. O'er the land of the free and the home of the brave.'

Once the thunderous applause subsided, party organizers continued hyping the ecstatic crowds by having them chant in unison the slogans posted on each of the six digital screens: "Enough is Enough"—"We the People"—"Go Green: Recycle Congress"—"President Harris: I'm Not Your ATM"—"Jesus, Not Harris, Is my Messiah!"

After the final slogan was posted, top country singer Willy Blackstone's name was flashed across each mega-screen in exploding red, white and blue colors. For the next several minutes or so, millions of emotion-filled voices joined in with Willy singing his number-one country hit entitled, "Bring My America Back Home to Me."

At the conclusion of Blackstone's touching song, the rally's announcer made a request to the cheering, flag-waving masses: "Everybody, put your hands together and give a welcoming cheer to our first scheduled speaker, the honorable U.S. Congressman from the great southern state of Alabama, Elijah Weaver!"

"Hello, free people!" the very popular black Republican Congressman shouted. "How's your government treating you today?"

A chorus of expected boos immediately followed the congressman's opening question. But what Congressman Weaver said next would literally send this record-breaking crowd into a total uproar. "I have come here today because I want more than anything else, for America to see firsthand," Weaver paused and smiled broadly at the crowd, then shouted into the microphone, "that a black man can actually speak to an audience without the aid of a teleprompter!"

Even before the words came out of his mouth, Weaver knew he was taking a calculated risk telling this mostly all-white conservative crowd a racial joke. He also knew that only another black man could tell a racial joke concerning a black president's reliance on teleprompters, without being brutally chastised by the liberal media.

The very moment Congressman Weaver finished telling his joke, everyone, including the congressman, broke into spontaneous laughter. In a minute or two after the laughter subsided, someone in the crowd, directly below the stage's platform, shouted another racially charged statement that grabbed everyone's attention. "Did you hear what that guy just said over there?" the flabbergasted NBC News anchor, Katie Reynolds, asked her speechless cameraman. "He just said it again! Quick, get him on camera!"

Everyone, including Congressman Weaver, stood speechless, stunned that anyone would dare shout out such a blatantly appalling declaration. Within moments of hearing the racially charged words, each of the television crews was given the order by their respective networks to redirect their cameramen's attention away from Congressman Weaver and onto a particular figure standing only feet away from the edge of the stage.

"Boy, you get your big fat black rear off that stage!" a scruffy-looking middle-aged man shouted. He wore sandals and a white tee shirt, cut off jeans, and his exposed skin, except for his face, was completely covered in faded bluish-green tattoos.

"I didn't come all this way to Washington D.C. to listen some black congressman telling me about our black president's fear of standin' up in front of a lot of white folk without his fancy tele-whatever showin him what to say next. I came here for someone to tell me how, in God's name, I'm gonna get my shrimpin' job back!"

Before he had the chance to spew out of his toothless mouth another vulgar word, the tattooed man was descended upon from all sides by over a dozen United States Park Police officers. As fast as the incident had started, it was over. The Park Police made their arrest, but not before irrevocable damage had been inflicted on the rally's perceived persona of representing the true values of the average American. As he was being led away in handcuffs by the U.S. Park Police, the tattooed toothless man smiled broadly, knowing that he had just earned every single penny of his $500,000 price tag. Samuel Tucker's brief two-minute performance on the National Mall had just provided the progressives the very ammunition they were all awaiting. No matter what was said and how elegantly and heartfelt it was expressed, only one speech and one message from today's conservative rally would be broadcast across the vast liberal media landscape—The American Values Party is a racist organization and its conservative narrow-minded social agenda helps spawn bigotry and racism across America.

Watching everything transpire from the close-up vantage point of the nearby stage, Amducious turned to his arch demon counterpart,

Allahzah and sneered. "Samuel Tucker has just earned his supper in a D.C jail cell!"

"Admit it, Destroyer!" Allahzad said with a smile. "As far as humans go, Tucker was brilliant. I am going to personally make sure that every single one of Tucker's words are broadcast daily nonstop for the next week or so on Al Jazerra television throughout the entire Middle East."

"And when I'm finished twisting and distorting Tucker's story in the American media," Amducious boasted, "this toothless human scab will be known across America as the new poster boy for the American Values Party. So help me, Satan!"

"Praise be to Lord Satan!" Allahzad responded in turn with a raised left fist.

Friday, June 12th, 2015
4:59 p.m.
Lola's Barracks Bar & Grill
8th & I Streets SE
Washington D.C.

Everyone was standing at their assigned posts. With the beers chilled, the crabs hot, and most important of all, the President of the United States out of town, all of the necessary ingredients were now in place for the weekly onslaught of U.S. Marines from the 8th and I Streets Barracks. Located just a stone's throw away from the oldest active post of the United States Marine Corps, the dozen or so employees of Lola's Barracks Bar & Grill were counting down the minutes on the kitchen's large mounted wall clock until the first Marine crossed over the threshold of this popular D.C. restaurant.

For the fifty or so Marines assigned to the prestigious 8th & I Streets Barracks, tonight was also a very special occasion. Tonight was the last free Friday night these honored Marines, assigned to perform in ceremonial parades, funerals, and other ceremonies for the president and other national dignitaries, had off duty until summer's end. The nicest benefit of their highly esteemed assignment was, when the president was out of town, the entire Unit was also on liberty. With President Harris out of town until Monday, every Marine sitting inside the 8th & I Streets Barrack's recreation room had their eyes fixed on the large wall clock hanging beside the pool table. As the 5 o'clock hour neared, all fifty voices began counting down the seconds in unison to the official start of their planned weekend activities: "Five, four, three, two, one, blast off!" With less time than it takes Marines to shout their famous HOOAH!, the large rec room emptied with every one heading directly toward the barrack's 8th Street front entrance. Only one Marine remained behind, sitting in the solitude of the empty rec room, or at least that's what he thought.

"Hey Kassel, aren't you joining us at Lola's?"

What the hell's he still doing here? Looking up, a stunned Sergeant Kassel recognized the fellow Marine standing at the entrance to the room. Quickly mustering his thoughts, Kassel managed to mumble out a somewhat logical response. "Ah, sorry Dave, but I won't be able to make it tonight! It's our last free Friday, and I've already promised Helen that I'd take her out to a fancy downtown restaurant and then to a movie."

Shaking his head before leaving, Sergeant David Liddy chided, "Kassel, has anybody ever told you that you're just a henpecked sucker?"

"Hey Dave," Sergeant Kassel called to his departing buddy, "this is for you, and also, for any of those likeminded friends of yours down at Lola's!" Kassel extended his finger in an obscene gesture.

With Sergeant Liddy's departure, with sweat streaming down his face, Kassel had a distinct sense of being alone. Before getting up, the Sergeant Major wiped every drop of perspiration from his face and forehead with a handkerchief. Nervously, he looked down at his watch and mumbled to himself, "*Get a hold of yourself, idiot. You've already given your commitment; there's no turning back, now!"*

With that being his last word, at 5:12 PM, Sergeant Major Brad Kassel exited the 8th & I Streets Barracks. Turning left, he strained his eyes in the direction of Lola's Barracks Bar & Grill. Had it been any other night, he too would be sitting inside Lola's, celebrating along side his 8th & I Streets buddies. With his mind already made up, Kassel turned to his right and proceeded down 8th Street in the direction of another close by restaurant, The Ugly Mug Bistro. It was here that Sergeant Kassel determined to keep his previously scheduled 5:30 appointment.

Friday, June 12th, 2015
5:27 p.m.
The Ugly Mug Bistro
732 8 Street SE
Washington D.C.

Known simply by locals as The Mug, what this popular Barracks Row watering hole lacked in the way of restaurant ambiance, it more than made up for in offering good ol' pub grub featuring some of the best pasta dishes and roast-beef stacked sandwiches in all of D.C. With a large TV monitor playing a live Washington Nationals' game directly above the bar, a lone busboy scurried about the narrow dining area, readying an available table for its next customer.

"Sergeant Kassel, you are more than welcome to sit here," Benny Bishop commented as he pulled a chair away from the table he just bused. "If you'd like, you can order now, or wait until the arrival of your friend."

"Thanks, Benny, but I'm a little bit early." Kassel replied as he graciously accepted the busboy's offer. "I think I'll wait for a few minutes."

"That's great, Sergeant Kassel, I'll tell your waiter."

In just a few minutes, the person he had been waiting for was standing directly on the other side of the table. "Brad, please excuse me. Traffic was a horrendous mess, backed up all the way to the beltway."

Kassel stood and extended his right hand to greet Buck Jamison, a man he had previously met twice before. Buck stood about five foot nine inches tall, and looked no different than any other, thirty-something, sandy haired Caucasian.

"No apologies needed, Buck. Have a seat, man."

"Thanks, Brad! I am literally straight-up starving!" Jamison replied, rubbing his stomach. "Tell me, what's good around here?"

"Buck, this place may not look like much, but a former top D.C. chef created The Mug menu, so everything they serve is good, right down to the beer. My favorite's the French dip sandwich platter. Picture this, Buck: a large brioche roll, stuffed to the max with thinly sliced roast beef, coated with a mixture of their own house creamy French dressing, a side of crispy thin oven-baked onion rings. dusted with grated parmesan cheese, and a thick slice of dill pickle on the side. All served with your choice of domestically homebrewed beer."

"Ooh-wee, say no more brother!" Jamison replied, hand-butting Brad Kassel from across the table.

"You sold me, Kassel, but under one condition."

"What's that?"

"I'm paying!"

"You'll get no complaints from me, Buck."

"Would you like a Bud?"

"Doesn't everybody?" replied the smiling, sandy haired imposter.

"Hey, Frankie," Kassel motioned to the approaching waiter. "Two Buds, please!"

"Coming right up, Sergeant Kassel!"

With their beers on order, Kassel looked across the table and stated nervously, "Look, Buck, I've got to tell you straight off, I'm beginning to get second thoughts about all this."

"Isn't the money enough for you, Brad?"

"No-no, your offer is more than enough. In fact, I still have every penny you gave me, all twenty-five thousand dollars of it."

"Then what's the problem, man?"

Appearing both frustrated and nervous at the same time, Kassel sat back in his seat and confessed what was truly troubling him. "The problem is, Buck, I'm a Marine. I have sworn on oath to protect my country with my life and I will never go back on that oath."

"Brad, stop right there!" Jamison curtly demanded. "I am not asking you to go back on your oath one iota! Once we have taken care of that Muslim, you will be fulfilling that oath you took, and you will be protecting the country you love with your very life."

"That's the other thing. I've also sworn an oath to protect the President of the United States with my life, even if that president happens to be a blood-sucking Muslim."

"Brad, listen to me and listen well. Rashid Jabbar Harris is president in name only. He is a fraud. Rashid Harris is a smooth-talking Muslim imposter, who has conned his way to the top of the political ladder with the financial backing of hating, socialist liberals like George Kaufman. Don't you remember my showing you, when we meet two months ago, positive proof that Harris was actually born in Kenya? Has anyone ever held up Rashid Harris's long form birth certificate in front of the world, proving once and for all that he is a legitimate American citizen, and giving him the Constitutional right to even become president? No, Brad—never—and nobody ever will. Rashid Harris is not an American."

Sergeant Kassel quietly sat back in his seat, silently listening as Jamison stated his case.

"Brad, just put aside totally the fact that Harris was born in Kenya. His father was a Kenyan nationalist and his fifteen-year-old white American mother was too young at the time to legally and legitimately pass her America citizenship onto him.

His mother remarried another Muslim named Kolo Kalapebo and in 1967, they all moved to Indonesia where Rashid was not only raised Muslim, but attended a Muslim school in Jakarta. His school's official registration papers had his nationality listed at the time as being Indonesian, and his religion, not Christian, as he now contends, but Muslim. Need I say more?"

"I don't know," a thoroughly perplexed Marine replied.

"Brad, look me in the eye," demanded a clearly determined Jamison. "There are two things I need to remind you of: First and foremost, you're not going to get caught! As long as you follow our plan to a "T" there is absolutely no way anyone could ever trace anything back to you. All the money you will be receiving, and I have half of it with me today, is in cash—all in small bills and all perfect legal tender."

"Brad, this one is really important! The people over me have direct ties to the White House. Like us, they are true American patriots. They, too, want America restored to its Constitutional roots—with no Muslim-loving socialists having any part in governing it whatsoever!"

"Ok, Buck," Kassel conceded. "What's the plan?"

A relieved Jamison (Habeeb Quadri) sat back and said in a calm voice, "Sergeant Kassel, I knew you would never let your country down."

Reaching under the table, Jamison proceeded to shift the briefcase he had carried into the restaurant over to Sergeant Kassel's side of the table. "It's all there, Brad," he commented with a smile. "There's more than enough here to keep the banks from foreclosing on your parent's home. After next month's successful Fourth of July celebration, that amount will be doubled."

Overwhelmed by it all, Sergeant Kassel closed his eyes and sat back in his chair.

"Ok, Buck Jamison, or whomever you say you are, I'm ready; tell me the plan!"

Pleased with himself, a relieved Jamison folded his hands and sat back.

"As you know better than anyone, Sergeant Kassel, a multi-layered, seemingly impenetrable wall of human security is in place 24/7 to protect the lives of President Harris and other important heads of state. As you also are so keenly aware, the only way to breach such an elaborate security system is to have someone in place who has gained trust on the protected side of the wall, open a small, but penetrable crack, just wide enough for someone on the outside to slip in, carry out the job and slip back out again without ever being detected."

"And you have such a plan?"

"I assure you, this plan is better than any James Bond could have conceived."

"You, Sergeant Kassel, have two very small, but extremely important parts to play in all this."

Habeeb Quadri, alias Buck Jamison, paused momentarily to look around at the faces of all the other Ugly Mug patrons seated round-about before proceeding. "Okay, Brad, when you first arrive at your scheduled 6 a.m. starting time on the 4th of July, you and over four dozen other members of 8th & I Streets Barracks Marines will be dropped off directly in front of the West Lawn of the U.S. Capitol Building. You will then go directly to your assigned post, checking the IDs of all those given special orange access badges to sit within the fenced off area directly in front of the bleachers where the president and his family will be seated. Then, after the 8 p.m. live concert performance by the National Symphony Orchestra, the fireworks display will be launched in back of the Washington Monument. Your first task, Sergeant Kassell, is simple. When you see this man, you are to check his credentials, as you would for anyone else, and allow him to pass unimpeded through the metal detector beyond your checkpoint."

"My God, Buck, do you have any idea who this man is?" Kassel questioned. "This is that stupid brainless idiot whose picture has been plastered on the front page of every liberal newspaper in the country. He's a blatant redneck racist. There's no way in hell that he's going to get the security clearance to get within ten miles of the President of the United States."

"Buck, don't ask me how, because I'm not privileged to that level of information— and even if I were, I couldn't tell you. In three short weeks from now, Mr. Samuel James Tucker will be seated amongst his fellow Americans on the West Lawn in front of the United States Capitol Building. At 9:10 p.m. on that same evening, with all eyes, including those of the President of the United States, fixed on the exploding fireworks display over the top of the Washington Monument, Mr. Tucker will perform a Fourth of July fireworks display of his own that this country will never soon forget."

"One thing I don't understand, where is he getting the gun? There's no way he could even pass though a metal detector without a gun being detected."

"Not to worry," smiled Jamison. "When the time is right, you will personally make sure that Mr. Tucker has all that he needs to take care of that very small matter."

Friday, June 12th, 2015
6 p.m.
Living Hope Christian Church
1210 Wisconsin Avenue NW
Washington DC

On most Friday evenings, the blacktop parking lot that surrounds the Wisconsin Avenue's Living Hope Christian Church was usually empty, but tonight was an exception. Two vehicles, one, a late model six passenger Chevy SUV, the other, a shiny new red Ford Mustang, were parked just outside the Church's side entrance.

Just inside the entrance door, the distinct sounds of a female's sobs could be heard coming from the head pastor's office just down the hallway. The three humans now seated in a small circle had absolutely no clue that the simple prayer they were about to agree on would not only have spiritual implications, but in the natural, this seemingly insignificant petition would soon set in motion a course of events that would change American history forever.

"Honey, it's all right to cry, but you haven't done anything wrong," consoled Jean Aldrich, the wife of Pastor Jim Aldrich.

"But Mrs. Aldrich," cried the young woman, "I've been disobedient to the Lord. Doesn't the Bible say Christians are not supposed to be unequally yoked with unbelievers? I've been dating one for over six months now!"

"Helen, honey," Pastor Jim Aldrich smiled as he looked directly into the young woman's teary brown eyes. "As my wife just said, you didn't do anything wrong. Falling in love with someone isn't a sin. In fact, from everything you told Jean and me, you've done everything right."

"But Pastor Jim, when Brad and I first started dating around Christmas time, Brad was willing to go to church with me, and he seemed very open to my sharing my faith." Helen stopped momentarily to wipe the tears from her eyes before continuing.

"But in the last month or two, I have noticed a big change in his attitude toward any Christian. The moment I even mention Jesus' name, Brad will either change the subject or withdraw into silence. Pastor Jim, I really love Brad, but according to the Bible, unless he accepts Jesus as his Lord and Savior, I have to stop seeing him. Pastor Jim, please tell me, what should I do?"

"Helen, whenever a person refuses repeatedly to hear the truth, the only thing we can do is pray," the Pastor said, "For now, let's just lift this entire situation to the Lord in prayer."

Helen once again wiped the tears from her eyes as she joined hands with her Pastor and his wife. With hands held tightly, Pastor

Jim Aldrich stared once again into her eyes and compassionately said, "Helen, the Bible clearly states that when two or three are gathered together in Jesus' name, He is there in the room with us. The Bible also says that if we ask anything in Jesus' name, He will grant that request and His Father will be glorified. Let us all bow our heads in prayer.

"Dear Heavenly Father,

Father, we thank You for providing all of us salvation and eternal life in Heaven through Jesus' sacrifice on the cross for our sins. We ask you now to save Brad Kassel. Father, we ask that he will not perish in hell, but that Brad will accept Jesus as his Lord and Savior, and receive salvation by accepting Jesus' sacrifice for him. We stand here before you in one accord agreeing for the salvation of Brad Kassel.

Father, we ask this all in the Holy Name of Jesus,

Amen"

Even though their eyes remained closed during the entire prayer, the three humans were totally unaware of the presence of two massive supernatural beings intently listening to every word the pastor prayed.

"So be it!" said Yahriel turning to his archangel counterpart, Muriel. "Whether he accepts it or not, Sergeant Brad Kassel is now marked for salvation."

"Whom do you suggest that I assign guardian over this human?" asked Muriel.

"For what this mortal is soon going to face, Kassel really needs our best warrior assigned to him," Yahriel, the angelic prince of prophetic wisdom and worldly affairs, replied.

"So be it!" declared Muriel. "When he arises tomorrow morning, Sergeant Brad Kassel will have Kiel at his side!"

Chapter Nine

"Satan, the god of this evil world, has blinded the minds
of those who don't believe, so they are unable to see the
glorious light of the Good News that is shining upon them."

~2 Corinthians 4:4

Thursday, June 18th, 2015
4:45 a.m. Israel Standard Time
Prime Minister's Residence
Beit Aghion
9 Smolenskin St., Jerusalem

While the majority of the city's nearly 750,000 residents slept, two
large government vehicles left the darkened upscale neighborhood
of Rehavia traveling northeast toward their intended destination,
the prime minister's office located at 3 Kaplan St., Jerusalem.
Unknown to the human occupants inside, atop the roofs of each
vehicle sat four angelic warriors. Their Commander, the Archangel
Michael, assigned these eight trusted angels to protect the Israeli
Prime Minister, Yacov Ben Yizri, sitting in the lead SUV. Two
massive winged warriors remained behind, standing shoulder-
to-shoulder at the front-gated entrance leading up to the Israeli
Prime Minister's Beit Aghion residence. They carefully watched
as the faint red glow from the moving vehicle's taillights gradually
diminished as it disappeard into the distant Jerusalem darkness.

"*Commander, what do you think the Prime Minister's decision will be?*" Michael's curious angelic companion, Pethel, inquired.

"*It's hard to tell,*" Michael admitted. "*These Israelis are sometimes hard to read. They say one thing with their mouths, but their hearts say something else. I must admit I, too, am curious to hear Ben Yizri's decision.*"

"*What happens if he goes along with the demands of the American president?*" Pethel asked. "*Will we move all of our warriors back to the pre-1967 borders?*"

"*That decision must come from the Lord,*" Michael replied. "*Unless the Lord, Himself, says differently, we must not intervene.*"

"*Michael, I know we have discussed this matter a thousand times before, but why is it that Jews always make the wrong choices? Don't they realize that they are covered by the Covenant? They have God's eternal promises. They also have you and legions of angelic warriors to constantly watch over and protect them.*"

The inquisitive angel briefly paused and looked directly into his commander's crystal blue eyes. "*I know exactly what you are going to tell me, Commander. They are humans, and humans are rebellious!*"

Michael smiled. He fully understood his comrade's frustration with the weak human spirit, but Michael also knew that in spite of the human's shortcomings, their Creator still loved them.

"*My friend, regardless of what the prime minister decides,*" Michael reassured, "*have confidence that God's prophetic plans will be fulfilled. Our warriors will be ready for anything Satan has in store.*"

Thursday, June 22nd, 2015
1:02 p.m. Israel Standard Time
Prime Minister's Office
3 Kaplan St., Jerusalem

From the moment he arrived at work shortly before daybreak, the Israeli Prime Minister, Yacov Ben Yizri, had not left his Jerusalem office, not even to eat. For the past several hours he had been meeting behind closed doors with a small group of his most trusted Likud party cabinet members. Also seated in the same large conference room were two intelligence officers from Mossad, the Israeli government's equivalent to America's top security agency, the CIA.

After sitting through what seemed like hours of hearing classified intelligence reports privy to no other person on Earth, Prime Minister Ben Yizri finally sat back in his chair, put up his hands and chuckled out loud "Enough!" Shaking his head back and forth, the Likud prime minister smiled as he looked around the room at all the surprised faces.

"Where is King Solomon when you really need him?" the Prime Minister joked as he once again leaned forward in his chair to direct his full attention toward the two Mossad agents sitting directly across the long conference room table.

"Mr. Yatom and Mr. Halevy, when you return to your Tel Aviv Mossad headquarters, I want you to extend my heartfelt appreciation to all those agents who diligently worked hard gathering this critical information vital to our nation's survival."

The Prime Minister momentarily paused, staring intently into the eyes of his top intelligence officers. "But, before you leave," the Prime Minister continued, "I don't have to tell you two how heavy a weight has been placed upon my shoulders. Before I make my decision on what to do, I would like the two of you to summarize one last time, in as few words as possible, everything you presented."

"That's fine, Mr. Prime Minister, and if it's all right, I will go first."

"Thank you, Ephraim; please proceed."

"As we have extensively covered and discussed, as far as sanctions go, every single engagement policy President Harris has attempted to impose on the Tehran government has failed to budge Iran one iota in its quest for uranium enrichment. Diplomacy backed by timid U.N. Security Council sanctions has not persuaded Iran from discontinuing its nuclear weapons program. It is the opinion of Mossad that it is now too late in the game, and Tehran has invested too many scarce economic resources, human capital, and prestige to refrain from taking the final steps to attaining nuclear capability. Moreover, the Iranian hardliners, who have established an increasingly firm grip on power, are vehemently opposed to better relations with the United States. In summary, Mr. Prime Minister, as far as imposing sanctions in stopping Iran from developing nuclear weapons, it has been, and will continue to be, an exercise in futility."

"Mr. Halevy?" the Prime Minister queried.

"Mr. Prime Minister, I completely concur with my colleague's summary. All past international diplomatic efforts to diffuse this serious situation have failed to secure the desired results. The Iranian regime's drive to obtain nuclear weapons, its rapid progress in building up its ballistic missile arsenal, and its ominous rhetoric about destroying Israel has potentially created an explosive situation. While the United States was trying to engage Tehran in talks over the past year, the Iranians have nearly doubled their stock of 5% enriched uranium to 6,300 pounds. A recent report from the International Atomic Energy Agency says Iran has enriched a growing stockpile of uranium up to 20%, installing new centrifuges for that purpose. These steps have taken Iran closer to the nuclear brink. Enriching fuel from 20% to the 90% or so needed for a Hiroshima-style atomic bomb would take only a few weeks. Based on these numbers, our intelligence believes that Iran now has produced enough nuclear fuel to make at least two low-grade atomic weapons. It is also my opinion, Mr. Prime Minister, that Israel may see no other choice than to launch a preventive strike against Iran's nuclear facilities."

Standing, the Prime Minister extended his hand of sincere thanks to his Mossad officers. "Thank you, gentlemen, for your tireless efforts and endless dedication to your country," the gracious Israeli leader commented with a broad smile.

Once the Mossad officers left the room, Israel's Minister of Defense, Ehud Levy, turned to his boss and said, "Yacov, how much more time can we afford to waste? Diplomacy, backed by punishing sanctions has failed. President Harris has proven repeatedly that Israel cannot depend on him. It was only last month that Harris stopped the shipment of bunker-busting bombs to Israel, and has maintained an embargo of cutting-edge weapons that Israel wants. He has allowed votes at the UN against Israel that he could have vetoed. His Cairo speech alone makes him untrustworthy from Israel's viewpoint. So Israel has to decide whether to take the serious risk of a possible first strike by Iran. Israel is too small. If Tel Aviv is hit by radioactive material, the consequences are far too serious to contemplate."

Staring intently into his Defense Minister's fiery brown eyes, Yacov Ben Yizri responded to his life-long friend in a compassionate tone, "Ehud, you are a dear friend; I know your heart. You love Israel as much as I do. You and I have been serving our country together since the days when we were both young IDF (Israel Defense Forces) commandos fighting for our country's very survival during the 1973 Yom Kippur War. You formerly served as the prime minister, and now you are my Defense Minister."

"Nothing seems to change, Yacov," Ehud Levy, reminiscing in agreement, replied. "It was bad then. It's bad now."

"Except in 1973, we were the only players on the block with atomic weapons. I'm afraid if we don't act quickly, that will soon change."

Turning his full attention toward a rather tall, attractive middle-aged woman seated to his right, the Prime Minister smiled and said, "Yanny, I want to thank you once again for coming."

"Thank you, Yacov, for inviting me." Yanny Herzog, the present opposition leader of Israel's Kadima Party, responded politely with a handshake.

"You have graciously accepted my offer to come and play the opposition's role of devil's advocate," the Prime Minister affirmed. "As a trusted member of our Knesset, I want to hear how you view everything you have heard this morning."

"Yacov, think about the severe consequences of any attack on Iran." Herzog frankly stated. "This is exactly what this crazy Iranian president wants and you will be playing right into President Rouhani's hands. If we attack the Iranian nuclear facilities, he will say this attack was American supported, if not American orchestrated. The aircraft used in any strike will be American-produced, supplied and funded F-15s and F-16s, and most of the Israeli ordnances used will be from American stocks. The Iranians will almost certainly retaliate against both the U.S. and Israeli targets. Think very hard about it, Yacov, before you make up your mind! This could very easily lead all of us into World War III!"

Thursday, June 18th, 2015
6:35 a.m. (Eastern Daylight Savings Time)
Washington D.C.
Oval Office, White House

At the same time Israeli Prime Minister Yacov Ben Yizri was meeting in his Jerusalem office with a select group of his Israeli cabinet members, nearly six thousand miles away, a very similar discussion was being held by the President of the United States and a small group of his closest presidential cabinet members.

Like clockwork, the first person seen by the President every morning was his Director of National Intelligence, Dr. Jensen Everett. From 6:30 until 7:00 AM, no one else was permitted access to the Oval Office until the President's chief intelligence advisor had thoroughly briefed America's Commander in Chief on all matters related to national security.

Due to the explosive events unfolding in the Middle East, the president deemed it necessary to invite three other strategic members of his own cabinet to be present for this morning's daily presidential brief. Joining the DNI chief was the Vice President, Roen Morris, the Secretary of State, Andrea Jacobs, and the Secretary of Defense, Jonathan Bates.

Each person entered quietly through the Oval Office's side entrance door and proceeded to sit at prearranged chairs that had a top-secret folder with their names labeled on the front cover.

"Good morning, everyone."

"Good morning, Mr. President." All four stood and respectfully greeted their Commander in Chief, President Rashid Harris, as he entered the room through the Oval Office's front entrance door. Trying hard not to stare, everyone was taken back by the president's atypical unkempt appearance.

"Guys, forgive me for my appearance this morning," a disgruntled, unshaven President Harris commented as he proceeded to walk past his trusted advisors, not stopping to give his customary cordial handshake greeting. "I haven't had much sleep in the past twenty four hours."

Looking aged and vulnerable, wearing a white wrinkled shirt and opened collar, the person presently standing behind the desk stood in stark contrast to the person who sat there only a year earlier—a vibrant, immaculately dressed, self-assured person who genuinely felt that he could change the world all by himself.

"Thank you all for coming out on such short notice," the president said with a forced smile, "but needless to say, I deemed it necessary for you to be present for this morning's intelligence briefing. With that said, I will turn this briefing over to our Director of National Intelligence, Dr. Everett Jensen."

"Good morning, everyone," the DNI chief commented with a brief smile and a welcoming handshake extended to each person standing to his left.

"Thank you, again, everyone,' the president acknowledged. "You can all be seated."

"Even though as cabinet members we possess the highest security clearance," Dr. Jensen cautioned, "the information I am about to share must never leave this room. Only the president has the authority to say otherwise."

Each person nodded, affirming the DNI's explicit terms of secrecy. They knew Dr. Everett Jensen as a straightforward man who never minced his words. But each also knew Jensen well enough to sense a slight uneasiness in his voice. The president also appeared nervous as he silently sat behind his desk fiddling with his fingers.

"Will everyone break the seal on your folders and open to the first paragraph found on page one," Jensen commented as he too proceeded to unseal the top-secret folder on his lap.

The DNI chief waited a moment longer while the president, the vice president, and his secretaries opened their folders.

"Gentlemen and Secretary Jacobs," Jensen continued, "my role as Director of National Intelligence is to meet with the president every morning at 6:30 a.m. and read to him verbatim every word that is in this intelligence brief. When I finish reading, I then proceed to answer to the best of my knowledge any questions the president may have in respect to the report. I answer only to the president. This is the protocol we will follow here today."

Again, each person nodded, agreeing to the DNI's terms.

"Please refer to paragraph one as I read it aloud."

"As has been the stated public position of the United States Government and also, the larger international bodies of the world, the nation of Iran has every right to develop peaceful nuclear power that meets the energy needs of its people, but, as this intelligence report will show, Iran has been and still is, breaking all the rules that nuclear nations must follow. On numerous occasions, Iran has been caught concealing information about its nuclear program from the international community. This report will show conclusive evidence that Iran is threatening the fragile stability and the security of the entire Middle East region, and also, the world.

"Last year, our own national intelligence agencies, the CIA and NSA, discovered through a combination of aerial, satellite and ground based surveillance, that Iran has been building a clandestine, underground nuclear enrichment facility. Its exact location is on the grounds of the Islamic Revolutionary Guards Base located 100 miles southwest of Tehran near the holy city of Qom. The size and the configuration of this illegal facility are inconsistent with any peaceful nuclear power program and is in direct violation of all international nuclear-control agreements.

"Three months ago, International Atomic Energy Agency inspectors reportedly found that the amount of enriched uranium stored at the Iranian Natanz nuclear power facility far exceeded the specified agreed five percent level suitable for civilian energy production. At that time, IAEA inspectors found over 6,000 pounds of low-enriched uranium at the Iranian Natanz nuclear facility, enough radioactive material to produce about two nuclear weapons. As a direct result of those findings, the U.N. Security Council levied its toughest sanctions against Iran for its noncompliance, cutting off their access to foreign capital and blocking their ships from certain foreign ports."

The DNI chief stopped momentarily and looked up from his folder. Turning his attention to the three presidential cabinet members seated to his left, Dr. Jensen said with serious, but straightforward expression: "At approximately 11 p.m. Eastern Standard Time last night, this disturbing information I am about to read came across my desk. After reading it, I deemed it necessary to immediately contact the president. After a brief discussion, President Harris made the decision to have the three of you present at this morning's intelligence briefing to hear what I am about to say."

Jensen turned his head and nodded ever so slightly at the sullen president seated behind his Oval Office desk. The DNI chief looked down at his opened folder and stated this request, "Will everyone please turn to the next page of this report?"

Without a hint of emotion, Jensen once again began reading the ominous statement typed in bold red letters on the top line of the second page.

"CIA operatives covertly working in Iran have confirmed that Iran has illegally collected enough nuclear plutonium—over the 90 percent threshold—needed at its Natanz nuclear power facility to successfully produce at least one, and possibly two, of these untested low-yield nuclear weapons.

The DNI chief stopped momentarily to look up from his folder and address the president directly. "Mr. President, it was the unanimous consensus of the intelligence agencies I represent that this information has the highest level of credibility."

"Are the Israelis aware of this report?" the president asked.

"I wouldn't be a bit surprised. Mossad usually has this type of intelligence long before we do."

"Mr President, may I speak candidly?" the DNI Director asked.

"By all means."

"I believe we share some of the responsibility for what has taken place over night." Dr. Jensen boldly proclaimed.

"You need to explain yourself, Dr. Jensen," the president curtly responded.

"Please, don't get me wrong, Mr. President." Jensen clarified. "Our nation's attempt to stop Iran's nuclear ambitions through imposing stiff international sanctions was a noble cause. But in our own zeal to facilitate this outcome, we completely ignored the fact that the Iranian regime's entire focus has been, and still is, the complete annihilation of Israel from the face of this earth."

"Dr. Jensen, what is your point?" demanded a clearly irritated president.

"With all due respect, Mr. President, in retrospect, pressuring the Israelis into believing that sanctions alone would stop the Iranian hardliners from going forward with their nuclear ambitions was a mistake. We inadvertently prompted the Israeli government to drop its guard just long enough to allow their sworn enemies the time needed to achieve what the Iranian President Hassan Rouhani has been publicly stating all along, "To wipe Israel off the face of the earth."

"That's quite enough, Dr. Jensen," the president abruptly admonished. "Thank you for your report. If you don't mind, I would now like to discuss what was just said with my cabinet members in private."

"I understand, Mr. President," Dr. Jensen acknowledged with a nod. Without saying another word, the DNI chief got up from his chair and exited the room through the side entrance door.

The moment the door closed behind the DNI chief, the president stood up behind his Oval Office desk and blatantly declared to the three seated cabinet members, "If I had the power right now, I'd love to get rid of that disrespectful Republican so-and- so!"

"Isn't there something you can do, Mr. President?" a puzzled Vice President Morris asked.

"Roan, believe me, I've tried to get him replaced almost from the first day I took office. Jensen happens to be the top Pentagon dinosaur left over from the last administration. I'll be long dead before he leaves this office."

Everybody chuckled before the president continued. "Seriously, does anybody have any suggestions on what we should do?"

"Let's just assume the Israelis have the same intelligence report we have. In their minds, this leaves them with no other option but to plan an immediate strike on Iran's Natanz nuclear power facility."

"That's the very reason I didn't sleep last night. My question is to you. How can we prevent this from happening and, at the same time, still achieve our ultimate goal of getting the Israeli government to sign a peace treaty with the Palestinians?"

Okay, Mr. President, I believe I might have the answer to that question," the smiling Secretary of State, Andrea Jacobs, exclaimed. "It's the same answer we all agreed would work if ever the opportunity would present itself."

"Mr. President," interrupted the Secretary of Defense, Jonathan Bates, "reading that smile on her face, I believe I know exactly what Andrea is about to propose, and if my hunch is true, I believe it will work."

"That's the very reason I invited you guys to be with me today," President Harris commented with a smug grin. "Let's work out the details before I make a long distance phone call to Ben Yizri."

Thursday, June 18th, 2015
3:02 p.m. Israel Standard Time
Prime Minister's Office
3 Kaplan St. HaKirya, Jerusalem

At the conclusion of Yanny Herzog's response to the question the Israeli prime minister had proposed to her concerning her oppositional views on attacking Iran's nuclear facilities, Yacov Ben Yizri stood and walked to the front of the room. "Yanny, the right side of my brain agrees with every word you have spoken, but my logical left-brain still shouts the same words spoken to the world on the day I was sworn into office. What I said then, I still believe now: You don't want a messianic apocalyptic cult leader controlling atomic bombs. Just think what might have taken place in the world if Adolph Hitler would have obtained the atomic bomb before anyone else. When a crazy wide-eye fanatic gets hold of the reins of power and the weapons of mass death, then the entire world should start worrying, and that is what I see happening in Iran. Living in the shadow of the Holocaust, Israel must shout out to the world the words of over six million of our slain countrymen, "Never again!" And I say to the Iranian president Rouhani and any other crazy person who agrees with his twisted way of thinking—people who say the Holocaust didn't happen are people who wish it will happen again! So far, we have done everything humanly possibly to avert an all out regional war an…."

Before Prime Minister Ben Yizri had a chance to finish his concluding statement his personal secretary, Mira Halbani burst into the room. "Yacov! President Harris is on the phone!"

"Put the president's call on speaker phone, Mira. I want everyone to hear what President Harris has to say."

"Yacov, my good friend."

Everyone in the room smiled at the insincerity of President Harris' comment.

"Yes, President Harris," Prime Minister Ben Yizri acknowledged with a straight forward tone, "such a busy man as yourself usually doesn't make social calls, so I am assumming that you have something of importance to discuss with me."

"Yacov, of all the world leaders I get the privilege to talk with on a daily basis, you my friend, are one person who does not mince words."

"I, Mr. President, cannot afford that luxury," Ben Yizri said with a smile.

"Yacov, I will be the first one to admit this, your country's intelligence is, hands down, the best in the world."

"Thank you, Mr. President," the Prime Minister chuckled. "On that note we both firmly agree."

"Yacov, what I am about to ask, I want you to be totally honest with me." President Harris stated in a firm tone.

"With all due respect, Mr. President," the Israeli Prime Minister responded boldly, "before I commit myself to answering anything, I want you to be totally honest with me. No games here, Mr. President. We are dealing with the lives of millions of our citizens."

"Mr. Prime Minister, no games!" President Rashard Harris agreed. "What has Mossad told you in respect to Iran's most recent nuclear advances?"

The shrewd prime minister smiled, knowing full well that the United States president was verbally fishing for details that he may or may not already have. Not knowing exactly how to respond, the savvy Israel Prime Minister tapped into a source of information that his ancient people have depended on for eons past. *"Adoni (Lord), what shall I say?"* he silently petitioned.

With all eyes fixed on the man standing at the front of the room, the Israeli prime minister boldly responded with only slight hesitation, "The Iranians presently have in their possession as least two untested low-yield nuclear weapons, each one equivalent in magnitude to those used on the Japanese cities of Nagasaki and Hiroshima."

Everyone in the conference room, especially the Prime Minister, held their breath waiting for the American president's response. "As of last night at 11 p.m., that's exactly what our intelligence agencies have told me."

Everyone in the prime minister's conference room sat amazed that the Prime Minister was bold enough to affirm privileged information that he didn't have.

"Thank you, Adoni!" Yacov Ben Yizri looked up and smiled.

"Yacov, I want you to promise me you will not order an attack on any Iranian nuclear facility until you have thoroughly examined the proposal I have ordered hand delivered to your office today before 2 p.m."

"Mr. President, could you briefly supply me now with an overview of your proposal?"

"Mr. Prime Minister, I will give, as we say here in America, a nutshell view of my proposal. If you agree to my plan to start, within two months, direct, face-to-face peace talks with the Palestinians, placing everything on the table for discussion, West Bank Settlements and the status of East Jerusalem, then I will promise you that those two Iranian nuclear weapons will never leave the borders of Iran."

"Mr. President, I promise, Israel will not make an attempt to attack any nuclear facility found within the borders of Iran until I have thoroughly taken my time inspecting every single word found in your proposal. I will get back to you, Mr. President, as soon as possible."

Monday, June 22nd, 2015
9:45 a.m.
International Atomic Energy Agency Headquarters
Wagramer Strasse 5
Vienna, Austria

As the ten o'clock hour approached, U.N. International Atomic Energy Agency ambassadors from around the world entered the large chambers used specifically to rule on global concerns related to nuclear issues. Cameras flashed as each U.N. ambassador took his or her seat at designated booths located alphabetically in English, according to the country they represented. In a few short minutes, the ambassadors present would be asked to vote on a new resolution to place further sanctions on Iran for their country's refusal to allow U.N. IAEA inspectors complete access to a newly discovered underground nuclear power facility.

Along with the world's representative nuclear nations, sat Iran's IAEA ambassador, Ali Asghar Soltanieh, nervously awaiting the 10 a.m. start of the IAEA's Board of Ambassadors meeting at the International Center, in Vienna, Austria.

With the humans preoccupied with the events going on in the front of the chamber, an informal meeting was about to adjourn in the chamber's far back corner just in time to watch the human vote.

"Well, comrades, everything appears to be going as planned," *Apollon, Satan's second in command commented. He was dressed for today's special occasion in a floor-length black robe. The arch demon*

remained seated on the edge of the back row bench as his two generals stood before him.

Before we end our business, I want the two of you to briefly state your specific assignments to me one more time."

Except for their yellowish facial features, the physical identities of each of the standing princes were totally concealed within their floor-length hooded robes. Apollon turned first to the taller of the two princes standing to his left, with visible locks of jet-black hair resting on his high-browed forehead.

"Amducious, get right to the point and state your mission!" Apollon demanded.

"My pleasure, Commander," Amducious replied with an evil sneer. "The moment after the first skyrocket explodes over the skies of Washington D.C. at next week's 4th of July celebration, America will also explode, once again, into racial turmoil, the likes of which have not been seen since my demons had Martin Luther King, Jr. killed in 1968. I assure you, Lord Apollon, our plans are foolproof. Once the president is shot, all blame will be cast directly on the leaders of the American Values Party."

"Excellent," Apollon grinned in approval.

"My demons and I are honored to do our part, Lord Apollon," Amducious commented with his left fist raised high in honor of Satan.

Apollon now turned his attention to the dark-skinned demonic prince standing in the center.

"Allahzad, state your mission!" Known by his superiors and fellow demons as the Prince of Persia, Allahzad had served his assigned mission longer than any other. His earthly kingdoms were well known in the annals of human history: the Babylonians, the Edomites, the Philistines, the Assyrians, and the Persians to name a few. Throughout human time, it has been his charge to do whatever it takes to destroy God's chosen people. It was also he who appeared before Muhammad in the cave on Mt. Hera pretending to be the Archangel Gabriel. Day after day, Muhammad returned to the same cave, believing the entire time that he was receiving revelation about Allah from the angel Gabriel. In truth, it was Allahzad, posing as an angel of light, who

deceived Muhammad into memorizing all of his visions and teaching his Muslim followers to submit to a pagan deity that Satan himself had named after the Arabian moon god, Allah.

Calm and methodical, Allahzad stated his mission. "I assure you, Lord Apollon, I have very good news," declared the Persian Prince with an evil grin. "Our Iranian friends have accomplished the first phase of their assigned task. They now have in their possession enough nuclear plutonium, over the 90 percent threshold, needed to produce nuclear weapons. As I speak, our Iranian scientists are in the process of securing, within the underground confines of the Natanz nuclear power facility, the first of our arsenal of nuclear weapons. These are the very weapons that will one day be used to annihilate Israel from the face of this earth, once and for all!"

"Don't be deceived into believing your plans are infallible!" Apollon admonished Allahzad. "Michael knows exactly what you're doing."

"Don't worry Commander, I have plans to take care of Michael," sneered Allahzad.

"That is why Lord Satan has selected you for this mission." Apollon smugly commented as he turned his attention to the human activity at the front of the chamber. "I see the humans are about to vote. Let's go over and cheer them on!"

Thursday, June 29th
11a.m.
Natanz Nuclear Power Plant
Natanz, Iran

It was exactly 11 a.m. when what appeared to be a small military convoy pulled up to the heavily guarded front entrance gate to the Natanz Nuclear Power Plant. Just beyond the facility's fenced in perimeter a number of administrative buildings was acting as a superficial façade for something more sinister buried beneath. Concealed about twenty feet beneath the main administrative building was a massive underground nuclear enrichment plant covering over 100,000 square meters, protected by a concrete wall and ceiling five meters thick.

Leading the convoy was a black limousine followed closely behind by a security detail consisting of a half dozen fully armed Iranian Revolutionary Guard vehicles. They had finally come to the end of their journey, a three-hour, 250-kilometer long trek across the scorching Iranian desert. Once safely inside the facility's guarded perimeters, the black limo separated from its military escort and proceeded in the direction of the main adminstration building. Within moments of stopping under the shaded protection provided by the main administration building's front portico, the limo's back door opened and a rather short, thin man stepped out. To some, this very familiar person standing alone by the limousine was considered a peaceful family man who sometimes drove his 30-year-old Peugeot to work. To others, he was viewed as a brilliant soft-spoken intellect, a college educated PhD, who lectured from time to time at the University of Tehran. But to his critics, both inside and outside of Iran, he was feared as the single most dangerous individual to the stability of the world. Recent Western headlines had painted him as a man crazy enough to nuke Israel and wipe out the Jews, even if it meant igniting a nuclear war that ended all civilization.

Before taking another step toward the front entrance of the adjacent air conditioned administration building, the Iranian president looked up toward the portico ceiling above, closed his eyes and silently prayed, "Lord Allah, I stand here before you and your people as your humble servant, a willing vessel here to do your bidding. Now is the time to bring an end to your enemies, the godless infidel and the hated Jew."

The moment the Iranian president opened his eyes, a burly framed, full bearded man, dressed entirely from the neck down in a white gown, was walking in his direction with an entourage of similarly dressed people following closely behind.

"President Rouhani," the facility's head engineer, Ali Abbar Salehi, declared as he greeted the Iranian president with a traditional hug and kiss. "What a great honor it is to have you visit our Natanz Nuclear facility."

"Thank you, my friend, for having me," the Iranian President graciously commented. "I'd like to start our tour as soon as possible."

"No sooner said than done, Mr. President!" Salehi responded by extending a guiding hand in the direction of the opened front door to his administration office. "Mr. President, if you would follow me to get out of this intense heat into our air conditioned administrative building, we will immediately begin our tour."

After making a long awaited bathroom stop, the Iranian president, now dressed from toe to chin in a protective white radiation suit, followed his cordial host down a long corridor that ended at a closed metal elevator door.

"Mr. President, for your information, this elevator shaft was constructed along the cement reinforced perimeter of our facility's buried outer wall. The elevator itself can descend to an underground depth equivalent to that of a forty-five-story building. Once we step in and begin our descent, we will pass through 22 meters of packed earth. Directly below that, we will pass within a meter or two of the complex's steel reinforced, four-meter thick concrete roof."

The Iranian president responded to Mr. Salehi's factual comments with an occasional headshake. As the numbers on the elevator's digital display moved ever closer to the president's requested floor, the head engineer commented. "I know you have a very busy schedule ahead of you, Mr. President, so I will take you directly to your specified destination to begin today's tour, our fifth floor, the site of the Islamic Republic's only 164 machine centrifuge cascades."

Once again, the Iranian president recognized the engineer's attentiveness to detail with just a simple head nod.

"We've arrived, Mr. President!" Ali Abbar Salehi declared as the elevator came to a complete halt. "All personnel entering Level Five must have protective radiation headgear on at all times."

Before pressing the open button, Salehi did a quick inspection of not only the Iranian president's protective body, but also the president's two accompanying security escorts as well.

"Good, everyone get ready! We are about to enter the most amazing site anyone will ever see in all the Middle East!"

Once said, Salehi pressed the elevator button and the doors opened to a truly amazing sight. Ali Abbar Salehi was not exaggerating in the slightest.

"Ali Abbar Salehi," the Iranian President stated as he stared in awe through the transparent covering of his protective headgear.

"You were wrong when you said that this is the most amazing sight anyone will ever see in all the Middle East," President Rouhani declared. "This is truly the most amazing sight anyone has ever seen!"

"It truly is and Allah has blessed me by seeing it everyday," affirmed the nuclear plant's proud head engineer.

As the four men stepped out from the metal elevator's narrow confines, the surrounding scene was virtually overwhelming. In every direction their eyes were met by countless twelve-foot-high columns of gold-covered gas-filled centrifuges used specifically to enrich uranium.

"How many are there in all?" the awestruck Iranian President asked.

"Over 7000!" Salehi proudly acknowledged. "That number is 5,000 more than international law allows."

"I won't tell anybody," Rouhani turned to his host and smiled.

"Nor will I, Mr. President," Salehi added with a smile.

"Tell me, Salehi, how do these centrifuges extract enough uranium to make a bomb?"

Sahehi smiled. Without saying a word, the moment the Iranian president's eyes fixed on the wide expanse of glittering golden centrifuges, his curiosity peaked like that of a schoolboy.

"It's really quite simple, Mr. President." Salehi comment, directing the president's attention to a row of partially immersed narrow cylinders to his far right. "Those are called uranium centrifuge cascades, Mr. President. We are not supposed to have those either."

"Once again, I promise," the President smiled, "I won't tell."

"Good, neither will I, Mr. President!" Sahehi laughed out loud. Once he was able to regain his composure, the head nuclear engineer continued explaining for his curious guest how to enrich uranium to make a nuclear bomb.

"Here is how simple the process is, Mr. President." Sahehi continued. "We start first by extracting uranium oxide from the raw uranium ore. Now, uranium oxide contains two different type or isotopes, uranium 235 and uranium 238. It is the U-235 that we need to extract to make either a bomb or to fuel a nuclear power plant. The process of concentrating the U-235 is called enrichment and that is done in a centrifuge. The more centrifuges we have to separate U-235, the more enriched uranium we can make. It is that simple."

"And we have enough centrifuges now to make nuclear bombs?" Rouhani excitedly asked.

"More than we'll ever need, Mr. President."

"All praise be to Allah!" " Rouhani cried out.

"Praise be to Allah, Mr. President!"

"And where are they, now?"

"They, Mr. President?"

"The bombs. Where have you hidden them?"

Salehi smiled. "Mr. President, please follow me back to the elevator."

This was the very moment this soft-spoken son of a blacksmith, the former mayor of Tehran, the elected president of the Republic of Iran, had long awaited and he wasted no time following Ali

Salehi's directions. As he stepped into the opened elevator, Iranian President Rouhani allowed only one solitary thought to enter his mind: *The next time those metal doors open, my life's mission on earth will be fulfilled.* After all, as the most powerful member of the semi-clandestine Iranian organization Hojjatieh, he had sworn to his followers to provoke chaos on a global scale in order to hasten the arrival of the apocalyptic 12th Imam. What better way to assure that this catastrophic event would happen than to strike an atomic deathblow against the Israeli coastal city of Tel Aviv?

Two subterranean floors below the Level Five reactor room, two very impatient demonic beings stared intently with their squinty yellow eyes fixed on the closed elevator door.

"What's taking your humans so long?" complained an irritated Apollon .

"I sense his presence coming now." Allahzad turn toward his superior and smiled. No sooner had he professed those prophetic words than the elevator doors opened and out walked the Persian Prince's favorite human in the entire world.

"There he is now, your new Hitler," Apollon sarcastically mocked his demonic subordinate.

"I disagree with you, Lord Apollon," Allahzad smiled. "Where Hitler failed in his mission to eradicate the Jews, Rouhani will make sure it is fulfilled."

"There is still one major obstacle that stands in your way or have you forgotten?"

"As I said before, Lord Apollon, when the time is right, I will deal with Michael."

Chapter Ten

"Blessed is the nation whose God is the LORD; and the people whom He hath chosen for His own inheritance."

~Psalm 33:12 (KJV)

Saturday, July 4ᵗʰ, 2015
6:00 a.m.
National Mall
Washington D.C.

Shortly after the Declaration of Independence was ratified on July 4, 1776, John Adams, one of the document's five authors (along with Franklin, Jefferson, Sherman and Livingston) said, "I am apt to believe that it (July 4ᵗʰ) will be celebrated by succeeding generations as the great anniversary festival. It ought to be commemorated as the day of deliverance; it ought to be solemnized with pomp and parade, with shows, games, sports, guns, bells, bonfires and illuminations from one end of this continent to the other, from this time forward forever more." Call him a prophet or visionary, but every word spoken over two centuries ago by America's second president has since come to pass. In every corner of our nation, in every city, town and suburb—large and small—plans were now under way to celebrate America's Independence with even more pomp and pageantry than Adams could ever have envisioned.

Even before the rising of the sun, preparations had begun in earnest for making this the best 4th of July celebration Washington D.C. had witnessed. For the past two days, U.S. government workmen were out in full force setting up a huge canopied covered performance stage on the West Lawn of the U.S. Capitol, large enough to support the entire National Symphony Orchestra. On the same side of the street, bleachers were also erected giving invited high ranking government officials, including the President of the United States and his family, not only a clear close-up view of the concert, but also, of the fireworks display that was to follow.

As the sun rose higher in the eastern sky above the Nation's capital, only those with the highest security clearance were allowed inside the roped-off perimeters within a four-block radius surrounding the U.S. capitol. In exactly eight hours, public access to the West Lawn would once again be resuming through a series of security checkpoints. After 3 p.m., anyone headed in the direction of the Capitol would be required to stop at one or more of these screening areas to have the U.S. Park Police thoroughly search all bags, coolers, backpacks and closed containers to make absolutely certain that no concealed weapon of any sort entered through these protected barriers.

At the present moment, in every visible direction surrounding the U.S. Capitol, everything appeared to be secure. No one had the slightest clue that security within this fenced off area had been breached. A deadly weapon had already been hidden in the least conceivable of places. Later on today, someone gaining access to this secured area would remove this weapon from its concealed confines with the intent of targeting its deadly force against the most protected human on Earth, the President of the United States of America.

Saturday, July 4th, 2015
7:04 a.m. Eastern Time
238 Aspen St. N.W
Washington D.C.

It wasn't the alarm clock on her nightstand that woke Helen McAllister from a sound sleep. Instead, it was the familiar ring tone from her favorite Christian song that forced her to open her eyes on this holiday morning.

"Okay, I'm up!" she grudgingly admitted, while at the same time, attempting to feel her way around the cluttered nightstand adjacent to her bed for her ringing cell phone.

Who would call me this early in the morning on my day off? The moment she located the phone a broad smile came to her face. "Brad!" she announced aloud after seeing her boyfriend's name digitally displayed on the phone's caller ID. "Honey, what's wrong?" she instinctively asked.

After a brief pause, the voice on the other end said, "Helen, we need to talk."

Sensing the sincerity of his voice, a concerned Helen asked once again "Brad, tell me now, what is wrong?"

"Helen, look outside of your bedroom window."

Without hesitation, she immediately followed her boyfriend's instructions. The moment she opened the louvered shades to her second floor bedroom window, a broad smile appeared on her face. Standing in the driveway, along the side of her red Ford Mustang, was her boyfriend, Brad Kassel, dressed in civilian attire.

"Brad, what are you doing out there? I thought you were on duty today! Won't you get in trouble?"

"Helen, could you please come out here? I'll explain everything to you."

"Brad, hold on. I'll be right there!" With that said, she quickly grabbed a brightly colored robe draped over a cedar chest at the foot of her bed, and dashed down the flight of steps toward the front entry of her family's suburban Washington home. Once outside, she looked in the direction of her parked red car in the driveway, but, to her surprise, nobody was standing there.

"Hello, Helen." To her surprise, her boyfriend was sitting on the wooden porch glider, directly in back of her.

"Sergeant Brad Kassel, aren't you considered AWOL?"

"Not until 0900." He smiled. "So, I really don't have a lot of time."

"Brad, I don't see your car. Where did you park?"

"Down by McDonald's, about four blocks away."

With all of her senses literally spinning in overdrive, Helen asked again, but this time in a firm, compassionate voice, "Brad Kassel, I want you to tell me exactly the reason you left your barracks to travel all the way here, and don't you dare leave anything out!"

"Yes, ma'am!" Kassel replied with a smile. "Helen, I didn't sleep more than an hour or two last night. I just lay there thinking over and over again about everything you've been telling me about the Lord." "Hon, I believe I'm ready to accept Jesus into my heart."

For a split moment, Helen McAllister sat on her family's porch glider too shocked to say a word.

"Helen , please forgive me for being such a self-centered jerk. I've had a lot to think about lately, the state of our country,my family back home in Michigan, and especially about you, Helen, and I've come to the conclusion that I simply have to trust God with everything or I'm going to drive myself nuts."

By now, tears of joy were literally streaming down Helen's cheeks. Even though she had prayed constantly for this very moment, never in her wildest dreams did she believe her prayers would be answered this fast, this soon.

"Brad, did you do it? Did you ask Jesus into your life?"

"That's why I'm here. I didn't want to say anything without having you being there as my witness. Tell me what to say and I'll not only say it with my lips, I'll mean it with my heart."

For Helen, this was too good to be true. After wiping the tears from her eyes and face, she gave her boyfriend a joyful embrace that lasted well over a minute. Forcing herself to pull back, she looked Brad Kassel directly in the eyes and said, "Brad, before you say a word, I want you to fully understand the importance of your decision to accept Jesus into your life."

"Go for it Helen, Sergeant Kassel is ready to receive his orders."

"Brad, two thousand years ago, Jesus said to a religious leader named Nicodemus that he must be born again in order to enter the Kingdom of Heaven. That means that once you commit your life over to Jesus, your spirit, the real Brad Kassel, is literally transformed into a brand new creation. As the Bible says, *"Therefore, if anyone is in Christ, he is a new creation; old things have passed away; behold, all things have become new."* The Bible also says that once you have made this conscious decision to make Jesus your Lord and Savior, God's Holy Spirit enters you, equipping you with supernatural gifts to battle and defeat the devil."

"Woo, Helen, if you don't mind. Let's put the devil on the back burner for now and concentrate on the first part, making Jesus my Lord and Savior.

Helen looked her boyfriend directly in the eye. She had seen far too many times the wiles of the devil come immediately to attack a new naïve Christian's testimony and leave them doubting their commitment to Jesus.

"Okay, but just for now," she reluctantly agreed. "But beginning next week, you are going with me to our church's Wednesday night Bible study."

"I promise, you Helen McAllister. Unless the President of the United States says differently, I will be there for every single meeting."

Monday, July 4th
9:53 a.m. Eastern Time
Washington D.C.
Oval Office, White House

"Okay guys, we really need to wrap this up," President Harris stated with a smile as he looked at the affirming nods of the four people seated in front of him on two parallel couches. "In two hours from now, my wife and I will be hosting a gathering of my top party supporters right outside those doors in the Rose Garden."

Today being a midweek holiday, the president's morning schedule was usually kept to a bare minimum of non-essential appointments, but for the past hour or so, the president had been meeting behind the closed doors of the Oval Office with four of his top secretaries and advisors. With the president seated on a leather wing backed chair at the forefront of the group of four, he turned his attention first to the man seated on the end of the couch to his left.

"Jonathan, if you would please, tell me your plan."

"Thank you, Mr. President," acknowledged Jonathan Bates, the Secretary of Defense. "As soon as I arrive back at my office, I plan to personally contact the Israeli Minister of Defense, Ehud Levy, and pass along a detailed account of our $60 billion arms deal with the Saudis which would include 84 F-15 fighter planes, 70 Apache attack helicopters, 72 Blackhawk troop-transport helicopters, and 36 Little Bird surveillance copters, all with the specific strategic purpose of containing Iran and preventing the possibility of a unilateral Israeli military strike against Iran's nuclear facilities."

"Do you think Levy will buy it?" the President asked in a serious tone.

"I believe he will once I tell him that as part of the arms package, the Saudis have agreed to give Israel unimpeded airspace in an eventual attack against Iran."

Turning then to the former Massachusetts U.S. Senator and presently, his Special Middle East Envoy, Robert Michaels, the president commented, "Bob, I hope you've already packed your bags for you have a big trip ahead of you."

The elderly statesman smiled and said, "Mr. President, before the first skyrocket explodes over the skies of Washington tonight, I will have in my hand a complete itinerary of my next Middle Eastern trip. At each stop along the way, I will sit down with the leaders of Syria, Turkey, Jordan, and Egypt and solicit their full support for not only our proposed peace plan timeline, but to bring pressure to bear on both militant groups, Hezbollah and Hamas, to accept these agreements."

Finally, the president turned to his Secretary of State, Andrea Jacobs and smiled. "Well, Andrea, you have been given the toughest assignment of all—selling this proposal during your Jerusalem trip next week to two men who, not only don't trust each other, they don't even trust you or me."

Andrea Jacobs chuckled at the frankness of the president's comment. "You're absolutely right, Mr. President," his Secretary of State affirmed with a smile. "This thing has gone on since the Carter Administration. I'm afraid the Middle East peace process has become a literal graveyard of timelines and deadlines. With so many past promises being made and broken, nobody actually believes that a peace agreement between the Israelis and Palestinians is at all possible."

"With that said, Andrea, what makes you believe that this next proposal will be any different?"

"Good question, Mr. President," the Secretary of State conceded. "As we have all discussed here in great depth, it is crunch time as far as the Israeli Prime Minister Yacov Ben Yizri's making a decision to attack Iran's nuclear facilities. He told me to my face, when I first met him two years ago, that sanctions against Tehran would not work, and he was right. Now we have something he wants more than anything else and that something is Iran. I will promise Yacov Ben Yizri that if he agrees to our three-point proposal, then the United States will guarantee America's full military backing in preventing Iran from ever using any weapons of mass destruction against Israel."

"One more time, Andrea," the president persisted, "what are the three proposals you will presenting to Yacov Ben Yizri?"

"Yes, Mr. President," Jacobs continued. "First, the Israeli prime minister must order an immediate freeze on any further settlement construction going on in the West Bank and also in east Jerusalem. Second, starting next month with an initial meeting held here in the White House, Ben Yizri must agree to a rigorous schedule of direct talks to be held every two weeks with his Palestinian counterpart, President Abu Mazen. Third, and the most ambitious part of this entire proposal, in exchange for United States granting Israel full military support and protection from any future Iranian attack, Israel must agree to a one-year goal of working out the details on all the core issues dividing them and the Palestinians—final borders, Jerusalem, water rights and the status of the Palestinian refugees."

Looking directly into the eyes of his four subordinates, the President adamantly declared, "An ambitious plan, but this time it has to work. There are no other options!"

"Mr. President," Secretary Jonathan Bates said with a smile, "We mustn't forget the proverbial 'icing on the cake' offer Andrea is going to make Yacov Ben Yizri at next week's meeting in Jerusalem."

"Twenty F 35 stealth aircraft worth nearly three billion dollars!" the president responded with a finger pointed directly into the face of the secretary of defense. "That offer's only good if Israel agrees to conclude a peace deal with the Palestinians on our terms and on our deadlines."

All eyebrows immediately lifted, shocked by the hostile tone of the president's voice toward the Jewish State. Sensing his error, the president quickly recovered by concluding this morning's impromptu meeting with a cordial smile and this well-worded release. "Thank you all for coming out this morning, and as your Commander-in-Chief, once you've wrapped up all your unsettled business, I order you to take the rest of the day off and enjoy this splendid day with your friends and family. You are dismissed. Have a wonderful 4th of July!"

Saturday, July 4th, 2015
11 a.m. Eastern Time
109 Clinton Street
Schenectady, New York

Everyone living in and around Schenectady, New York could sense the excitement. Nothing like this had taken place in this city of over 61,000, located close to where the Mohawk and Hudson Rivers meet, at least not in recent memory. Not since Schenectady's heyday a century ago, when it was known worldwide as the home to the corporate headquarters of both the Edison Electric Company (now General Electric) and the American Locomotive Company, had so many people gathered at one time in the city's once thriving business district. A sizable crowd had assembled on a closed off section of downtown Schenectady's Clinton Street. Several large television communication vans with satellite dishes mounted on their side began pulling up along reserved yellow painted curbs in front of the Town Hall. All of the major cable news networks were present, busily setting up and positioning their cameras, aimed toward the entrance of Schenectady's main municipal building. All this was was being done in anticipation of a big announcement that was soon to be made.

As the time for the eleven o'clock announcement neared, the crowd's excitement peaked the moment the front entrance doors to the Schenectady Town Hall opened and out walked the former New York Governor, Robert Berry. With the general election for President of the United States still over a year away, all the latest national polls showed the Schenectady native the favored frontrunner for capturing the Republican nomination for President of the United States. As he waved to the large crowd of cheering supporters, an entourage of over a dozen or so nationally recognized politicians followed Berry up the steps leading to a raised platform, constructed on the Town Hall's front lawn. The boisterous cheers died down quickly the moment Berry raised his hands signaling it was time to give his highly touted speech. With his Republican friends standing in the background, Berry stepped up to the center stage microphone and opened his speech with a challenging question.

"Does anyone here recall the name of the city that was once known for both lighting and hauling the world?"

In a thunderous response, the crowd shouted back in near unison, "Schenectady!"

Acting in jest, Berry put his right hand up to his ear and asked the hyped up crowd, "Can you all repeat that again? The noise was so loud, I didn't quite hear you."

The deafening response that followed played right into Robert Berry's prepared speech. With thousands looking on, the ever so confident former Republican governor started his speech.

"In my memory, it wasn't that long ago that the word Schenectady was used synonymously with two other celebrated American words—jobs and pride. I also remember, as if it were only yesterday, my Dad coming home each night with a sense of pride in his eyes. We would sit down at the dining room table and Dad would tell all of us about how many diesel locomotives he and his fellow workers at the American Locomotive Company had assembled that day. Today, few families in Schenectady have the privilege that I had—growing up with a father as the sole provider for his family, who came home and bragged about how much he loved his job. In fact, after the American Locomotive Company was bought out in the late 1970s by the Montreal Locomotive Works and moved to Canada, all the good paying jobs in Schenectady seemed to disappear. And folks, we're not alone. Simply get in your car and start driving in any direction away from Schenectady. Go north into New England—west toward Pittsburgh, Pennsylvania or Cleveland Ohio; go south toward the Carolinas, to Georgia, Florida, and Alabama—go up and down the Gulf Coast and you'll find that the same problem exists—there are few, if any, good paying American jobs left anywhere in America. Other than Ronald Reagan, for the past quarter century or so, no politician in America, either Democrat or Republican, has stepped up to the political plate to fully support and fight for the protection of precious American jobs.

Berry stopped momentarily, allowing the crowd to vent their support with a rousing applause and cheers. Pausing long enough to make eye connect with the surrounding crowd, the former governor continued his speech.

"No one has to stand here and tell you that our nation is in trouble. We know in our hearts that unless something is done quickly, the America we all know and love could very possibly be lost forever. For that reason, we have assembled here today in this great American city that has so many people completely stymied and tongue-tied when asked to either pronounce or spell its name. I have been given the honor to stand here today before both my fellow New Yorkers and all Americans to read the words of my party's pledge to not only restore jobs back to America, but also, more importantly, to restore America, the country once known for its freedom of innovation, back to its jobs."

In pausing, Berry turned his attention toward the dozen or so Republican senators and congressmen who had traveled long and far to show their solidarity for the man chosen to voice their renewed political cause to America. One by one, each Republican representative acknowledged his or her support for Berry with either a nod or a symbolic thumbs up gesture of approval. Turning once again toward the anticipating crowd, Robert Berry introduced all listeners to the Republican Party's Pledge to America.

"America is more than a country. America is an idea—an idea that free people can govern themselves, that government's powers are derived from the consent of the governed, that each of us is endowed by their Creator with the unalienable rights to life, liberty, and the pursuit of happiness. America is based on the belief that all men and women can, when given the economic, political, and religious liberty, advance themselves, their families, and the common good.

"America is an inspiration to those who yearn to be free and have the ability and the dignity to determine their own destiny. Whenever the agenda of government becomes destructive of these ends, it is the right of the people to institute a new governing agenda and set a different course. These first principles were proclaimed in the Declaration of Independence, enshrined in the Constitution, and have endured through hard sacrifice and commitment by generations of Americans. In a self-governing society, the only bulwark against the power of the state is the consent of the governed, and regarding the policies of the current government, the governed do not consent.

"An unchecked executive, a compliant legislature, and an overreaching judiciary have combined to thwart the will of the people and overturn their votes and their values, striking down long-standing laws and institutions, scorning the deepest beliefs of the American people. An arrogant and out-of-touch government of self-appointed elites make decisions, issue mandates, and enact laws without accepting or requesting the input of the many. Rising joblessness, crushing debt, and a polarizing political environment are fraying the bonds among our people and blurring our sense of national purpose.

"Like free peoples of the past, our citizens refuse to accommodate a government that believes it can replace the will of the people with its own. The American people are speaking out, demanding that we realign our country's compass with its founding principles and apply those principles to solve our common problems for the common good.

"The need for urgent action to repair our economy and reclaim our government for the people cannot be overstated. With this document, we pledge to dedicate ourselves to the task of reconnecting our highest aspirations to the permanent truths of our Founding Fathers by keeping faith with the values our nation was founded on, the principles we stand for, and the priorities of our people. This is our pledge to America.

"We pledge to honor the Constitution as constructed by its framers, and honor the original intent of those precepts that have been consistently ignored—particularly the Tenth Amendment, which grants that all powers not delegated to the United States by the Constitution, nor prohibited by it to the states, are reserved to the states respectively, or to the people.

"We pledge to advance policies that promote greater liberty, wider opportunity, a robust defense, and national economic prosperity. We pledge to make government more transparent in its actions, careful in its stewardship, and honest in its dealings.

"We pledge to uphold the purpose and promise of a better America, knowing that to whom much is given, much is expected and that the blessings of our liberty buoy the hopes of mankind. We make this pledge bearing true faith and allegiance to the people we represent, and we invite fellow citizens and patriots to join us in forming a new governing agenda for America."

Berry stopped his speech just long enough to pass a nod in the direction of his campaign manager, Griffin Gunson. On cue, Gunson, standing at the bottom of the stage, signaled his assistant, Casey Engle, that it was now time for her volunteer workers, already dispersed throughout the large crowd, to begin passing out the laminated cards.

Holding high one of the cards for all to see, Berry continued, "Our volunteer staff of workers is now giving everyone a small card with the entirety of the Republican Pledge to America printed on both sides. I have been informed that by the end of this week, these same cards will be mailed to every household in America. When you leave here today, please tell somebody who hasn't heard the good news, that the Republican Party has a real plan to restore America and restore American jobs. On behalf of my fellow Republicans, I want to thank all of you for coming out on this 4th of July morning to join me in endorsing a new declaration for rebirth of the greatest nation this world has ever known, the United States of America!"

Saturday, July 4th, 2015
10 a.m. Central Time
The Graham Estate
15 miles North of Trinity Mills, Texas

It was the 4th of July, a Graham family tradition to be gathered together—all two dozen Graham family members—Rosemary and Eliot Graham, their seven children, five spouses, and ten grandchildren at their Texas family home to celebrate, in full blown Texas-style, the birth of their beloved country. After literally devouring a hardy Texas breakfast consisting of dozens of fried eggs, slabs of crispy bacon, mounds of buttery toast and gallons of orange juice, the Graham men quickly exited the large eat-in kitchen for their favored location, sitting around the large screened family television. Under any other condition, Rosemary Graham would have stopped the scoundrels dead in their tracks, at least having them wash off their dirty dishes in the sink and placing them in the dishwasher before making their getaway. But just for today, the family matriarch gave the Graham men her blessing to escape the kitchen duties in order to watch the highly publicize Republican Pledge to America broadcast nationwide on the Fox News Channel.

During the entirety of Robert Berry's televised message, not a sound could be heard in the large family room. All eyes were fixed on the large television screen strategically placed in the center of the room. As the twenty minute speech came to its carefully scripted conclusion, the former New York Governor stood proudly at the center stage microphone and closed with the same familiar words that American politicians have used to end their speeches for multiple decades past, "May God bless all of you and may God bless America."

Aaron, Graham's son, the lawyer, looked across the room at his father, seated comfortably at his designated place of honor, the leather wingback chair placed closest to the television, and asked, "Well?"

"Well scripted!" Graham replied.

"Dad, is that all you have to say?" asked his puzzled lawyer son. "Berry intentionally left out everything that's going wrong with this country in order to appease the independent voters."

"Aaron, I knew exactly what Berry was going to say even before he opened his mouth to speak," the elder Graham firmly stated in response to his son's poignant question.

"How's that, Dad?" inquired his oldest son, Eliot Jr.

With a total of six onlookers, Graham proceeded to remove a small white card from his shirt pocket and display it to the amazement of his four sons and two sons-in-law.

"Dad, that isn't what I think it is, is it?" Mary Elizabeth's husband, Cody Ketterman, asked.

"If you mean, Cody, is this the same card that Robert Berry's volunteers were just seen passing out to crowds in Schenectady, New York, the answer is yes. This small card in my hand has the same Republican Pledge to America printed on each side that Robert Berry just finished reading to all America."

"I guess being the host of the world's number conservative radio talk show has its advantages," Cody said with a smile.

"So, Dad, being that you already knew the Republican Party wants to maintain status quo, what do you plan to do about it?" Aaron questioned.

"Personally, I believe we need to change the status quo," Graham admitted with a tone of complacency. "But realistically, the way things now stand, there's a lot of people out there, especially in the Republican Party, who are not supportive of change. You guys have all seen the latest polls. Berry has almost a twenty point lead over anyone else in the Republican Party, and that includes both Democrats, Analise DeVoe and Rashid Harris!

"Dad, I didn't hear anywhere in the Republican Pledge for a call to honor families, hold up traditional marriage, protect the sanctity of life, and support the private faith-based organizations that form the core of our American values."

"Okay, I'm all in favor of doing everything we can to bring jobs back to America," Cody admitted, "but I heard nothing said in that shallow statement about eliminating government earmarks, lowering the national debt, dealing with China, or for supporting Israel."

"What about supporting God, Dad?" Eliot Jr. interjected. "Other than the general platitudes to God's name offered at the end of Robert Berry's speech, I didn't hear anything in the Republicans' Pledge for a need to honor God and beseech His divine help in guiding America back on the right path. The problems plaguing America go well beyond economics. All issues are moral—whether it's economics, border control, health care, marriage or abortion. In fact, even most of the economic problems we face are a direct or indirect result of a fundamental breakdown in our ability to discern right from wrong, to adhere to tried-and-true standards of morality, to follow the path set out for us by our founders, to recognize that we are 'endowed by our Creator with certain unalienable rights, that among these are life, liberty and the pursuit of happiness.' You simply can't have a self-governing society without having an operational consensus that God's laws are our standards of morality."

"Well said, everybody," the family patriarch humbly admitted. "I couldn't have expressed it any better myself."

"You need to run, Dad; you'll win hands down. There is nobody out there supporting the true values that America was founded on."

"On what ticket?"

"The only ticket," interjected his lawyer son, Aaron. "The American Values Party will support your run in a heartbeat."

"What about money?" Graham asked. "If you've checked lately, my bank account doesn't quite match the $150 million needed to run a successful campaign."

"What about the offer George Kaufman made you?"

"Aaron, his offer was just a cheap ploy to use me as a type of Ross Perot to siphon Republican votes away from Berry and make sure another liberal Democrat ends up back in office! And besides," Graham added, "Kaufman's a socialist who hates democracy and everything that goes with it. He's is also a Jew who hates Israel and will stop at nothing to destroy his own people's homeland."

"Dad, don't even worry about where the money would come from if you decide to run," Aaron commented. "All the polls show that the majority of people think more highly of you than any person in America today. You just say yes and I guarantee, the money will be there."

Saturday, July 4th, 2015
3:03 p.m. Eastern Time
U.S. Capitol's West Lawn
Washington D.C.

What a great plan: spending a 4th of July under the stars with friends and family while listening to magnificently orchestrated music and watching the best fireworks display seen anywhere on the planet. It was no wonder that on this special holiday, thousands of local residents decided to forgo the comforts of their air-conditioned homes and take the metro into the Nation's Capitol to celebrate the anniversary of America's birth. But for a core group of over five hundred or more very determined people who had been standing all morning in long lines on Constitution and Pennsylvania Avenues, their goal was a bit more specific. They were willing to endure the intense summer mid-day heat just to secure a three-by-three foot grassy spot literally feet away from the same stage where, six hours from now, the National Symphony Orchestra would be performing Tchaikovsky's "1812 Overture" as fireworks explode in the skies over the Nation's Capital. *Before claiming their coveted location on the* Capitol's West Lawn, *they were required to subject themselves* one last time *to having their* bodies scanned and their personal belongings thoroughly searched by members of the Capitol Police. At the very end of their long arduous journey, that for some, started over two miles away on Massachusetts Avenue at the Union Train Station, stood two U.S. Marines, fully dressed in their ceremonial white capped-white gloved attire, checking the IDs of every single adult attempting to enter this highly secured area. To expedite the line's flow and also, more importantly, to make absolutely sure every person entering the fenced in area was not deemed a security risk, two other U.S. Marines, all from the 8th & I Street Barracks, sat at a small desk adjacent to their standing partners, using a wireless laptop computer to run a quick background check on every person standing in line.

"Identification, please," a young Marine standing at the gated entrance asked politely.

"Is all of this security really needed, Sergeant?" a middle-aged woman with long stringy gray hair inquired. She was struggling with a folded chair under one arm and a water cooler in the other.

"Yes, ma'am," the Marine cordially replied, directing the women's attention toward their immediate right. "Do you see those bleachers setup over there?"

"Yah, so what?"

"Well, ma'am," the young Marine replied with a friendly smile. "After we finish checking your driver's license, you have the same privilege of watching the fireworks explode over the Washington Monument as some very important people. Sometime this evening, the President of the United States and his family will be seated in those same bleachers along with several important members of Congress."

"Wow, that is too cool!"

"Here is your driver's license, ma'am," the seated Marine, Master Sergeant Brad Kassel said with a smile.

"Brad, you seem mighty quiet today," Kassel's concerned partner, Sergeant Corey Strong, commented. "Is something bothering you?"

"No, nothing. I guess I'm really tired. I don't know why, but I didn't get a whole lot of sleep last night."

"Well, after all the fireworks are over, go back to the barracks and get a good night's sleep."

I will if Tucker doesn't show up in this line.

Sergeant Kassel didn't have to wait long for his answer. Standing only five persons back, a toothless tattooed man stared in his direction.

"Kassel has made eye contact with Tucker, Demon Slayer," Aniel commented. He was one of two massive angelic warriors assigned to divinely protect Brad Kassel from spiritual harm.

"Keep a close watch on Kielon, Samuel Tucker's assigned mid-level demon," cautioned Kiel, "What I wouldn't give right now to take this sword and slice that smirk right off Kielon's black crusty face."

"Just say the word, Demon Slayer, and I'll totally remove his ugly face as well."

"You know as well I, Aniel, our mission here today is to protect Kassel from spiritual attack. As long as Kielon keeps his claws buried deep in Tucker's back, he can shout all the blasphemies and profanities he wants. But if he raises just one of his scaly clawed hands in the direction of Kassel, you have my permission to slice that repulsive demon into a puff of smoke."

One by one, the line of humans moved forward until it was Samuel Tucker's turn to present his mortal credentials to the awaiting Marines.

With his worst nightmare standing only a few feet away, Sergeant Kassel's full attention was fixed on the man handing his driver's license over to his partner, Sergeant Cory Strong.

There is no way this redneck's ever going to pass a background check. Once Tucker's arrest record flashes across this laptop's screen, the Capitol police will be all over that crazy jacka-s faster than he can say "Louisiana."

"Sergeant Kassel, here is Mr. Kevin Johnson's Virginia driver's license," Sergeant Strong cordially commented as the standing Marine handed him the small laminated card.

No, no way. Kassel thought to himself. Hastily, the nervous Marine pressed his fingers against the laptop's keyboard and began typing in the name and driver's license number that appeared on the front side of the official looking document. Within mere seconds of querying the National Data Bank, the man's name and address—Kevin Leroy Johnson; 53 year old; 209 Old Mill Run Rd. Sterling, Virginia—appeared on the LCD screen, with no mention of any arrests and no criminal record.

"Is everything in proper order, Sergeant Kassel, Sir?" the tattooed man asked, toting under his arm what appeared to be a tightly rolled red blanket.

Without saying a word, the mystified Marine Sergeant returned the driver's license to the smiling Kevin Johnson—alias Samuel Tucker.

"Thank you, Sergeant Kassel," the tattooed imposter commented with a wide toothless grin. After he slipped his driver's license into the back pocket of his cutoff blue jeans, Tucker mockingly saluted both Marines before making his exit. "Carry on soldiers. Hope you will enjoy tonight's fireworks as much as I will."

As he watched Samuel Tucker casually stroll inside the fenced in grassy confines of the U.S. Capitol's West Lawn, Kassel sat back in his chair just staring at what he alone knew to be a manufactured lie of monumental proportions. *How far up the political ladder does this thing go?* Before he had time to ponder another thought, his military colleague, standing to his immediate right, passed along another driver's license to be inspected. *Lord, I don't know how you're going to do it, but I need you to get me out of this gigantic mess I've gotten myself into.*

As Tucker entered the Capitol's fenced in West Lawn, his attached demon rotated its scaly black head around 180 degrees in the direction of the two angelic warriors standing guard over Sergeant Kassel. In a shrill screeching voice, Kielon defiantly proclaimed. "Kiel, you are wasting your efforts protecting that human. As the popular song goes, when the bombs begin bursting in air, the President of the United States will die and your assigned human, Brad Kassel, will die with him, burning in hell forever!"

With an uncharacteristic expression of concern on his face, Kiel turned to his angelic subordinate and said, "I will remain here with Kassel." Watching intently as the demon-controlled mortal joined the ranks of other humans already inside the fenced in borders of the Capitol's West Lawn, Aniel intuitively responded to his angelic superior's non-verbal request. "Rest assured, Demon Slayer, I will neither let the mortal nor demon out of my sight."

With the U.S. Capitol Building as a picturesque backdrop on this cloudless 4th of July afternoon, hundreds of fortunate humans, granted privileged access to this highly secured area, scurried about the manicured lawns looking for a prime location somewhere near the stage where the National Symphony Orchestra would be performing at tonight's dazzling fireworks display. But there was one human walking about these prestigious grounds, interested in neither classical music nor fireworks. From the moment he entered the West Lawn's protected confines, to keep himself inconspicuous from the ever-watchful eyes of the roaming secret service agents, he casually followed closely behind a group of college-aged students who were searching for an unclaimed spot to unfold their blankets. It didn't take long before he was able to locate his intended destination—six brightly colored portable toilets strategically placed under the protected shade of a cluster of trees. For the remainder of the afternoon until twilight, Samuel Leroy Tucker would claim portable toilet number three as his temporary residence.

Saturday, July 4th, 2015
6:00 p.m. Eastern Time
Independence Mall
Philadelphia, Pennsylvania

No matter where you stood on Philadelphia's Independence Mall, you could literally dance to the beat of the toe-tapping music blaring out of dozens of strategically placed electronic loudspeakers. With local street vendors on every corner, the tantalizing aroma of hot Philly cheese steak sandwiches permeated the surrounding air. The excitement at the Mall was now at feverish pitch. Very soon, one of the most popular women politicians in America would be addressing this crowd of over 18,000.

You would never know by her unbridled enthusiasm, or the crowd's electrified energy, that Analise DeVoe, a Democratic contender for her party's nomination for President of the United States, was presently five points behind the Nation's beleaguered President, Rashid Harris, and more than fifteen points behind the current Republican frontrunner, Robert Berry. But those discouraging numbers meant absolutely nothing to the thousands of Philadelphians who had come out on this picture-perfect 4th of July evening to celebrate their Nation's birthday. In moments, Analise DeVoe would announce the only numbers these mostly unemployed and underemployed Americans were interested in hearing. As she stepped up to the microphone, placed stragically within shouting distance of where her nation's founders declared their independence from British rule on July 4, 1776, the confident former U.S Attorney General began her speech by quoting an unexpected source.

"I will begin my speech today by quoting what former President Reagan would say at the end of his speeches, "If not us, who? If not now, when?" A few months ago, when my husband, Ethan, and I were sitting around our dining room table planning our summer trips, we had no trouble deciding where we were going to celebrate the 4th of July this year. I believe you will agree with our decision. At this present moment in time, there is no other place on Earth better to celebrate the birth of our beloved nation than Philadelphia, the city where our Nation was birthed. I believe you will also agree with me when I say, that unless we act now, with the same tenacity and courage demonstrated by our Founding Fathers—to develop a job friendly America—where the economic environment is primarily focused on innovation and domestic job creation, backed by a federal government that is willing to enforce restrictions to put an end, once and for all, to outsourcing our good paying jobs to those working outside of our country's borders…then America, as we now know it, will be no more."

No dazzling fireworks display anywhere could simulate the thunderous response generated by the thousands of cheering, agreeing Pennsylvanians. For the next twenty minutes, Analise DeVoe kept repeating her campaign mantra over and over again: jobs, jobs, jobs to the desperate ears of those who needed to hear her message of hope. At the close of her poignant speech, DeVoe declared: "If elected president, I will do everything within my power to reestablish America once again to the innovative economic superpower that she was a century ago."

Saturday, July 4ᵗʰ, 2015
7:30 p.m. Eastern Time
U.S. Capitol's West Lawn
Washington D.C.

They would soon be surrounded by the best security protection afforded to anyone on the entire planet. Each VIP, with their respective family members, would be assigned tailor-made seats with an unsurpassed view of both the National Symphony Orchestra and the accompanying fireworks display over the distant Washington Monument. As each U.S. senator and congressperson and accompanying family members exited their limousines, they were escorted only a short distance to their assigned bleacher seats by Secret Service agents dressed in their standard black suits and ties.

With the exact precision of a finely tuned clock, at exactly 8 p.m., a final black limousine arrived at the designated First Street drop-off area, accompanied by two sets of Secret Service escort vehicles. Another detail of no less than a dozen Secret Service agents surrounded the vehicle. An agent opened the vehicle's side door and President Harris, followed by his wife Yolanda and their twin twelve-year-old daughters, Dianna and Deyonna, stepped out. As they walked toward their reserved front row bleacher seats, everyone within a one-block radius of the Capitol's West Lawn stood as the National Symphony Orchestra played "Hail to the Chief."

At the time "Hail to the Chief" was being performed by the National Symphony Orchestra, only a few hundred feet away from where the President and his family were being seated, in one of the most inconspicuous of all places imaginable, the words from a popular song from the past, *You Ain't Nothin But A Hound Dog*, awakened the sleeping occupant locked inside a portable toilet. In the dimly lit narrow chamber where Samuel Tucker called home for the past five hours, the former shrimper from Louisiana reached waist-ward to locate the small leather holster attached to his belt. Once located, Tucker removed its contents and placed his cell phone against his ear.

"Yah?" the half-awake Tucker managed to grunt.

"Sam, it's 8:05—the exact time you asked me to call ya," the familiar voice of Tucker's girlfriend, Cheyanne Rogers, said. "You sound all groggy, Honey. Did I wake you up?"

"You're not the first one, darling," Tucker replied with a quick smirk. "They've been waking me up pounding on this damn plastic door all day long."

"Sam, listen to me, darling," Rogers implored. "Wherever you are, I want you to leave there right now and come home. Don't even think about going through with it!"

Tucker rubbed his eyes and face, then sat back against the red blanket he used to prop himself up against the bathroom wall.

"Sam, darling, don't do it! He's not worth the money! Come home now!"

Despite his girlfriend's passionate plea for him to abort his plans to kill the president, another more familiar voice took preeminence over Tucker's troubled mind.

"Don't even think about leaving," chastened the voice of his familiar spirit, Kielon. *"You've come all this way and there's no going back. Finish the job, Tucker. Only you can stop that n-ger from destroying America. No one else can do it. Besides, when this is all over, Cheyanne Rogers is going to be a rich Southern gal beyond her wildest dreams."*

Refusing to listen any longer to his girlfriend's ardent pleas, Tucker deposited his cell phone down the darkened hole of the adjacent toilet.

Full of intense rage, the demon-controlled man stood and wrapped both hands tightly around a six inch thick PVC pipe used to vent fresh outside air from the portable bathroom's roof all the way down to the top of the toilet's holding tank. With a single forceful twist, Tucker removed the entire six foot length of plastic tubing and placed it at a diagonal angle on the floor below. Wasting no time, the enraged mortal inserted his right hand down the length of the hollow plastic cylinder until his fingertips made contact with yet another cylinder, but this one felt cold and metallic. Turning the plastic tubing over once again, Tucker was able to grasp a firm hold on the wooden base of the object of his search. With another quick turn of the wrist, the duct-taped bonds that held the object securely in place snapped and out slid a small semi-automatic rifle with a plastic 25-round magazine taped to its wooden stock.

"Hello Ruger 10/22," Tucker proudly proclaimed, while inspecting the deadly rapid-fire weapon with a scope attached.

Carefully removing the bullet-filled magazine, firmly taped against the gun's wooden stock, Tucker snapped the magazine in place and made his final statement before departing his temporary hiding place, "Tucker, you've never amounted to anything in your entire life. You're a loser and you'll always be a loser."

As he exited the portable toilet number three with the deadly weapon carefully concealed inside the red blanket tucked tightly under his armpit, Tucker's familiar spirit, Kielon, declared, "Say goodbye, Tucker, it's time to die and take that n-ger president along with ya!"

Saturday, July 4th, 2015
8:56 p.m. Eastern Time
U.S. Capitol's West Lawn
Washington D.C.

For the two Marines assigned to check IDs of those leaving and reentering the highly secured Capitol's West Lawn, the scheduled 9:15 start time for Washington D.C.'s fireworks display could not have come any sooner.

"Once we hear the cannons go off in the background and we see the fireworks' grand finale explode over the Monument, we are out of here!" declared a tired, but still exuberant Marine Sergeant Cory Strong. "And remember, Kassel, tomorrow is a day off!"

"Yah!" Master Sergeant Brad Kassel agreed somberly.

"Kassel, what the hell's bugging you, man?" inquired the clearly frustrated sergeant. "You've been acting depressed like this all night and, to tell you the truth, you're really getting on my nerves!"

Oh, God, I wish I could tell him and everyone else for that matter! I don't care what happens to me now. I don't care if they put me in jail and throw away the key, but, whatever it takes, I have to stop this from happening. I have to find Tucker before it's too late!

Without saying a word, Kassel stood, left his assigned post, and walked in the direction of the fenced in West Lawn.

"Brad, where the hell are you going, man?" demanded his puzzled partner.

"I'll be back, Cory. I've got to go to the bathroom."

Saturday, July 4th, 2015
9:08 p.m. Eastern Time
U.S. Capitol's West Lawn
Washington D.C.

Everyone was ready. All eyes were focused on the distant darkened outline of the 555' 5-1/8" tall obelisk built to commemorate a man who led his country to independence and then became its first president. In a matter of mere moments from now, the U.S. Marine Drum and Bugle Corps will accompany the start of one of the greatest fireworks displays seen. The only eyes not looking upward toward the western horizon belonged to the hundred or so highly trained secret service agents disbursed throughout this massive crowd. Their assignment was to actively search for something or someone other than fireworks.

On this 4th of July evening, hundreds of other eyes were also intently focused on another exploding event other than fireworks that was soon to take place on the Eastern end of the National Mall. In fact, their clandestine attention was exclusively directed on a drama being played out on the Capitol's West Lawn among three mortals, Marine Sergeant Major Brad Daniel Kassel, Samuel Leroy Tucker, and Rashid Jabbar Harris, the President of the United States.

"Sergeant, is everything all right?"

Stunned, the startled Marine Sergeant Major turned around to face his second worst nightmare other than locating Samuel Tucker. Thinking fast, Kassel extended his right hand toward the gentleman standing only feet away.

"Yes Sir, I am Sergeant Major Brad Kassel."

"Sergeant Kassel, I am agent Brady Ross," the straight-faced man flawlessly dressed in a black suit and tie, said. "Sergeant, I've been watching you for several minutes. You seem to be looking for someone or something amongst the crowd."

After a brief handshake, a panic-stricken Sergeant Kassel responded to the secret service agent's suspicious stares. Mixing fact with fiction, Sergeant Kassel nervously stated his case.

"Sir, I am also on duty here tonight. I am a member of the 8th and I Street Barracks. My assignment has been to run background checks on all persons entering the West Lawn through the gated First Street entrance with my assigned partner, Sergeant Cory Strong. Agent Ross, I seem to have misplaced my cell phone earlier this afternoon so I decided to take a short break away from gate duty and come out here and look for it."

"Sergeant Kassel, may I see your credentials?"

"Absolutely, sir," Kassel respectfully responded.

Removing a small flashlight from his inside jacket pocket, the secret service agent thoroughly examined Kassel's military credentials before handing the card back to the nervous Marine.

"Sergeant Kassel," Agent Ross replied with the briefest of smiles. "Sorry I had to stop you, but with the president in the house, we must take all precautions."

"Believe me Agent Ross, I fully understand."

"I hope you locate your cell phone, Sergeant."

"I am persistent, Agent Ross. If it's all right with you, I'll keep looking out here until I find it."

"Good Luck, Sergeant."

Saturday, July 4th, 2015
9:15 p.m. Eastern Time
U.S. Capitol's West Lawn
Washington D.C.

Every day for the past week or so, Samuel Leroy Tucker had wandered unassumingly onto the manicured lawns in front of the U.S. Capitol Building practicing mentally what he is about to do in reality. Within minutes of leaving the confines of his afternoon hiding place, Tucker exchanged the yellow plastic walls of a portable bathroom for a patch of unclaimed green turf only a few feet away from the chain link security fence that encircled the entire perimeter of the Capitol's West Lawn. It was here that Tucker planned to spend the duration of his time, not only at the National Mall, but quite possibly, on planet earth.

With all eyes focused westward on the skies above the Washington Monument, Samuel Tucker reclined on the grassy turf, comfortably resting his head on his red folded blanket. With nobody paying the least bit of attention to his actions, Tucker removed what appeared to be a small black metal cylinder from his back pocket and placed one end of the narrow tube up to his right eye.

BOOM! BOOM! BOOM! The Washington D.C. July 4th fireworks display was officially underway. Soon, awe inspired oohs and ahs were accompanied by the rat-tat-tats and trumpet blasts from the combined talents of the U.S. Marine Drum and Bugle Corps and U.S. Army Herald Trumpets.

"It's about time," Tucker said with his toothless grin. Steadying his elbow against his chest, he carefully aligned the minute crosshairs of the small, but powerful gun scope on his intended target, seated with his family, over one hundred and fifty yards away.

Saturday, July 4th, 2015
9:38 p.m. Eastern Time
U.S. Capitol's West Lawn
Washington D.C.

From the moment public access to the U.S. Capitol grounds opened earlier in the afternoon, hundreds of sword drawn warrior angels were ordered by Commander Kiel to stand guard along the entire fenced in perimeter of the West Lawn. They were also charged with the difficult task of denying street roaming D.C. demons entrance to the Capitol's West Lawn, and at the same time, not to interfere in any way with the natural outcome of today's events.

Undaunted by hours of exposure to mind-boggling taunts and cursing far beyond the range of human tolerance, Kiel's angelic warriors obediently stood their post, holding back their temptation to slice through the midriffs of each of the grotesque apparitions that blasphemed God's Holy Name. With mere moments remaining before the explosive grand finale took place above and below the darkened skies of Washington, the Lord of Hosts declared a divine directive, composed of four simple words, to His angelic creation, Kiel: "now is the time!"

In less time than it takes for a twinkling of an eye to occur, on a raised stage centrally located in the middle of the West Lawn, over one hundred human musicians, gifted by the Creator to perform heavenly harmonies with human-made instruments, began playing Tchaikovsky's "1812 Overture." At the same moment, the first note of the 1812 Overture was played, and live cannon fire, provided by the United States Army Presidential Salute Battery commenced. Technicians, seated nearly a quarter mile to the west, gave orders to launch the last of their pyrotechnic missiles over the skies of Washington.

"It's time!" Kielon proudly announced. Acting on his demon's command, Tucker withdrew the concealed weapon hidden under the red blanket. Carefully snapping the optical scope into its aligned position, the demon-control human focused his instrument of death on its intended target, the President of the United States of America.

At the same moment, acting on a nod from his commander, Kiel, who had been hiding behind an adjacent tree, removed his golden sword from its sheath and sliced the oblivious demon, Kielon, into a red sulfurous puff of smoke.

"Turn to your right!" Kiel commanded.

Immediately acting on what he perceived to be his own intuitive thought, Sergeant Brad Kassel turned his head to the right and instantly spotted the target of his search.

"Go!" Kiel's supernatural command instructed Kassel's mortal mind.

The moment Tucker pulled back on the automatic weapon's trigger, without fear or contemplation, the human warrior instinctively thrust his entire body directly on top of the pointed weapon's muzzle.

Tat-tat-tat-tat... Four rounds of ammunition penetrated the human soldier's torso, ripping through bones, organs and flesh, as the metallic projectiles exited the mortal warrior's body.

Unnerved by his unseen attacker, Tucker stood, in a desperate attempt to re-gather his thoughts.

"The gun!" he thought out loud.

"Freeze!" shouted a voice in the darkness.

Fear was now rampant. With frightened people running and screaming in all directions, a man, dressed in a dark suit and tie, shouted one last command before firing his service revolver. "Sir, stand where you are and don't move a muscle."

Standing less than fifty feet away, Samuel Tucker spotted the wooden stock of his semiautomatic rifle buried beneath Sergeant Kassel's blood soaked body.

"Sh-t!" Tucker shouted out, making a last ditch effort to salvage his twisted plans.

"I said stop!" Agent Ross commanded, aiming the sight of his handheld pistol dead center at the assailant's chest.

Bam!

The single bullet fired from Agent Ross's service revolver instantly penetrated Samuel Leroy Tucker's heart. Tucker died before his body hit the ground.

"Who are you?"

The massive angel smiled before answering.

"I am Kiel, an angel of the Most High."

"Am I dead?"

"The human body that you are standing over is dead, but you, Brad Daniel Kassel, are alive forevermore."

"I don't understand."

Aniel, standing alongside his commander, Kiel, answered Brad Kassel's question.

"In your former life, you made a conscious decision to accept Jesus' blood sacrifice on the cross as a complete atonement for your sins. At that exact moment in human time, when you made Jesus, Son of the Living God, your Lord and Savior, you entered the eternal Kingdom of God."

"*What about him?*" Brad Kassel asked as he pointed to the other human body lying on the ground to the right of his own.

"*Unfortunately,*" Aniel continued, "*Samuel Tucker rejected salvation for the wiles of the devil. As a child, and also a young adult, Tucker's faithful Christian grandmother presented him the simple Gospel message of God's perfect love at every opportunity. But, like the vast majority of his fellow humans, Samuel Leroy Tucker desired Satan's lies of temporal earthly bliss over God's free gift of eternal life.*"

"*Brad Kassel, beloved of the Most High, welcome to Eternity!*"

"*Who was that?*" the excited newcomer asked.

"*Follow us, Brad Daniel Kassel,*" Kiel answered with a smile. "*You will find out momentarily!*"

Chapter Eleven

"You used to live just like the rest of the world, full of sin, obeying Satan, the mighty prince of the power of the air. He is the spirit at work in the hearts of those who refuse to obey God."

~Ephesians 2:2 (NLT)

Saturday, July 4ᵗʰ, 2015
9:44 p.m. Eastern Time
CNN Global Headquarters
Atlanta, Georgia

The last public building tour had ended hours ago at the bustling CNN's Global Headquarters in Atlanta, Georgia. Even so, it was standing room only in the small fifty-seat theater used to offer visiting tourists a 'behind the scenes' look at a virtual CNN control room. With every seat taken and both side of the aisles filled to capacity, a bizarre spectacle was about to take place within the walls of this global news giant that went totally unnoticed by human eyes.

No sooner had the first of the two scheduled speakers stepped onto the small front stage, an ominous hush permeated every square inch of this replicated theater. Except for the pair of black bat-like wings that jutted out from his massive shoulders, the demon appeared strikingly angelic. Standing over ten feet tall, his jet-black hair flowed freely over his muscular broad shoulders as he walked. His true identity as an arch demon was easily revealed by the combination of his distinctively yellowish-black skin, a high protruding brow, and a deep-set pair of piercingly yellow eyes. Stopping just short at the edge of the small stage, the arch demon Amducious raised his clenched left fist and belted out a thunderous opening salute.

"Praise be to Satan!"

"Praise be to Satan!" A deafening roar filled the room.

The arch demon, charged by his Lord Satan with the destruction of the United States, stared intently into the yellow eyes of each of his scaly skinned subordinates, either seated or standing before him. In eons past, he knew every one of these grotesque winged apparitions as angelic princes, magnificent in stature and endowed by their Creator, God, with uniquely tailored supernatural gifts and superior intelligence. Except for retaining a keen intellect, little remained of their former angelic glory.

"It is an honor to be in the company of such a distinguished gathering of princes to oversee America's power media outlets," Amducious boasted with a prideful sneer. "You have each left your distant assignments to join me here tonight at our Atlanta headquarters, used specifically to broadcast our unique gospel message to a daily audience of more than one billion humans in 212 countries across the world."

Of the vast myriad of fallen spirits assigned by Satan to Amducious' command, the sixty or so gathered in this one room represented the "cream of his crop." Each demonic prince was gifted with the crafty ability to manipulate and maneuver their assigned media outlet in any direction they chose.

"You may have heard it said that the media tends to stretch and exaggerate information, making 'mountains out of mole hills.'" Amducious commented with a rare smile. "Little do these naïve mortals know that the actual root word for their word media means 'medium' and that we, demons, are the 'medium' responsible for distorting the information they present in the first place. You are the ones who deserve recognition for twisting the news each night, not those self-serving mortals who sit in front of a camera, microphone or computer and take credit for all of your hard work."

While his sixty or so subordinates vented a litany of curses and blasphemies against their respective human media counterparts, Amducious pointed his clawed finger at a particularly handsome yellow skinned demon seated directly in front of him in the theater's front row.

"Before I ask Prince Zagam to share the reason I have called you to assemble here tonight, I want to recognize the ingenious craftiness of two of your fellow princes." With a prideful sneer from ear to ear, the arch demon announced, "Pyro, stand up and be recognized!"

As the handsome demon stood, an aura of arrogance could be sensed permeating throughout the entire room of demons. With all yellow eyes focused on Pyro, affectionately known as the prince of lies, Amducious made known his subordinate's achievements.

"Pyro told me when we first started our media campaign back in the 1940s that the easiest way to bring down a large oak tree was to poison its roots. I have to admit, he was absolutely right! Pyro's plan was also quite simple. Change the way Americans think and you'll change the way Americans act. The roots of America are its children and Pyro's plan of attack was to infiltrate and bring fundamental changes to the ways Americans think, through both their public schools and the university systems. It's hard for even me to appreciate the speed of his plan. Before 1947, a large majority of America's universities, including Harvard, advocated conservative Christian principles as one of their basic tenets. For over 150 years, more than half of Harvard's graduates were Christian pastors. Up until 1963, open prayer and Bible readings were accepted practices in public schools all across America, and the Ten Commandments were posted somewhere in every public school building. Children were also encouraged to believe that they were created in the image of God."

Those last few statements produced a spontaneous round of booing and hissing throughout the small theater.

"Pyro's first plan of attack was to replace the thoroughly established conservatively minded college professors with a new breed of free thinking, liberal idealists. It wasn't long before the subversive attitudes

of our 'open minded' professors filtered down to their students. These enlightened students went on to become America's present lawyers, judges, and politicians. Beginning in the early 1960's, our new breed of progressive judges and policymakers were now being elected by their naïve constituents to powerful positions in all levels of government. So began Pyro's ingeniously divisive plan to distort the original intent of Thomas Jefferson's reference to a 'wall of separation between church and state'. This famous statement was written in a letter Jefferson sent to the Danbury Connecticut Baptist Association in 1802 expressing his concern that the newly formed American government should not be allowed to give favored governmental status to one particular established Christian church over that of another. Few Americans are aware that there is absolutely no mention in the United States' Constitution at all about the existence of any 'wall' prohibiting the free exercise and expression of a human's religious faith. It is only through their sheer ignorance of historical facts that Pyro was able to convince these fearful mortals to ban all prayer and Bible reading, and even the singing of innocent Christmas carols, from every public school across America. By the 1980s, using his satanically inspired 'wall of separation' lie once again, Pyro was successful in having the Ten Commandments legally removed from the walls of every public school building throughout America. Public school children were now taught a curriculum, approved by science committees, that evolution was a scientific fact and humans were not placed on Earth by a special act of God, but by some accidental process that I personally like to call, slime and time. Once we were able to teech that they were nothing more than mere animals, it wasn't hard to convince them that what had been called 'sinning' was nothing more than acting out their own basic animal instincts. It was amazing that they bought it all, hook, line and sinker. They would much rather believe the big lies we told than the absolute truth that God created them! Because of Pyro's genius, the mere mention of God, Jesus and moral absolutes, has now been legally legislated out of every public school building in America. What a stupid, gullible lot is man!"

Amducious raised his arms to the cheers and hisses of his agreeing audiences before continuing. "And the final outcome," Amducious arrogantly boasted, "Americans today don't really believe in anything. They think they do, but in reality, they don't! They have allowed themselves to be brainwashed into believing the big lie of multiculturalism, that there are no such things as moral absolutes. The ethics of multiculturalism are the accepted practices in today's educational systems. Children are now taught to be tolerant of the strange behavior of others and not be judgmental. Children are even encouraged to read books about likable wizards where they are eventually drawn into the belief that dark magic and witchcraft are cool and acceptable practices."

Amducious paused, allowing his squirming horde a brief moment to verbally vent some more cheers and hisses.

"I personally consider this final feat of Pyro's to be his greatest achievement." Amducious said with a prideful sneer, pausing momentarily to place his clawed hand affectionately on his subordinate's shoulder. "Even the vast majority of so-called mainline denominational Christian churches have replaced their belief in God's absolutes with the big lie of moral tolerance. In mainline churches today, one seldom hears a discouraging word like 'repentance or sin.' With that I say, Praise be to Satan!"

"Praise be to Satan!" The demon-filled audience thundered back in unison.

Turning his attention toward the back row of the small theater, the arch demon announced the name of the final prince to be recognized.

"There is one prince seated here amongst you whom I trust more than any other," Amducious declared. "We served together in Heaven long before the fall and he has remained my trusted and faithful follower throughout the eons of human time."

Pointing his clawed index finger in the direction of what appeared to be a rather minute goblin seated in the midst of several towering winged giants in the theater's back row, Amducious announced, "Lasmodious, stand and be recognized!"

As far as an outward appearance goes, this particular high-ranking demon was hideous indeed. Like Zagam, Lasmodious represented a special breed of imps identified as ogres—short in stature, covered from their horn-crested heads to their claw-tipped toes by thick bulging layers of sagging multicolored reptilian-like scales. What this malformed ogre lacked in external appeal, he more than made up for with his exceptional cunning and guile.

Fully aware that his blatant remarks showing favoritism toward any one demon might provoke jealousy among the ranks, the arch demon proceeded to intently glare at the entire assembly as if they were a room full of disobedient school children. Satisfied that all murmurings had ceased, the crafty demon continued his speech by asking this probing question with a threatening scowl, "What English word did Prince Lasmodious solely invent?"

"Desensitize!"

"And what single adverb did Prince Lasmodious say to use to achieve it?

"Subtly!" *they all replied.*

"Correct again!" *their impressed commander acknowledged with a smiling sneer.* "When Lasmodious first approached me at the beginning of the twentieth century with a specific request to place him in charge of an up and coming media trend known as Hollywood motion pictures, once again, what one word did he say would work best to divert America's attention away from God?

"Desensitize!"

"How did he do it?" *Amducious asked with a sneer.*

"Subtly!" *they replied.*

"Good! You're truly impressing me tonight! Can you also name two powerful visual images Lasmodious subtly introduced to the American public through our medium of motion pictures?"

"Violence and sex!"

"Exactly!" *affirmed their proud commander.* "It was Lasmodious' idea alone to introduce a steady flow of subtle sexual images and violent content into every film Hollywood released. It wasn't long *before Americans became completely and utterly desensitized to subtle portrayals of sex and violence viewed weekly at their local big-screened movie theaters."*

"What was the name of the next medium used by Lasmodious to desensitize Americans to sex and violence on a daily basis right in their own family living rooms?"

"Television!"

Your astuteness to detail is truly amazing!" Amducious commented with a rewarding sneer. "It was at this same time, from the early 1960s and throughout the 70s, that Lasmodious cunningly invented and began implementing his favorite expression, 'keep it below the radar.' To keep a safe distance from the ever-watchful eyes of the FCC (the Federal Communications Commission), Lasmodious ingeniously chose to release sexual and violent content gradually into every home in America. During the 1960's, it was his brilliant idea to conceal acceptable violence within the innocent guise of popular cowboy and Indian shows. He then allowed his demons, specializing in violence and crime, to gradually implement ever-increasing graphic images depicting shootings and senseless gore into the entertaining format of police shows during the 1970s and 80s. At the same time Lasmodious's specialty demons were desensitizing the American public to gross acts of violence, his demons of lust and perversion were busily scripting the roles of trendy daytime television soap opera actors and actresses to perform passionate love scenes where their daily acts of sensual adultery would soon set the stage for accepted normal American marital behavior. Does anyone here recall the name of Lasmodious' next highly successful media venture?"

"Cable Television!"

"Absolutely! The very building that presently surrounds us is a glorious testimony to the powerful medium of cable television. Literally overnight, cable television provided Americans everywhere, of all ages, the chance to choose whatever entertaining program their self-serving minds desired from a list of over hundreds of digital channels. You name it, they pay for it, and we'll offer it: endless

hours of watching movies of all ratings, indoor and outdoor sports for all seasons, 24/7 news coverage, cooking shows, sex and violence on demand, mindless science fiction, stupid cartoon channels, fantasy channels galore, just enough visual entertainment to keep the mortal masses totally preoccupied watching empty images on a digital screen, never realizing until it was far too late that they had wasted most of their precious time on earth serving their own selfish needs instead of the needs of those around them."

Before continuing, Amducious paused. With his left clenched fist extended outward, the arch demon proceeded to beat his chest three times and then pointed his clawed index finger in the direction of the ugly imp standing in the back row. "I am honored, Lasmodious, to call you my friend," declared the clearly emotional arch demon. "Before I call on Prince Zagam, I must not forget to mention the greatest of all accolades accredited to Lasmodious' long list of achievements. In 1985, with the insatiable demand for cable television literally exploding on every continent, Lasmodious astounded me once again by asking my permission to take on a brand new challenge called the Internet. Even back then, with the advent of home computers, he was able to perceive the endless possibilities for this new venture."

Before closing, Amudicous recalled the exact prophetic words pronounced from Lasmodious' scaly lips over a quarter of a century prior. "Destroyer, think about the infinite possibilities of having a high speed digital information center in every single American home. Ten years from now, even the youngest unsupervised school aged child with just a basic knowledge of the alphabet, could instantly access anything their evil intuitive little minds desired, including hardcore pornography.

"Needless to say," Amducious boasted, "Lasmodious couldn't have been more on target! Today, over 88.9% of all American households own a high-speed Internet computer, 68% of Americans have one or more smartphones, and 45% have tablet computers."

Sensing jealous murmurings arising once again from his impetuous ranks, Amuducious decided it best to close by summarizing the gathering's vast range of media achievements.

"Thanks to the concerted efforts of each of you, America is no longer perceived by the world as a society based on moral responsibility and commitment. America today is a sexually enlightened society, decadent, and void of any thoughts of decency or shame, driven by self-gratifying relationships. As a direct effect of your individual efforts of saturating the media with a whole host of tantalizing, self-serving sensual diversions, Americans are completely disconnected from one another. For example, in 1947, the number of marriages ending in divorce was under ten percent. Today, the American divorce rate has increased to almost sixty percent! Better yet, the overwhelming number of failed marriages has helped foster a rejection of marriage altogether. In America today, cohabitation is in and marriage is out! Love them and leave them with a sexually transmitted disease is the common lot for these unfulfilled relationships. The vast majority of their children grow up to be insecure, disconnected, dysfunctional adults. The final outcome of your tireless efforts—God's ways are now viewed by the majority of Americans as boring and utterly useless in their cluttered lives. On the other hand, sin is now widely accepted as being normal everyday behavior throughout America from sea to shining sea."

Like a heavy metal rock star standing on stage, the arch demon brazenly raised both arms above his head. His left fist was tightly clenched in defiance of God, and his right, proudly displaying the sign of Satan. With arms raised high, the arch demon look up toward the ceiling and bellowed out his closing mantra in shrill reverberating pitch, "Praise be to Satan!"

"Praise be to Satan!" resounded the same defiant chant from the room full of demons.

Before exiting, the arch demon pointed his clawed left index finger at each and every one of his subordinates in recognition of their individual contributions to the cause. After beating his massive chest three times as a symbolic gesture of demonic solidarity, he turned his *attention away from his audience toward a rather ugly imp sitting alone at the end of the first row.*

"The stage is now yours Prince Zagam," he graciously sneered before exiting to the small theater's darkened back recesses.

Tonight's final speaker looked nothing like his predecessor. Where, moments ago, a stately ten-foot tall giant had stood; now an ugly scaly yellow skinned dwarf occupied center stage. As with others in his special class of demons, this ogre also possessed the gifted superior intelligence that more than made up for his lack of visual appeal.

"Before I say another word," Zagam announced, "I want every one of you to bow your heads in honor of a mortal, who only moments ago, surrendered his earthly life for the continuation of our great cause."

Except for Amducious and Zagam, every demon in the room cringed and scowled at the thought of paying homage to a lowly human mortal.

"Why do all of you look so perplexed? Haven't you ever been asked to pay homage to a mortal before?" Zagam questioned with a sarcastic glare. "No? Well let me now introduce all of you to a special human mortal."

In an instant, the soul of Samuel Leroy Tucker appeared, standing center stage.

"My fellow demons, I would like you to meet Samuel Leroy Tucker."

The entire audience of demonic princes immediately began hissing or growling uncontrollably in response to having a quivering human soul standing in their midst.

"Get him out of here!" demanded Aznel, shaking his clawed fists in the air from his standing position along the right side aisle.

"Have you lost your mind?" Mazdor questioned. "Send him to hell now!"

"I hate the sight of human souls!" screamed another irate demon from the back of the theater.

"All in good time," Zagam said with devious smile.

Being a member of their fallen ranks, Zagam completely understood the reason for his fellow princes' intense ire. Contrary to popular belief, it wasn't their hatred toward humans that drove his fellow princes into such a rage. It was their intense jealousy that human mortals are redeemable beings and demons are not. Long ago, demons had forfeited all claims to their Heavenly rights when they willfully rebelled against their Creator.

"Show respect!" blasted an unnerving call from the far corner of the room.

"Thank you, Destroyer," Zagam acknowledged with a nod from his horn-covered head. With every yellow eye intently fixed in the direction of the theater's small center stage, the terrified shivering soul began to talk.

"Am I in hell?" the petrified human soul asked in a quivering voice.

"Not quite, but very, very close!" chuckled the amused ugly imp standing mere inches away.

"If this isn't hell, who are they?" Tucker demanded, staring out at the most hideous scene a human mind could ever imagine.

Like an erupting super volcano, all pandemonium instantly broke out in response to the human's last question. The laughter became so intense that the actual walls of the massive CNN headquarters began to noticeably vibrate, sending fear into the human inhabitants inside that they had been struck by a minor earthquake. Allowing his demonic counterparts a moment longer to vent their amusement, Zagam continued.

"As I said only moments ago, we are indebted to the actions of this single human."

As Zagam started to speak, Tucker's confused soul turned toward the grotesque monster standing beside him in order to garner what possible role he may have unwittingly played to place himself now in such a hellish bizarre situation.

"In life," began Zagam, "Mr. Tucker was a shrimper by trade from the bayous of Louisiana—until a little oil spill polluted all the little shrimp he used to catch in the Gulf of Mexico. It was then that Mr. Tucker met some of our best career advising demons. They assisted in *redirecting Mr. Tucker's interests and talents toward a new and better paying occupation as a professional assassin."*

"Ooh!" a host of impressed demon voices resonated throughout the room.

"Enough said for now! In a few moments, you will all be returning to your specific media assignments with a detailed written account of Mr. Tucker's recent historic performance. The moment you arrive, your responsibility begins. You are to make sure that every demon under your control has his assignment— to either print, report or broadcast every single word written about Samuel Leroy Tucker's recent act of heroism."

Zagam was notorious for never mincing his words. Knowing his dominion on earth was rapidly coming to an end, he used his allotted time to expedite his cunning attempts to thwart God's prophetic plan to send him, along with the millions of his other demonic cohorts, to their final future destination, the Lake of Fire.

With every demon's full attention focused front and center, Zagam pointed his clawed gnarled finger in the direction of each prince standing before him and commanded, "Every prince responsible for the printed content published in every major newspaper and magazine read daily across America, stand to your feet. You are to leave the moment you receive this printed message in your hands. Make absolutely sure your human reporters and editors type every single word printed!"

With a snap of his finger, each demon had in his clawed hands a completely written transcript of every detail Zagam wanted each and every one of their subscribers to read in tomorrow's magazine or newspaper.

"Now be off and let our truth be known to all of your daily readers!"

The exact moment Zagam completed his command, nearly a quarter of the room's sixty or so princes instantly vanished.

Those remaining forty or so princes were now fully focused, waiting patiently for Zagam's next command.

"*Every prince responsible for the televising of major news broadcasts to America by means of satellite-linked dishes or cable networks, stand to you feet.*"

In a mere moment of time, nearly thirty princes stood to their feet.

"*You,*" Zagam again pointed the same gnarled finger in the direction of each standing prince, "*are directly responsible for the content broadcast to American households from each of the major televised news networks. You are to leave the moment you receive this printed message in your hands. You are to make sure that each of your assigned human television anchors broadcast clearly and precisely every word on this transcript, and make sure not a single word is left out! Now be off and let our truth be known to all of your viewing audience,*" Zagam commanded. In an instant, in a twinkling of an eye, over ninety percent of the room was vacated.

Turning to face his remaining five princes, one being Amducious' friend, Lasmodious, Zagam said with a smile, "*You five remaining princes are solely responsible for the content posted on the world's five major Internet web servers and their related search engines. Together, the information you send out daily covers the entire world. Once you receive your transcripts, you are to return immediately and begin posting our messages of truth to the entire digital world. Now be off and let our truth be known to all of your viewing audience!*"

In an instant, in a twinkling of an eye, in the fifty-seat theater, where mere moments ago stood an overflow crowd of hideous demonic beings of all shapes and sizes, now only four supernatural beings remained—a massive arch demon, an ugly ogre, a thoroughly terrorized human soul, and a winged eagle-headed apparition named Griffin. With three pairs of yellow eyes focused on the frightened human soul, a voice from above posed this final question. "*Sam Tucker, before you're sent to hell, is there anything you'd like to ask?*"

"*Yes,*" Tucker replied, mustering enough nerve to look up and courageously face the towering giant. "*What exactly was written about me on the message that was sent out to broadcast to all America?*"

"*Your request will be answered.*" *Amudcious replied.* "*Look upon the wall in front of you and read about how you, Samuel Leroy Tucker, have single handedly brought down the once mighty, but briefly lived, American Values Party. With all heads turned, the entire text of Zagam's media message began slowly scrolling up the adjacent twenty-foot high, white paneled wall used specifically by human technicians to project virtual images of an actual CNN media control room.*

"*On Wednesday, July 4, at approximately 9:40 p.m. Eastern Time, Samuel Leroy Tucker, a resident of Grande Isle, Louisiana, carried out an unsuccessful assassination attempt on the life of Rashid Jabbar Harris, the President of the United States of America. According to written testimonies of several eyewitnesses on the scene at the time when the shooting took place on the U.S. Capitol's West Lawn, the assassination attempt was thwarted by the brave sacrificial actions of a valiant Marine Sergeant named Brad Kassel. According to eyewitness accounts, the very moment Samuel Leroy Tucker aimed and was preparing to fire his automatic weapon in the direction of the bleachers where the president and his family were seated together watching the grand finale of the National Mall's fireworks display, Sergeant Kassel literally dove on top of the assailant's weapon, his body fatally receiving several fired bullets at point-blank range. Moments later, Samuel Leroy Tucker was shot dead by an alert White House Secret Service agent.*

Of special note: Samuel Leroy Tucker has been positively identified as the same gentleman who was arrested at last month's American Values Party National Mall Rally for shouting out threatening racial epithets directed specifically at the president. After his arrest by D.C. Park Police, it was thoroughly established by extensive background checks that Mr. Samuel Leroy Tucker was both a card-carrying member of the popular southern white supremacy group named the Christian Defense League and also, an accepted member of the American Values Party. It has been long reported, and actively denied by the leadership within the American Values Party, that members of several white racist groups had infiltrated their ranks and were actively involved in promoting and supporting the American Values Party's conservative causes to return America back to her foundational roots. Contrary to the conservative grassroots charter supported by the American Values Party, tonight's unsuccessful assassination of America's first elected black president only highlights the fact that racism is another sad legacy that has been passed on to our present generation by our America's Founding Fathers.

After reading the entire scripted message, a dejected Samuel Tucker looked down at the wooden stage below.

"Why so sad, Mr. Tucker?" Zagam asked in a sarcastic condescending tone.

"Cheer up, Tucker," Amducious sneered. "As we demons like to say, you're about to leave on an everlasting vacation to eternity's popular alternative destination."

"Go to hell, you ugly b-stard," a defiant Samuel Tucker boldly declared as he looked up into the massive demon's yellow piercing eyes.

"No, you, Mr. Samuel Leroy Tucker," the equally defiant and clearly irritated arch demon, Amducious, declared, "will go to hell."

That very instant, the human soul, that had been standing in their midst, vanished, leaving behind three demonic spirits huddled closely together on the small wooden stage. With all introductions over and no more assignments to pass along, the relieved arch demon turned his attention to the winged chimera and inquired,

"With the American Values Party possibly out of the political picture for good, your role in next year's presidential elections is about to take center stage. How do future political prospects look at this time for the popular Republican candidate, Robert Berry?"

"Let me describe for you, Destroyer, Robert Berry's political future in weather forecasting terms," Griffin answered in a hissing tone of voice. "I foresee in my long-range political forecast that Governor Berry's chances remain exceedingly hot in capturing next spring's GOP's nomination for President of the United States. But once his nomination has been made official, I have personally arranged for a massive big-breasted cold front named Sheila to move in and put an *instant chill on any hope he might have of becoming the next President of the United States."*

"Out of curiosity, Griffin," Zagam inquired with a smile, "what does your extended forecast look like for next year's presidential elections?"

"Barring some unseen act of God," Griffin replied, shaking its feathered head in jest, "I guarantee come Election Day next November, the Democratic nominee, Analise DeVoe, will be elected to the office of President of the United States of America."

Chapter Twelve

"The enemy who planted the weeds among the wheat is the Devil. The harvest is the end of the world, and the harvesters are the angels."

~Matthew 13:39 (NLT)

Saturday, July 4th, 2015
9:33 p.m. Central Time
102 Lea Street
Hastings, Minnesota

For Sean and Lindsey Wiggins, today's 4th of July backyard barbecue represented much more than celebrating their beloved country's birthday with invited friends and family. It marked four years of their seemingly endless effort and joint determination to see the nation they loved return to its founding fathers' original beliefs and established doctrines. For the past several hours, the cofounders of the American Values Party played host at their beautiful lakefront Minnesota home to a who's who of local, state and national political personalities. Present at their backyard celebration was the Minnesota Governor, Sarah Booker, three local members of Congress—Scott Jeffers, Lance Baylor, Ben Christy, and two U.S. Senators—Evan Gleason and Maggie Holts. Each conservative official had won his or her elected seat with the full backing of the American Values Party. In fact, over 40% of the candidates the American Values Party supported during last year's National mid-term election captured political positions ranging from 9 state governors, 5 U.S. Senators, and 40 new members of the U.S. House of Representatives. As Sean and Lindsey Wiggins stood at the end of their driveway waving to the last of their departing guests, little did they realize that another, more ominous round of fireworks was just about ready to explode, but this time, not in the skies above, but over the medium of America's air waves.

"Honey, I'll make you a deal," Sean Wiggins smiled as he reached out and affectionately locked fingers with his wife of thirty-seven years.

"Well, that entirely depends on what you have to offer me, Mr. Wiggins." Lindsey responded with a playful nod.

"Okay, Mrs. Wiggins, here's my generous offer, take it or leave it."

"Ooh, this sound really serious!" his wife smiled as the happily married couple walked slowly hand-in-hand along the paved driveway leading toward their brightly lit home.

"What if I say I would be willing to get up early tomorrow morning and do all the dishes?" her husband challenged with a serious stare.

"You definitely have my attention, Mr. Sean Wiggins. What else do you have in mind?"

"Well, to tell you the truth," Wiggins replied with a mischievous grin, "how's about you and me just going upstairs and setting off some fireworks of our own before calling it a night?"

"Is that all you have to offer me, Mr. Wiggins?" Lindsey jokingly asked.

"What else would you have me do, my fair lady?" her husband questioned with a put-on British accent.

"Being that we don't have to be into the office until noon tomorrow," she flirtatiously said, "what about you serving me breakfast in bed tomorrow morning?"

"And how would you like me to cook your egg?"

"A veggie omelet sounds really tempting right now."

"Coffee or orange juice?"

"Definitely coffee, no sugar, and a spot of hazelnut creamer would be nice."

"Anything else on your list, Mrs. Wiggins?"

"Yes, one more thing." Lindsey innocently admitted. As she opened the French entrance doors leading into their home's great room, she turned to her husband and asked, "Could you please make sure all the downstairs doors are locked and the lights are all turned out? I'll be waiting for you upstairs to continue our 4th of July celebration."

After following his wife inside the house, the phone rang and Sean said, "Lindsey, whoever that is, please tell them we're not home."

"Wiggins, you are one crazy man!" Lindsey laughed as she picked up the cordless phone from its tabletop base station. "Hello, this is the Wiggins residence. Lindsey speaking."

As Sean Wiggins proceeded to turn off the lights in the kitchen and dining room, his attention was immediately diverted to his wife, who was holding the phone by her side with a strange sullen expression on her face.

"Lindsey, honey, what's wrong?"

Startled, she instantly snapped out of her momentary trance. "Sean, turn on the television, now! Charlie Mitchell just called and said there's been an assassination attempt on the president at D.C.'s National Mall."

"President Harris?"

"Yes, turn on the television!" Lindsey demanded.

Without saying another word, Sean ran over and snatched the television remote control off the nearby coffee table. In a matter of moments, he and his wife stood shoulder-to-shoulder staring at their wall-mounted television in disbelief at a scene where frantic people appeared running in all directions.

"Sean, what channel are we watching?

"I don't know! I think MSNBC!"

"Try another channel. This one has too much confusion going on."

Wiggins continued pressing the buttons on his handheld remote until finally, a familiar face appeared on the large flat-paneled monitor.

"Thank God, it's Keenan!" Wiggins declared, stopping his search when he spotted the popular FOX news reporter.

With emergency lights flashing all around him and sirens blaring in the distance, Keenan McShea held his microphone close to his face and summarized for his FOX audience what had just taken place directly across the street on the National Mall.

"Folks, this is what we know right now. At approximately 9:45 p.m. Eastern Time tonight, moments after the grand finale fireworks were released into the skies above the National Mall, several shots were fired from an automatic weapon by a man identified by U.S. Park Police on the scene as Samuel Leroy Tucker."

"Oh my God, Sean! That's the same man who was arrested by Park Police at last month's rally on the Mall. He's a known white supremacist! How did they ever allow him in there?"

"I have no idea, Linds, but there he is, big as life, on the screen for the entire world to see!"

Wiggins continued surfing through the channels, hoping to find a news broadcast that would supply further information on the shooting. No matter where he stopped on the remote control, the only image presented on the screen was the same exact smiling picture of a toothless Louisiana shrimper named Samuel Leroy Tucker.

"Sean, go back to Keenan. I want to hear what he has to say!"

"Done!" In an instant, Keenan McShea was back live, summarizing the details as they were handed him, of what had taken place less than an hour earlier on the West Lawn of the U.S. Capitol.

"Because of the heroic actions of this one man, Brad Daniel Kassel, a Marine Sergeant Major stationed at the 8th & I Streets Barracks, the President of the United States, Rashid Harris, is alive and unharmed tonight. According to signed written testimonies from several eyewitnesses on the scene, this is what we now know:

Sergeant Major Kassel, while actually on duty tonight at the National Mall, stumbled on the assailant only moments before Samuel Leroy Tucker would have fired his fully loaded assault rifle in the direction of the president. Once again, according to eyewitness accounts of those on the scene, without thought or hesitation, Sergeant Major Brad Kassel dove directly on top of the gun's barrel as the assailant fired. According to the U.S. Park Police reports just handed me, Sergeant Major Brad Kassel died instantly, after being shot in the chest by four exploding 22-caliber bullets at point blank range. According to the same police report, no other person or persons received injuries as a direct result of tonight's assassination attempt. Moments after Sergeant Kassel was fatally shot, the assailant, Samuel Leroy Tucker was shot dead by an on-duty Secret Service officer. I cannot overemphasize this singular fact—as a direct result of Sergeant Major Brad Daniel Kassel's sacrificial actions tonight at the U.S. Capitol's West Lawn, the President of the United States, Rashid Jabbar Harris, remains alive and well and able to serve America until the end of his term."

Saturday, July 4th, 2015
10:41 p.m. Eastern Time
238 Aspen St. N.W
Washington D.C.

The headlights from Helen McAllister's Mustang illuminated not only the family's paved driveway, but also, James and Anne McAllister's front living room as well. She had just arrived home from her girlfriend Nancy's 4th of July party.

"She's home," James McAllister, Helen's teary-eyed father, commented.

For the past fifteen minutes, since they first heard the horrific news reported about the actual identity of the young Marine killed at tonight's shooting on the National Mall, James and Anne McAllister stood glued at their living room's front window.

"James, what are you going to say?"

"There's only one thing I can say, Anne, and that is the truth," he released his grip on the window's side curtains he had been holding for the past few minutes.

"But James, how on earth are you going to break it to her?"

"Believe me, Anne, I haven't stopped thinking about that question since we found Helen's cell phone resting on top of the kitchen countertop."

"Maybe it was a blessing that she forgot it," Helen McAllister's mom reflected. "I wouldn't want to think about her driving all the way home from Nancy's house in Gaithersburg, knowing that her boyfriend was murdered while on duty at the National Mall. I just pray she didn't turn on the radio and hear the news."

"If she did," James said with a reassuring smile, "we'll know in a moment."

At that moment, with both heads bowed, the father of Helen McAllister prayed these heartfelt words, "Father God, Anne and I humbly come before you with one of the biggest requests we have ever made. We ask that you give me the right words to say when our daughter walks through that door. In Jesus' name we ask, amen."

At the moment he ended his prayer, the front entrance door opened to the sound of this joyful greeting, "Hi, Guys, I'm home! Happy 4th of July!"

At the same moment, the voice of the angel, Mekiel, spoke these biblical words of comfort over his assigned family: "My peace I give you," declares the Lord Jesus. "I do not give you peace as the world gives. Do not let your hearts be troubled, little ones, and do not be afraid. My peace is now upon the McAllister family."

Saturday, July 4ᵗʰ, 2015
11:12 p.m. Central Time
The Graham Estate
15 miles North of Trinity Mills, Texas

Except for the youngest four grandchildren who were fast asleep in their assigned upstairs bedrooms, the remainder of the Graham family was still wide-awake. For the past two hours, each Graham family member sat, fixated, as were millions of others Americans across the country, in front of the television, watching the rapidly unfolding events taking place in the Nation's Capitol, Washington D.C.

"Dad, turn back to the C-SPAN reporter on channel 212. I'm not sure if you caught it, but he made a very interesting point just a moment ago."

Acting immediately on Aaron's request, Eliot turned the channel, and the image projected was not that of a C-SPAN reporter, but that of Samuel Leroy Tucker.

"It has been brought to our attention," Drew Paterson announced, "that this man, Samuel Leroy Tucker, the alleged gunman in tonight's presidential assassination attempt, had two interesting documents on his possession that are beginning to shed more light on how it was possible for a known white supremacist to have gained access to one of the most highly secured five acres on planet earth."

The image of a Virginia driver's license displaying Tucker's picture was projected on the screen, and the name of a 53-year-old, Sterling, Virginia man, Kevin Leroy Johnson, was printed on its front cover.

"This Virginia state-issued driver's license, released to the media minutes ago, is the exact I.D. U.S. Park Police found tonight on the body of Samuel Leroy Tucker. It is also the assumed I.D. Samuel Leroy Tucker used to gain access to the Capitol's West Lawn sometime between 3 and 5 p.m. this afternoon. With all the intensive pre-screening involved before entering the West Lawn's secured confines, it is still not known how it was possible for Samuel Leroy Tucker to have in his possession such a deadly weapon, identified by police as a Ruger 10/22 semi-automatic rifle."

Pausing for a brief moment, the scene reverted to the image of the well-known C-SPAN host reporter, now seated in the familiar surroundings of the Cable-Satellite Public Affairs Network's home studio.

"There is one more worrisome puzzle to the rapidly unfolding mystery behind tonight's attempted presidential assassination that has just been brought to our attention. This, just released document, was also found by U.S. Park Police on the body of Samuel Leroy Tucker."

Not a single sound could be heard in the room as the next mysterious document was projected on the television screen. The C-SPAN reporter commented, "This, to me, is very disturbing." Up on the television screen, enlarged and visually enhanced for all to see and read, was an image of a National American Values Party Membership card with Samuel Leroy Tucker's signature legibly signed on the front.

"That's an outright fraudulent lie!" a furious Eliot Graham shouted. "As far as I know, the American Values Party never issued a membership card to anyone."

"Quick, Dad, turn the channel to another station. I bet you a dollar they're feeding their audiences the same exact lie."

"Keep your dollar, son; I already know what they're doing," the perceptive Graham fumed.

Both Grahams were right. As the senior Graham proceeded to change the news channels, one by one, they displayed the same hellish distortions, created and released to the worldwide media hours earlier by a demonic prince named Zagam.

Saturday, July 4th, 2015
11:22 p.m. Central Time
102 Lea Street
Hastings, Minnesota

"Sean, please tell me that I'm dreaming," pleaded Lindsey Wiggins, sitting by herself on her great room's leather loveseat, aimlessly staring at a darkened television screen.

"Lindsey," Wiggins replied, looking at his clearly distraught wife from across the room, "this is worse than any nightmare I could ever imagine."

"Sean, the media's playing this thing up as if we hired Tucker to shoot the president."

"No, it's much more than that," Wiggins reflected as he walked across the room toward his wife. With tears welling up in his eyes, Sean Wiggins knelt on the floor beside his equally crushed spouse. Looking up, Wiggins proclaimed, "Lindsey, I don't know who's behind this or how they were able to pull it off, but I know there is a righteous God in Heaven, and this entire fiasco wasn't orchestrated to assassinate the President of the United States. That assassin's bullet was aimed directly at us and the very character and existence of the American Values Party."

Tuesday, July 5th
1:22 a.m. Eastern Time
526 Patrick Lane
Schenectady, New York

Like a lone star shining in the night, a singular light went on in the upstairs bedroom of one of Schenectady's most exclusive neighborhoods, briefly illuminating the darkened sky surrounding the well-known Berry residence.

"Honey, it's useless. I can't sleep!" a restless Robert Berry commented as he sat on the edge of his large king-sided bed.

"Bob, you really need to get some rest," Elizabeth admonished as she sat up in bed, her back resting against raised pillows pressing against the headboard. "Honey, I don't have to tell you, but you have a big day ahead of you tomorrow."

Standing, Berry walked over to the opened bedroom door. Before leaving, he turned to face his concerned wife and said, "I need talk to Grif."

"Bob, it's almost 1:30. I'm sure Grif's sound asleep by now."

"Griffin, sleeping?" Berry shook his head and smiled. "No way, especially not with all this excitement going on. Right now, Griffin Gunson is sitting in front of his television set eating this stuff up as if it were candy."

Knowing the hectic schedule of the day ahead, Elizabeth Berry made one last attempt to reason with her visibly tired husband, but very determined Republican candidate for president.

"Bob, for God's sake, you can talk to Griffin in the morning. It's over an hour and a half's drive from here to your first speaking engagement in Hartford, Connecticut. You're scheduled to give your speech at 11 a.m. at Hartford University, and after we leave there, we have less than an hour and a half to be at the Bradley International Airport to catch our flight for Denver."

Knowing that his wife had his best interests at heart, Berry responded with a smile.

"Lizz, honey, I appreciate your concern, but calling Griffin is something I have to do, or I won't be able sleep at all."

Stepping into the darkened hallway beyond the bedroom door, Berry commented,

"Don't you worry about me, Lizz. I'll be sleeping in Julie's old bedroom tonight. So, Honey, just go back to sleep!"

Sunday, July 5ᵗʰ, 2015
1:25 a.m. Eastern Time
The Reilly Farm
120 Country Line Rd.
Schenectady, New York

Ever since the new renters moved into the old Reilly Farm at the end of Country Line Road, the local horses from the nearby farms had been acting quite bizarre. There was even one incident recently reported to police where two prize thoroughbreds from a neighboring large estate had jumped a four-foot fence. The horses were discovered the very next day with unexplained lacerations covering their bodies, and wandering aimlessly in a dazed state of confusion along New York Interstate 90.

The local residents living along Country Line Road also noticed a strange habit about their new young neighbors that were giving them concern. No matter what time of day one drove by the old Reilly farm, all the downstairs lights of the old farmhouse remained lit throughout, and tonight was no exception.

"Griffin, will you turn off that blasted television and computer and come up to bed, already!" the shrill voice of Gunson's girlfriend exploded from the couple's upstairs bedroom.

"Let's compromise, Sheila," Gunson responded, looking up from his wireless laptop computer with a grin. "You can stay up there until I'm done or come down here and have some fun."

Seemingly unfazed by his girlfriend's complaints, Gunson shut the living room television off with a TV remote resting on the arm of his chair. He immediately turned his full attention to the screen of his laptop computer, continuing to surf the Internet for the latest details on last night's assassination attempt on the president.

"Griffin Gunson, you lied to me!" a feminine voice whined in close proximity.

With his attention diverted away from his computer, Gunson looked up at a sensual scene that would have driven most men his age into a passionate frenzy. Pressing her nearly nude body against the back of his chair, his big-breasted brunette girlfriend, Sheila Brewster, was clad in the sheerest of nighties. "You promised me that if I went with you to that boring 4th of July party at Bob Berry's house, we'd come home early and have fun in bed all night!" Brewster complained.

"Sheila, when are you ever going to learn that your persistent nagging ranks right up there with toothaches and hemorrhoids?" Gunson countered with an impish grin. "Besides, Bob's your boss, too."

"He's only my boss during the day," Sheila responded in seductive tone, repositioning her exposed body on the arm of the chair within inches of Griffin Gunson's face. "You're the man of my nighttime fantasies."

As she bent low to give Gunson a sensual kiss, the phone rang. "Who in the Sam Hill could be calling at this late hour?" Brewster threw up her hands and complained.

"Sheila, just pick up the phone and hand it to me."

Looking at the phone's digital caller ID, Brewster cried out in frustration, "It's Robert Berry!"

"Don't say another word!" Gunson commanded in a strange, completely foreign tone of voice, two octaves lower than normal.

Out of fear, Brewster reluctantly handed the phone to her live-in boyfriend. Covering the entire cordless receiver with his hand, Gunson looked at his girlfriend and said in a calm, firm voice, "Go up to bed, now Sheila. I promise you, I will join you upstairs the very moment I hang up this phone."

"When am I ever going to learn that you love politics more than you love me?" an infuriated Brewster responded, flashing two raised middle fingers in Gunson's smiling face before leaving.

When he was absolutely sure all distractions were over, Griffin Gunson turned his full attention to the person patiently waiting for his response on the other end of the phone. "Yes, Bob. Is there a problem?" Gunson asked in a cool, respectful tone of voice.

"Griffin, how can you speak so calmly at a time like this?"

Gunson smiled before answering his boss. "Bob, if you're referring to yesterday's incident down at the D.C. National Mall, the way I see it, it can only be a win-win situation for us. Mr. Samuel Leroy Tucker did the Republican Party a big favor."

"Explain yourself, Grif."

"Okay," Gunson continued, "thanks to that little business card discovered on Mr. Tucker's dead body, all heat for last night's assassination attempt will be directed at the American Values Party, not us."

"Go on."

"Before I do that, Bob, I need to go back and review some facts."

Just make it quick, Grif, I'm starting to get tired."

"I'll make it brief," Gunson affirmed. "After their rapid rise to fame following last year's mid-term election victories, the American Values Party clearly emerged in the public view as the militant wing of the GOP. Their popularity rose as a direct result of the public's reaction to the increase in government spending of President Harris' administration and the socialist tactics of the Democratic-controlled Congress. If the Values Party would have stopped their self-righteous crusade right there, the GOP would have gladly embraced them with open arms, but unfortunately, they didn't. Their party's organizers, specifically Sean and Lindsey Wiggins, ignored all logical reasoning and went with the radical social agenda put forth by that 'holier-than-thou' radio fundamentalist preacher, Eliot Graham. If you remember, I told you back then that this kind of reaction might occur if we opened the Republican Party up to the view of those religious right-wing nuts."

"I remember," Berry recalled. "You were the only one who said before last year's primaries that it would be political suicide for the Republican Party to adopt the Value Party's far right agenda.

I have to admit, what you said then is even truer today. If we would have advocated support for either the Defense of Marriage Act or banning abortions, we not only would have lost the vast majority of our independent voters, but we would have picked up every Samuel Leroy Tucker and backwoods redneck along the way. So what do you suggest we do now?"

"Bob, what do we always do when a crisis comes our way?" Gunson countered with a question of his own.

"Wait until it passes."

"That's exactly right, Bob," Gunson affirmed. "Sure, an assassination attempt on the life of America's first elected black president makes for great headlines. The NAACP and liberal Democrats are going to use this story to their advantage and I don't blame them! "

"Grif, do you foresee any rioting taking place?"

"Possibly," Gunson conceded. "As I told you before, no matter how bad his poll numbers might appear, Harris has a solid lead among the illegal immigrants, the working-class poor and inner city blacks. To them, Harris represents their dreams come true. They are the very ones who have benefited directly from his socialist agenda of taxing the rich working class and rewarding the poor welfare class with money they didn't earn. They also view Harris as their Robin Hood and this might very well be the catalyst they've been waiting for to make their silent voices known."

"If rioting is going to occur, then how can you say this won't hurt us?"

"Bob, relax! Your present polling numbers are higher than all the other candidates combined, and besides, in a month or two from now, no one's going to even remember the name Samuel Leroy Tucker."

"I'll take your word on that, Griff."

"Boss, I have absolutely no doubt that come next November the 2nd, the President of the United States will be Robert Winslow Berry."

"You haven't been wrong yet, Grif," a clearly tired Robert Berry admitted.

"And I never will be!" declared his self-assured campaign manager. "I suggest that you try to get some sleep, boss. As we both know, you have a really big day ahead of you tomorrow."

After hanging up the phone, Griffin Gunson turned his full attention toward a large mirror hanging on the nearby living room wall. Positioning himself directly in front of the mirror's oval-shaped frame, Gunson removed his shirt exposing a large tattoo of a black pentagram covering his entire lower chest and abdomen. He smiled with pride at two inverted black crosses tattooed on each side of his chest. At the base of each cross were tattooed droplets of red blood appearing to flow outward from the gold rings that pierced each of his nipples. Before retiring to his upstairs bedroom to fulfill a promise he had made earlier to Sheila Brewster, Gunson stood in front of the mirror a moment longer, totally captivated by the reflected images of his demonic tattoos. Covering the entire center of the star-like tattoo with his left hand, Gunson began reciting the words to an oath that he had repeated nightly ever since surrendering his eternal soul to the devil.

"Lord Satan, I once again offer my life and my eternal soul for the continuance of your kingdom here on earth. Use me as you so choose. I am at your service. In your unholy name I ask. Amen!"

Chapter Thirteen

"They even sacrificed their sons and their daughters to the demons. They shed innocent blood, the blood of their sons and daughters. By sacrificing them to the idols of Canaan, they polluted the land with murder. They defiled themselves by their evil deeds, and their love of idols was adultery in the Lord's sight. That is why the Lord's anger burned against His people, and He abhorred his own special possession."–Psalm 106: 37-40 (NKJV)

Tuesday, July 14th, 2015
11:47 a.m.
200 Farmington Ave., Apt. D
Bristol, Connecticut

"For land sakes, Millie," Joanne Hanson exclaimed, her face pressed against the small kitchen window. "Another one has just arrived!"

"And how many does that make so far?" Mildred Duncan inquired calmly. She was sitting a few feet away on her favorite burgundy recliner.

So far, six," Joanne replied, pressing her wrinkled brow further against the doubled pane glass of her kitchen window in order to get a more accurate count of the number of television vans parked along Farmington Avenue just outside their second floor apartment.

"Oops, make that seven, Millie!" Joanne rescinded with a girlish grin. "A big white van with a CBS logo has just pulled up to the curb across the street."

Though Millie Duncan was usually somewhat more reserved in nature than Joanne, her legally married same-sex spouse of three years, the excitement of today's big announcement was beginning to show. Millie, once an energetic Connecticut state social worker, slowly walked over to join her elderly spouse at the small kitchen window. Time had visibly taken its toll on her seventy-six year old body, now ravaged by the debilitating effects of osteoarthritis.

"Oh my, word!" Joanne stated, overwhelmed by the strange sight of seeing so many of her favorite news and TV personalities standing just outside her kitchen window. "There's the CBS's Morning Show host, Brent Newsom, standing shoulder-to-shoulder with NBC's Good Morning USA host, Janet Styles."

"Look Joannie, they're all waving at us!" her elated lesbian partner of over fifteen years declared with a big smile.

"Joannie, I believe they're also trying to tell us something," Millie affirmed with tears in her eyes.

"I believe they're telling us to turn on the television!" Joanne declared. Without a moment's hesitation, Joanne Hanson left Millie standing at the window and made a quick beeline, as she likes to say, over to the old 25-inch console television positioned against the far living room wall.

No more than a split second after pressing the console's power-on button, Joanne Hanson stepped away from the archaic television's semi-oval screen. Speechless at first, only able to click her fingers to get Millie's attention, Joanne finally was able to muster three profound words, "We're on television!"

To the elderly lesbian couple's complete amazement, their favorite TV personality, MSNBC's primetime news host, Rachel Meadows, was on television as she stood directly below their upstairs balcony.

"At any moment now," Meadows announced, "the highest court in the land is poised to pass a decision making these two unassuming women from Bristol, Connecticut instant national, and perhaps, international celebrities."

"Millie!" a wide-eyed Joanne Hanson declared, "that's us!"

As she painfully made her way back to her favorite cushioned recliner, Millie froze, her heavily wrinkled eyes stared in a state of total disbelief. Only a few feet away, displayed on her living room television screen, was her three-year-old wedding picture which showed Millie with a beaming smile, proudly holding hands with her equally elated newly married same-sex spouse, Joanne. With her wedding picture on the screen for all the world to see, the reporter, Rachel Meadows, made this carefully scripted comment, "I believe I can say with all confidence that for this loving same-sex couple, and perhaps, the millions of other gay couples all across the United States, either married, or waiting to be legally married, today is a day they never, ever dreamed could possibly happen."

"Oh my gosh! Oh my gosh! Oh my gosh!" screamed an ecstatic Joanne, excitedly shaking her clenched fist in front of her.

"Shush-up!" Millie demanded with a scowl on her face. "I want to hear what else Rachel has to say!"

With her MSNBC cameramen standing a few feet away from the world-renowned reporter, Rachel Meadows began verbally documenting the details behind the three-year plight of these two unpretentious elderly lesbian women from Bristol, Connecticut, whose previously untold story could possibly change the entire world.

"Their story began one month to the day after Connecticut's Governor, Milton Fenton, signed into law a bill making Connecticut the third state in America to legalize same-sex marriage. In December 2008, Joanne Hanson, a retired civilian employee from the Department of Intelligence, attempted to enroll her newly married seventy-three-year-old spouse, Mildred

Duncan, into her federal employee health benefits program—a move that could have saved the newlyweds hundreds of dollars a month. To her dismay, the local benefits coordinator told Joanne that although she was legally married to Mildred Duncan under Connecticut law, federal law did not recognize same-sex unions. That very same day, Millie contacted a friend in the Connecticut State legislature who immediately put both women in touch with the Boston-based gay rights organization, Gay and Lesbian Legal Services. Within twenty-four hours of making that first phone call, a lawsuit was filed on behalf of Mildred Duncan and Joanne Hanson making them the plaintiffs against the federal government in an effort to strike down the Defense of Marriage Act, a 1996 law passed by the U.S. Congress and signed by then President Bill Clinton, prohibiting the federal government from recognizing marriages of same-sex couples. Ever since the day Mildred Duncan and Joanne Hanson first filed their 2008 lawsuit in federal court, five states in all, plus the District of Columbia, had passed laws allowing same-sex marriages to be performed. Since that time, scores of new lawsuits, involving plaintiffs from New Hampshire, Massachusetts, Connecticut, Iowa, and Vermont have geographically expanded the legal attack on the Defense of Marriage Act. Even Rashid Harris, who up until now had been quiet on the issue, recently released an official White House statement in support of Millie and Joanne's legal challenge saying the Defense of Marriage Act is blatantly discriminatory and that he, as President of the United States, is now calling for its immediate repeal."

By now, both Millie and Joanne had locked arms and began slowly prancing in a circle, square-dance fashion, around their small living room.

"I must also mention," Meadows continued, carefully following her scripted report, "both these women had been previously married before to men, and have grown children. The fact that the law values one of their marriage relationships over the other is a source of consternation. If Millie and Joanne were married heterosexuals, we wouldn't be talking today, because they would have the benefits."

The savvy reporter paused momentarily, signaling her news crew with a nod to play a prepared video clip taken three years earlier on the steps of the Hartford, Connecticut Federal Courthouse, the same day Millie and Joanne first filed their case.

"Millie," Joanne jumped up and declared, "They're playing that old tape made the day we first filed our lawsuit!"

Playing to the sympathy of their liberal audience, MSNBC played the three-year old clip showing a local news reporter stopping the two elderly lesbians as they walked down the courthouse steps. With a large microphone placed directly in front of Joanne Hanson's face, the reporters asked, "Ms. Hanson, what do you and Ms. Duncan plan to accomplish by filing a lawsuit against the federal government?"

"Millie and I would like our federal government to recognize our marriage as real as everybody else's."

The timing of the small video clip was perfect. With seconds rapidly ticking away toward the noon hour, the U.S. Supreme Court was scheduled to announce its decision on one of the most contentious and controversial cases since the January 22, 1973, the landmark Roe vs. Wade decision that made the practice of supervised medical abortions legal nationwide for the first time in American history.

"Folks," a visibly anxious Rachel Meadows announced, "in mere minutes, the final opinion by the U.S. Supreme Court case, Hanson and Duncan vs. the Federal Government, should be publicly announced. MSNBC will let you know the outcome of that monumental decision the very moment we receive confirmation, but before we do, allow me a few minutes to go over the staggering obstacles that are involved in even getting a case, like Millie and Joanne's, heard by this high court."

All across America, liberals, conservatives, and millions of others, who still have yet to form an opinion on the matter of legalizing homosexual marriage, stopped whatever they were doing and turned on their televisions and radios to hear the Supreme Court's big announcement.

"Each year," Meadows continued, "the Supreme Court is asked to hear approximately five thousand cases. However, because of time and resource constraints, and because not all cases are of equal merit, the Court selects only a handful to formally review. When formal appeals are filed before the Supreme Court, legal briefs outlining the reasons behind the appeals are circulated among the Justices who sit on the Court. Justices then compile and circulate a "Discuss List" of cases that might warrant Supreme Court review. Finally, the Justices meet and vote on which cases to hear. The Court uses an informal "Rule of Four" in deciding whether or not to hear a case—only four of the nine Justices need to vote to hear a case. Through this process, the Court chooses 150 to 200 cases to hear each year.

"As they narrow the number of cases on the "Discuss List," the Justices use several standards to determine whether or not a case is "justifiable." First and foremost, the Court must decide if it has jurisdiction in a case. If it does not, it will almost certainly not hear the case. The Court has heard fewer than 200 original jurisdiction cases in its entire history. The Court will also generally refuse to rule on "political questions," cases that it believes are better addressed through the regular political process by other branches of government. Cases in which no real controversy or dispute exists will also be rejected by the Court. Similarly, the person or persons who bring cases before the Court must have "standing." They must be able to show that they have sustained "injury in fact," that they have been harmed in some real way.

"Once the Supreme Court has decided to hear a case, it orders lower courts that have handled the case to surrender all records and supporting documents related to it. As an appeals court, the Supreme Court does not convene new jury trials, but rather reviews the decisions of lower court judges and juries. As the Justices on the Court begin to weigh the merits of the cases that come before them, attorneys on both sides of the case present oral arguments in the Supreme Court chamber. These sessions are open to the public and are the most visible phase of the Court's decision-making process. Oral arguments, however, are rarely the deciding factor in the Court's decisions. Much more important are the legal briefs filed by each side, as well as numerous "friend of the court" briefs filed by interested parties who want the Court to consider particular aspects or ramifications of the case. Ultimately, a majority of the Court—five or more Justices— decides the outcome of the case, and a final opinion is written and announced to the public. When the Supreme Court announces its decisions, the outcome in a particular case is often of only secondary importance. Far more important are the implications of the Court's decision in that case for a host of other lower court cases and controversies. The extent of the applicability of the Court's decision in a particular case to other cases is usually spelled out in detail in the Court's opinion.

With less than a minute remaining before today's landmark Supreme Court ruling was to be announced, Rachel Meadows looked directly into the camera in front of her and made this closing remark: "A prominent attorney who had argued hundreds of cases before the Supreme Court once told me something I'll never forget. The Supreme Court decision is not final because it's right, it is right because it is final. The Court's position as the court of last appeal, and as the highest court in the land, means that its decisions are binding and unchangeable. Once the Court has ruled, its decisions have all the effect and permanency of law."

Rachel Meadows paused, her face blazing with raw emotion.

"Folks, my MSNBC supervisors have just contacted me. Only seconds ago, the Supreme Court of the United States has handed down the following ruling on Duncan and Hanson vs. the Federal Government...

Tuesday, July 14th, 2015
10:58 a.m.
Mall USA
50 East Broadway
Bloomington, Minnesota

Nobody took notice. Not even Mall USA's highly-trained security staff, recognized world-wide for their state-of-the-art surveillance technology, had the slightest clue that something so indescribably horrific was about to take place within the 4,200,000 square foot enclosure of America's largest mall. As the noon hour approached, this innovative mall, known throughout the country for revolutionizing the American shopping experience was, once again, literally packed to overflowing. Nowhere else in America could shoppers find top-named retail stores, restaurants, entertainment attractions, and amusement rides—complete with an indoor roller coaster—all under one roof. A virtual city within a city, Mall USA has also earned a national reputation as one of America's top rated tourist destinations, entertaining guests from all parts of the country. From musical acts, fashion shows, and staging grand premiere movie openings, Mall USA is now known as the Hollywood of the Midwest. Along with coverage in many national and local television broadcasts, the Mall has also become the place where fans can meet and greet their favorite celebrities.

Today was their day. Five years in the making, more than six months of meeting weekly at America's largest mall, they were more than ready to become the first Muslim martyrs to sacrifice their lives on American soil since the infamous day of September 11th, 2001. Over twenty members of a clandestine sleeper cell, an offshoot of the international terrorist group, Al Qaeda, were now evenly dispersed throughout America's largest mall, all awaiting their leader's cell phone signal to begin their attack. A sleeper cell is a dormant, on standby, group of individuals that were smuggled in, arrived legally or were possibly born in the country that is the point of attack. The members live among the general population and participate within the guidelines of that society, attempting to blend in and not draw any unwanted attention until the time when the cell is to carry out a terrorist attack. They smiled and waved at the passing families, never giving the slightest clue, not even to the passing security police, that concealed within the contents of their inconspicuous shopping bags and wrapped packages were weapons so sophisticated and deadly that their likes have never been seen before on American soil. Within eye contact of one another, each cell member began nodding to each other, signaling the next terrorist to begin counting down the seconds to the noon hour. At exactly 12 p.m. noon, within the walled confines of America's largest mall, twenty cell phones spontaneously began ringing. Instantaneously, before anyone had a chance to react, the deafening sounds from detonated bombs, whizzing bullets, shattering glass, collapsing walls, and blood-curdling hellish screams could be heard echoing from one end of this scorched out blood-filled chamber to the other. In less time than it takes to sit down and take a few sips of coffee, it was all over. Over five thousand innocent Americans of all ages, races, and ethnic backgrounds were murdered once again in another despicable act carried out by an organized team of Muslim extremists for the sole purpose of inflicting the diabolical fear of Allah into the hearts of the hated American infidels.

Tuesday, July 14th, 2015
10:58 a.m.
Memphis, Tennessee

Though long predicted, no one wanted to believe the fact that it could happen again in their lifetime. Not even Mattie Metzger and Angela Johnston, the two University of Memphis geologists assigned with the daily task of monitoring the site of America's most colossal earthquake, could foresee its reoccurrence, especially not today.

It happened nine days before Christmas on December 16, 1811. An earthquake of unimaginable proportions struck Memphis, Tennessee without warning. At exactly 2 a.m., a violent shaking and a roaring sound so deafening as to shatter eardrums abruptly awakened the terrified residents in Memphis. Rising mounds of fractured earth instantly swallowed up the entire countryside surrounding the town of 2,000 residents. Surrounding forests were flattened, islands disappeared, and the Mississippi River shifted its course by over three miles. Survivors reported that the ground they stood on actually rolled, rising and falling like ocean waves. Damage was reported as far away as Charleston, South Carolina, and Washington, D.C. with brick chimneys reportedly collapsing in Maine. So intense was the shaking that President James Madison was awakened from a deep sleep, thinking intruders were in the White House. It has been estimated that what is now known as the New Madrid Earthquake of 1811 affected more than 1 million square miles. Except for the 9.3 magnitude Good Friday Earthquake that struck Anchorage, Alaska in 1964, no other North American natural disaster compares to that legendary event.

Time has since erased most of the earthquake's visible scars, but the cause of this great natural disaster, a 150-mile-long subterranean line of weakness known as the New Madrid Fault, remains forever hidden beneath the tons of sediment deposited by the Mississippi River from America's heartland. Unlike the more elastic faults that underlie California and Japan, the ground above the New Madrid Fault is brittle. When it moves, there is no elasticity. The vibrations produced are so devastating and widespread that the ground has been known to actually liquefy, causing surface features such as buildings and bridges to sink as if in quicksand.

Within a few seconds of 11 a.m. Central Time, without the slightest hint of any previous warning signs from the vast array of sensitive seismic equipment scattered throughout the University of Memphis' Earthquake Research office, it happened. Staff seismologist, Angela Johnston, was sitting quietly at her desk when she took notice of a flashing red light at the bottom of her desktop computer screen, indicating a possible undetermined shift had just occurred somewhere along the 150 mile course of the New Madrid seismic fault.

"Mattie," Angela Johnston called out to her fellow colleague, Mattie Metzger, also a University of Memphis trained seismologist. "Could you do a quick check on the GPS sensors? I'm getting a flashing light that a shift has just occurred somewhere along the New Madrid."

"That's weird," Mattie commented as she looked up from the magazine she was reading. "I just checked all the seismographs a few minutes ago. There hasn't been even the slightest tremor recorded along the entire New Madrid all morning.

Even before Mattie Metzger had a chance to stand, she was literally lurched backward into her seat by a thrusting force of unimaginable proportions. All around the small University of Memphis office, used specifically to record, pinpoint, and predict earthquakes along the New Madrid Fault, expensive earthquake recording equipment—computers, seismographs or other sensitive electronic recording devices—instantly became airborne projectiles before crashing to the oscillating floor below.

"Angie, let's get the hell out of here!" screamed her frightened co-worker.

"Head for the window, Mattie!" Johnston quickly asserted, pointing her index finger in the direction of the crushed glassless opening that only a few moments prior, was a large double-paned window.

Without hesitation, both women were forced to painfully crawl across the buckling tiled floor now covered with bouncing slivers of skin-piercing glass as they made their way to their only source of possible escape. First to arrive at the shard-covered opening, Angela thought fast and picked a broken piece of wood that once framed the window. With the instinctive determination to survive, she pushed out the remaining razor-edged glass slivers before making her safe exit unto the grass-covered ground below. Once both women were safely outside, without giving thought to the currents of free-flowing blood streaming from the numerous punctured openings that riddled their knees and hands, they managed to dash as fast as they could toward a distant campus clearing far enough away from any danger from a collapsing building or a falling tree. Once they safely arrived on the grass-covered knoll, along with scores of other terrified University of Memphis students and faculty, Angela Johnston and Mattie Metzger looked up to witness one of the most incredible sights imaginable. What could only be described as a giant tsunami made up of a combination of land, buildings, and concrete was now coming right toward them out of the west-northwest. This indescribable monster literally lifted the surrounding landscape at least twenty feet into the air before depositing everything into a crushing heap of crumpled and twisted smoldering rubble. Up and down the meandering Mississippi River, as far as St. Louis, Missouri to the north and Vicksburg, Mississippi to the south, manmade riverfront structures such as bridges, highways, overpasses, pipelines and buildings vanished, swallowed up in an instant under the liquefied casing of the earth's tortured still-quivering surface. Only now, billowing plumes of blackened poisonous smoke were being carried by high altitude jet stream winds toward the myriad of American cities and towns to the north and east of this hellish site of unspeakable disaster.

Tuesday, July 14th, 2015
4:43 a.m.
The Graham Estate
15 miles North of Trinity Mills, Texas

"God, no! No!"

The piercing predawn cry instantly shattered the peaceful solitude that moments earlier prevailed throughout the darkened Graham estate.

"Honey, what is it?" Eliot Graham's startled wife cried as she attempted to reach over and turn on the adjacent nightstand lamp. "Eliot, tell me, what's wrong?"

Never in all their married years had Rosemary Graham seen her husband's usual calm, collected demeanor exhibit what was now visible on his sweat-covered face. As a terrified Eliot Graham sat up in bed, with streams of perspiration drenching the collar of the pajama top, the only word he was able to utter was his wife's nickname, "Rosie!"

"Eliot, take all the time you need to gather your thoughts, honey." Rosemary Graham calmly stated.

Taking his wife's wise advice, Graham slowly took in a few more deep, but evenly controlled, breaths before saying, "Rosie, you know me better than anyone else. You know that I have a tendency to joke around from time to time." He paused momentarily and looked into his wife's dark brown eyes. "Honey," he continued, "what I am about to tell you, I sincerely want to assure you, I am in no way joking."

Before Eliot Graham could say another word, a clearly shaken Sydni Graham entered through the bedroom door.

"Mommy, Daddy, what's wrong?" asked the trembling voice of their youngest child. "I was sound asleep and all of a sudden, I was awakened by a scream that sounded a lot like Daddy!"

"Sydni, it was nothing. Your Dad's all right. He was just having some sort of nightmare, that's all it was—a nightmare, right Eliot?"

Not wanting to place any fear in his youngest child's mind, Graham smiled calmly at his concerned daughter, who was still in the bedroom door, and said, "Go back to sleep, Syd. Your Mom's exactly right. I had a bad nightmare. Boy, was it ever a nightmare!"

"You guys are absolutely sure everything's all right?"

Sitting up in their large king-sized bed, each parent responded with a reassuring "Yes!"

Alone again, Rosemary Graham turned to face her husband and asked. "Okay, Eliot, now that's Sydni's gone back to her room, tell me all about your dream."

"Rosie, you know that when I am serious about something, I never mince words," Graham firmly stated.

"What is it, Eliot?" she asked with a voice of concern. "Tell me!"

"What I just had wasn't a dream, Rosie" Graham flatly stated. "It was a vision!"

"Eliot, how do you know for certain that it was a vision?"

"Rosie, you have no idea. It was so real!" Graham stated with a sigh in relief. He could now share his surreal experience with the only person in the entire world he knew would never doubt a single word. "I can actually give you the names, Rosie—names of real people who I have never met before."

"Really? What else?"

Staring into his wife's puzzled eyes, Eliot Graham, a man known to millions as a beacon of sound reasoning and bedrock stability, was about to step out of character and make one of the most outlandish proclamations of his life. "Rosie, I believe that God's about ready to pass severe judgment on America. This country is about to see disasters of unimaginable proportions!"

"Eliot, tell me! Why would God do that?"

"Because America has totally forsaken Him," Graham tearfully replied. "I believe it all goes back to 1963 when the Supreme Court ruled to take prayer out of public school. Then, ten years later, we legalized murder and called it abortion. The blood of the innocent now covers our entire country. I can't even fathom how many babies our country has murdered since that infamous day in January of 1973. But that wasn't what I saw in my vision that brought the wrath of God's judgment upon America!"

"What was it, Eliot?"

"God's judgment falls the moment America legally annuls his sacred institution of marriage between a man and a woman." Turning to his wife, Graham smiled once again. "Rosemary, we need to call all the children for a family meeting, right away! I have a long-awaited big announcement that needs to be said."

Even though their daughter was once again sound asleep down the hall, Rosemary and Eliot Graham were not alone in their bedroom. Two massive supernatural beings were imperceptibly standing at the foot of the Grahams' bed, intently listening to every single word spoken by the two married humans.

Turning toward his angelic counterpart, Yahriel said with a smile, "The prophetic vision you showed Graham accomplished phase one of your current assignment."

Returning with his own smile, a relieved Muriel, the archangel God charged with America's protection, replied, "I believe Eliot Graham fully understands the dire importance of his running for the office of President of the United States."

"Do you think Graham will change his mind?" queried Yahriel.

"Some humans might, but not this one," Muriel replied with a nod. "Eliot Graham is truly a man of his word."

"Muriel, you know as well as I do, with such a staunchly conservative Christian like Eliot Graham running for president, Satan's attacks on Graham will be ruthless. I suggest that now would be a good time to call on Kiel and his warriors to protect the entire Graham family from Satan's onslaught."

"Say no more," Muriel responded with a reassuring smile of confidence. "I've personally taken care of that little matter. From this day forward, the Graham family will have the best angelic protection afforded to any group of humans on planet earth."

Chapter Fourteen

"*For evil to flourish, all that is needed is for good people to do nothing.*"

~Edmund Burke

Thursday, July 16ᵗʰ, 2015
5:25 a.m. Israel Standard Time
Tel Hai, Israel

It wasn't supposed to happen, not in the natural, at least not until sunrise. A brilliant flash of golden light radiated outward and skyward in all directions, momentarily illuminating the darkened hilly landscape surrounding the ancient northern Galilee settlement of Tel Hai. With thousands of blazing golden swords held high, their voices combined in unison to shout out toward Heaven the Name of the God they were all created to serve, "Jehovah Sabaoth—Lord God of Hosts."

Removing his sword from its sheath, the highly esteemed Archangel looked out in humility at all the fearless angelic warriors who served under his command. Tal Hai was the final stop on his whirlwind cross-country tour. He had just spent the entire morning traveling the length of Israel's borders with Egypt, Jordan, Syria, and Lebanon, both encouraging and preparing his warriors for a possible battle with a formidable enemy.

"Some of you should remember vividly the heroic battle that was fought on this very spot not so long ago," Michael, the Commander

of the Heavenly Host, declared. With his brilliant golden sword held high over his head, he recounted the events of that fateful day. "Eight Zionist settlers fought valiantly and died here on March 2ⁿᵈ in the human year 1920. Fighting along side of the humans were also a dozen of our finest warriors."

The renowned Archangel, respected by his warriors for his insurmountable strength and valor, was also known for his passion to serve. Instilled within the being of this exalted servant was the freedom to demonstrate the same range of heartfelt emotions as his Creator.

"Unfortunately," Michael paused briefly to muster enough inward strength to continue, "my warriors found themselves vastly outnumbered and totally overwhelmed by the ferocity of the enemy attack. Four of my best warriors were lost on that day. A day after the battle, I stood right where I am standing now, vowing to myself, 'never again!'" The Archangel, with tears in his eyes, repeated the vow, 'Never Again!'

"Never again!" his warriors returned the same charge.

"Six months later," Michael continued, "a group of over twenty fellow Zionists returned to Tel Hai to bury their loved ones and to resettle the land given to them under the covenant. Once again, this small group of Zionist settlers was attacked from all sides by an overwhelming numbers of Arabs."

Michael paused once again, lowering his sword to chest height. "I was there on that day," he openly declared. "Once again, my warriors and I were outnumbered, but unlike the previous attack, we were prepared!"

Pressing his sword across his chest, the Commander of the Heavenly Hosts thundered a declaration to all the warriors standing before him, "I stand here now as a witness before my Lord and Creator to testify to the valor and determination on that battlefield. When humans and warriors stand together united, prepared to do battle and to hold fast to the promises found in God's Holy Covenant, then no powers on earth or in hell can stop them!"

"Never again!" the warriors again shouted in unison.

"Together, we won the battle that day!" Michael declared. "It marked the first time in over two thousand years that Abraham's covenant descendants living in their covenant land fought back from insurmountable odds and defeated their enemies!"

Turning to face the monument in back of him, Michael continued, "This stone lion has fought many battles alongside Abraham's descendants, each time outnumbered, and each time victorious! What is our charge?"

"Never again!" the warriors answered in unison.

"The lion not only represents the valor and courage demonstrated here so long ago. It is a monument dedicated to the true Lion of Judah, the Holy One, Our Lord and Creator who's Name is above all names. This is His covenant land. We will fight and defend Israel with all of our strength and all of our might!"

Raising his sword once again high into the air, Michael vowed one last charge to his warriors, "All the powers of hell will not prevail against us!"

"Never again! Never again! Amen!" thundered the combined voices from a legion of angelic warriors.

Thursday, July 16th, 2015
11:00 a.m. Israel Standard Time
Bint Jbeil
Southern Lebanon

They arrived from all over the Middle East. Many had traveled to be here today from as far away as the snowcapped Himalayas that line both Afghanistan's and Pakistan's eastern borders. Others left their assignments in the oil-rich desert nations of Iran, Saudi Arabia, and Egypt to the south. Still, thousands of others arrived this morning from as far north as Turkey's Black Sea shorelines. This show of demonic solidarity had not been seen in this tumultuous region since the Israel-Hezbollah War was fought here in 2006. Black-winged demons of all hierarchies, bizarre shapes and sizes lined both sides of a forty-kilometer route beginning at the Mediterranean coastal city of Beirut, Lebanon, and ending, literally a stone's thrown away from the contentious Israeli border. These grotesque apparitions rallied and cheered alongside tens of thousands of totally oblivious humans who proudly waved Iranian flags from village rooftops and roadside shoulders as a single solitary mortal passed by their location en route to an obscure human outpost in the middle of the sweltering hot Lebanese desert.

Within an hour's drive from the air-conditioned comforts of his five-star Beirut hotel room, Iran's controversial president, Hassan Rouhani, arrived at the final destination of his two-day stay in Lebanon—a visit the United States and the Israeli governments called intentionally provocative. The Iranian president's choice in using Bint Jbeil, a southern Lebanese border town as the backdrop for his carefully scripted speech, was by no means, an accident. This obscure desert village, barely two and a half miles (four kilometers) from the Israeli border, had been dubbed by locals, "the capital of resistance." During the Jewish state's 18-year occupation of southern Lebanon, it was the center for Hezbollah guerrilla action against Israel that ended in 2000. Six years later, during the 2006 war between Hezbollah and Israel, Bint Jbeil was literally turned to rubble. It has since been largely rebuilt, thanks in part to large infusions of cash generously donated by Iran. For this reason, and more, tens of thousands of grateful Lebanese supporters of all ages have left their homes and schools and traveled to this desert border town. From as far away as neighboring Syria, they have assembled here today to listen to their Iranian benefactor's highly touted speech vowing his nation's continued support to stand by Lebanon and Hezbollah against their nation's neighboring archenemy, the Jewish State of Israel.

As the Iran president's motorcade slowly traveled through the rebuilt streets of this southern Lebanese outpost, the outpouring from the massive supportive crowd touched his heart. Everywhere he looked, people were standing along the village roadsides and on nearby rooftops, holding up portraits of relatives and loved ones who died in the various wars against Israel. The five car motorcade came to a complete halt on a paved parking lot within walking distance of the Bint Jbeil soccer stadium. As he opened the limousine's rear door, Rouhani stepped outside to the deafening roar of his cheering Lebanese fans. No matter where he looked, in every direction, there were numerous billboards and signs bearing photos of his hand waving image and the Persian words "Khosh amadeed," meaning "welcome."

Today was the day, Hassan Rouhani, the former mayor of Tehran, and now, the elected President of the Republic of Iran, had long awaited. As the most powerful member of the semi-clandestine apolitical organization Hojjatieh, this soft-spoken son of a blacksmith believes he, alone, has been called by Allah to fulfill the prophetic role of an end-time Islamic John the Baptist. His divine mission—to provoke his Islamic followers to bring chaos to the world on a global scale in order to hasten the arrival of Islam's predicted messianic 12th Imam.

An entourage of a dozen or more bodyguards quickly ushered the Iranian president to the stadium's main gate, where he was greeted by another large banner reading, "Welcome Mr. President," in both Persian and Arabic. The Lebanese president, the prime minister, and the parliament speaker were all assembled to greet the Iranian president before he made his final ascent up a flight of steps leading to a raised stadium stage. After a brief introductory statement by Amel Hassad, Bint Jbeil's mayor, expressing his village's overwhelming gratitude toward the Iranian president's generosity, President Hassan Rouhani stepped up to the microphone.

Before saying a word, the Iranian president looked toward heaven and silently prayed, "Lord Allah, I stand here before you and your people as your humble servant, a willing vessel here to do your bidding. Now is the time to bring an end to your enemies, the godless infidel and the hated Jews."

With his claw-like hands buried deep within the Iranian president's torso, Allahzad, the demon Prince of Persia, began to speak through Hassan Rouhani the same kind of mesmerizing message he spoke through Adolf Hitler, his assigned human host less than a century before.

"The world will soon be witness to a new miracle from Allah. Palestine will be liberated!"

The speaker's premeditated introductory statement, televised to billions of Muslims around the world, sparked an immediate and thunderous response of approval from thousands of his flag-waving supporters standing throughout the stadium. As video cameras zoomed in on Rouhani's face, the crowds marveled as the Iranian president's calm demeanor transformed before their eyes to a commanding presence the likes of which they had never seen.

"There's no doubt that your enemies fear your unity," Rouhani told his supporters. "Unity is the symbol of endurance, steadfastness and victory."

As Allahzad inserted his clawed hands deeper into the human's small torso, the Iranian president's voice deepened, taking on a more pronounced tone.

"The world should know that the Zionists will soon perish," Hassan Rouhani, declared. "The last hour is about to come. We, the defenders of the faith, are called here today to hunt down every last Jew and kill him. Allah cries out to all of you these very words found in his blessed Koran, "O Muslims, O servants of God, if the Jews will hide behind stones, the stone will say, 'There is a Jew behind me; come and kill him.' Only in Muslim unity will Israel be wiped off the map!"

A foreboding smile appeared on Rouhani's face as he glared at his mesmerized audience. Allahzad also gloated at the expression of fear on the faces of the awestruck humans. Reaching down to the wooden stage floor below, Roudani picked up what appeared to be a medium-sized rock.

Holding the rock outward for all to see, he said with a smile, "Allah, himself has told me to perform this small demonstration in your presence today. Soon, the promised Mahdi will arise. Just as I have effortlessly picked up this rock from the floor below, the Mahdi will pluck up and remove every illegal Zionist Jew now squatting on Palestinian land. Shortly, the Mahdi will remove each one of these thieves and place the Israeli pigs in their new homeland, fifty kilometers out into the deep waters of the Mediterranean where they belong!"

In closing, the crafty Iranian president stepped away from the microphone just long enough to allow his boisterous followers time to vent their approval. With his rowdy cheering supporters looking on in a symbolic act equivalent to the messianic Mahdi tossing the Jewish nation of Israel into the Mediterranean Sea, Rouhani tossed the rock he had been holding in his right hand onto the green turf below.

"Death to the Jews!" the demon-controlled Iranian born mortal, shouted with his left fist held high in defiance of his enemies. "Praise be to Allah!"

"Praise be to Satan!" a thunderous, but totally imperceptible shout exploded, a response to mortal man's finite senses from Allahzad and tens of thousands of his agreeing demonic subordinates.

Thursday, July 14th, 2105
3:45 p.m. Israel Standard Time
Prime Minister's Office
3 Kaplan St., Jerusalem

Just moments ago, a highly-secured motorcade ushered off the American Secretary of State, Andrea Jacobs, to her next scheduled stop along her three-day visit to the Middle East, a meeting with the Palestinian President Abu Mazen at his West Bank headquarters in the city of Ramallah. Left standing outside the prime minister's office on Kaplan Street was a small contingency of Israeli government officials, including the Israeli Prime Minister, Yacov Ben Yizri, and his Minister of Defense, Ehud Levy.

"Is she finally gone?"

"You can open your eyes now, Yacov," Ehud Levy responded with a smile, "She's gone."

"I pray to Adoni that I never have to see that woman again," said the relieved Israeli prime minister.

"Your meeting was that bad?" Levy asked with a serious stare.

"Let's just say," Ben Yizri answered his friend's blunt question with his own raised eyebrow stare, "Andrea Jacobs has left us with a lot to talk about."

Today was a day that Ben Yizri had long prayed would never happen. What started as a cordial mid-morning luncheon with the American Secretary of State and the full Israeli Cabinet, ended less than ten minutes ago as a cataclysmic political nightmare. Not since assuming his nation's highest office for the second time in his long illustrious career as an Israeli politician, had Yacov Ben Yizri imagined that the once strong bonds that existed between his tiny Jewish State and its staunchest friend and ally, the United States of America, could ever be tested to this degree—at least not, until two hours ago. He had just completed a one-on-one, and, at times, verbally contentious meeting in his private upstairs office with America's Secretary of State. They had been discussing items with such strategic worldwide implications that no other human ears, outside his room, were privy to hear. Now, a nerve-rattled Ben Yizri knew he needed some time alone to process everything that had just transpired.

With the secretary's motorcade now long gone, those left standing outside the prime minister's office soon dispersed inside the prime minister's office to carry on the business of the day. Before returning to his own upstairs office, Yacov Ben Yizri looked into his friend's hazel eyes and made this request, "Ehud, will you do me the honor of calling a meeting of our seven senior ministers?"

Without hesitation, his faithful friend responded, "When and where, Yacov?"

"Have everyone convene in the cabinet room exactly one hour from now," the Prime Minister responded with a solemn smile.

"And if anyone asks me where they might find you in the meanwhile, Yacov?"

"Tell them I'll be alone in my office, praying."

Thursday, July 14th
4:47 p.m. Israel Standard Time
Prime Minister's Office
3 Kaplan St., Jerusalem

For the past minute or so, all eyes in the Israeli Cabinet Room were fixed on a wall clock hanging on the adjacent front wall of this large, but mostly empty room. Its hands were now showing nearly two minutes had passed by since their scheduled 4:45 p.m. meeting was called to convene. Never had these seven men known the Prime Minister to be counted late for any meeting, especially for one of such vital national importance. Seven men in all, known collectively as the "Forum of Seven" —four members of the conservative Likud party, one from the liberal Labor Party, and two from the ultraconservative Shas party—made up Prime Minister Yacov Ben Yizri's most trusted inner circle.

At exactly 4:47 p.m., Yacov Ben Yizri made his belated entrance into the Israeli Cabinet Room holding in his right hand what appeared to be a large copy of the Torah. As he walked over to claim his designated seat of honor at the head of the large oval-shaped conference table, those present stood and welcomed their leader with a rousing round of applause. The prime minister accepted his seven subordinates' warm welcome with a brief, but humorous apology.

"I want to thank each and every one of you for your gracious display of short-term memory loss," he responded with a smile. "You may all be seated."

Everyone enjoyed one last laugh before sitting down and discussing the serious matters of today's meeting.

"I'm not sure if Ehud told you what I have been doing for the past hour," a more somber-faced Ben Yizri admitted. "I've been locked in my office reading an old familiar biblical story that somewhat parallels what is going on right now in Israel."

With the full attention of his seven cabinet ministers, the Israeli prime minister opened the Torah to the Book of Numbers and began reading aloud a well-known Torah story that each man present in the room had heard many times over since they were little children.

"The story begins in Numbers, Chapter 13 when G-d tells Moses to send out twelve men, one from each of the twelve Israelite tribes, on a secret forty day fact-finding mission into the land of Canaan. Before leaving, Moses strictly instructs each of the Hebrew spies to do the following: *'See what the land is like. Find out whether the people living there are strong or weak, few or many. Do their towns have walls or are they unprotected? Is the land itself good or bad? Is the soil fertile or poor? Are there many trees? Enter the land boldly, and bring back samples of the crops you see.'* At the end of forty days all twelve Jewish spies returned from exploring the land and this is what they reported back to Moses and the people. *'We arrived in the land you sent us to see, and it is indeed a magnificent country—a land flowing with milk and honey. But the people living there are powerful, and their cities and towns are fortified and very large. We also saw the descendants of Anak who are living there! The Amalekites live in the Negev, and the Hittites, Jebusites, and Amorites live in the hill country. The Canaanites live along the coast of the Mediterranean Sea and along the Jordan Valley. We can't go up against them! They are stronger than we are! The land we explored will swallow up any who go to live there. All the people we saw were huge. We even saw giants, the descendants of Anak. We felt like grasshoppers next to them, and that's what we looked like to them!"*

Ben Yizri stopped momentarily to address the confused stares he was receiving from his fellow ministers.

"I know some of you are not religious by nature," he said with a reassuring smile, but if you will humor me for a moment longer, I promise, I will get to the point of this story."

With all heads present nodding in agreement, the Prime Minister continued reading:

"After hearing all of the negative reports, the people began weeping and crying aloud as they were telling Moses and Aaron. *'We wish we had died in Egypt, or even here in the wilderness! Why is the LORD taking us to this country only to have us die in battle? Our wives and our children will be carried off as slaves! Let's return to Egypt!'* But Joshua, the son of Nun, and Caleb, the son of Jephunneh, spoke: *'The land we passed through to spy out is an exceedingly good land. And if the LORD is pleased with us, he will bring us safely into that land and give it to us. It is a rich land flowing with milk and honey, and he will give it to us! Do not rebel against the LORD, and don't be afraid of the people of the land. They are only helpless prey to us! They have no protection, but the LORD is with us! Don't be afraid of them!'*

Before saying another word, the Israeli Prime Minister closed the Torah and looked directly into the eyes of each of his seven senior ministers.

"My friends," a somber-faced Yacov Ben Yizri began, "whether or not you believe the events that took place in that ancient story actually happened, I am presently standing here to tell you that we, the elected leaders of the present day Nation of Israel, are confronted with the same situation today."

"Yacov, you, of all people, understand how long of a day this has been," commented Vice Israeli Prime Minister, Silvan Shalom, with a smile. "I am hungry, as we all are. As I speak, my wife, Sarah, is at home in the kitchen preparing a delicious meal. Could you please cut to the chase, and explain how this child's Bible story has any relevance with your meeting today with the American Secretary of State, Andrea Jacobs?"

Smiling once again, Prime Minister Ben Yizri looked directly at his Vice Prime Minister and said, "I promise, Silvan, I won't keep any of you longer than I have to, but unfortunately, what I am about to say may spoil your appetite for dinner tonight.

"Yacov, you're beginning to scare me a little," said Eli Yishai, the Minister of Internal Affairs.

"Gentlemen, as Silvan so aptly puts it, I will cut right to the chase. Most of what I discussed in private with Andrea Jaocbs, we have gone over in this room many times before. The only thing different today was the size of America's bribe to get us to sell off our birthright."

"Tell us, Yacov," interjected Moshe Ya'alon, the Israeli Minister of Strategic Affairs, "what is America's new proposal?"

"In a nutshell," Ben Yizri replied, "for the price of twenty F 35 stealth aircraft valued at nearly three billion dollars, we must agree to freeze all construction presently going on inside the entire West Bank for a period of six months. Jacobs also presented me with a long list of American favors the Harris Administration is willing to agree to in exchange for this extension of the building freeze."

"What types of favors are the Americans offering us?"

"Well, for one, there's an offer by the Harris Administration to increase our annual three billion dollar security aid package," the Prime Minister replied. "Jacobs also presented me additional U.S. commitments, including guarantees to prevent the smuggling of weapons and missiles into a Palestinian state, a lengthy period of interim security arrangements in the Jordan Valley, and a comprehensive regional defense pact for protection from Iran to follow the establishment of a Palestinian State on the West Bank of the Jordan."

"What about a commitment from Rashid Harris to veto any unilateral resolution presented before the UN Security Council calling for the immediate establishment of a Palestinian State?" Deputy Prime Minister, Meshulam Nahari, asked.

"That happened to be my very first question," nodded the Prime Minister. "Andrea Jacobs explicitly stated that Rashid Harris's offer includes a verbal agreement to veto any anti-Israel UN Security Council resolution through the end of his term next year."

"I would like to get that in writing!" Israeli Minister of Strategic Affairs, Moshe Ya'alon, declared.

"I'm afraid to ask what the American Secretary of State is asking Israel to do in return for this more than generous offer?" Deputy Prime Minister, Meshulam Nahari, commented.

"Our heads on a plate!" Israeli Prime Minister exclaimed with a poignant stare. "In exchange for Israel's acceptance of all of these U.S. security agreements, including the United States granting Israel full military support and protection from any future Iranian attack, beyond the six month building freeze, Israel must also agree to a one-year goal of working out the details on all the core issues dividing them and the Palestinians—final borders, Jerusalem, water rights and the status of the Palestinian refugees."

"Yacov, in hypothetical terms only, if we did agree to a Palestinian State, was there any mention of leasing the Jordan Valley from the PA?" Avigdor Lieberman, Minister of Internal Affairs, questioned.

"Good question, Avigdor!" responded the Prime Minister. "The answer is 'yes', but only in chunks of seven year lease agreements."

"What do you mean by 'chunks'?" Lieberman asked out of curiosity.

"According to the American proposal, once the entire Jordanian Valley is incorporated within the borders of a Palestinian State, any Israeli enclave remaining inside the Palestinian borders must agree to relinquish all property rights to that land and be willing to sign a renewable lease in order to occupy their present homes."

"And how long will that lease be?"

"That number hasn't been determined."

Turning next to his personal confidant and Minister of Defense, Ben Yizri, Yacov asked, "Ehud, you've been silent this entire time. What do you think about all this?"

"I don't have to tell anyone sitting here that our people are desperate for peace. As the Israeli Minister of Defense, the question in my mind is, 'at what expense?' The Jordan Valley encompasses a massive swath of territory. Our own Israeli military analysts have long agreed that our country is indefensible without the valley."

The Jordan Valley, being discussed, runs from Lake Tiberias in the north, to the northern Dead Sea in the south. It continues another 96 miles south of the Dead Sea to Aqaba along the Jordanian border. The Jordan Valley forms the border between Israel and Jordan in the north, and the eastern strip of the strategic West Bank in the south.

"Yacov," interjected Moshe Ya'alon, "You have stated on multiple occasions that the Jordan Valley is so vital to Israel's security that Israel must control it in the future. This past February, I remember that you stood in front of the entire Knesset and said that Israel could never agree to withdraw from the Jordan Valley under any peace agreement signed with the Palestinians. You also told Israel's Foreign Affairs and Defense Committee that the Jordan Valley's strategic importance along the eastern border of the West Bank made it impossible for Israel to withdraw. Are you changing your stance on the Jordan Valley now?"

"No, never!" Ben Yizri flatly declared. "As the Israeli Prime Minister, I stand by my word. I will never relinquish complete control over the Jordan Valley, no matter how big a military bribe the Americans offer us."

"What about Iran?" the Minister of Intelligence and Atomic Energy, Danny Meridor, questioned.

"Iran," Ben Yizri pondered out loud. Now was his chance to tie in the ancient Biblical account recorded in the Book of Numbers with the challenging decision he, alone, had to make concerning Israel's security and future.

"Before I answer Danny's question, allow me to take a moment or two longer to return to our biblical story concerning the twelve Israelites Moses sent out to spy the land. If you recall, out of the twelve men sent to spy out the land of Canaan, ten came back with negative reports saying the odds were virtually impossible for the twelve Israelite tribes to conquer such an occupied, fortified land as Canaan. Only two men, Joshua and Caleb, differed in their opinions."

Pausing once again, Ben Yizri opened his Torah to the Book of Numbers and read aloud the same biblical passage he had read earlier:

The land we passed through to spy out is an exceedingly good land. And if Adoni (Lord) is pleased with us, he will bring us safely into that land and give it to us. It is a rich land flowing with milk and honey, and He will give it to us! Do not rebel against Adoni, and don't be afraid of the people of the land. They are only helpless prey to us! They have no protection, but Adoni is with us! Don't be afraid of them!'

Closing the Torah for the final time, Ben Yizri stared intently into the eyes of each of his seven ministers and said, "Whether or not you believe these ancient accounts are fact or fabled fiction is completely irrelevant to me. What is important here is the fact that shortly, all the world's media outlets will be reporting the details of my meeting with the American Secretary of State. Once everyone out there is fully informed about the 'generous offer' made to us by the United States, Israel will receive relentless pressure from every conceivable direction to accept America's proposal, or face, once again, the 'world's wrath.' The pressure to submit to America's demands will be even greater in our own Knesset where my liberal political enemies have been waiting for such a moment to declare that I never wanted peace with the Palestinians; that I have only been posturing for peace all along."

Yacov Ben Yizri paused momentarily to take a sip from a glass of water placed within arm's reach on the table before him.

"Whether you want to accept this or not," he continued, "the decisions we are facing today are exactly what faced Israel thousands of years ago. The vast majority of voices will be soon shouting at us from the rooftops, "Accept the American offer!" Sign away our Biblical birthrights for the promises of a man desperate to leave some sort of legacy for himself that he has yet to accomplish on his own."

"Yocav, stop for a second! You just lost me," Danny Meridor said. "Who is that person you are talking about?"

"None other than Rashid Jabbar Harris," Ben Yizri declared. "With over one year left in his term as President of the United States of America, Rashid Jabbar Harris has accomplished nothing on his domestic agenda. His administration squandered away almost a trillion-dollars in stimulus money without making a dent in America's high unemployment rate. His Harris-care medical relief program has ended up a huge financial disaster. He has been unable to reach any form of a cap-and-trade agreement. America's financial deficit, both domestic and foreign, is now three times higher than it was when Harris took office three years ago. His governing ineptitude was a key factor in his fellow Democrats losing their solid majority holding in the U.S. Congress."

"Again, I'm not exactly sure where you're going with this, "the Minister of Intelligence and Atomic Energy, commented. "I asked you about Iran, not President Harris."

"Follow along with my argument, Danny." Ben Yizri emphatically stated. "You'll see in a moment that Iran is exactly where I am going."

Danny Meridor conceded to the Prime Minister's request with an affirming nod, allowing Ben Yizri to finish his argument.

"The only frontier left for Harris to accomplish his political legacy is foreign policy. That leaves the Arab-Israel conflict as the most likely place for Harris to make his mark in the international sphere. Consider the fact that President Harris has been on record stating that the historic justice in this conflict resides not with Israel, but with the Palestinian people. As a probable one-term president, he really sees this as his big chance to make another historical mark for himself. And what is the one most obvious candidate left for his foreign attention other than the Arab-Israel conflict?" asked Ben Yizri.

"Iran," Danny Meridor answered with an affirming nod.

"Nothing will determine history's verdict on the Harris presidency as to whether or not Iran achieves nuclear weapon capacity," Ben Yizri continued. "Yet there are few indications that President Harris would ever exercise the military option to prevent that outcome. He has never fully articulated to the American people how dangerous a nuclear Iran would be for America and Europe—not just Israel. It is far from clear that he is convinced that some form of Cold War-type nuclear containment is not possible with Iran. Secretary of State Jacobs has spoken of the United States spreading its nuclear umbrella over its allies, as if the United States were assuming the inevitability of a nuclear-armed Iran. The Harris administration was slow in putting any sanctions on the regime in place, and failed to seize upon the widespread citizen unrest after the stolen Iranian elections in 2009 to increase pressure on the regime."

Ehud Levy once again interrupted his friend by asking Ben Yizri this crucial question. "Yacov, what exactly are you suggesting we do, unilaterally bomb Iran without American support? You know better than anyone in this room, without America's support, the Saudis will never agree to allow a single Israeli jet to fly over their airspace."

Instinctively, Yacov Ben Yizri knew now was the critical time to sell his plan to his seven colleagues, or lose their support entirely. Standing once again, he appealed to them.

"Everyone, please just listen to me for two more minutes!" he passionately requested. "Just for a moment, I want each of us to imagine we are sitting here before Moses. We are called to present Moses a logical argument, using only the details presented here today as the backdrop for our decision."

With everyone nodding his head in agreement, Ben Yizri continued. "The first situation appears to be impossibly hopeless. We, Israelis, are few in number and our Arab enemies are many. We are completely surrounded on every side with no hope of possible escape. We are given no other choice but to forfeit our covenant land back into the hands of our enemies as we did with the Gaza Strip in August of 2005.

"The second situation appears on the surface to be equally as hopeless, but we are determined to stand united on the time-tested argument stated from the lips of brave Caleb, *"Don't be afraid of our enemies and do not rebel against ADONI. Don't be afraid of the people of the land. They are only helpless prey to us! They have no protection, but ADONI is with us!"*

Totally unaware of his presence, Ramiel, Yacov Ben Yitzri assigned angelic guardian, blew a puff of his divine breath directly into the prime minister's nostrils, literally flooding the human's entire body with a sensation of total peace, strength, and mental acuity like he had never experienced before.

Without explanation, Yacov Ben Yizri suddenly sensed a surge of both mental and physical energy. "What I propose we do is rather quite simple," asserted the energized Israeli Prime Minister. "As long as we get everything America has promised us in writing, I see nothing wrong with going along with Andrea Jacob's proposal and accept a building freeze for six months. We'll sit down with the Palestinians once again and discuss everything we have already discussed a thousand times over.

In the meanwhile, we will set a date to have two of our newly acquired stealth bombers pay a visit on Iran's Natanz Nuclear Power Plant."

While Ramiel maintained his assigned position, standing no more then an angelic arm's length away from his assigned human, Yacov Ben Yitri, two other tall angelic beings stood at the far end of the room carefully observing and listening to every word that was being said. "Job well done, Ramiel!" Muriel commented with an approving smile and thumbs up, giving a touch of personal angelic recognition to the ministering angel assigned to guard and protect the Israeli Prime Minister. Muriel also gave his nodding approval in the direction of the angel standing to his right.

"Time is growing short, Muriel, my good friend," acknowledged Michael, God's appointed Captain of His Heavenly Host. "We will soon be entering into what God's Word calls in the Book of Revelation, 'The Days of Woe!'"

Chapter Fifteen

"Give no regard to mediums and familiar spirits; do not seek after them, to be defiled by them: I am the LORD your God."

~Leviticus 19:31

Monday, July 20ᵗʰ, 2015
7:15 a.m. EST
Berry Campaign Headquarters
317 State Street, Albany, N.Y.

She had arrived long before anyone else at the Robert Berry campaign headquarters, located in the heart of downtown Albany's business district, but Sheila Brewster was far from being alone. As she busily scurried about the large conference room setting up for this morning's scheduled 10 a.m. brunch, little did she realize that she was being carefully watched from the back of the room.

The day after returning home from a whirlwind six-day, four-state campaign tour, Sheila Brewster, Robert Berry's perky public relations director, stopped momentarily, smiling broadly at her reflection in the conference room's large metallic coffeepot.

Brewster, you did it! She proudly thought to herself, at the same time admiring her revealing chesty form, magnified from the pot's curved reflective surface. *"It took some doing, but honey, you have finally arrived."*

Three demonic beings, all clustered together in front of the conference room's window facing State Street, nodded in agreement with the unsuspecting human's thoughts.

"I commend you, Malzar," the tallest of the trio, affirmed, "job well done!"

The smallest of the three apparitions in the room stared upward in awe, thoroughly shocked by the complimentary words spoken by his towering commander.

"Thank you, Destroyer," the lizard-skinned imp with a prideful grin responded. "For the past thirty-two years now, I followed every single detail of your instructions. I believe she is now ready."

"Excellent! That is why I selected you, Malzar, above all of my familiar spirits for this very important mission," Amducious followed with a sneer. "Your past record of preparing your assigned human females for a lust-filled lifestyle of sexual addiction is impeccable."

"There's nothing to it!" Malzar immodestly declared. "A little bit of fondling here and there, especially by a close relative when they are young and impressionable, always seems to work."

"You're being far too modest, Malzar." Amducious sneered, looking down at the gloating lizard-faced chimera. "Without your being aware of it, I've been watching you carefully over the eons. You've been a true mentor to multitudes, instructing my demons of sexual perversion on the fine art of using trusted relatives such as brothers, stepfathers, fathers and even grandfathers into sexually molesting their assigned female and male children. Thanks to your resourcefulness, Malzar, one out of every six adult American females, including many who call themselves Christians, conceal a hidden sexual time bomb that will eventually destroy, not only their lives, but as in the case of your present assignment, Sheila Brewster, as well as everyone who comes in contact with her."

Amducious turned his attention next to the winged apparition standing to his right on two sets of clawed lion paws.

"Griffin, tell me what I want to hear," the massive arch demon sneered.

"Of course, Destroyer," acknowledged the feathery-winged, lion-torso griffin, bowing its eagle-shaped head low in submission to its commander. *"Working through my human host, Griffin Gunson, I've accomplished all of my assigned tasks, including, having Elizabeth Berry stricken with a demon of infirmity."*

"How did you manage that, Griffin?" Amducious asked out of curiosity.

"That part was really quite easy, Destroyer," the griffin answered, raising its curved beaked head high in a display of pride. *"While her husband, Robert Berry, spoke in front of a human assemblage at his final campaign stop in Austin, Texas, I had Griffin Gunson seat Elizabeth Berry beside a Texas senator's wife who had been stricken earlier in the day with a potent little demon who specializes in attacking a human's upper respiratory tract. Humans simply call this highly contagious spirit of infirmity, the common cold."*

"I assume then that Elizabeth Berry will not be joining her husband at this morning's celebration."

"Your assumption is correct, Destroyer," replied the griffin with a nod. *"Mrs. Berry is presently at home suffering uncomfortably in bed from the ill effects of a sore throat and a sinus infection she picked up somewhere on this past week's campaign trail."*

"And when should we expect the governor to arrive?" the sneering arch demon inquired.

"I expect the governor to be arriving here any moment now, Destroyer," the griffin answered with another nod of his feathery head. *"Thanks to Malzar's assistance, he arranged to have Shelia Brewster drive herself into work this morning, while I had Griffin Gunson pick the Governor up at his Schenectady home and drive him the fifteen mile distance into Albany. Any moment now, Gunson's car will be stopping outside of this window, dropping off Governor Berry right here, at our door step."*

"How will you be keeping Gunson occupied in the meanwhile?" Amducious asked.

"Gunson has a very busy morning ahead of him. He has been assigned the task of securing all of the food items needed for this morning's brunch. I expect him back here no sooner than 9 a.m."

Sneering, Amducious looked down at the griffin and asked one final question.

"And what happens if an employee or campaign volunteer arrives here unexpectedly before 9 a.m.?"

"I can assure you, Destroyer, I've also taken care of that small matter," replied the griffin. "I've instructed two of my local associates, Pajzar and Nozad, to post two street derelicts on the sidewalk just outside the entrance to this building. If a human makes an attempt to enter the campaign headquarters before 8:30 a.m., these demons of alcoholism will have their drunken human hosts physically escort the unwanted intruders immediately away from the building."

"I'm truly impressed by your diligence to detail, Griffin," acknowledged the arch demon.

"The Governor has arrived!" Malzar gleefully declared, his piercing yellow eyes staring down at the busy street directly below the conference room window. Malzar's eyes were soon joined by two other pair of gloating yellow orbs, each set focused on a sleek jet-black BMW sports car parked at the street side curb, just three stories below where all three demons stood.

A sudden noise coming from somewhere outside the conference room walls caught Sheila Brewster's immediate attention. Startled, she looked away from her reflected coffeepot image in the direction of the room just beyond the opened conference room door. "Griffin, is that you?" she cautiously asked.

"Try again?" responded another very familiar voice from somewhere in close proximity. Before she could speak his name, the unannounced person was now standing under the threshold of the conference room door.

"Woo! Bob," a relieved Brewster exclaimed, "you really did startle me!"

"Sheila, I am so sorry! That was so inconsiderate of me," the former New York Governor apologized. "I should have announced my presence in the intercom as soon as I unlocked the office's main door."

"That's alright, Bob," a much calmer Sheila Brewster responded, now noticing the Governor's eyes securely fixed on her bulging midriff.

"Bob, wait a minute, where's Grif?" she questioned with a playful smile.

Before answering, Berry displayed a mischievous grin of his own.

"Griffin Gunson is out on a very important mission," Berry replied with a wink. "I sent him shopping for a whole list of food items and other goodies needed for this morning's celebration, and best of all, I don't expect him back here until sometime after 9 a.m."

"Does that mean you and I are all alone here in this great big office all by ourselves?"

"That's right." Berry replied with an affirming nod. "It's just you and me, Brewster, and that big fat spider on the wall in back of you."

"Ooh!" Brewster screamed as she propelled herself forward into Berry's waiting opened arms.

With their faces now only inches apart, Robert Berry whispered in her ear, "I have a small confession to make. There was no spider on the wall in back of you."

"Robert Berry, you're a very naughty boy!" Brewster said in girlish tone of voice. "You just said that to get me into your arms."

"Whatever works," Berry smugly commented, grinning from ear-to-ear. He proceeded to kiss Brewster on her lips before making this provocative comment. "We have a little less than an hour before people start arriving."

"What about your wife?"

"Poor Liz," Berry responded with an impassioned stare. "Unfortunately, she won't be able to make it here today. My dear wife woke up early this morning with a scratchy throat and a very stuffy head."

"Then, time is a wasting," Brewster declared while pressing her large protruding chest over closer against Berry. "Where should we go?"

"My office," smiled a highly aroused Berry. "I'll pull the shades and lock the door."

"You lead the way, big boy," Sheila Brewster said with a seductive smile. "I'll join you in just minute. I first need to pay a short visit to the little girl's room."

Sheila Brewster released her firm grip from around Berry's waistline, leaving her highly aroused boss standing in the conference room all by himself.

As the perfectly formed female made her exit from the room, Berry remained at the conference door, his thoughts consumed by lustful passion and arrogant pride.

It doesn't get any better than this! In every poll, I'm over twenty points ahead of both Harris and Devoe, and no one else comes close. Except for some liberal Democrats, mostly everyone in America loves me; and hot chicks, like Brewster, who will do anything I ask of them, surround me wherever I go.

"Pride before the fall," Amudicious stated, directing his scowled stare at the boastful human standing on the other side of the room. "Of all the Bible verses, I truly believe I hate that one the most, but in this situation, it works perfectly."

With a click of his clawed fingers, Amducious utilized a small vestige reserved from his former angelic past to momentarily stop natural time just long enough to walk the short distance across the conference room, stopping within inches of Berry's motionless form. Bending low, the arch demon briefly entertained himself by blowing yellowish puffs of his putrid sulfur-laden breath directly into the human's nostrils.

"Robert Berry, you better prepare yourself for a great big fall," the sneering demonic prince declared. *"Very soon, those magnificent polling numbers you constantly brag about and all those beautiful hot chicks will become a very distant memory."*

Clicking his clawed fingers together once again, natural time returned in an instant to the Robert Berry's campaign headquarters.

"Pew! Berry declared, clenching his nostrils tightly between his right thumb and index finger. *"Where the hell did that smell come from! It stinks worse than burnt sh-t!"*

Nauseated by the overpowering foreign stench that was permeating the air throughout the entire conference room, Berry quickly exited the room in the direction of the same bathroom presently occupied by Sheila Brewster. In his wake, the plaster walls throughout the entire three-story State Street building noticeably vibrated from the imperceptive laughter now coming from the third floor conference room.

Monday, July 20th 2015
11:07 a.m. Eastern Time
Berry Campaign Headquarters
317 State Street, Albany, N.Y.

For the past hour or so, over two dozen of Robert Berry's paid and volunteer campaign staffers had gathered at their downtown Albany's headquarters to celebrate, with food and drink, the former New York governor's phenomenal rise to the pinnacle of political stardom. According to the latest national polling tallies, their boss's present lead ahead of the upcoming presidential primaries eclipsed all other rivals, be they Republican, Democrat, or Independent. Now, standing at the far end of the large conference room holding a glass filled with bubbling champagne high above his head, Robert Berry attempted to present a toast in a noise-filled room where partying was the order of the day.

"Shush, everybody," Berry signaled, pressing his left index finger against his mouth.

Standing directly in front of the threshold of the conference room door, he continued, "You've all heard it said, 'It ain't over until the fat lady sings.'

"Well, excuse me if I sound a little presumptuous at the moment, especially with the presidential primaries still over six months away, but thanks to all of your tireless efforts over these past six months. I think that now I'm beginning to hear someone singing that familiar tune."

Stepping aside from the opened door, Berry allowed two heavyset, bare-chested male staffers to enter the room. Everyone present pointed and laughed hysterically at their strange attire. Besides being bare-chested, these burly men were dressed identically, from head to toe, in Uncle Sam costumes, complete with white beards, patriotic red, white and blue top hats, bow ties and matching red, white and blue striped pants and opened vests.

On cue, raising their arms as if they were about to conduct an orchestra, the two men began singing, "Berry, Berry, Berry—Berry's going to win. Come next November, it's a clinch that he'll be in. President of the United States, nothing else will do! This dream will be a reality, and it is all because of you! Hey!"

For the next few minutes, everyone present joined in singing the now familiar lines: "Berry, Berry, Berry—Berry's going to win!" Once the final crescendo was sung, Robert Berry presented his long awaited toast.

"Thank you!" he said, once again raising his champagne glass high above his head, "From the bottom of my heart, I personally thank each and every one of you."

With everyone present holding their individual champagne filled glasses in front of them, Berry spoke: "I present this toast to you who are standing with me. You share my vision of an America, economically and militarily strong once again, of an America, free from the socialist restraints that are presently crippling its progress, stifling job growth and draining all of its future resources, an American nation, whose future is securely anchored and sustained by the very words spoken over two hundred years ago by our nation's third president, Thomas Jefferson: *"America will only experience future happiness if Americans can prevent their government from wasting the labors of the people under the pretense of taking care of them."*

Extending his champagne glass to the people standing before him, Robert Berry declared, "To America's future!"

"To America's future!" *thirty voices responded in unison.*

"Humans never cease to amaze me," Amducious declared, shaking his head back and forth in disbelief as to the gullibility of humankind. "These weak-minded mortals are so easily deceived into trusting all of their future hopes and dreams on the carefully crafted words of such a fallible impostor of a human as Robert Berry."

With his clawed hands buried deep within Berry's upper torso, Amducious stared down into the yellow eyes of his demonic subordinate standing to his left and said with a sneer, "Malzar, I believe it's now time."

Nothing else needed to be said. The lizard-shaped chimera knew exactly what he had to do. By simply clicking his spindly black fingers together, Malzar initiated the distinct muffled sound from a concealed cell phone's ring tone that captured every human's attention.

"Oh my God!" Sheila Brewster exclaimed. "I could have sworn I turned off my cell phone over an hour ago." Embarrassed, Brewster reached into her small shoulder strapped purse and removed the still ringing object. Looking down at its digital display, she smiled. "It's only my mom!" she said in relief. "I'll be back in a moment."

Before exiting the room, Brewster winked in the direction of the man standing at the door.

"I'll be right back, Mr. Berry, sir," she teasingly commented, wiggling her bottom back and forth in an enticing feminine fashion as she passed by her smiling boss.

No one, not even Brewster's boyfriend, Griffin Gunson, took notice of the flirtatious actions taking place in the front of the room. Gone for only a short time, Sheila Brewster quickly returned to the conference room door expressing a grave look of concern. Breezing by Berry, she immediately located her boyfriend, Griffin Gunson, standing alone by the food table with a bottle of beer in his hand. Pulling him aside, Brewster whispered something into Gunson's ear. Gunson wasted no time contemplating her message. In his usual cool, collective manner, he casually approached Berry, quietly passing along everything he had just been told. Smiling cordially as to not attract anyone's attention, one by one, the trio of Berry, Brewster, and Gunson, quietly exited the room in a nonchalant manner.

At first, only a few Berry staffers took notice that their boss was missing from their midst. But as time went on, others became concerned when Berry had not returned to the conference room. It didn't take long before the concerned staffers discovered the whereabouts of the missing trio. All three were found seated beside one another in a tight semicircle at a small desk in the far corner of the first floor's hospitality room—their eyes fixed on a small desktop computer monitor displaying a streaming video televised live from Trinity Mills, Texas.

Monday, July 20th, 2105
10:24 a.m. Central Time
The Graham Estate
Along the southern banks of Lake Lewisville
15 miles North of Trinity Mills, Texas

It was hard to keep it a secret, especially after breaking the exciting news to over twenty of his closest family members at an emergency family meeting held over three days ago at the Graham's family's Texas estate. But soon, possibly within minutes, the entire world would hear the same electrifying news, that up until now, only a select few of Eliot Graham's closest confidants had heard from his own lips.

Never in his entire life was Eliot Graham so nervous. The man known by millions of his faithful radio listeners as the conservative voice of America was about to take a quantum leap forward into an area that he had sworn to himself he would never, ever permit himself to go.

With a spectacular view of Lake Lewisville as a backdrop, Eliot Graham momentarily stepped away from all the surrounding confusion. With the muffled clamor from television news crews readying their cameras, invited political dignitaries mixing and mingling, and excited family members running to and fro only a short distance away, Eliot Graham knelt down in the solitude of his backyard gazebo, humbly bowing his head and praying these exact words: "Lord, You alone know my deepest inner thoughts. You know how much I dread doing what I am about to do. Except for my wife, Rosemary, You, Lord, know me better than anyone. You know how much I loathe involving myself in the current political arena, but more importantly, You also know I love my country. Lord, it breaks my heart to sit back and do nothing while America's being ravaged from what I believe to be Satanic forces out to destroy her. Whatever happens from this day on, I surrender it all to you, Lord. Not my will, but Your will be done in my life. As the Apostle Paul so aptly expressed in Romans 12:1, I make myself a living sacrifice. I ask You now to endow me with Your divine wisdom and insight to meet the multitude of unforeseen challenges that lie ahead along this uncertain path. I need Your strength to never waiver in my convictions in spite of all the compromising voices shouting otherwise. To You alone be the glory, Lord. I ask this all in the name of my Lord and Savior, Jesus Christ. Amen."

"Dad, it's time."

Eliot Graham opened his eyes to the welcoming sight of his oldest son, Eliot, Jr., who extended a supporting hand.

"I'm ready," the senior Graham sighed, firmly gripping his son's hand as he stood.

As he and his dad were facing each other, eye to eye, Graham Jr. nervously shook his head back and forth as he made this confession, "Dad, I have to admit something to you."

"Go ahead, Son," Graham smiled. "We've never held anything back from one another.

"I can't believe you're actually doing this!"

"Ditto!" the elder Graham confessed with a chuckle. With that said, the father and son duo left the confines of the backyard gazebo and laughed all the way back to the estate's front lawn, where hundreds were now gathered to hear Eliot Graham announce to the world a decision that could rock the political landscape of America for many years to come.

Monday, July 20th, 2015
11:30 a.m. Eastern Time
Berry Campaign Headquarters
317 State Street, Albany, N.Y.

Not everyone could join the boss, Robert Berry, in viewing Eliot Graham's soon-to-be-made big announcement. For the dozen or so Berry staffers who couldn't squeeze into the already cramped first floor reception room, they were forced to resort to using a variety of other available media devices such as digital cell phones, iPods, laptops, and other desktop computers scattered in private offices throughout the three-story Robert Berry campaign headquarters. For the dozen or so fortunate Berry staffers who managed to find a reasonably comfortable position, either standing or sitting, within the small confines of this modestly decorated room used solely as a waiting lounge for those with scheduled appointments to meet with Governor Berry, their diligence was about to pay off. A very familiar conservative face soon appeared on the computer monitor's twenty-six inch digital screen.

"Look, everyone, it's Keenan Wiggins!"

"Shush, everybody! Let's listen. Keenan's about ready to speak."

Monday, July 20th, 2015
10:30 a.m. Central Time
The Graham Estate
Along the southern banks of Lake Lewisville
15 miles North of Trinity Mills, Texas

"If someone would have told me this a couple of months ago, I wouldn't have believed it was possible," admitted the popular Fox News reporter, Keenan Wiggins. "But in the crazy world of presidential politics, this proves once again that anything is possible."

Keenan Wiggins momentarily paused, intercepting a message just sent to him via his Bluetooth headset. "Ladies and gentlemen, I just received word from my news director that Eliot Graham is about to make his big announcement known to the entire world."

With his entire family of twenty-four seated on folding chairs in the background, and scores of television cameras and their respective news crews strategically posted all around, Eliot Graham stood alone at the microphone. Before saying a single word, he momentarily closed his eyes and silently quoted one of his favorite Bible verses, *"Lord, I can do all things through Christ who strengthens me."* Opening his eyes once again, Graham turned his head, facing his most precious earthly possession.

"Before I say anything, I want to thank my wife, Rosemary, for everything."

Eliot Graham paused momentarily, giving honor to the woman whose faithful loving companionship he had cherished for the past thirty-seven years.

"Now, if I started telling 'you-all' what 'everything' means," he said with a strong Texas accent, "we'll probably be here for the rest of the night, and then some."

Graham's dry sense of humor was an instant hit, especially for those who were less familiar with his quick wit, personable sincerity and uncompromising Godly character.

"I also want to thank my seven children, who are all seated in back of me next to their 'mama' from oldest to youngest."

Everybody clapped as the seven Graham children stood up and took a bow.

"Last, but far from being least," chuckled Graham, "I want to thank my children's spouses, and all ten of my grandchildren for their love, wisdom and most importantly, their continued support in helping me reach this monumental decision."

With his heartfelt acknowledgments completed, a confident Eliot Graham turned around to face a new form of media directed entirely at him. He was no longer seated in the glass-enclosed confines of a radio broadcast booth. For the unforeseeable future, he had to get used to the fact that television cameras and not microphones would be his media of choice to communicate his conservative ideals to a new audience of Americans that had never heard mention his name. Boldly, the former Baptist minister, turned conservative communicator, opened his mouth and spoke.

"There are many of you watching right now who know all about me. You know who I am and what I stand for. Some of you watching may have only heard about me. You may have accidentally turned your radio dial in the wrong direction one morning and heard this strange Texas accent blaring out at you from your car's radio speakers. But to the millions upon millions of American citizens, who never heard my name mentioned in casual conversation and heard the words of my voice on the American airwaves, allow me the honor and privilege right now to introduce myself. My name is Eliot Graham and I humbly stand here today in the presence of God and before millions of my fellow Americans and boldly declare: I love America! I was born here in Trinity Mills in Texas, not far from where our family home is presently located. Folks, I can stand here before you and read an elaborate political speech, but I am sick and tired, as I'm sure all of you are, of listening to politicians speak beautifully crafted words that have no substance or real meaning to the lives of those folk whom they have sworn on oath to serve.

"For years now, I've asked God to raise-up a political leader, especially in the office of the presidency, who would fulfill our founding fathers' heartfelt mandates to keep America free of being tainted from the destructive effects of what I like to call humanistic socialism and Godless pragmatism. These two corrupt forces know no political boundaries. They are as prevalent in the Republican Party as they are in the Democratic Party. You may be scratching your heads right now, wondering what this crazy Texan is talking about when he mentions highfalutin words such as humanistic socialism and Godless pragmatism.

"Folks, I'll make it plain and simple for you all. Humanistic socialism simply means that government wants to step in to our lives and tell us the big fat lie that they can solve all our problems. Many of my Democratic friends from Washington D.C. gnash their teeth together when I expose their little secret. If you strip away all their political rhetoric, this is what our Democratic congressman and senators really are saying. "If you elect me, I'll vote in favor of taxing everything. You name it, we'll find a way of taxing it. This way, the government is guaranteed to take in tons of money. With all of your money in our treasury, we can provide all of you with everything you will ever need. And best of all, you'll never have to work for it! From cradle to grave, your government will take good care of you. We'll provide you with food stamps, free health care, free education, a variety of good paying government created jobs, low-cost government subsidized housing, and, best of all, early retirement."

Some clapped, some squirmed, and some even nodded their heads in agreement, but everyone was touched by the sincerity of Graham's message. From here Graham's message took on a more serious tone.

"The reason humanistic socialism doesn't work is rather quite simple. Simply put, it puts a damper on a person's internal drive to better himself. Once a nation's innovative spark is gone, all that you are left with is a welfare state. Folks, that is why our American kids are doing so poorly in public schools compared with their same peers in Europe, Asia and elsewhere. Despite spending more money per capita on public school education than any other nation on earth, despite having the best technology that money can buy in every American classroom, a large percentage of American kids are being immersed daily, at home, on television, and at school into accepting socialist ideals that promote mediocrity. Because of humanistic socialism, America is presently buried in so much mind-boggling accumulated debt, almost 18 trillion dollars at last count, that unless we are willing to take bold steps now, in less than a generation, the America we now know will be no more."

Everyone stood frozen in place, finding it difficult to mentally absorb the stark reality of Graham's words.

"The second destructive force that is destroying America is Godless pragmatism. Godless pragmatism simply means that whatever seems to be working at the moment, regardless of whether it's right or wrong, moral or immoral, we count it all good and call it truth."

With a look of fire in his eyes, Graham now went on to attack the very political party that he once proudly called his own.

"My many capitalist friends in the Republican Party will wholeheartedly agree with everything I just stated concerning the destructive effects of socialism on a free society, but they are spineless cowards when it comes to admitting that Godless pragmatism is just as destructive to America as socialism. Many of my Republican friends might hate my guts after what I am about to say, but America, here's the truth about the Republican Party in a nutshell. Did 'you all' ever see the picture of the three monkeys? One has its hands over its ears; another one has its hands covering its eyes, the last one over its mouth. To me, those three monkeys represent the Republican Party—they see no evil, they hear no evil, and they especially, speak no evil."

Now, even the liberal news reporters were clapping at the animated antics displayed by the former Texas preacher standing at the microphone.

"Why do they do that, you may ask? Well shucks, folks, the answer is easy. Those Republican cowards are afraid of losing the independent voters to the liberal socialist Democrats. They're so afraid if they come out speaking against the hot-button moral issues such as gay marriage and abortion, they can just kiss their independent voters goodbye. And that, America, is the truth, plain and simple."

Everyone stood in awe of this middle-aged man from Trinity Mills, Texas, who, up until now, was only heard, but never seen, by the American public.

"Well folks, that's about all I have to say." Eliot Graham commented as he proceeded to walk away from the microphone. Taking a step or two forward, Graham returned to the microphone making one final comment.

"You all, I did forget one small item of business," he said with a broad mischievous smile. "Shucks folks, I've decided that being there is presently nobody out there brave enough or bold enough to tackle these hardcore issues that I just mentioned, I stand here now, humbly asking those of you out there who still believe in our national motto, In God We Trust, to back my run for the office of President of the United States of America on the American Values Party ticket come next November."

Everybody present, even the dozen or so news reporters who didn't agree with his politics, stood and applauded the tenacious character of the man standing alone at the microphone. Graham knew he was on a roll. In spite of the almost deafening response from the surrounding standing ovation, he continued with his blistering impromptu speech.

"If you elect me president, I promise that I will recognize God as the source of inspiration behind the powerful words written by our Founding Fathers: that all men are created equal, that they are endowed by their Creator with certain unalienable Rights, that among these are Life, Liberty and the pursuit of Happiness. We must never forget that it is God and God alone who endows each of us with Life, Liberty, and the freedom needed to pursue happiness. Contrary to the tenets of socialism, happiness is not a right. To pursue something means you must be willing to work hard in order to obtain it. Jobs will come back to America, but only if America is willing to once again pursue life's challenges with the same innovative tenacity and determination as did Thomas Edison and his black assistant, Lewis Latimer, when they co-invented the first electric light bulb."

Even as Graham spoke, the ovation continued.

"If you elect me president, I promise I will fight for the passage of The Fair Tax Plan. What is the The Fair Tax Plan you ask? The Fair Tax plan is nonpartisan legislation. It increases a worker's take-home pay by at least 25.3 percent. It abolishes all federal personal and corporate income taxes, gift, estate, capital gains, alternative minimum, Social Security, Medicare, and self-employment taxes and replaces them with one simple, visible, federal retail sales tax administered primarily by existing state sales tax authorities. The Fair Tax Plan taxes us only on what we choose to spend on new goods or services, not on what we earn. It is a fair, efficient, transparent, and intelligent solution to the frustration and inequity of our current tax system. It enables workers to keep their entire paychecks. More importantly, it refunds in advance the tax on purchases of basic necessities for people living below the poverty level. It allows American products to compete fairly with foreign competitors. It closes all loopholes and brings transparency and accountability to tax policy. It ensures Social Security and Medicare funding and solubility far into the future. And most importantly, The Fair Tax Plan abolishes the IRS!"

A round of deafening cheers immediately followed Graham's last statement.

"If you elect me president, I promise I will fight to my dying breath to protect the sanctity of every American life, from a newly fertilized human embryo to a ninety-nine year old elderly American on life-support. I will also fight to my dying breath to protect the sanctity of marriage, between one man and one woman, the very institution that keeps America strong and viable. If we ever choose to forfeit this fundamental institution established by God Almighty, we would surely forfeit all that America stands for."

Graham paused momentarily and smiled. Being a former preacher and presently, a talk show host, he instinctively knew when it was time to stop talking. Whether the people accepted what he had to say or not, he spoke what was in his heart and he was satisfied.

"Folks, I end with an apology." Graham this said with a serious expression.

Rosemary Graham sat in back of her husband just shaking her head back and forth. So many times she had seen her husband end his sermons using the same familiar ploy.

"I said at the very beginning, I wouldn't be giving you all a speech. I kept my promise. Some highly paid speechwriter did not craft my words. I spoke to you from my heart. I shared with every American listening to my voice my deepest thoughts and convictions. Folks, plain and simple, I just want what you all want. I want America back. I want America strong. I want America blessed. I want America debt free. I want to see good paying jobs return to our shores. I want to see everything I buy stamped in the bold red, white, and blue colors—made in America. If you share that same vision for America, then vote for Eliot Graham come November of next year. I close now by admonishing all Americans to live by this standard recorded in the Old Testament book of 2nd Chronicles:

'If My people, who are called by My Name will humble themselves and pray, and seek My face, and turn from their wicked ways, then I will hear from Heaven and I will forgive their sin and heal their land.'"

With all the conviction and boldness of an evangelical preacher, Eliot Graham ended his speech by proclaiming this familiar presidential closing over all who were presently listening to the sound of his voice.

"God bless you and may God bless America!"

Monday, July 20th, 2015
11:55 a.m. Eastern Time
Robert Berry Campaign Headquarters
317 State Street, Albany, N.Y.

While scores of elated people, unashamedly shouting out the words, 'God bless America!" rushed forward to shake the hand of the man from Trinity Mills, Texas, who had just expressed, in so many heartfelt words, the missing hope that most Americans were so desperately wanting to hear, over a thousand miles away, in a three-story building in downtown Albany, New York, an eerie silence now prevailed. Throughout the Robert Berry campaign headquarters, where the deafening sounds of revelry were heard less than an hour before, now, an overwhelming sense of shock and dismay from what they had just digitally witnessed, was only now taking effect.

Looking into the dazed eyes of his usually cool, levelheaded campaign manager, a clearly flustered Robert Berry asked, "Grif, how is this going to effect us?"

"Calm down, Bob, your poll numbers are safe," Gunson reassured his panicked boss with a confident smile, "but we need to go on the offensive, immediately. The way I see it, Graham is no different from Samuel Leroy Tucker. They're both extremists. They're far right-winged members of the American Values Party. Once we inform America about who he really is, I promise you, we'll have no problem with Elect Graham come next November, whatsoever."

"Bravo!" declared the impressed arch demon, Amducious, standing beside his two demonic subordinates at the entrance to the small reception room. "Gunson said that all on his own."

"I've trained him well, Destroyer," proudly declared the winged griffin.

"Unfortunate man, Robert Berry," sneered the massive ten-foot giant. "For what we have planned for the governor not even Griffin Gunson's smooth-talking words will be able to salvage his run for the presidency come election day next November."

Chapter Sixteen

"The coming of the lawless one is according to the working of Satan, with all power, signs, and lying wonders, and with all unrighteous deception among those who perish, because they did not receive the love of the truth, that they might be saved.

~2 Thessalonians 2:9-10

One year later
Monday, July 29ᵗʰ, 2016
4 p.m. Eastern Time
The Republican National Convention
Quicken Loans Arena
Cleveland, Ohio

With the upbeat sounds of contemporary rock music blaring out in all directions, Robert Berry looked up at the large digital clock suspended from the ceiling of the Quicken Loan Arena and smiled. In less than four hours from now, his lifetime dream would officially become a reality. That is when the final roll call of individual state delegates would be made, publicly certifying him, Robert Winston Berry, the Republican Party's choice to represent his party during the next two months leading up to the November 2ⁿᵈ presidential elections.

After patiently waiting through three exhilarating days, filled, from morning to night, with red, white and blue signs and banners, noisy partying, longwinded speeches, mingling, hobnobbing and fraternizing with a who's who of celebrities, political supporters, corporate executives and financial contributors, it would almost be over. All that was left now was for his good friend and former New Jersey Republican Governor, Janet Weisman, Berry's choice for his vice-presidential running mate, to give her scheduled 7 p.m. speech. Once she stepped away from the raised stage podium, the Chairman of the Republican National Committee, Michael Carson, would follow; at that time he would call the noisy convention floor to order to begin the delegate count. Even though the convention's outcome was a foregone conclusion, the roll must be counted to certify the vote. Each state gets to make a brief statement and announce which candidate will get their delegates' votes—as decided by the primary elections.

Only a few hundred feet away from the arena floor's noise and confusion, in a large room utilized mainly for banquets, an invitation only, sit-down dinner was about to begin in Robert Berry's honor. All the invited guests, their security clearances checked and rechecked by a team of secret service agents stationed at the dining room's entrance, took their assigned places at tables where red elephant figurines held up signs displaying the individual's names. All the high-ranking Republican Party officials were present, including two former presidents, the Republican National Chairman, and the GOP Speaker of the House of Representative, California congresswoman, Barbara Ann Raushback. As waiters and waitresses scurried about, from table to table, taking dinner orders, all the reserved seats in the large dining hall seemed to be taken, with the exception of three; two of the three seats were reserved on the left side of the room for Robert Berry's campaign director, Griffin Gunson, and Gunson's girlfriend, Sheila Brewster. But the most talked about empty seat was reserved at the head table where all eyes were now focused. Without any explanation at all given for her absence, the seat left empty to Robert Berry's immediate right was reserved for his wife, Elizabeth Berry.

Earlier that day

Monday, July 29th
8:39 a.m. EST
The Embassy Suites Hotel
5800 Rockside Woods Blvd
Cleveland, Ohio

When Elizabeth Berry's eyes opened early this morning, one thought was going through her mind, shopping. If only for an hour or two, she desperately knew in her heart that she needed to get away from all the fake glitter and empty platitudes involved with living, once again, an unfulfilled life in the shadow of a political rock star. Not wanting to disturb her sleeping husband, she quietly got out of bed, showered, and dressed herself in a casual, unassuming outfit that would not draw public attention to her true identity.

"Liz, what time is it?" mumbled a voice from the nearby bedroom.

Stepping out of the bathroom, Elizabeth quietly commented, "Go back to sleep, Honey! I'll be back in a couple hours."

"Where are you headed off to so early?" Berry inquired with a concerned tone.

"You know me, Bob!" she said with a smile while tying her long blonde hair in a ponytail. "I gotta check out the stores! I spotted a mall a few blocks from here. Don't worry, Robert, I'll be back here with plenty of time to spare."

"Just remember, Liz, this is a really big day," cautioned Berry. "I just want everything to go smoothly today."

"You'll get your day, Bob," Elizabeth Berry calmly stated as she unlocked the entrance door to their top floor executive suite. Before exiting into the hallway, she turned and made this final comment, "I promise you, of anyone, I won't be the one to spoil it!"

Monday, July 29ᵗʰʰ
9:14 a.m. ES
Tower City Mall
Two Blocks North of Quicken Loans Arena
Cleveland, Ohio

Elizabeth Berry was in luck this morning. For this week only, the Tower City Mall decided to open their doors an hour earlier to accommodate the large influx of out-of-town-shoppers attending the nearby Republican National Convention.

With two plain-clothed secret service agents leisurely strolling close behind, Elizabeth Berry walked down the length of the mall's central walkway looking for her favorite place to shop. With scores of shoppers all-around, the unassuming trio was totally unaware that they, too, were being followed.

After walking for several minutes, casually stopping only to browse the numerous window displays that lined both sides of the long corridor, Elizabeth Berry smiled. She had finally located her diversionary oasis that would, if only momentarily, help her forget the lifestyle she had grown to hate over the years. Posted directly above its entrance doors in big bold black letters was the name of her favorite women's clothing store, Chico's. For the next half hour or so, Elizabeth Berry challenged herself to totally forget the outside world and indulge herself in the fantasy world of high-end women's fashions.

After spending several minutes perusing through rows of colorful blouses, a rack of fashionable ladies' jackets caught Elizabeth Berry's discerning eye.

"Mrs. Berry?"

Not wanting to draw the attention of the two Secret Service agents standing directly behind her, Elizabeth Berry decided to respond.

"Yes, I'm Elizabeth Berry, and who are you?'

"Mrs. Berry, before I tell you who am I, we need to sit down and talk in private."

"Honey, whoever you are, for the moment, this is as private as it gets," Elizabeth Berry said in a low audible voice. "Now, tell me exactly who you are and what it is you want to say, or I will personally inform those two Secret Service agents standing directly in back of me to arrest you and hall your ass immediately out of this mall. Do I make myself clear?"

After a long pause, the woman hidden behind the rack of jackets spoke. "Mrs. Berry, my name is Jennifer. I'm twenty-six years old. I'm a college grad with a master's degree from the University of Pittsburgh in political science. This past spring, I was working in D.C. as a junior intern for Republican Senator Tony Ladles. It was then that I met your husband."

Elizabeth Berry immediately interrupted. "That's a lie! At no time during this past spring did my husband ever set foot in Washington D.C.!"

"Have it your way, Mrs. Berry!" the woman replied, loud enough to capture the attention of everyone present in the popular women's apparel store, including the two secret service agents assigned to protect Elizabeth Berry.

"I'll make it plain and simple, Mrs. Berry," the young woman continued. "Senator Ladles introduced me to your husband during a campaign stop in Cincinnati, Ohio. That happened during the first week of April. You weren't there at the time, Mrs. Berry!"

Immediately, the two Secret Service agents located their target, a young woman ranting and raving from the opposite side of the row of jackets where Mrs. Berry was standing. Acting quickly, they secured the woman by her arms and shoulder as she continued shouting out her explicit story for all ears to hear.

"When I first met your husband, he invited me to lunch, then to his hotel suite for sex. I was stupid. I said yes, and now, Mrs. Berry, I'm four months pregnant with your husband's child!"

Thinking fast, one of the two federal agents led the kicking and screaming woman into a fitting room in back of the clothing store.

"Let her go, now!" a firm voice from somewhere in the front of the store demanded.

Everyone focused on an attractive tall brunette standing to the left of a totally shocked cashier who was manning the front checkout desk.

"Everyone out of the store, now!" the agent, standing directly in front of a quivering Elizabeth Berry, demanded. Shoppers quickly acted on his order, then the same agent shouted one final order, "Will the store manager please close the front security gates behind you as you leave?"

In moments, the metal front security doors were securely closed. The only individuals remaining inside the locked downed clothing store were the two Secret Service agents, a teary-eyed Elizabeth Berry, a young woman named Jennifer, and an attractive unnamed brunette.

"Mrs. Berry, do you know this woman?" Agent Tom Ingle was referring to the brunette.

"Yes, Tom, unfortunately I do," a tearful Berry admitted.

Turning to face the agent in the back of the store, Berry calmly made a request, "It's okay, Don. Let her go."

Agent Don Meekins released his firm grip on the young woman's upper arm.

Completely in charge, Elizabeth Berry made her final petition to the two Secret Service agents assigned by their superiors to give her twenty-four hour protection. "Tom, Don, if you don't mind, I want to talk to both of these ladies alone."

Both men nodded in agreement. While the Secret Service agents positioned themselves on adjacent sides of the front cash register, the three women were left alone in the back of the store. For the next half hour, three women, almost virtual strangers before entering the store, in the privacy of a Chico's fitting room, discussed how the hidden secrets of just one man named Robert

Berry had not only affected their personal lives, but quite possibly, once the truth would be revealed, the entire political landscape of America.

Monday, July 29th, 2016
10:37 a.m. Eastern Time
The Embassy Suites Hotel
5800 Rockside Woods Blvd
Cleveland, Ohio

Robert Berry was livid. Standing alone in the living room of his top-floor executive suite, he looked down again at his wristwatch and began to panic. *We're already late! Where the hell is she?*

Berry had every right to be panicked. In less than thirty minutes, he was scheduled to be present on the convention stage with his wife, Elizabeth, who was to have been seated at his immediate left. His vice presidential running mate, Janet Weisman, and her husband, Jerry, were to have been seated on his right. Before he could express another negative thought, the front entrance door opened and in walked his smiling wife.

"Where the hell have you been, Liz?" ranted her clearly irate husband. "You promised me you'd be back here over a half hour ago! Liz, you're not even dressed!"

"That's right, Bob," Elizabeth Berry calmly agreed. "The reason I'm not dressed is really quite simple."

Totally composed, Elizabeth closed the door and defiantly said, "I am not going."

"What!" fumed Berry, "What does that mean? You're not going? Have you lost your mind?"

"No, Bob," she said with a smile. "On the contrary, you self-centered, power-hungry bast-rd." For the first time in my entire life, I believe I have finally found my mind!"

Now Berry was truly in a panic. Somehow, he could sense that this woman, with a confident grin on her face, was not the the same person who left him, half-awake, a couple hours before.

"Look, Liz honey, we don't have time now to discuss whatever you think is going on here." In a more appeasing tone he pleaded, "Go in and get ready, I'll just stay out here and wait."

"You just go to your coronation on your own, King Robert!" Liz chuckled to herself as she picked up a phone receiver on a nearby table. "I'm calling the airport. I'm leaving Cleveland on the next available flight back to Albany."

"Liz, honey, tell me, what happened? Where have you been? Who did you talk to?"

"If I told you, you bast-rd, you wouldn't even know," his wife admonished with an icy glare. "You've slept with so many young, pretty women over the years, you've probably lost count."

"Who talked with you, Liz?" Berry demanded. In an act of desperation, Robert Berry forcefully jerked the phone receiver from his wife's hand and tossed it across the room.

"Does the name Sheila Brewster ring a bell?"

"You believe what that bit-h says?"

"Maybe not her," but I do believe what Jennifer Thomas has to say." She walked across the room to pick up the phone.

"Who the hell is Jennifer Thomas?"

"Like I said, Bob, you've had sex with so many girls; you can't even remember their names."

"Whoever this Jennifer is, Liz, she's lying! She's lying I tell you!"

"They're all lying, Bob," his wife calmly said, but what about your baby growing in her womb? Is your baby also lying, Bob?"

"My God, she's pregnant?"

"My! My! My!" Elizabeth mocked, as she circled her quivering, lying husband. "The man who would be King of America now stands before little old me, shaking like a frightened child!"

"Look Liz, don't leave me! Please don't leave now! I can fix this. Everything is coming together. I promise, I'll never cheat on you again. Liz, just sit down and think this over. In two short months from now, I'm going to be the president, and you're going to be the First Lady! Think, Liz! Think how wonderful our lives will be!"

"You dumb stupid b—t—rd!" Elizabeth Berry defiantly declared, stepping back a foot or two before looking directly into her husband's frightened eyes. "You still don't get it, you dumb ass! I don't want to be the first lady. At least, not with someone who didn't think twice about the real possibility of passing along to his wife a sexually transmitted disease that could have possibly killed her, or made her life a living hell until she died in misery!"

"Please, Liz, forgive me. I'm so, so sorry." Berry cried out, begging from his knees.

"I'm sorry, too Robert," she calmly stated, as she walked toward the door. Stopping only to pick up her red purse from a nearby chair, she turned once more to look back at her teary-eyed, kneeling husband. Feeling no pity for the man she had spent the last twenty-seven years faithfully serving both day and night, she made this final comment." Bob, don't worry about my clothes," she said with a forced smile. "I'll send somebody here I truly trust to get them later." With all the courage she could muster, she closed with this stinging pronouncement. "Listen to me, Robert Wilson Berry, and never forget these words. My first name is not Hillary and yours isn't Bill. If the American people still want you after all of this hits the fan, buddy, they can have you. I don't want you anymore!"

With her red purse in hand, Elizabeth Berry opened the door to the top-floor suite and left, never again to return.

The entrance door to executive suite 900 opened wide and this human female walked out. As she entered the hall, beyond the room where her husband stood crying, she took no notice of the three spirits carefully observing every determined step of her rapidly paced walk down the carpeted corridor to the elevator. Wasting no time, she pressed the button, the metallic door opened, then closed, transporting the human nine stories below.

She would now begin her journey in a new life, leaving behind the empty façade of power and politics that she had grown to hate.

"Congratulations, Destroyer!"

"Thank you, Malzar," Amducious pridefully acknowledged wiith a broad sneering grin, as he stared down at his two grotesque subordinates. "Phase one of our plan to get Analise Devoe elected president has now been accomplished. Thanks to your superlative efforts, the king of the Republican Party has been dethroned.

"What about Eliot Graham?"

"I'll personally take care of Graham, myself," Amducious replied with a sneer. "For now, you two are free to do as you will, at least until I call for your special services again sometime in the very near future. I release you both from your present assigned hosts. Griffin, go find some horses to mutilate. Malzar, check out some prospective children whose lives may need your special touch. Due to your diligence for detail, you have assured that the souls of both Griffin Gunson and Sheila Brewster will spend an eternity, along with all of us, forever and ever in hell."

All three demons laughed in agreement.

Monday, July 29th
8 p.m. Eastern Time
The Republican National Convention
Quicken Loans Arena
Cleveland, Ohio

Like a master conductor directing her full symphony orchestra toward a climaxing crescendo, Janet Weisman, Berry's choice for his vice- presidential running mate, ended her thirty-five minute speech with this blistering attack on the Democrats' choice to represent their party at the November 2nd election.

"In closing, allow me a moment or two longer to strip away the 'job facade' label given to this darling of the liberal media, and expose the real Analise Devoe for who she really is and what she represents."

With over two thousand Republicans looking on, Janet Weisman reiterated the stark differences between her party's platform and that of her opponent.

"Who is Analise Devoe? Strip away her 'jobs' mantra and you will clearly see that she is no different than her progressive predecessor, Rashid Jabbar Harris. Over the past four years, Analise Devoe has gone on record fully supporting the Harris administration's efforts to raise taxes on both the wealthy and the hardworking middle class wage earner in order to create a whole host of federal budget-busting social programs. Her past actions speak much louder than her words. No matter how well-crafted her words may sound, she was, is, and will always be, a left-winged, tax-raising socialist, and like her predecessor, Rashid Jabbar Harris, she is in favor of the 'redistribution of American wealth'. As smart as she appears in the media, what she and her entire party of liberal Democrats fail to grasp is this fundamental economic principle. You cannot create jobs in a toxic economic environment that removes the basic incentives for companies and businesses to increase and restore productivity.

"On the other hand, our Republican Party's platform fully supports policies intended to advance rapid job growth solely within our borders. We intend to reduce corporate taxes for American companies, large and small, who commit themselves to ending the destructive practice of outsourcing American jobs to foreign countries. We will give added tax breaks to those businesses that compensate their workers with incentives and bonuses to increase productivity. We plan to pay down the massive federal budget deficit by eliminating all governmental waste, including, the myriad of budget draining social programs instituted over the past four years by the progressive Democrats.

"I close with this sobering statement. In a democracy, the people get the government they deserve. The only way to achieve a better government is to establish policies that address the country's problems in the approximate order of their importance. Tax policies should only be designed to stimulate economic growth, especially toward higher productivity, and finance the necessary activities of the government. This will be the policy of the Berry – Weisman White House. The choice is clear. The choice is America's. Thank you for listening to me today. God bless you all, and may God bless America!"

The moment Janet Weisman stepped away from the podium, she was joined, center stage, by a host of her fellow Republican friends and colleagues, including her husband Jerry, and possibly, her future boss, Robert Berry. After hugs and handshakes, everyone returned to their assigned onstage seats for the grand finale of tonight's events.

Michael Carson, the Chairman of the Republican National Committee, stepped up to the microphone to announce the long awaited roll call of state delegates. One-by-one, the Republican National Committee Chairperson announced the roll call of states in alphabetical order, starting with the representative from Alabama.

"We call James O'Donnell to the podium, the representative from the great state of Alabama." Carson stepped away from the microphone to allow a tall lanky farmer from Jefferson County, Alabama, to address the two thousand plus Republican packed arena. "Mr. Chairman," his rich deep voice, highlighted by a strong southern accent, "the 48 delegates from our great State of Alabama, known 'as the Yellowhammer State, the Heart of Dixie, and the Cotton State, cast all 48 of their votes for the former governor of New York, Robert Berry."

Seated in back of the center stage podium were a host of invited dignitaries, including the ten Republican presidential candidates, all of whom were aware of their political fate long before tonight's vote count. Still, two reserved seats remained empty on the raised platform; one was set-aside for Robert Berry's wife, Elizabeth, and the other for Berry's campaign manager, Griffin Gunson.

While the delegate vote continued, one man had been sitting alone in the back, listening to Janet Weisman's speech. Earlier in the day, this same man was on top of the world. Two hours ago, he had a reserved seat on the same stage where his boss, Robert Berry, was sitting. He should have been ecstatic, counting down the remaining votes to declare victory before the whole world, but he wasn't. Now, the only thing that totally captivated his full attention was a single piece of paper he held tightly in his right hand.

"Grif, thank God I found you!" a rather thin, short-statured thirty-two year old man, declared. "I've covered every inch of this place looking for you."

"Get the hell away from me, Sam!" mumbled the disgruntled man, slouching on a folding chair he set up for himself by an exit corridor in the back of the arena. "I'm in no mood to talk, Sam."

"Grif, man, I completely understand exactly how you feel! Berry fired me, too!"

Gunson looked up at the smiling face of his former administrative assistant and said in a cold, firm voice, "Well Sam, since you no longer work for me, could you do three last favors for me?"

"Sure, Grif!" Price wholeheartedly agreed. "I'll be more than happy to do anything for you, man."

"Good." Gunson followed with a forced smile. "Now, listen very carefully."

Sam Price stood silently by, not saying a word until Gunson made his requests known.

"One, don't ever use that name, GOD, in my presence again! Is that understood?"

To Gunson's surprise, for the first time in their two year association, Price did not respond.

"Two, don't ever go looking for me again, and three, and most importantly, get the hell away from me and never let me see your stupid smiling face again."

Again, Griffin Gunson was dumbfounded and speechless. The person, who immediately jumped at his every command, remained standing defiantly before him.

"Didn't I make myself clear enough, Sam?" Gunson asked in a raised voice, loud enough to capture the attention of two security guards standing a short distance away.

"Do I have to punch that asinine smile off your face before I finally get rid of you?" Gunson continued to rant.

"If that's what you feel like doing," Price boldly replied, "then punch me, but I'm not leaving you."

"What's wrong with you, man? I told you to leave me alone."

"You're wasting your breath, Grif." Price calmly responded. "You can punch me if that makes you feel any better, but I've made up my mind, man, I'm not leaving you."

"Gentlemen, what seems to be the problem here?"

Unaware that anyone else was listening in on their conversation, Sam Price turned around to face two uniformed security guards standing only a few feet away.

"Officers, I'm so sorry if I raised my voice," Price apologized, again shocking his former boss by taking full responsibility for Gunson's rude behavior.

"As I was just telling my friend, Grif, here," Price continued, addressing the skeptical on-looking guards with a convincing story. "I had just lost something of great importance, and I guess I got a little carried away, officers. I promise, I won't let it happen again."

"Buddy, I'm holding you to that promise," said the taller of the two guards. "Any more loud noise coming from either of you, you're both out of here! Have I made myself clear?"

"Absolutely," Sam Price ardently agreed. "You'll have no more problems from me, officers."

Appearing satisfied with Price's apologetic statement, the two convention center guards cautiously returned to their former post, leaving the two men alone once again, one man standing, the other sitting on a folding chair in front of the arena's back exit.

Looking up at Sam Price, Gunson smiled. "Oh, man, I am so stupid! Sam, buddy, I should have seen this coming a long time ago!"

Knowing Gunson as well as he did, Price looked down at his former boss with a suspicious stare.

"Sammy, buddy, you should have told me the truth about yourself." Gunson chuckled. "You're queer and you've got the hots for me!"

"No, Grif," Price calmly stated, shaking his head in disagreement. "None of the above."

"Then why won't you just leave me alone?" Gunson whispered in a low tone, not wanting to draw further attention from the on looking guards. "Go find a life for yourself, Sam!"

"You just nailed it, man." Price agreed with an affirming nod. "I did find a life—a new life that is now completely opposite of the one I used to live."

"Sam, don't tell me that you found Jesus or Buddha or someone else," Griffin Gunson scoffed. "You have no idea how sick I am of hearing about the great benefits of that religious rubbish. I've heard about religion and Jesus my whole life and there's absolutely nothing you can tell me that's ever going to change my mind."

"Okay, Grif, I'll make you a deal," Price commented with a smile. "If you tell me exactly why you hate Jesus so much, I promise you, Grif, I'll leave you alone and never bother you again."

"Now that's a deal," nodded Gunson, "with one condition attached."

"What's the condition, Grif?"

"That you sit down here on the floor beside me and you shut your mouth until I'm finished telling my story. Agree?"

"Absolutely!" Wasting no time, he quietly sat down on the cement floor beside his former boss.

"Okay, Sam, first, I want you to know this right off the bat." Gunson paused, taking in a deep breath before continuing. "What I'm about to tell you, I've never told anyone before."

"I promise you, man," Price looked up with a sincere smile, "I'll never repeat anything you tell me, Grif, so help me God!"

"Okay!" Taking in another deep breath, Gunson began his story:

"From my earliest recollection, I remember being raised by a hardcore religious father who dictated every move my family made. My father was assigned as a lay pastor at the church we attended. My mother never pushed religion on me. I also remember at an early age being forced to attend nightly Bible studies in our house which involved studying the Book of Revelation. Because of that, I developed this deep fear of the world coming to an end. My view of God was no better. I was taught to live my life according to rigid stipulations found in Old Testament law. I can also remember just waiting and waiting every Saturday for the Sabbath to be over, just so that I could do something fun.

"I also remember at the age of ten going on vacation to visit some family members in Scranton, Pennsylvania. Before leaving, I was told that my Dad couldn't join my Mom and me on our trip due to his previous work commitments. It was while we were still on vacation in Pennsylvania that Dad called Mom and told her that he didn't love her anymore, and that he was having an affair with another woman.

"Needless to say, at that moment, my entire world was shattered. My Mom and I returned to our home outside of Albany, faced with a nasty long-term divorce process. In the midst of all of this mess, my brother, Mike, was born. My Mom desperately needed somebody to help her pay the mortgage, so a woman named Janet moved into our house. Before long, Janet became my babysitter. During the summer months, after my Mom left for work, Janet would take my young brother and me to a nude beach down along the Hudson River. It was there that Janet taught me things that I should have never learned at the age of 11. I was so confused that by the age of twelve, I actually contemplated committing suicide. I felt that I was the cause of my parents' divorce. A voice in my head kept telling me that if I had never been born, none of this would ever have happened. One day, Mom found cocaine in Janet's bedroom in our home. The police were called and that was the end of that fiasco, with many more to follow.

"Even with Janet gone, my mother was still a complete emotional wreck. Many times she told me that my brother and I were the only two things that were still keeping her alive. Since my parents' divorce, Mom had also completely lost her faith in God, and so had I. I could not understand that if God was so loving, as I had been told, why did he sit back and do nothing to prevent our family from being destroyed? I began to develop a deep anger and hatred toward God, and for that matter, all Christians. One day, when I was home alone, I found this giant steak knife in the kitchen. I remember going into the bathroom and locking the door behind me, planning to use the knife to help me escape the pain I was suffering. As I held the knife to my wrist, my entire childhood flashed before my eyes. Out of nowhere, a sudden fear came over me. Staring down with the knife in my hand, this thought instantly popped into my mind. *What would happen to me after I died?* It scared me so bad that I dropped the knife and ran out of the bathroom.

"As I got older, I vividly remember my mother bringing home different men she had met at the various bars she visited. I also remember how lonely I was at that time. Other than my brother, Mike, I had absolutely no friends. All that changed when I reached the 7th grade. It was then that I met some really cool Gothic kids, the ones at school who dressed in all black clothing. I instantly took to these guys and they began teaching me their ways. From 7th grade on, I grew my hair long, dyed it jet-black, wore heavy dark makeup, listened constantly to satanic music and carried chains under my trench coat. One night, while I slept over at a friend's house, I was forced to do drugs, touch women and get drunk. This caused even a deeper hatred and depression to rise up within me. Needless to say, I failed seventh grade and had to repeat it. By the age of 14, I was an alcoholic. I would drink pure alcohol morning, noon, and night. I smoked various drugs and studied my satanic bible that I had been given as a gift. Suddenly, all of my friends around me began to die. One of my good friends was accidentally run over by his mother's car. Another one died of cystic fibrosis and the list goes on and on. It was at that same time that I began to practice heavy occultism and witchcraft, including attending séances, worshiping the dead, playing with Ouija boards, and casting black magic spells on people I didn't like. As I descended deeper and deeper into Satanism, I began having more interactions with the spiritual realm, and also with demons.

"The turning point in my life came the very day I was invited to attend a Motley Crue Concert with some friends. While the band was up on the stage performing their famous song, 'Shout at the devil', I was in the audience praying to my father, Satan. I remember what happened next as if it just now happened. At the very moment the lead singer, Vince Neil, screamed out the words, 'shout at the devil,' I sold my soul to Satan in exchange for the power that I requested of him.

In the years that followed, many of the things I desired came to pass, but not all of it was good. At the age of 16, I had moved out of Mom's home and in with a witch who taught me everything she knew including astrology and palm reading. Before long, she took all my belongings and ran off with another man. Most of my high school friends were either expelled from school or in jail for various reasons such as bomb threats and drug busts. With all of this happening all around me, I remember going back to the same church I had attended as a child with my parents, to see if I could find any hope there. I'll never forget the cold stares I received as I sat quietly by myself during that Saturday morning service in the back pew. No one had to say a word. I could read the expression on their faces. They were all judging me by the way I looked. As far as Christianity was concerned, that was my last straw. From then on, I was determined to live my life hating God. I began to listen to music that spoke of torturing, raping, killing and mutilating Christians, and then destroying their churches. I even built a small altar in my room to Satan and I have been worshiping Satan ever since!"

With visible tears in his eyes, a much calmer Griffin Gunson looked down at his former administrative assistant and said, "I hope I didn't scare you too much with all that devil talk, Sam."

"No Grif, quite the opposite," Price admitted with a relieved smile. "Whether you believe it or not, your story sounds an awful lot like mine."

"What do you mean, Sam? You're not a devil worshipper! Forgive me for my candor, man, but you're a straight up nerd."

"No Grif," Sam looked up and chuckled, "in my case, looks truly are deceiving!"

"Well Sam," Gunson responded with a sigh, "I guess it's your turn to tell me your story."

Sam Price sat truly amazed by the sudden change in Griffin Gunson's attitude. Not wanting to hinder this positive change of events in any way, Price nodded his head in agreement and began sharing his parallel story with a man, who only a moment before, was threatening to punch him in the face.

"I would be honored, Grif," Price acknowledged with a nod. "I was also brought up in a really religious home in northern New Jersey, directly across the Hudson River from New York City. I had a Bar Mitzvah when I was thirteen. Growing up, my family only ate kosher food. My family was so religiously strict that I wasn't allowed to drive a car on the Sabbath or even date girls who weren't raised in an Orthodox Jewish family. Just like in your family, my Orthodox Jewish parents divorced when I was only fifteen years old, and I, too, blamed God for it, big time! There are so many details in your story that I can identify with, but let me stop here and tell you some of the good parts of my story."

"I'm glad you found a good part or two to latch onto, man, because I never did," Gunson soberly admitted.

Not wanting to distract Gunson's attention, Sam Price continued with his story.

"I was still in high school, getting drunk, doing drugs and a whole lot of other stupid, self-destructive things, until one day, a friend of mine invited me to attend my first ever Heavy Metal Christian concert at this big open-air stadium. I have to admit, I loved metal music at the time, and I absolutely loved that concert, except for one small detail. The band members proclaimed the name of Jesus with the same fervor in their music that I thought was only reserved for Satan. After the concert, I had a chance to meet with the lead guitarist. We talked for a long time. He told me that he was once a Satan worshipper, and that Jesus had changed his life. I had never in my life heard a story like his before. I also instantly rejected it. A few nights later, I went to check out an advertised worship concert that was being held in that same stadium. Once again, to my total amazement, I witnessed many of the people in this concert clapping, dancing, singing, crying, and lifting their hands toward the sky. I had never seen anything like this before that week. Being brought up in a strict Jewish home, most of these things were prohibited. Drums and electric guitars accompanied every single worship band. The musicians even encouraged the people in the audience to dance and go crazy for God. To say the least, I was very intrigued by everything I was witnessing. Before long, I felt this unexplainable hunger well up deep inside of me. More than anything else, I needed to know if this God they were all singing to was actually real.

"At that moment, being surrounded on all sides by strangers I had never met, I cried out to God. I told Him that I would give Him one more chance to reveal Himself to me. I asked

Him specifically to show Himself to me—to make His presence more real to me than all the people standing around me. Before I knew what had happened, something that felt like a strong wind knocked me to the ground! No one else around me felt it, only I did! I found myself literally stuck to the ground in a near fetal position. No matter how hard I tried, I could not get up! It was like someone had placed a twenty-ton weight on top of my body. The next thing I felt was this strange tingling sensation moving throughout my arms and then, my entire body. At that moment, I actually heard an audible voice whisper to me these exact words. "I love you, Sam Price, and I forgive you." No one had to tell me who that was. I knew that it was Jesus Himself speaking to me! And I could do nothing more but cry and repent before God for my many sins and ask Him to save me. I then heard Him say, 'Everything that you have been through in your life will now be turned around and used for My Glory!' "

Sam Price ended his story. He then looked up, smiling at a scene he never thought possible. Griffin Gunson was crying. Somehow, Price just knew in his spirit that God had used every single word he had just spoken to penetrate a small place left protected from Satan's lies somewhere deep inside Griffin Gunson's broken heart.

With tears streaming down his face, all Gunson could manage to say was, "Wow!"

Sam Price began laughing uncontrollably with joy.

"How do you feel, Grif?" a giddy Price managed to ask.

"I can't really answer that," an astonished Gunson replied. "I've never felt like this before!"

Without saying a word or performing a religious ritual, Griffin Gunson asked Jesus into his heart. Instantly, God's Holy Spirit entered his entire being. In a moment, in the twinkling of an eye, all the thick layers of Satanic lies and worldly self-deception vanished from Griffin Gunson's totally regenerated spirit, never again to return.

"Grif," Sam continued, with tears of unspeakable joy welling up in his own eyes, "I don't know if you know the words to this song, but if you do, I want you to softly sing them with me, right here and right now. Sing them, just as if you would have sung them, so long ago, when you sat in church with your mom and dad. Grif, I'll start you off."

With tearing streaming down his face, Sam Price began singing the first verse of the classical hymn song by millions.

"My hope is built on nothing less than Jesus' blood and righteousness. I dare not trust the sweetest frame, but wholly lean on Jesus' Name."

With the roll call of Republican state delegates still continuing on the distant arena stage, Griffin Gunson stood. With two thoroughly astonished security guards looking on, in the presence of Sam Price and a host of unseen angelic companions, a former demon-possessed man renounced Satan and committed his life and future to the King of Kings and the Lord of Lords. Without fear of reprisal, Sam Price and Griffin Gunson sang aloud in Christian unison the last verse of a very old hymn.

"On Christ the solid Rock I stand, all other ground is sinking sand; all other ground is sinking sand."–Amen and Amen!

Chapter Seventeen

And have no fellowship with the unfruitful works of darkness, but rather expose them. For it is shameful even to speak of those things, which are done by them in secret. But all things that are exposed are made manifest by the light, for whatever makes manifest—is light.

~Ephesians 5: 11-13 NKJV

Saturday, October 29ᵗʰ, 2016
5:57 a.m. CST
Texas Health Presbyterian Hospital
8200 Walnut Hill Lane
Dallas, Texas

The scene at the front entrance to Texas Health Presbyterian Hospital's ER appeared quite normal, at least, for this time of the morning. Just moments ago a local ambulance departed after dropping off a very pregnant mother in labor with twin boys. Her nervous husband, holding hands with the couple's three-year daughter and two-year-old son, made their way through the emergency room's main entrance door. Once inside, the children sat with their daddy in a nearby waiting room, anxiously awaiting word that their expectant mommy had delivered their newborn baby brothers.

Just beyond the range of human perception, this natural scene was anything but normal. Scores of massive sword-drawn angels were posted at every conceivable entranceway leading in and out of the hospital. Teams of two warriors were stationed every fifty feet along a maze of walled corridors that comprised the internal framework of Texas Health Presbyterian Hospital. By Kiel's order, this impenetrable wall of angelic defense was called for the sole protection of a single human female, who slept in the curtain-drawn privacy of an ER examination room.

For the first time since she arrived at Texas Health Presbyterian Hospital's emergency department late last night, no doctors, nurses, technicians, or family members entered the exam room assigned to Rosemary Graham. After spending a tumultuous, painful night of being subjected to a host of invasive and non-invasive medical tests, scans and procedures to help doctors determine the exact cause of her abdominal attack, she rested. Her mentally exhausted husband of thirty-seven years sat quietly by her bedside, his heart breaking at the thought of losing his most precious earthly possession. As he stared intently at his wife, sleeping peacefully, his tormented mind bombarded God with the same petition over and over.

"Lord, I beg You from the depths of my being, please wake me up from this nightmare. I do not want to live in this world without my wife. I will do anything You ask of me. I will give up my job, sell my home and all of my earthly possessions, Lord, just to live out the rest of my days with Rosemary."

Rosemary Graham opened her eyes immediately after Eliot's prayer, and turned to greet her apprehensive husband with a radiant smile.

"Eliot, I just had the most wonderful dream," she said softly with a peaceful gleam in her eyes. To her husband's complete amazement, she sat up in bed and began to describe her dream in intricate detail. "In my dream," she continued with the zeal of a young excited child, "I saw myself clothed in a long white robe, sitting on white marble steps. "I don't know how I knew it, but I knew I was young again, probably in my twenties. Directly in front of me was a beautiful golden veil partially pulled back from the center. At first, I didn't know what was on the other side of the golden veil, but I knew that I had to wait outside on the marble steps until I was called. Eventually, I heard my name called. I remember passing through the opening in the golden veil and entering into God's Throne Room. Eliot, I can't even begin to describe the beauty that surrounded me. Once inside, I met Jesus."

Rosemary paused and wiped the joyful tears from her eyes before she continued.

"Eliot, the Lord put his arms around me and told me that He loved me so much!"

Again, Rosemary Graham paused to wipe the freely flowing tears from her face.

"He then stepped back, smiled, and said, "Rosemary, I want you to give this message from Me to your husband, Eliot. Tell him that no matter what, he is to trust Me with all of his heart, soul, and mind. Tell him not to listen to the words of man that speak death, but to stand on My words alone that speak life. Tell Eliot that My love for him is unfathomable. Tell him that My Spirit dwells within him and to trust only in my Holy Spirit. Tell Eliot, that no matter what his natural ears might hear, he is to claim this one verse from the book of Psalms over you night and day: "Rosemary Graham will not die, but live, and declare the works of the Lord."

Saturday, October 29th
10:55 a.m. EST
1 Reservoir Ave.
Charleroi, Pennsylvania

All was quiet in the Hileman household, at least, for the moment. Mel was praying behind closed doors at the far end of his large sprawling brick rancher, just as he did every morning, in the quiet solitude of his home office. Ocie, on the other hand, was on the opposite side of the house, scurrying about her large kitchen, creating her husband's favorite weekend breakfast—a large platter piled high with two eggs, sunny-side up, over two thick buttermilk pancakes, covered with a rich golden maple syrup. Diligently searching the shelves of her refrigerator through a maze of pickle jars, salad dressings and other condiments, she finally found what she was looking for—Hazelnut Delight—Mel's favorite coffee creamer, hidden behind a large jar of mayonnaise. Closing the refrigerator door, she detected a familiar melody coming from the hallway.

He's done, Ocie quietly affirmed with a smile. To Ocie Hileman, that melody represented much more than an old song in Mel's vast repertoire of Gospel hymns. As long as she could remember, Mel signaled the end to his daily hour-long prayer time by singing aloud these exact words: "Oh to be His hands extended, reaching out to the oppressed. Let me touch Him, let me touch Jesus, so that others may know and be blessed."

Being married to the same man since they were practically kids, she knew better than anyone the virtues of this true man of God. A retired car salesman by trade was not the only title of Mel's calling. For the past fifty year, he had been affectionately known as Brother Mel, a pastor of a small Pentecostal church, built high atop a steep Western Pennsylvania hillside overlooking the river town of Charleroi. Preaching aside, the one attribute that made Brother Mel the most trusted man in the Monongahela Valley was his sincere faithfulness to God's calling. Not only did he believe that every single word in the Bible was the inerrant word of God, he lived it. He, and his lifelong loyal companion, Ocie, his wife of over sixty years, truly loved God with every fiber of their beings. Together, they demonstrated Godly love to all who crossed their paths. With the collapse of the local steel industry, sending thousands of hardworking Mon Valley residents into unemployment for the first time, Brother Mel and Ocie were right there to support and assist in any way they could. It made no difference whether a person was a member of their congregation or not. No matter what the need, big or small, they were always there to meet it.

The moment Mel stepped into the kitchen, his eyes widened. "Yummy!" he declared as he pointed to a breakfast feast fit for a king.

"Now if it isn't Mel Hileman! You just sit yourself right down and start eating your breakfast before it begins to get cold."

Even before Mel had a chance to act on his wife's orders, the kitchen phone rang. Mel picked up the cordless receiver. "Hello, Brother Mel speaking."

It didn't take long before Mel's facial expression went from joyful bliss to that of deep concern. By the despairing look on her husband's face, Ocie immediately knew in her spirit something was wrong.

"Thanks, Jerry," Mel quietly commented as he hung up the receiver. Without saying another word, Hileman turned and walked down the long central hallway in the direction of the living room.

"Mel, was that Jerry Banks?" his concerned wife asked, attempting to keep pace with her silent husband. "Honey, tell me what's wrong."

Stopping just short of the entrance to the living room, Mel Hileman turned to face his thoroughly confused wife. "I'm sorry, Ocie. You're right. That was Jerry Banks on the phone. He told me something about Eliot Graham withdrawing from the presidential race."

"No, that can't true! Why would Eliot do something crazy like that with only two weeks to go before the election?"

Looking into his wife's brown eyes, he responded emphatically. "Honey, Jerry said it has something to do with Rosemary. Apparently, he just found out this morning that Rosemary's very sick. He's going to contact the airport now and make arrangements to catch the next flight to Dallas."

"Don't tell me that! Not Rosemary, Lord, not now!"

Aside from her family, no one knew Rosemary Graham better than Ocie Hileman. Ocie Hileman and Rosemary's mother, Jeannie Banks, were the best of friends. In fact, Ocie and Jeannie graduated from Charleroi High School together. Ocie was Jeannie's matron of honor when Jeannie married Jerry Banks. Ocie was right there at Jeannie's side when she gave birth, over fifty-five years ago, to a little baby girl named Rosemary. She was also there, by her bedside, when Jeannie Banks went home to be with the Lord three years ago. With a look of pure compassion, Mel Hileman continued. "Jerry also said that Eliot had called for a press conference that should be starting any moment now. Let's turn on the television and listen to what Eliot has to say."

In a state of shock, Ocie silently nodded in agreement. Following Mel into the living room, she stood by while Mel located the television remote and turned on the old 32-inch console television. A host of familiar faces appeared on the television screen.

"Mel, it's Eliot and the kids," Ocie stated in a trembling voice. "Where's Rosemary?"

"Honey, come here and sit here on the couch with me to listen. Look, Ocie, Eliot's about to speak."

Saturday, October 29th
10:00 a.m. CST
The Graham Estate
15 miles North of Trinity Mills, Texas

Never, in his worst nightmare, or in his wildest dreams, had Eliot Graham imagined that this could be possible. It was a little more than one year ago when he stood at the same spot on his estate's front lawn, surrounded then, as he is now, by scores of television cameras and their respective crews. On that hot August afternoon, a passionate Eliot Graham announced to the world his sincere intention of running for the office of President of the United States. On that exhilarating day, his future appeared bright, his direction clear. He truly believed then that God Almighty had directed his life to be the conservative voice, which would bring America back from the brink of moral and economic disaster.

What a difference a year can make? Encircled by the loving support of his seven children, Eliot Graham closed his eyes and silently prayed the same words he would always pray before speaking in front of a gathering.

Lord, I know your Word says that I can do all things through Christ who strengthens me. Father, more than ever before, please supply me with Your strength to say and do all that I must. As always, I ask this in Jesus' precious name. Amen.

Opening his eyes, Graham stepped up to the microphone. Putting aside any and all fearful thoughts, he began to speak, trembling at first, but gaining strength and clarity as he continued. "Folks, I want to thank you-all for coming this morning on such short notice. With my family's help, only hours ago, I made a decision to call for this press conference in order to dispel any rumors you-all may have been hearing. Late last night, my wife, Rosemary, was rushed by ambulance to Texas Health Presbyterian Hospital."

Struggling to fight back tears, Graham continued. "Without any prior symptoms, just before she went to bed last night, Rosemary began experiencing severe abdominal pain and vomiting. Not wanting to take any chances, I immediately called for an ambulance. When she arrived at Presbyterian Hospital, the emergency room doctors ordered a battery of tests. From then on, a team of highly qualified specialists worked throughout the night trying to pinpoint the exact source of Rosemary's attack. As of 5:30 this morning, Doctor Sal Goldstein, the chief surgical resident at Presbyterian Hospital explained the result of my wife's numerous medical tests.

With all the strength he could muster, Eliot Graham announced his wife's medical diagnosis. "After a definitive biopsy taken early this morning, the good doctors at Presbyterian Hospital determined that Mrs. Graham's symptoms were the result of an extremely rare cancerous tumor called Cholangiocarcinoma. A definitive MRI scan taken last night has also shown that at present, nearly 80% of my wife's liver has been consumed by this malignancy."

Stopping only momentarily to clear his voice, Graham pushed himself to continue. "Due to the nature of these unfolding events and the advanced progression of my wife's disease, I see no other choice at this moment but to withdraw my name from the American Values Party's ballot for President of the United States."

Saturday, October 29th
11:10 a.m. EST
1 Reservoir Ave.
Charleroi, Pennsylvania

"Oh Lord, Jesus, please!" Ocie pleaded in a quivering voice, "This can't be happening! Not to Rosemary! Lord please, I beg you, touch her body! Heal her! Heal her now in the Name of Jesus!"

"My God!" Mel cried out with an expression of anger. "Ocie, do you realize what's happening here?

"Without a doubt!" Ocie defiantly declared. "This is a blatant attack of the devil. He doesn't want Eliot to become president! Honey, what are we going to do?"

For the first time since he picked up the kitchen phone ten minutes ago, Mel Hileman, the uncompromising man of God, knew exactly what he had to do. "First of all, we're going to get down on our knees and pray!"

"Amen, Mel!"

"We're going to pray like we've never prayed before, Ocie! After that, we're calling Eliot."

"Honey, what are you going to tell him?"

"The simple Gospel truth, Ocie," Mel boldly declared. "Rosemary Graham, that little girl who attended your children's Sunday School class over fifty years ago, that nineteen year old woman who asked me to marry her to a young Texas seminary student named Eliot Graham over thirty-seven years ago, is not going to die. Rosemary Graham is going to live and declare the works of the Lord!"

"Amen, Mel. Amen! Get down on those old bony knees, Brother Mel, and let's get busy!"

Saturday, October 29th
7:52 p.m. Israel Standard Time
26 Meah Shearim Street
Jerusalem, Israel

When the Sabbath arrives, an aura of peace seems to blanket the entire Holy City of Jerusalem—the shops close early, buses stop running, and the Orthodox Jews park their cars in front of their homes for the rest of the weekend. Because commerce and driving are two practices Israeli Jews refrain from doing on the Sabbath, the numerous roads leading in and out of Jerusalem also become empty.

No sooner had the sun set with another Sabbath came to a close, that the lights from a lone car illuminated the darkened kosher shops and two story dwellings that lined both sides of Meah Shearim Street, the oldest neighborhood in all of west Jerusalem. Among the thousand plus ultra-Orthodox Hungarian Jewish residences, who called the Meah Shearim sector of Jerusalem their home, a hundred year old man by the name of Benzion Yizri resided. The old man was considered by fundamentalists to be more radical in his Zionistic ideals than any other Jew living in the land of Israel.

With his first name meaning 'son of Zion', this staunchly independent ultra-conservative centenarian viewed himself as Israel's revolutionary vanguard. As such, Benzion saw the present state of Israel much differently from the vast majority of his conservative secular peers. Benzion totally rejected any notion that Israel was destined to forfeit a single inch of God's covenant land, and co-exist with their Arab neighbors in a state of misguided mutual peace. On the contrary, Benzion saw Israel's very existence—after returning from two thousand years of Diaspora—as part of God's overall prophetic plan for his people. As one of the original framers of Israel's Zionist doctrine, Benzion also regarded his nation's 1967 victory in recapturing East Jerusalem from the hands of the Jordanians a clear-cut signal that a new phase of God's divine plan was about to take place.

Three men, not including the driver, exited a car parked in front of 26 Meah Shearim Street. With men flanking him on each side, a third man, a yarmulke crowning the top of his head and dressed in casual attire, walked up to the front entrance of the two-story residence and pressed the outside intercom button. After a moment, he received a brief response.

"Who is it?" Benzion Yizri asked in an audibly weak, but clearly recognizable voice.

"It's me, Papa! Yacov!" Benzion's relieved son, Yacov Ben Yizri, the Israeli Prime Minister, answered.

Few outsiders were privy to the strong bonds of paternal influence Benzion Yizri had over his three sons, especially his middle son, Yacov. All three boys grew up in an ultra-Orthodox household, where the strict adherence to every word of the Torah was considered as important to sustaining life as were the needed staples of oxygen, food and water. So strong were the paternal bonds established in Yacov's early childhood, that even at his present age of 60 years, he obeyed his father's every command—with one major exception.

An incident occurred in the late 1990s, during Yacov Ben Yizri's first term as Israel's prime minister. For the first time in his memory, Ben Yizri blatantly broke the Fifth Commandment. He went against his father's stern warning to never concede any of Israel's God-covenant land from Judea and Samaria, the biblical names given for the West Bank. Instead, he listened to the compromising secular voices of his father's political adversaries, and handed over the West Bank city of Hebron to the Palestine Authority, a historical mistake Ben Yizri swore to himself he would never repeat, at least, not while his father was still alive.

With the ever-vigilant eyes of two highly trained and fully armed IDF officers safeguarding his immediate flank, and a full security detail inconspicuously stationed along the entire length of Meah Shearim Street, Yacov Ben Yizri stood outside his father's residence, patiently waiting for someone to answer the door. No more than a second or two after responding to his father's voice, the front entrance door to Benzion Yizri's residence opened to the welcoming smile of a very familiar face.

"Yacov!" Standing inside Benzion's doorstep, a rather short, stout man, greeted the visitor with a big smile.

"Uncle Mordi!" Yacov acknowledged, as he greeted his father's younger brother with a welcoming hug and a hardy pat on the back. So strong was their initial embrace that the gold trim skullcap that adorned the elder Ben Yizri's head became dislodged and fell to the floor just inside the door.

"Sorry Uncle Mordi," the younger Ben Yizri apologized as he stooped down to pick up his uncle's yarmulke from the carpeted surface.

"No apology necessary, Yacov! Why is it that my yarmulke never fell off my head when I had hair?"

"Uncle Mordecai, I believe I read the answer to your question somewhere in the Book of Proverbs," Yizri smiled as he graciously returned the circular cloth headpiece to its place of origin.

"Yacov, are you sure that's in the Bible?"

"I believe the proverb goes something like this," the young Ben Yizri responded, staring intently into his uncle's aging grayish blue eyes. "God gives youth hair, so people won't stare. God instructs old bald men to wear yarmulkes, so people won't care to stare."

"Chapter and verse?"

"Uncle Morti, I won't lie to you," smiled his nephew with a mischievous grin.. "I asked God to add that verse ten years ago when I, too, started going bald."

To Yacov Ben Yizri, his 84-year-old uncle, Mordecai, was a true Godsend. After the death of his mother, Zila, his father managed to live by himself for only a short period of time until his eyesight began failing him. Then, for the past five years or so, his Uncle Benjamin, a widower himself, moved into his brother's Meah Shearim Street residence to be both a companion and a caregiver to his elderly sibling.

"How's Papa?"

"Grimfaced and foreboding, as usual," shrugged the older Ben Yizri. "I don't have to tell you, Yacov, but despite your father's advanced age and failing senses, Benzion Yizri's mind is as sharp as ever."

Before saying another word, Mordecai Ben Yizri paused momentarily, staring into his nephew's eyes with a look of deep concern.

"Yacov, why am I getting this feeling that you have come here with a heavy burden on your heart?"

The younger Ben Yizri gently placed a reassuring hand on his uncle's shoulder and smiled. "Uncle Mordi, all I can tell you is that I have a very big decision to make and I need to talk to Papa before I make up my mind."

"I completely understand, Yacov," his uncle responded with an affirming nod, knowing by the troubled expression on his nephew's face that this burden he was carrying was a matter of utmost importance.

Saying no more, the younger Ben Yizri followed his uncle the short distance into the entrance foyer and downstairs to the parlor. Stopping just short of the parlor's entrance, Mordecai Ben Yizri affectionately placed his hand on his nephew's shoulder and softly commented, "Yacov, he's in there waiting for you."

"Thanks, Uncle Morti."

As his Uncle Morti departed to the privacy of his upstairs bedroom, Yacov Ben Yizri stood alone, his eyes fixed on the shadow of a great man quietly resting in the solitude of the downstairs sitting room. For a brief moment, the Israeli prime minister allowed his mind to wander back to a time when his father was not only young and vibrant, but a time when the world had very little faith in his father's Zionist dream for a homeland for his people, Israel. In those days, many, including some of his own Jewish people, had said there would never be a Jewish State. They said recognizing a Jewish enclave with established borders in the Muslim-dominated Middle East was unrealistic, but Papa said otherwise.

In all of these years, nothing has changed, thought Yacov Ben Yirzi to himself. *They were wrong then, and they're still wrong today.*

Quietly, Yacov Ben Yizri stepped into his father's first floor sitting room. A cloth-cushioned couch, where Benzion was now comfortably resting with eyes closed was positioned against one wall and a winged-back chair and a leather recliner were tastefully placed against the other.

"Hello Papa, it's Yacov."

Benzion opened his eyes and smiled. "Yacov, Son, sit down here on the couch beside me so I can see you better."

Following his father's instructions, Yacov Ben Yizri positioned himself on the couch only inches away from his father. Leaning forward, Ben Yirzi affectionately gave his father a kiss on the cheek and said, "Papa, you know I love you."

"I love you, too, my son."

"As always, Papa, I have come here today seeking once again your wise counsel."

With all the strength he could muster, the elderly Benzion leaned forward, staring directly into his son's eyes and said, "Yacov, my son, my counsel to you hasn't changed since the last time you asked for it."

With a glaring fiery stare, the elder statesman continued. "You came to me asking for my advice three years ago after President Harris promised you that U.N. sanctions against Iran would stop Hassan Rouhani 's plans to build a nuclear bomb. I told you then that sanctions would never stop a crazy man. Crazy men don't care about the needs of their people. All Rouhani wants is Tel Aviv destroyed and Israel wiped off the face of the map. Sanctions didn't stop him and never will."

"You're so right, Papa."

"I'm not done, Yacov. You came to me two years ago, asking for my opinion concerning freezing settlement construction in Judea and Samaria. I told you then that the two-state solution doesn't exist. There are no two people here. There is a Jewish people and an Arab population. There is no Palestinian people, so you don't create a state for an imaginary nation. They only call themselves a people in order to fight the Jews."

"Papa, as always, you were right. You are always right, Papa! When am I ever going to get that fact into my thick head and listen?"

"My son, lift up your head and listen now to my words and never forget what I am about to say."

Though the toll of years had weakened his lungs, the intensity of his youthful Zionist passion spoke clearly through Benzion's age-worn voice. "This land belongs to G-d, no one else! We are simply stewards of His will." declared Benzion Yizri, his head defiantly shaking back and forth. "G-d has given title deed to His land to Abraham's descendants through Isaac, not Ishmael, which this deceived world likes to believe."

With a cautious stare mixed with fatherly pride, Benzion once again firmly admonished his son, the Israeli prime minister. "Yacov, listen to me. G-d has chosen you for such a time as this to guide His people through these tumultuous times. Next month, I will be one hundred and one years old. Who knows how much longer I will be with you, my son. That is why you must trust in Adoni with all your heart and listen to His voice only. As Solomon did so long ago, Yacov, allow Adoni alone to guide your thoughts and give you all the wisdom you will need to make decisions to protect His people from their enemies."

Humbled almost to the point of tears, the younger Ben Yizri stated the true reason for tonight's visit. "Forgive me Papa," confessed his remorseful son. "I admit before you and G-d, for the past four years, I have listened to the voices of men instead of Adoni. The economic sanctions placed on Iran only gave the Rouhani regime the time needed to build nuclear bombs."

Yacov Ben Yizri paused momentarily, wiping the tears from his eyes before continuing. "I then waited to see the result of America's presidential elections, hoping that either the Republican candidate, Robert Berry, or the Independent candidate, Eliot Graham, would be elected president and stop Iran's insane pursuit to wipe Israel off the face of the earth. The way it looks now, neither of these conservative American candidates will be elected. In all likeliness, the ultra-liberal, Analise Devoe will be the next American president, and I believe this will have very serious implications for Israel. Analise Devoe has gone on public record stating that she intends to cut deeply into the present aid we receive from the United States if Israel does not give in to the Arabs' demands for a Palestinian state with east Jerusalem as its capitol."

Again, the younger Ben Yizri momentarily paused, this time noticing a marked widening of his father's eyes, as if the elder Yizri was staring at something or someone standing directly behind them.

"Papa, what's wrong?"

"Yacov, I want you to do me a favor," his father asserted with a strange expression of amazement on his face.

"Anything, Papa!" Ben Yizri replied with a voice of concern.

"Go into the kitchen and bring me back my Tanakh. You will find it on the kitchen table."

"I'll be right back, Papa."

Without hesitation, Ben Yizra acted on his father's request. No more than a minute had past when Yacov Ben Yizri arrived back in the parlor. "I'm back, Papa," Ben Yizri declared, holding tightly under his right arm his father's oversized Hebrew Bible. "I have your Tanakh with me, Papa."

With the same dazed expression on his face, the elderly Benzion looked at his son and said, "Sit down again beside me and open the Tanakh to the eighth chapter of the Book of Ezra, and translate for me in English the 31st verse.

After a moment or two of searching through pages and pages of the large print Hebrew text, Yacov Ben Yirzi stopped his search somewhere in the middle of the Hebrew Bible. "Okay, I found the verse you asked for Papa, Ezra 8:31."

"That's it!" the old man declared. "Read it out loud, my son."

Translating from Hebrew to English, the Israeli Prime Minister read aloud an ancient biblical account that had taken place thousands of years ago along the shores of the Persian Gulf in what is now present day Kuwait.

"Then we journeyed from the river Ahava on the twelfth of the first month to go to Jerusalem; and the hand of our God was over us, and He delivered us from the hand of the enemy and the ambushes by the way."

Confused, the younger Ben Yizri looked up from the large print Hebrew text and asked, Papa, I don't understand. What significance does this particular verse have?"

"Son, as you were speaking a moment ago, I distinctly heard a voice inside my head say, "read aloud Ezra 8:31." Benzion replied with a broad smile.

"What?"

"I know it must sound crazy, Yacov, but I know what I heard." Benzion declared.

"If it were truly a voice that you heard, Papa, what do you think it means?"

Instead of answering his son's poignant question, Benzion Yizri proceeded to close his eyes and bow his head. After a moment or two of silence, he lifted his head high, and to the complete astonishment of his son, began speaking the following statement aloud in perfect Hebrew. "Yacov Ben Yirzi, you are the chosen leader of my people, Israel. As I had instructed my prophet Ezra, so long ago, to lead my people along a safe journey from where the river Ahava (Euphrates) flows into the Persian Gulf, across the dry deserts of ancient Babylon and Assyria, all the way to Jerusalem, I now give you this charge. Yacov Ben Yirzi, you are to call together an assembly of only those ministers whom I have placed directly under your authority. When they have all assembled, you are to authorize your ministers to follow the exact instructions I had given my prophet, Ezra."

Yacov Ben Yizri sat spellbound. At no time in his memory could he recall anyone, let alone his century old father, speak with such clarity and authority.

"First, you must instruct your ministers that prayer and fasting is a priority of the utmost importance. Before setting out on their journey back to Jerusalem, I instructed Ezra to lead his people in both prayer and fasting that they might have a safe journey. Even with multitudes of bandits and ambushes along their entire route back to Jerusalem, I, Adoni, delivered my people from the hands of their enemies. Listen carefully to my instructions, Yacov Ben Yirzi, for this is your hour to bring Me glory!"

*This is not my father speaking, h*e reasoned. *This has to be G-d!*

"Beginning next Wednesday at sunset and ending at sunset after next Saturday's Sabbath, you and your selected ministers are to fast. During that time, no solid food shall touch your lips. You may drink only liquids. While you fast, you and your ministers are to earnestly pray and endeavor to seek My face and My wisdom only. I, in turn, will instruct all of you as to My plan to bring Me glory. Thus saith Adoni."

"Enough said!" declared the Archangel Michael, as he withdrew his hand from the head of the human, Benzion Yizri. Turning to the angel standing to his right, the massive Archangel commented, "If these humans are obedient and will fast and pray as instructed, God will honor His Word and reveal His plan to keep Israel safe from Satan's soon planned attack."

"What happens to Israel if Yacov Ben Yizri's ministers fail to heed God's instructions?" Ramiel, Yacov Ben Yizri's assigned ministering angel, asked.

"As always, humans have a free will," God's appointed Captain of His Heavenly Host replied. "The consequences for willful disobedience to God's specific charge will be severe. All we can do now is pray that Yacov Ben Yizri's ministers will listen to God's directive to pray and seek His face only."

Saturday, October 29th
12:16 p.m. EST
1 Reservoir Ave.
Charleroi, Pennsylvania

Two massive angelic beings stood silently by, carefully watching in awed admiration as the two human occupants of the dwelling humbly lay on their living floor, obediently beseeching God to miraculously intervene and save the life of Rosemary Graham. After several minutes listening to Ocie and Mel Hileman's earnest petitions, quoting aloud such specific verses as First Peter 2:24, "By Jesus' stripes, Rosemary Graham has already been healed", the angels broke their silence.

"I believe it is time, my friend." Standing to Yahriel's left was Muriel, the angelic prince whose vital mission was to spread throughout the entire earth the message of God's Gospel Truth.

With a simple nod of Muriel's head, Ocie Hileman felt impressed to look up from her prostrate position on her living floor and witness a familiar face on the nearby television screen.

"Mel, honey, look who's on television!"

Following his wife's instructions, Mel lifted his head and smiled. "Ocie, it's Gene! He's being interviewed by Brenda Waters on KDKA news!"

Gene Binder was not only a respected deacon in Mel Hileman's church, he was also the President and CEO of the Monongahela Valley Hospital, a local community hospital built that met the medical needs for the residents of the entire Monongahela River valley.

"Mel, please turn up the sound so we can hear what's going on."

Standing outside the hospital's main entrance, the popular Pittsburgh News personality asked the hospital's president her first question. "Mr. Binder, it has been brought to our attention at KDKA News that you witnessed some kind of a miracle which took place recently at your hospital. Could you explain?"

"That's right Brenda," Binder proudly confirmed. "Medically speaking, what happened here two short days ago is nothing short of a miracle."

"How so, Mr. Binder?"

"Clinton Rhodes, a local resident of nearby Belle Vernon, Pa., was admitted earlier this past week, suffering from the severe effects of advanced liver cancer. When he was admitted into our emergency room, his condition was dire, to say the least. He was jaundiced, his abdomen was distended, and Mr. Rhodes was unable to eat or even drink small amounts of water. We were also told by his wife, Betty, that when Mr. Rhodes was first diagnosed with liver cancer back in early May, doctors from our nation's top cancer centers including Johns Hopkins, the Mayo Clinic, and Pittsburgh's UPMC liver transplant center, all concurred that Mr. Rhodes' condition was terminal, giving him less than six months to live."

"But all that has since changed, correct Mr. Binder?"

"Without a doubt, Brenda!" the hospital president acknowledged. "As of early yesterday morning, almost six months to the day that he was told he had terminal liver cancer, Clinton Rhodes is cancer free! Where his tumor marker, CA19-9, a protein that indicates the presence of cancer, was once over 37,000, as of this morning, Mr. Rhode's CA19-9 is less that 10. Where only days ago, Mr. Rhodes had a massive cancerous tumor almost a foot-long protruding from his abdomen, today the tumor is completely gone!"

Turning toward the television camera, the attractive African-American reporter smiled as she announced, "I'm sure by now everyone watching at home is sitting on the edge of their seat, waiting anxiously to find out for themselves how a man given a medical death sentence gets another chance at life. Stay tuned. We will be airing the rest of the story when we get back after a brief station break. Get ready to meet the real hero behind this amazing true story, a doctor named Jerome Canady."

During the short respite of time during the commercial break, a jubilant Ocie Hileman looked at her equally astonished husband and declared, "Mel, this has to be from God!"

"Honey, there's no doubt in my mind!" her husband confidently replied with an affirming nod. "Once again, the Lord is faithful to answer the prayers of His people!"

No sooner had her husband responded to her comment, than another thought entered Ocie's mind. "Mel, quick, you need to get Jerry Banks on the phone before the commercial ends. Tell him he needs to turn on KDKA News, now!"

"Jerry may have left already for the airport, but I have his cell phone number," Hileman replied. "Either way, I'll call him immediately!"

Saturday, October 29th
11:26 a.m. Central Time
The Graham Estate
15 miles North of Trinity Mills, Texas

Even though the last of the television news vans had departed over an hour before, vehicles, large and small, not only lined the paved driveway leading up to the main house of the Graham Estate, but also filled every conceivable space available on the estate's expansive front lawn. Inside the large two-story house owned by Rosemary and Eliot Graham, family members and close friends gathered together to offer their loving support to two people who had always unselfishly given everything they had to the welfare of others. In the kitchen and dining room, covering every square inch of both table and countertops, filling every available shelf in the large capacity refrigerator, there was every food item imaginable. Though people were assembled in various rooms throughout the expansive downstairs, it was in the large family room where an array of emotions ran the gamut from heart wrenching tears to victorious cheers. From the front entrance of the home's main foyer, a seemingly endless parade of children, grandchildren, and close friends lined up to take their turns hugging, kissing, crying and praying over the smiling woman now seated beside her husband on their family room couch.

Overwhelmed with the emotional atmosphere, the Graham's youngest child, Sydni, got up from the deacon bench positioned against a wall on the far side of the family room, and walked toward the kitchen. The moment she arrived, the wall phone located just inside the entrance to the kitchen rang.

"Hello, this is the Graham residence, Sydni Graham speaking."

"Sydni, honey, this is Grandpa Jerry."

"Grandpa, did you hear the news?"

Sydni, I want you to listen to me," a firm voice on the other end of the receiver, responded. "No matter what you have heard so far, you've got to believe me, honey, your mother is going to be all right."

"Grandpa, how do you know that for sure?"

"Syndi, all I can tell you is this. God has placed within me this unexplainable peace that tells me that He is in charge of this entire situation. He is also telling me to tell you, Honey, to trust Him. Trust Him, Syd, like never before, and everything is going to be all right. I just know your mom's going to be fine."

"Thank you, Grandpa–Thank you, Jesus!"

"Sydni, I need to talk to your father, Honey. Can you get him on the phone?"

"Grandpa, stay right there! I'll go get Daddy. He's seated right beside momma on the family room couch."

Saturday, October 29th
12:32 p.m. EST
Pittsburgh International Airport
Pittsburgh, Pennsylvania

His scheduled flight to Dallas had just left the tarmac outside Southwest Airlines Gate 10, but Jerry Banks was not onboard. He sat alone, watching with joy through a large glass-paned observation window the plane that took off without him. With his cell phone pressed firmly against his ear, Jerry Banks nervously waited for the sound of a familiar voice.

"Hello, this is Eliot!"

"Thank God, Eliot!" an anxious Jerry Banks sighed in relief. "Son, listen to me, I believe I've got good news."

"What are you talking about, Jerry?"

"Eliot, carefully listen to me!" his father-in-law implored in a firm tone of voice. "I believe I found a doctor here in Pittsburgh who has the tools to remove cancerous liver tumors."

"Who is this doctor?"

"His name is Jerome Canady," an emotional Banks, fighting hard to hold back his tears, replied. "He has invented a patented surgical procedure that uses an intense beam of plasma light to safely remove tumors that have entangled themselves around blood vessels. No one else in the world has ever successfully been able to do this before."

"How did you find out about this doctor?"

"I didn't!" Banks replied, now with torrents of joyful tears streaming down his face. "Eliot, this is a miracle from God. Mel Hileman just called me on my cell phone less than ten minutes ago and told me to watch this miraculous story on KDKA television about a local Mon Valley man, diagnosed with terminal liver cancer, who is now 100% cancer free. The moment Mel said goodbye, I immediately turned around, and right there, directly in back of where I am presently sitting, was a large wall-mounted flat screened television, already tuned to that same station."

"Jerry, are you absolutely sure this guy had terminal liver cancer?"

"Not only did he have terminal liver cancer, Eliot, over 60% of his liver was covered by the tumor and now he is cancer free!"

"Praise God, Jerry! Tell me, how can I get in touch with this doctor?"

"There's no need, Eliot. I just got off the phone with Doctor Canady only moments ago. You and Rosemary are scheduled to meet with Doctor Canady at the Mon Valley Hospital tomorrow at 10 a.m."

"Jerry, my ears must be deceiving me. Did you say Mon Valley Hospital?"

"Eliot, your ears are working perfectly fine. Doctor Canady is a resident surgeon at Mon Valley, the same hospital where Rosemary was born over fifty-five years ago."

Saturday, October 29th
11:37 a.m. Central Time
The Graham Estate
15 miles North of Trinity Mills, Texas

"Praise Jesus!" Eliot Graham cried, loud enough for everyone in the house to hear his voice. "Praise Jesus! Praise the Lord! Praise Jesus!"

As people gathered, Eliot Graham stood at the entrance to the kitchen, holding his hands high above his head and praising God with tears of joy streaming down his face.

"What is it, Daddy?" his concerned oldest daughter, Mary Elizabeth, asked.

"Honey, God has heard our prayers," an emotional Graham cried, wiping the tears from his face with the palms of his hand. "Sometime later on this afternoon, as soon as we can make arrangements, Rosemary and I are leaving on a flight to Pittsburgh, Pennsylvania to meet with a doctor named Jerome Canady."

Looking at all the confused faces staring in his direction, an emotionally overjoyed Eliot Graham continued, "Guys, I can't explain how I know this, but I believe with all of my heart that God has chosen this gifted surgeon to remove every vestige of cancer from your mother's body."

Chapter Eighteen

"Woe to the inhabitants of the earth and the sea! For the devil has come down to you, having great wrath, because he knows that he has a short time."

~Revelation 12:12 (NKJV)

Sunday, October 30ᵗʰ, 2016
9:15 a.m. Iranian Standard Time
Port of Shahid Rajai
Iran

As Sahid Mohammad strode across his ship's cargo deck, he paused momentarily and glanced upward. About one hundred feet above his head, a loading crane was lifting a large truck-sized container labeled "melons" from the ship's deck below. For a brief moment, the Pakistani born skipper of the Iran Deyanat, operated by the Islamic Republic of Iran Shipping Lines, smiled to himself. As far as Captain Mohammad was concerned, the contents inside this container, or any of his inventoried shipments for that matter, were correctly marked, even if they weren't. *We can take almost anything into and out of Iran*, he thought to himself with a grin. *The Revolutionary Guards have never confiscated my goods in the past, nor would they today.* The Iranian state-run company that owned this 44,458-pound dead weight bulk carrier, regularly falsifies shipping documents in order to hide the identity of end users, using generic terms to describe shipments to avoid the attention of shipping authorities. They also employ the use of cover entities to circumvent United Nations sanctions on a variety of illegally transported freight.

After leaving Shahid Rajai four months prior, following a nautical course with scheduled stops in India, Thailand, the Philippines, and finally China, as of 4:37 a.m. this morning, the Iran Deyanat finally completed its roundtrip journey. This Iranian government-owned, 200-meter floating transport, arrived home at its reserved spot along the loading docks of Iran's busiest commercial port. With its massive cargo deck stacked high with truck-sized containers filled with an endless assortment of Chinese goods ranging from electronic equipment to industrial products, its crew of 17 Iranians, 3 Indians, 2 Filipinos, and 8 Eastern Europeans, worked laboriously, nonstop, using a variety of manual and gas powered vehicles to unload the numerous crates that filled the Iran Deyanat's inside hull from bow to stern.

Standing precariously high atop the extended metal arm of a massive dockside crane, two sets of yellow eyes closely followed the progress of the first of four metal containers. With the first metal container resting on the flat bed of a tractor trailer truck below, the dark-skinned winged apparition turned to his taller yellow-skinned companion, and proudly proclaimed, "One down, three more to go."

"Allahzad," snarled the larger of the two evil spirits. "Are you absolutely sure these containers will be completely shield-proof to radiation detectors?"

"Yes, Lord Apollon," the demon prince of Persia affirmed with a nod of his scaly brown head. "The demons assigned to oversee the Chinese manufacturing plants where the shielding containers were made have absolutely assured me that they are 100% leak-proof."

"Did you actually see the tested results for yourself?" the skeptical arch demon inquired, "Or are you blindly taking the word of one of your lying associates?"

"Lord Apollon," Allahzad respectfully retorted, "these five-ton containers are internally lined with reinforced layers of lead and steel

shielding, more than enough to prevent a one-to-five kiloton nuclear weapon from ever being detected. If that wasn't enough to prevent the emission of further radiation, Cobalt-59 is infused between the layers of steel and lead to act as neutron absorbers. The Chinese have also lined the entire interior of each container with Zirconium casings, which bond immediately with neutrons before becoming radioactive."

With his clawed index finger held high above his scaly brown head, the Middle Eastern demonic prince ended his brief tirade with this final statement. "Lord Apollon, over six months ago, I stood directly behind the Iranian President, Rouhani, observing Chinese scientists, fully garbed in protective radiation suits, placing every known radioactive material—plutonium-239, uranium 235—inside a testing chamber, lined with the same materials that now line those four shielding containers. The testing room was lined with every radiation sensor available. Before the radioactive materials were placed inside the container, every sensor sounded a warning. Once the lid was securely closed, all warning sounds had stopped."

"You better be right, Allahzad," admonished his demonic superior with an evil grin." A month from now, when the Iran Deyanat arrives at theSuez Canal, I want to see four trucks leaving Port Suez with our little surprises, securely hidden inside those containers, at the bottom of a load of ripening Iranian melons.

"I assure you, my Lord," Allahzad said, "our precious cargo will arrive in Eqypt completely undetected."

No sooner had Allahzad finished his last statement when his perceptive eyes focused on a well-dressed human shaking hands with the captain of the Iran Deyanat.

"Your chosen human has arrived," Apollon commented with a grin.

"He has, my Lord," Allahzad affirmed with a prideful grin. "Meet Mr. Yihyeh Ayyasha, the senior Hamas commander I personally arranged to break out of an Egyptian jail over a year ago."

After a welcoming handshake and a traditional Middle Eastern embrace, the two men, standing in the midst of organized clamor, got right down to business. Opening what appeared to be some sort of hard covered black binder, the captain of the Iran Deyanat removed two stapled sheets of paper, and handed them to the man dressed in a business suit.

"Mr. Ayyasha," Captain Sahid Mohammad acknowledged, here is your shipment order for four Chinese built melon containers, paid in full. Just sign your name at the bottom of both sheets. You keep the top sheet for your records; the second sheet is mine."

After following the captain's instruction, Yihyeh Ayyasha returned the pen and a signed receipt for four, 3-by-7 meter-long, metal "melon" containers.

"As you have instructed," the captain continued, directing his client's attention to the second of the four metal containers being hoisted by the overhead crane off the deck of the Iran Deyanat, "your metal containers are presently being removed from our deck and placed onto the beds of two tractor trailer trucks."

"Excellent job, captain," the smiling Egyptian said with a firm handshake. "It has been a pleasure doing business with you."

Looking down at his receipt, Captain Mohammad made one last comment before the two men parted company. "Mr. Ayyasha, according to the note attached to my receipt, you will be returning these same four containers filled with melons back to our loading docks on November 7th."

"That is correct, Captain Mohammad! In fourteen days, my drivers will return to these same loading docks with four metal containers filled to the top with freshly picked Iranian melons. Two weeks later, you, Captain Mohammad, will once again order your men to unload those same containers filled with melons at the Egyptian city of Port Suez. From there, these melon-filled containers will be transported once more by truck, arriving at their final destination, Cairo, on the 24th of November.

"Mr. Ayyasha, tell me, will the melons be ripe at that time?"

"Oh, yes, Captain Mohammad, I assure you. They will be ripe."

Sunday, October 30ᵗʰ, 2016
8:58 a.m. Israeli Standard Time
Prime Minister's Office
3 Kaplan St., Jerusalem

Even on a usual day, anxiety levels could run high within the four walls of the Israeli prime minister's office. But as this new day began, the stress levels were already running far above normal inside this downtown Jerusalem landmark. Something had gone awry in the tumultuous Middle East, and no one, not even the savvy Israeli Prime Minister, knew its final outcome.

At exactly 8:58 a.m., Yacov Ben Yizri made his entrance into the Israeli cabinet room. His seven ministerial subordinates, already seated around the large oval-shaped conference table, were not looking directly at the Israeli prime minister, but at what he was holding under his right arm. For the second time in recent memory, the Israeli prime minister walked over to claim his designated seat of honor at the head of the Israeli conference room by placing a copy of the Torah in plain view on the tabletop.

"Yacov, why is it that every time I see you carrying the Torah around with you, I get the feeling that something bad is about to take place?" Eli Yishai, the Minister of Internal Affairs, asked.

Instead of directly addressing the question posed by his Minister of Internal Affairs, Ben Yizri looked directly into the eyes of his seven assembled ministers and calmly stated:

"I don't have to tell any of you that these are extremely dangerous times. Our surrounding Arab nations are presently in a state of revolutionary flux, and no one sitting here, including myself, has any answers. What started over a year ago with the fall of the government in Tunisia and then, Egypt, has now spread like wildfire throughout the entire Middle East with no end in sight. With last year's fall of Mubarak's long reigning Egyptian government, Israel lost a great stabilizing force of peaceful support along our southern borders. During all the chaos that took place in Cairo, not one international news outlet made mention of the fact that Yihyeh Ayyasha, the senior Hamas commander, broke out of an Egyptian jail along with thousands of other prisoners. This known terrorist was then able to traverse the Sinai Desert in a series of getaway cars. Arriving at the Gaza border, he then crawled on his belly through a smuggling tunnel and finally emerged back home in the Gaza Strip to a hero's welcome."

Ben Yizri paused momentarily, turning his attention back to his Minister of Internal Affairs.

"Eli," the Prime Minister replied, picking up the copy of the Torah he had placed on the tabletop for all to see, "in this insane world, where sometimes nothing seems to make any sense at all, I have recently discovered that this ancient book, passed along to us by our ancestors, has all the answers, but unfortunately, no one is willing to accept them."

"Does the Torah tell us why the surrounding Arab nations have suddenly gone crazy?"

"Silvan, the answer to your question is 'yes.'" Not wanting to be sidetracked into a lengthy discussion on biblical legitimacy, the savvy Israeli prime minister momentarily changed the subject to the main reason he had called for this impromptu meeting in the first place. Placing the Torah back down on the tabletop, Yacov Ben Yizri once again made eye contact with each of his seven most trusted ministers and said, "I don't have to tell you that we have a pressing item of business we have put off far too long. Gentleman, I'm afraid we cannot afford to put it off any longer."

"Yacov," Moshe Ya'alon, the Israeli Minister of Strategic Affairs, said, "I pray that you're not going to say what I think you are going to say, are you?"

"I am," calmly replied the Israeli Prime Minister. "No more than ten minutes ago, I just finished reading an intelligence report delivered to me this morning stating that Hezbollah is aggressively attempting to smuggle a crude nuclear device out of Iran via a ship or truck and deliver it to a highly populated Israeli city. According to the report, if the fissile device functioned poorly, it would result in an explosion with the power of 1,000 tons of TNT, resulting in radiation contamination and a "catastrophic" number of casualties. If such a device functioned properly, it could result in an explosion with the power of 15,000 to 20,000 tons of TNT, roughly equivalent to the bomb dropped on Hiroshima in 1945."

Ben Yizri paused, looking squarely at each of his ministers. "Gentlemen, the time for diplomacy has ended," he emphatically stressed, "I only pray that we didn't wait too long."

"Yacov, now I know you've gone completely insane!" Moshe Ya'alon stated. "With everything else going on in the Middle East, can't you see attacking Iran right now would be suicide?"

"I tend to agree with Yacov," the Minister of Intelligence and Atomic Energy, Danny Meridor, acknowledged.

"So do I," Ehud Levy, the Israeli Minister of Defense, agreed. "With the entire Middle East presently in complete turmoil, with each nation literally fighting against themselves, this might be our only window of opportunity to attack Iran's nuclear facilitates without having to worry about the repercussions of a united Arab attack."

Not wanting to put off the inevitable any longer, Yacov Ben Yizri proposed this most poignant question to the seven ministers. "Gentleman, which option shall we choose?"

"I highly suggest choosing the option at the top of practicality," Ehud Levy responded. "I've already discussed the list of scenarios at least a dozen or more times with my top intelligence officers."

"Then, which option do you suggest we attempt?" Ben Yizri questioned.

"I personally suggest sending them a team of eight F-16s fighter equipped with bunker-busting BLU-109 bombs. Their four targets would be the uranium-enrichment facility at Natanz, the enrichment site at Qom, the uranium conversion facility at Isfahan, and the heavy water reactor at Arak. These bombs are capable of penetrating deep enough underground to "severely" damage each of these targets without the fear of releasing deadly amounts of radiation into the surrounding countryside."

"What about the safety of the mission crew?"

"That, my friends, is our number one concern," acknowledged the solemn faced Israeli Defense Minister. "I don't have to tell you the dangers involved in such a risky mission. Once our pilots leave Israeli airspace, they will be flying over enemy territory the entire way to Iran. Throw into the mix that a roundtrip flight with a fully loaded F-16 fighter jet gets you only a little over a thousand miles of flying range without refueling. That leaves our pilots with a shortfall of at least 700 miles from the nearest Israeli runway."

"Talk about mission impossible!" commented Deputy Prime minister, Meshulam Nahari, with a glum expression on his face. "Once the actual attacks on the nuclear facilities are made, every Arab air force within a two thousand-kilometer radius of Iran will have their own jets in the sky to shoot ours down.

All eyes in the room were focused on the person sitting at the head of the table. Knowing that ultimately, the decision to order such a risky and potentially explosive mission of having Israeli fighter jets unilaterally attacking Iran's nuclear facilities rested solely on his shoulders, Ben Yizri looked down on the tabletop at the book that he had carried with him into this conference chamber. As his father, Benzion Yizri, had done in his presence only two days prior, Yacov Ben Yizri opened the Torah to a place he had already bookmarked and began reading aloud in Hebrew.

Now I gathered them by the river that flows to Ahava, and we camped there three days. Then I proclaimed a fast there at the river of Ahava, that we might humble ourselves before our God, to seek from Him the right way for us and our little ones and all our possessions. Then we journeyed from the river Ahava on the twelfth of the first month to go to Jerusalem; and the hand of our God was over us, and

He delivered us from the hand of the enemy and the ambushes by the way."

Once again, Ben Yizri looked up from the ancient Hebrew text to face a room filled with skeptical stares.

"Yacov has totally lost his mind," whispered Avigdor Lieberman, the Israeli Minister of Internal Affairs, into the ear of his fellow minister, Eli Yishai.

"No, that is definitely not Yacov Ben Yizri speaking," the Minister of Internal Affairs agreed. "Those are the words spoken by his crazy Zionist father, Benzion."

Seeing the telltale signs of skepticism on his subordinates' faces, Ben Yizri closed his eyes once more and silently prayed.

"Adoni, I alone cannot convince these men to accept the challenge I am about to propose to them. Please, Adoni, I am asking you now to intervene and impress upon their minds and hearts the vital importance of the role I will be asking them to take on behalf of the existence of your people, Israel."

Opening his eyes, the Israeli Prime Minister calmly spoke. "Just two short days ago, I would have completely agreed with everything you're thinking about me right now, but please, my friends, hear me out!" At this moment in time, whether you consider yourselves to be religious or not, is totally irrelevant. Whether you even believe in the words of the Torah doesn't really matter. The only thing that is relevant here is that the very existence of our people depends totally upon the actions I am asking each of you to apply to your lives this coming week."

With their full attention focused solely on him, Ben Yizri continued. "My fellow ministers, I will now endeavor to show each of you how that ancient journey taken by our people thousands of years ago has relevance to our present situation. Realizing they were about to enter a perilous country that was notorious for "the enemy on the road," Ezra ordered his people to stop along the banks of the Ahava River, known today as the Euphrates River, and enter into a three-day fast, praying without ceasing that they might have a safe journey back to Jerusalem. According to what I just read from the Torah, even with multitudes of bandits and ambushes along their entire route back to Jerusalem, Adoni delivered our people from the hands of their enemies."

Pausing once again Yirzi looked directly at each of his seven ministers and posed these poignant questions. "My friends, when it comes to our love and devotion to Israel, we are in complete solidarity. Each one of us was born here. Each one of us has served in the Israeli military. If called again, I know that each of us would be willing to give up our life for the protection and security of our people. We are presently serving in the capacity as sworn protectorates of our nation. With that in mind, I ask each of you to honestly search the depths of your heart and answer these questions. How dangerous to Israel is a nuclear Iran? To what length would the present Iranian regime go to carry out its planned agenda of wiping Israel off the face of the earth? And most importantly, can we sit here and afford to wait any longer?"

"Yacov, what do you propose that we do?" Meshulam Nahari asked.

Ben Yizri turned to his Deputy Prime Minister and commented, "Beginning at sunset this Wednesday and ending at sunset after Saturday's Sabbath, I believe G-d wants each of us to fast. During that time, we are to abstain from eating all solid foods. We are to drink only water. While we fast, we are to earnestly pray and endeavor to seek G-d's face and His wisdom only. If we perform this simple task of obedience, according to the Torah, Adoni promises that He will not only give us complete victory in attacking the Iranian nuclear sites, but He will also protect our homeland from enemy reprisal, and safely bring back home all of our pilots and planes."

Ben Yizri held his breath before making his final appeal. For the first time in his sixty years of life, he was consciously putting aside his own wisdom and understanding. He was truly trusting

G-d for a successful outcome of what first appeared to be an impossible request.

"All those willing to join me in entering into a three-day fast, beseeching G-d to give us complete victory in destroying the hidden weapons of an enemy sworn to our destruction, raise your hands high and be counted."

Yacov stood by watching this unexpected spectacle unfold in a state of silent wonder. Slowly at first, then one by one, each minister reluctantly raised a hand high above his head. The display of such unprecedented solidarity among his, sometime contentious, ministers brought Yacov Ben Yizri almost to the point of tears. Words could not express the pride and solidarity he felt at that moment toward these seven men. Never in his entire political career had he witnessed such selflessness coming from such a diverse group of ambitious politicians.

Beaming with pride, the Israeli Prime Minister boldly stated, "My fellow ministers, I stand here in awe of the loyal support you have demonstrated for both your nation, Israel, and for me, its prime minister. And in my capacity as the Israeli prime minister, I declare that our plan to attack the Iranian nuclear facilities has officially commenced! May the God of Abraham, Isaac, and Jacob bless and protect us all!"

Sunday, October 30th, 2016
10:00 a.m. EST
Monongahela Valley Hospital
1163 Country Club Road
Monongahela, Pennsylvania

News spreads quickly in the Mon Valley, especially when it had anything to do with a homegrown public celebrity named Rosemary Graham. Not wanting to draw any undue attention to their presence, Eliot and Rosemary Graham were given special permission to park their rented vehicle in the private space reserved for the hospital's top administrator. When they arrived at Mon Valley Hospital shortly before their 10 a.m. appointment time, they were met at the hospital's back entrance door by the hospital president and family friend, Gene Binder.

"Rosemary and Eliot, I only wish we were meeting under different circumstances," Binder confided as he gave Rosemary Graham a warm affectionate hug.

"Gene, all I can tell you is that God is in control," Eliot commented with a confident smile.

"Amen brother!" Gene replied, acknowledging Graham's words with a firm handshake and a nod of agreement. "If you both would kindly follow me. We'll go inside to meet Dr. Canady."

After walking through what seemed to be a confusing maze of hallways, back storage rooms and obscure offices, the group of three finally arrived at a door at the end of a long basement corridor marked "private, hospital personnel only." Once inside, they were met by the opened arms of two of their favorite people in the whole wide world.

"Ocie, Mel!" Rosemary cried out as the threesome embraced and let out a boisterous round of 'Praise Jesus!'

"Don't I get a hug?"

"Daddy!" Rosemary Graham cried as she clenched her arms tightly around the man who nurtured her from birth until the moment she committed her life to another man named Eliot Graham.

"What time did you guys get in last night?"

"Late!" Graham declared, shaking his head back and forth. "With such short notice, the only direct flight we could find out of Dallas left at 10:15 last night. We arrived here in Pittsburgh slightly after 1 a.m. and stayed at a nearby Hilton overnight."

"Guys," Mel Hileman said, "I hate to interrupt this homecoming, but why don't we pray now before Eliot and Rosemary go in to see the doctor?"

"Great idea, Brother Mel!" Jerry agreed.

Without hesitation, all six formed a close-knit circle of prayer. With eyes closed, Brother Mel Hileman prayed, "Dear Heavenly Father, from the very depths of our souls, we give You thanks. Our finite minds can't even begin to grasp the countless blessings You have bestowed to each of us with, but most importantly, we thank you, Lord, for providing eternal salvation by Jesus' sacrifice on the cross, and complete healing and restoration by Jesus' 39 stripes. Lord, You say in Isaiah 55:11, *"So shall My word be that goes forth from My mouth; It shall not return to Me void, but it shall accomplish what I please, And it shall prosper in the thing for which I sent it."* Dear Heavenly Father, Your word also says in Matthew 19, verses 19 and 20, *"For where two or three are gathered together in My name, I am there in the midst of them and that if two of you agree on earth concerning anything that they ask, it will be done for them by My Father in heaven."* Your word also says in John chapter 14, verses 13 and 14, *"And whatever you ask in My name, that I will do, that the Father may be glorified in the Son. If you ask anything in My name, I will do it."* Finally, dear Heavenly Father, we now stand before you in total agreement that according to Your written Word found in 1st Peter, chapter 2, verse 24, that by the stripes Jesus bore on His body before He was crucified on the tree, Rosemary Graham has already received her healing from the cancerous tumor that has attacked her liver. We stand here in complete agreement that you have endowed Dr. Canady with Your wisdom, Your skills, and Your divine ability to completely remove every cancerous cell from Rosemary Graham's body. We ask this in the Name above all Names, Jesus Christ, Yeshua Ha Mashiach, our Savior, our Lord, our Restorer, our Redeemer, and our Healer. Amen."

"Amen," reiterated everyone in the circle.

"Amen!"

"Dr. Canady," Gene Binder acknowledged the doctor with a smile.

On cue, everyone released hands and turned around to the smiling face of a completely bald, middle-aged African-American man, dressed in a white lab coat with a gray-colored stethoscope draped around his neck.

"Everyone, I would like you all to meet Dr. Jerome Canady, one of the most gifted, innovative surgeons I have had the honor of working with in all the years of my tenure as the chief administrator of Mon Valley Hospital."

"Hello everybody," Dr. Canady smiled, accepting the accolades of his success with a humble nod of recognition. Without saying a word, his eyes became fixed on the woman standing in the midst of the gathering of six.

"And you must be Mrs. Graham?" he intuitively asked, extending a hand to greet the woman who would soon trust her entire life into his care.

"I am," she affirmed with a cordial smile. "Please, Dr. Canady, call me Rosemary, and I would like for you to meet my husband, Eliot."

Immediately recognizing the smiling face of the gray-haired man standing to the left of his wife, Dr. Canady graciously received Eliot Graham's welcoming hand and said, "Mr. Graham, it is truly a privilege to finally meet you, Sir. Unfortunately, I wish we could have met under different circumstances."

"The privilege is all mine, Dr. Canady."

"With that said," Canady cordially nodded to the small gathering, "I need to discuss some very important matters with Mr. and Mrs. Graham in private. Mr. and Mrs. Graham, if the two of you could please follow me into the next room."

While the others remained behind in the lounge, Dr. Canady led Eliot and Rosemary into an adjacent room, equipped with all the latest medical technology presently available to man.

"Welcome to my world, Dr. and Mrs. Graham."

"Wow!" an impressed Rosemary Graham exclaimed.

"Double wow!" Eliot added.

"Mrs. and Mr. Graham, if you would both step over here. I have something I would like to show you." Dr. Canady stood alongside a long mesh of coiled tubing that ended with a small cylinder that resembled some sort of bladeless cutting tool. Picking up the surgical tool he invented, Dr. Canady proudly proclaimed, "I would like you to meet my baby, the plasma beam surgical knife."

With his tool in hand, Canady turned his full attention toward Rosemary Graham, now sitting on a stool beside him. What he was about to say would confirm everything that God had spoken to her one day prior as she lay in a confused state of mind in the emergency room at Texas Health Presbyterian Hospital.

"Mrs. Graham," Canady paused, then chuckled, "excuse me, Rosemary, does the image on that brightly lit monitor in front of us mean anything to you?"

"Yes," she acknowledged with a frown. "I believe that's the same MRI image taken of my liver while I was in the emergency room."

"Precisely! Rosemary, did the Dallas doctors tell you what that scan shows?"

"Yes," she bravely replied, "The doctors said that 80% of my liver had been consumed by a rare form of cancer called Cholangiocarcinoma."

"What else did the doctors in Dallas say?"

"They said that it is impossible to surgically remove or medically treat a tumor of that size."

"In other words, the doctors at Texas Health Presbyterian Hospital sent you home to die."

With an expression of confidence, Rosemary looked defiantly up into Dr. Canady's eyes and declared, "That's what they say, but my God spoke to me and said, that I will not die, but live and declare His works!"

"Amen!" her proud husband affirmed.

"And so it will be!" declared the doctor.

"What are you saying, Doctor Canady?" earnestly probed Rosemary Graham with a quiver in her voice.

Canady crouched down, then leaned forward, closing the gap between his eyes and his prospective patient to mere inches. In a soft-spoken voice, Dr. Canady replied. "Rosemary Graham, this is what I'm going to do for you."

The very moment Dr. Canady finished speaking, a visible transformation took over Rosemary Graham's entire demeanor.

"You can help me?" she quietly asked as tears of hope welled up in her eyes. Where only moments before she sat boldly upright, she now broke down and openly cried.

"Yes I can," Canady affirmed, embracing his new patient with a reassuring hug.

Standing only feet away from where his sobbing wife now sat and a smiling Dr. Canady knelt, Eliot Graham raised his hands high above his head and began praising Jesus.

After waiting a moment or two longer in order to allow sufficient time for the reality of hope to sink in, Dr. Canady once again directed Eliot and Rosemary Graham's attention to the MRI scan projected on the large monitor.

"Eliot and Rosemary," cautioned Canady in a more serious tone of voice. "I want to draw your attention now to that scan of Rosemary's liver. Notice the dark areas, verses the light. The dark areas are healthy liver tissue; the light area is cancer.

"My God," declared Eliot with a shocked look on his face. "Her liver is almost totally white."

"That's right, Eliot," confirmed Dr. Canady. "That's why the doctors at Texas Health told you that nothing can be medically done to remove it. No human has ever had that much cancer removed from the liver and survived."

"Well, if that's true, Dr. Canady, how can you now stand there and tell us that you can do something others can't?" Graham asked with a tone of skepticism in his voice.

Canady smiled as he shook his head and responded to Graham's doubt by posing this philosophical question, "Eliot, you can answer this question better than I can. Is there somewhere in the Bible where it says, 'all things are possible if you believe'?"

"That's right!" Graham acknowledged. "Jesus quoted that verse from Mark 9:23, *All things are possible to him who believes.*"

"For a non-religious man, I totally concur with Jesus' statement," Dr. Canady softly affirmed. "I am sure you are both aware by now that the liver is the only internal organ that has the innate ability to regenerate itself."

Both husband and wife nodded their heads in agreement.

"Good," Dr. Canady returned, with his own confident nod. "It's going to take me at least a week or more to get all of the people and equipment in place to pull this off, but here's our plan."

Chapter Nineteen

"So the great dragon was cast out, that serpent of old, called the Devil and Satan, who deceives the whole world; he was cast to the earth, and his angels were cast out with him."

~Revelation 12:9

Sunday, November 6th, 2016
8:10 p.m. EST
Monongahela Valley Hospital
1163 Country Club Road
Monongahela, Pennsylvania

Throughout the day, a steady procession of people patiently waited for their turn to visit with Mon Valley Hospital's star patient in room 403. Yet, even with visiting hours over, more than a dozen close relatives were granted an extra half hour to spend precious time with their beloved mother and grandmother, Rosemary Graham. The final person to enter room 403 before the evening oncology staff began prepping Mrs. Graham for her scheduled noontime operation was her sixteen-year daughter, Sydni.

With her father, Eliot, standing in the background, Sydni sat on a chair positioned against her mother's hospital bed. Trying hard to hold back her tears, the youngest child of Eliot and Rosemary Graham looked her mother in the eye and said, "Momma, I've been praying all day, asking God for just one thing. I told Him I will never ask Him for anything else the rest of my life."

"Did He answer you, Sydni?"

"Mommy, I believe God did!" No longer able to hold back her tears, Sydni Graham excitedly declared, "The Holy Spirit inside of me has given me so much peace, that I now know beyond a shadow of a doubt, Mommy, you're going to be all right!"

An overjoyed father agreed with every word. With tears of joy and hands held high above his head, Eliot Graham, the former presidential candidate, praised his Lord and Savior, Jesus Christ, with all of his heart, mind, and strength.

Monday, November 7th
2:46 p.m. Israel Standard Time
Tel Nof Airbase
Rehovot, Israel

A typical workday in the chaotic life of an air traffic control operator starts the moment he sits down at the assigned control tower station, and ends when his replacement arrives at the end of an eight-hour shift. During those eight hours of continuous sitting, the responsibilities of being assigned the control tower of Israel's busiest military airbase can be overwhelming. From take-off to landing, an air traffic controller is responsible for making sure that every single detail is taken into account to ensure the safest route of travel for their assigned aircraft.

When air traffic control specialist First Lieutenant Eliana Greenfield arrived at work today, she immediately realized that her usual 3 until 11 p.m. shift was going to be more than hectic; it would prove to be historic. In fact, the moment the elevator doors opened and she entered the glass-encased control tower, she instinctively knew something big was about to take place. No matter in which direction she turned, she saw high-ranking military brass from every branch of the IDF. But it was one man in particular, a civilian dressed in a dark business suit and tie that caught her attention.

"There she is now," Captain Eli Levitt, who was standing beside the man, announced. "Eliana, come here; there is someone here I want you to meet."

For a brief moment, Eliana Greensfield defied direct orders. *What's going on? These men are all big shot generals in the IDF!*

"Eliana, come over here," prompted her supervisor, "I assure you, he's not going to bite."

Reluctantly, she followed Captain Levitt's orders and walked from the elevator to where he stood with a man, who until now, had been only a digital image on her television screen.

"Mr. Prime Minister," Lieutenant Greenfield acknowledged with a puzzled look. "Sir, it is truly an honor to meet you, but, I am afraid I don't understand; what are you doing here?"

"Lieutenant Greenfield," Yacov Ben Yizri cordially interrupted, "Let me start off by saying that the pleasure of meeting you is all mine. I've been informed by your superiors that you are one of the best air traffic control operators presently working for the IDF."

"Mr. Prime Minister," the blushing Air Force Lieutenant whispered, "Sir, I don't know how to respond to something like that."

"Lieutenant, you don't have to respond," the Israeli Prime Minister said with a reassuring smile. "But I do have a big request to ask of you."

The Prime Minister's last statement caught Lieutenant Greenfield's full attention.

"Sir, I'll do anything for you and my country," Lieutenant Greenfield responded with patriotic zeal.

"Now, how did I know that you'd say that?" Ben Yizri replied with a smile.

Before parting company, the Israeli Prime Minister made one final comment. "Lieutenant Greenfield, Captain Levitt will fill you in on all of the details of your assignment. In the meanwhile, I have other pressing business awaiting my attention."

Extending out an appreciative hand to thank Lieutenant for her service to her country, Ben Yizri closed with these heartfelt words. "G-d bless you, Lieutenant Greenfield."

G-d bless you, also, Mr. Prime Minister, Sir!" she said with a blushing smile.

Monday, November 7th
7:00 p.m. Israel Standard Time
Tel Nof Airbase
Rehovot, Israel

Except for a handful of high-ranking military personnel, scattered in various locations throughout this highly secured desert outpost, no one had the slightest clue that something big was about take place. Security measures, both inside and outside the Tel Nof Airbase hadn't changed. The same number of armed security guards was posted at their assigned duty stations along the fenced-in perimeters surrounding this top-secret facility, known for conducting tests on experimental aircraft and advanced weapon systems. But just inside the brightly lit cavernous metal confines of aircraft Hangar Gimel (the Hebrew word for 3), things were far from routine.

Even before the break of dawn, preparations were underway to ready eight experimental aircrafts for an operation so secretive that not even the mission's assigned pilots were privy to their classified destination. Only feet away from where aviation mechanics scurried about making last minute checks to a multitude of digital sensors that covered the surfaces of each of the classified F-16 fighter jets, a top-secret meeting was about to convene.

"Good evening, pilots," General Iddo Nehushtan greeted. He was a white-haired, chiseled-chinned veteran of two of Israel's past wars with their Arab neighbors. "I assume by now you're all aware that this is not a drill. Before I inform you of the specifics of your mission, I need to share something with you that, up until now, I have never openly shared with anyone."

A silent hush permeated the entire Hangar Three briefing room. Everyone present, including the eight F-16 pilots and the two invited civilian dignitaries, seated on folding chairs directly behind the podium, sat at awe of being in the presence of this legendary Israeli warrior, who was about to disclose a secret.

"My fellow countrymen," the IDF Air Force General began as he turned to recognize the two dignitaries seated directly in back, "we are honored to have our Israeli Prime Minister, Mr. Yacov Ben Yizri, with us today."

Allotting the prime minister enough time for a nod of recognition, the Israeli general introduced the civilian dignitary at Ben Yizri's right.

"We are also honored to have our Minister of Defense, Mr. Ehud Levi, in attendance."

Facing his eight pilots once again, a composed General Nehushtan began his story.

"Before I issue your mission orders, I feel it necessary to share something that happened to me when I flew my very first combat mission. This incident took place in June of 1967. I was a young IDF air force officer right out of flight school."

To the pilots' dismay, a faint relaxed smile could be seen on the weathered face of this military man who was known for his expressionless demeanor.

"Only days before, Egyptian troops began moving into the Sinai, massing along the Israeli border to the south. At the same time, Syrian troops were prepared for battle along the Golan Heights to the north, and the Jordanian troops were mounting an offensive along the banks of the Jordan River to the west. Except for the Mediterranean Sea to the east, Israel was virtually surrounded by Arab enemies. Approximately 465,000 troops, more than 2,800 tanks, and 800 aircraft ringed Israel. The United States tried to prevent the war through negotiations, but it was not able to persuade Egypt's Nasser, or the other Arab states, to cease their belligerent statements and actions. Still, right before the war, President Johnson warned: "Israel will not be alone unless it decides to go alone." Then, when the war began, the U.S. State Department announced: "Our position is neutral in thought, word and deed." By contrast, the Soviets were supplying massive amounts of arms to the Arabs. Simultaneously, the armies of Kuwait, Algeria, Saudi Arabia, and Iraq were contributing troops and arms to the Egyptian, Syrian and Jordanian fronts.

"On June 5, 1967, Israel was alone indeed, but its military commanders had conceived a brilliant war strategy. The entire Israeli Air Force, with the exception of just 12 fighters assigned to defend Israeli air space, took off at 7:14 a.m. with the intent of bombing Egyptian airfields while the Egyptian pilots were eating breakfast. In less than 2 hours, roughly 300 Egyptian aircraft were destroyed. A few hours later, our Israeli fighter pilots, including myself, attacked the Jordanian and Syrian air forces, as well as one airfield in Iraq. By the end of the first day, nearly the entire Egyptian and Jordanian air forces, and half the Syrians', had been destroyed on the ground.

"The battle then moved to the ground, and some of history's greatest tank battles were fought between Egyptian and Israeli armor in the blast-furnace conditions of the Sinai desert. While most of our IDF units were fighting the Egyptians and Jordanians, a small, heroic group of soldiers were left to defend the northern border against the Syrians. It was not until the Jordanians and Egyptians were subdued that reinforcements could be sent to the Golan Heights, where Syrian gunners commanding the strategic high ground made it exceedingly difficult and costly for Israeli forces to penetrate. Finally, on June 9, after two days of heavy air bombardment, Israeli forces succeeded in breaking through the Syrian lines.

"After just six days of fighting, Israeli forces were in a position to march on Cairo, Damascus, and Amman. By this time, the principal objectives of capturing the Sinai and the Golan Heights had been accomplished, and Israeli political leaders had no desire to fight in the Arab capitals. Furthermore, the Soviet Union had become increasingly alarmed by the Israeli advances and was threatening to intervene. At this point, U.S. Secretary of State Dean Rusk advised the Israelis "in the strongest possible terms" to accept a cease-fire. On June 10, Israel did just that. By the end of the war, Israel had conquered enough territory to more than triple the size of the area it controlled, from 8,000 to 26,000 square miles. The victory enabled Israel to unify the entire city of Jerusalem for the first time since the Roman legions under Titus destroyed our capital city in 70 A.D. and led our people into captivity. Miraculously, Israeli forces had also captured the Sinai, the Golan Heights, the Gaza Strip, and the entire West Bank."

General Nehushtan paused, briefly clearing his throat before finishing his story.

"Don't ask me how I know this," a clearly emotional General Nehushtan continued, "but as I flew my assigned bombing mission over Jordan in the early morning hours on June 5th, 1967, I could sense an unseen presence protecting my jet. When I landed safely back in Israel, my fellow pilots, assigned to my squadron, all said that they experienced the same unexplained presence surrounding their jets. I want each of you to keep this true story in mind when you take off on your mission."

With his poignant story completed, General Nehushtan took a brief moment to look at a prepared memo on the podium's surface. Looking once again at a clock on a nearby wall, he proceeded to announce the reason for today's meeting.

"In a little less than a hour from now, at exactly 8:31 p.m., an F-16 jet, flown by Major Dani Weisman, your squadron leader, will take off on runway one. Once Major Weisman's jet is airborne, he will be followed by F-16 Viper jets flown by Major Micah Cohen, Captains Elon Kaufman, Abram Yitzel, Arie Herzog, Nathan Greenspan, and Moshe Ben Yuri."

The general paused again, staring at the two rows in the back. "And finally," General Nehushtan announced in a firm, but resoundingly proud voice, "protecting your squadron's rear will be our nation's first female fighter pilot, Major Roni Zuckerman!" Everyone stood to applaud the groundbreaking achievements of one of their fellow pilots. To her people, Major Roni Zucherman was already recognized as a national hero. But today, the woman who fought hard against all social odds to obtain her dream of using her innate piloting abilities to protect the nation she loved, was now being asked to place her very life on the line to ensure Israel's future survival.

After the standing ovation, General Nehushtan motioned for everyone to be seated. Never, in all his many years of issuing military orders, had he or would he ever again, ask his subordinates to risk their lives on such a dangerous mission. Looking directly at this squadron of elite jet fighters, he announced the planned decision: "Once you are all airborne, you will be following the flight plan Dalet."

Nervous relief immediately followed the general's announcement. Even though plan dalet (four) was not the most risky of the five attack scenarios the Israeli pilots were trained to carry out, it required flying their highly sophisticated F-16 fighter jets over a thousand miles of enemy airspace, dropping eight bunker-busting bombs on four Iranian nuclear power plants, and returning home to Israel with very little, if any, fuel left in their reserve tanks.

"Before I dismiss you," the general continued with a heartfelt expression of pride, "I will turn the remainder of this briefing over to a man you all know, our Prime Minister, Yacov Ben Yizri. Prime Minister Yizri will issue your final orders."

As the Israeli prime minister got up and walked the short distance to the podium, the eight pilots pondered why a civilian, even with the highest ranking of prime minister, would issue them their military orders.

"Before I say anything," the clearly emotional Israeli Prime Minister began, "I want each of you to know how proud and truly honored I am to be standing in the midst of you, our nation's very best."

Clearing his throat, the Israeli prime minister continued, "When I first arrived at the Airbase earlier this afternoon, I asked your commander, General Nehushtan, to do a big favor for me. I asked him to break established military precedent and allow me the honor of issuing your specific mission. Seated in back, to the immediate left of General Nehushtan, is our defense minister, Mr. Ehud Levy. After consulting our best intelligence officers, we have reached a decision on which of the five missions you will follow. It was determined that the best means of neutralizing Iran's present nuclear capabilities was to carry out what you have called plan Dalet. Also, we have reassigned the code name EZ 8:31 to this operation."

Feeling more at ease, Yacov Ben Yizri removed his suit jacket. After placing it across the top of the wooden podium, he stepped out among the seated pilots.

"That was truly a fascinating story that General Nehushtan shared with all of us," the Prime Minister acknowledged. "I'd like to believe that it is an example of G-d's divine protection over His people."

With that, Ben Yirzi picked an empty chair up at the side of the room and placed it directly in front of the eight pilots. Facing his audience, a relaxed Ben Yizri continued, "I came here tonight with a truly amazing story of my own. My story took place over a week ago in a conference room, not much larger than the one here. You may or may not know this, but I've been involved in Israeli politics for a long, long time, dealing specifically with issues involving our people, and there is this one overriding fact I have learned about Jews. Does any one want to venture a guess?"

"We Jews are hardheaded and stiff-necked!" Major Micah Cohen exclaimed.

"Absolutely correct!" Ben Yizri responded with an affirming nod. "Major Cohen, have you also served in Israeli politics?"

"No Sir," the Major acknowledged with a blushing smile. "I was brought up in a Jewish home with three brothers and two sisters."

"Well, in a Jewish family, it is nearly impossible to get Jews of differing political and religious viewpoints to agree on anything! That is why I am confirming that what happened in my office conference room last Sunday morning was a miracle."

Everyone chuckled as the Prime Minister made his point. Even Ehud Levy, the Israeli Defense Minister, smiled as his long time friend and political colleague went on to relate a story that he had witnessed in person.

"There's good reason that we renamed your mission EZ 8:31," Ben Yirzi continued. "Not only did all seven of my cabinet ministers agree on the planned mission that you are about to embark on, these same Israeli politicians proceeded to do something unimaginable—something so significant that it hasn't been attempted by the leaders of our nation for the past three thousand years. These seven men put aside their petty political, philosophical, and religious differences, and entered into a three-day fast. Allow me one moment longer to quote a verse from the Torah from the book of Ezra that I have since put to memory:

'Then we journeyed from the river Ahava on the twelfth of the first month to go to Jerusalem; and the hand of our God was over us, and He delivered us from the hand of the enemy and the ambushes by the way.'

"Before starting out on a long journey from Babylon to Jerusalem, the prophet Ezra instructed his people to camp along the banks of the Ahava River, the same river known today as the Euphrates River. Like you, their thousand-mile journey was about to take them through a hostile land, where enemies and ambushes awaited our Jewish ancestors along the entire route. But just as Ezra had instructed his people to fast three days before starting on their journey, your nation's leaders have done the same. For three days last week, my ministers and I fasted. During those three days, we not only went without food, we asked G-d to give you total success in fulfilling your mission's main objective of totally destroying Iranian nuclear capabilities. We also asked G-d to return each of you back safely without physical injury or harm to your aircraft."

Glancing at the time on the overhead wall clock, Yacov Ben Yirzi nodded to himself. He knew in his heart he had completed his mission. Even though he had expressed everything he intended to say, instead of turning the meeting back to General Nehushtan, he now did something unexpected; he even shocked himself with his boldness.

"Before we call this meeting adjourned, let's ask the G-d of Abraham, Isaac, and Jacob for His divine protection over this entire mission."

Without inquiry or censure, every person seated in Hangar Gimel's briefing room, bowed his head and prayed in silent agreement with every heartfelt word spoken by their Prime Minister, Yacov Ben Yizri.

Two towering angelic beings were also standing in the back of the briefing room, nodding their heads in agreement with every word spoken by the human, Yacov Ben Yizri. Once the prayer had ended, the massive being on his right, dressed in a brilliant white garment held securely at his waist with a golden belt, turned to his olive-skinned companion, garbed as an angelic warrior, and said three simple words, "It is Time."

Monday, November 7th, 2016
7:58 p.m.
Along Israel's northern, eastern, and southern borders

From a temporary command post set high atop the roof of Tel N Airbase's main control tower, the Archangel Michael consults with two of his most trusted comrades. Turning his full attention to the golden-haired warrior standing to his right, Michael asked, "Are our northern and western borders secure?"

"Yes Commander!" Rafael declared. He was second in charge of protecting Israel under Michael's command. "My warriors are prepared for anything the enemy could possibly send our way!"

"Anything?" Michael questioned with a querying eye. "Is it not true that our enemies have accumulated a hidden arsenal of over 20,000 rockets capable of striking targets deep within Israel?"

"And possibly more," Rafael affirmed with a nod. "Allahzad has been busily preparing for a future war with Israel since the day his Hezbollah militants were soundly defeated in 2006. This time, Allahzad has enough missile sites scattered throughout southern Lebanon and Syria to send over 400-600 rockets and missiles daily into Israel, with at least 100 missiles aimed directly at Tel Aviv."

"Tell me, Rafael, how do you plan to prevent this from happening?"

"Commander, you gave me specific orders in 1948 to develop an Iron Dome of protection around the entire state of Israel."

"And?" Michael asked in a resolute tone.

"It is finished, Commander," Rafael humbly replied. "Your request for an Iron Dome of protection is now fully operational and capable of intercepting any missile or rocket fired toward Israel. As of last month, the IDF has installed three batteries of the Rafael Advanced Defense System along the Gaza Strip, and three more batteries along Israel's northern borders with Lebanon and Syria."

The Archangel, charged by his Creator with the awesome responsibility of protecting God's covenant nation Israel from all harm, looked directly into his captain's crystal blue eyes and commented, "You have done exceedingly well, Rafael."

Michael then turned his attention to an armor-clad, dark-skinned angel at his left.

"Uriel," he said, placing his massive right hand firmly upon his muscular shoulder. "Why is it that every time I stand in your presence, I can distinctly smell a sulfurous stench?"

"Your nostrils serve you well, my friend. They detect the sweet smell of battle," smiled the archangel Uriel, whose name in Hebrew means 'Fire of God.'

"The battle rages?"

"If anything, it has intensified! Allahzad knows his time is quickly running out and he is getting desperate.

"Desperate enough to mount a direct attack against Israel?"

"If it means delaying his destiny with the Lake of Fire," Uriel smiled, *"the answer is yes."*

"Then let him come! I have over a million armed warriors positioned all along the Israeli borders, ready to greet him when he makes his move. Are your warriors ready?"

"More than ready," Uriel replied as he looked out toward the eastern horizon. *"Once the eight Israeli jets leave your protective air space, they will be more than well protected by an armed gauntlet of my most seasoned warriors along their entire route through enemy territory."*

"Then it is time," Michael declared, raising his golden sword high above his head. *"To God be the Glory!"*

"Forever and ever!" his fellow sword raised comrades exclaimed.

The moment the tips of their blazing golden swords made contact, the angelic three were instantly transformed into luminous beings, their outlines radiating brilliant light as bright as the sun. An epic battle between the forces of good and evil was about to commence. At stake was not only the continued existence of God's covenant land, Israel, but more importantly, the entire outcome of God's prophetic plan for mankind on planet earth.

Monday, November 7ᵗʰ
8:27 p.m. Israel Standard Time
Runway Aleph
Tel Nof Airbase
Rehovot, Israel

Major Dani Weisman sat alone inside the cockpit of the world's most technologically advanced weapon of warfare. He was silently awaiting his superior's orders to throttle his lead F-16 viper jet down the runway toward a perilous mission with a high probability of no return. As the anxious seconds ticked away, Weisman's thoughts drifted to a poignant conversation he recently had in the Tel Aviv apartment of Josef Weisman, his 81-year-old father. After a lengthy discussion concerning Israel's tenuous existence in the Middle East, Weisman recalled his father's exact words.

"Son, as an eyewitness to all that went on, it seems to me that the State of Israel has packed more history into her 63 years on this planet than other nations have in a millennia of time. There are many surprising things about our tiny feisty nation, but the most astonishing is that she has survived at all. I can recall the very day the U.N. declared Israel a nation after two thousand years of worldwide dispersion. The very next day, the armies of no fewer than five Arab countries invaded Israel, and she has been struggling for her right to exist ever since."

With a sincere expression of national pride gleaming from every furrowed groove of his wrinkled face, the elder Weisman continued, "Son, just consider these astonishing facts!" an overly exuberant Josef Weisman declared. "Our Jewish people constitute a mere fraction of one percent of the world's population, but our contribution to religion, science, literature, music, medicine, finance, philosophy, and entertainment is staggering. Between 1901 and 1950, Jews won 14 percent of all the Nobel Prizes awarded for Literature and Science, and between 1951 and 2000, Jews won 32 percent of the Nobel Prizes for Medicine, 32 percent for Physics, 39 percent for Economics and 29 percent for Science. Why are 20% of the professors in the most prestigious university in America Jewish? How come there is such disparity when you compare other people? Are Jews particularly smarter? Are they naturally more gifted? It was a Jew who created the first polio vaccine, who discovered insulin, who discovered that aspirin dealt with pain, who discovered chloral hydrate for convulsions, who discovered streptomycin, who discovered the origin and spread of infectious diseases, who invented the test for diagnosis of syphilis, who identified the first cancer virus, who discovered the cure for pellagra, and added to the knowledge about yellow fever, typhoid, typhus, measles, diphtheria and influenza. Today, Israel, a nation less than a century old, has emerged at the forefront of stem-cell research, which will, in the near future, give humanity unprecedented medical treatment for degenerative diseases."

Josef Weisman paused, allowing his emotionally charged thoughts to settle before continuing.

"My son, despite all this, how has the world rewarded us? During the 1930s and 1940s, the world sat silently by with blinders on their eyes as Adolf Hitler sent millions of our greatest scholars, scientists, doctors, entertainers, teachers, mothers, fathers, and children to their death to Nazi gas chambers. Civilization owes Judaism a debt it can never repay. Yet even today, the world still treats Israel like a leper on the international scene. Is it asking too much that all we Jews ask for is the world's support for our right to exist peacefully in the Jewish homeland of our ancestors?"

Directly in his line of vision, the digital numbers on Major Weisman's cockpit control panel now displayed the time as being 2030 hour. With less than a minute remaining before take-off, the mission's lead pilot's immediately refocused his wandering mind back to his mission at hand.

"EZ 8:31 group leader," the familiar voice of air traffic controller, Eliana Greenfield announced. "in less than a minute, you will be taking off on runway Aleph. Do you roger that?"

"That's affirmative, Tel Nof," Weisman answered. He was completely surrounded by a mind-boggling array of technical instruments.

Faced with the stark reality that within seconds, he would be commencing the most dangerous assignment of his life—far more risky than any offensive military mission his country had ever attempted. Even so, Weisman still remained confident that his mission's objective to eliminate Iran's nuclear threat on his homeland would be accomplished. For this reason, Major Dani Weisman, along with his seven fellow IDF pilots, were more than willing to place their lives on the line to carry out their perilous task.

There were still two more mission incentives that gave the eight seasoned pilots added peace of mind. Introduced for the first time in actual warfare, the entire surface of each of the eight F-16 fight jets had been pretreated with a top-secret microscopic coating that actually made the planes disappear off radar. In order to locate objects, the radar transmitter sends out electromagnetic waves. When these waves hit an object, they are scattered in all directions, with some being bounced back to the radar dish itself. The nanotechnology painted surface on the jets actually absorbs the radio waves emitted by the radar, and releases them as heat energy scattered in space. In doing so, the material disguises the object, making it difficult to identify by radar. The paint particles don't make the plane's detection on the radar disappear completely, but make it exceedingly difficult to positively identify the object as a plane or a flock of migratory birds. Even though the jets may not entirely disappear from enemy radar screens, as far as the Israeli military is concerned, this advanced technology is a considerably more cost-effective method to evade radar detection than purchasing an American F-32 stealth jet for $5 billion.

One additional highly classified defensive weapon was also integrated into the surface of Major Weisman's jet, making it virtually impregnable to damage by an incoming missile. Working like a futuristic force field, Israeli engineers equipped each jet's surface with the top-secret antimissile Trophy system that provides a virtual bubble of defensive protection. Using a multitude of strategically placed radar sensors to detect the range of any incoming missile, the Trophy system also employs a top-secret counter-measure to directly hit and neutralize the head of any incoming threat, thus detonating it before it makes contact with the targeted jet or land-based vehicle.

Totally undetectable to even the most sensitive of human instrumentation, the Archangel Michael, Israel's heavenly guardian, ordered each of the eight F-16 fighter jets be assigned an extra measure of added supernatural protection that would far exceed anything conceived by the mind of man.

Monday, November 7th
1:27 p.m. EST
Monongahela Valley Hospital
1163 Country Club Road
Monongahela, Pennsylvania

With scalpel in hand, Dr. Jerome Canady was ready to perform what his trained peers in the surgical medical profession called impossible—to successfully remove a cancerous tumor that had already consumed over 75% of his patient's liver. With special permission granted by the hospital's top administrator, Gene Binder, Canady had transformed Monongahela Valley Hospital's main operating room into a state of the art technological theater. Suspended from the ceiling directly above where the surgeon was standing beside his anesthetized patient, Rosemary Graham, was an overhead digital camera with connections leading to a surrounding array of laptop computers programmed with the latest advances in 3D imaging. He had spent the last week and a half assigning specific roles to each of the O.R. specialists who were more than ready to assist him.

Before placing the scalpel's razor sharp blade against the red surgical mark already outlined on Rosemary's Graham's abdomen, the gifted surgeon made an unprecedented gesture. With his facial expression concealed beneath the cloth confines of a surgical mask, for the very first time in his lengthy medical career, Dr. Jerome Canady silently prayed these words, "Lord, I truly need your help. Please, God, supply me with your wisdom to accomplish what man has called the impossible. Guide my hands throughout this entire procedure. I petition you now, God, as my mother taught me long ago as a child, to ask in the name of Jesus. Amen."

Taking in a deep breath, Canady looked around the room, acknowledging each of his assigned team members with a nod of confidence.

"You guys ready?"

Immediately after petioning his colleagues' agreement, he received his anticipated answer. A unanimous display of latex glove-covered thumbs up signaled the gifted doctor to proceed.

The very moment Jerome Canady made his initial cut deep into Rosemary Graham's exposed flesh, an unexplainable sense of confidence seem to permeate his entire being. From that moment on, until the final suture was tied, ending what would eventually turn out to be an extremely tedious, eleven-hour long operation, Rosemary Graham's assigned angel, Joveniel, would carefully guide Dr. Canady's hand along to human medical history.

Monday, November 7th
8:31 p.m. Israel Standard Time
The Air Traffic Control Tower
Tel Nof Airbase
Rehovot, Israel

With a host of military officials and political dignitaries observing in the background, air traffic control specialist Eliana Greenfield leaned forward in her chair, staring intently at her control panel screen as the seconds rapidly ticked off toward the start of the Israeli military operation coded name EZ 8:31.

"EZ 8:31 group leader, take off on runway aleph at my command. Five, four, three, two, one....,"

The very moment the time on her digital display screen registered 2031 or 8:31   p.m., First lieutenant Greenfield announced, "EZ 8:31 group leader, you are now free to take off on runway aleph."

A silent observer stood inches away from the control tower's plate glass observation window, watching in awe as each of the eight F-16 Israeli fighter jets took its assigned turn accelerating down the long runway toward an uncertain destiny. The moment the final jet's landing gear lost contact with the paved runway, an unusually subdued Israeli prime minister turned toward his minister of defense and calmly stated, "Ehud, I believe it's now time for you to make the call."

"No sooner said than done, Yacov," acknowledged his lifelong friend with an encouraging smile. "I'll notify my Chief of General Staff, Benny Gantz, to place all of our defense forces on immediate stage one notice."

"Good," Ben Yizri commented with a heavy sigh. "It's now time for me to make my phone call."

"My prayers are with you, my friend," Levi commented, giving Ben Yizri a sympathetic pat on the shoulder before following through with his task.

Staring out once again at the darkened desert expanse beyond the control tower's windows, Ben Yizri silently prayed, "G-d, before I make this phone call, allow President Harris' heart to be receptive of what I am about ask of him. Amen."

Monday, November 7th
8:52 p.m. Israel Standard Time
Along Israel's Eastern Border with Jordan

"This is EZ Boy 1 passing along this little bit of information to all my friends out there. It's time to say goodbye to the broad blue expanse of the Mediterranean waters below and proceed with the remainder of our wonderful Middle Eastern tour."

Everyone tuned into Major Weisman's transmitted frequency, including all those listening inside the confines of Tel Nof Airbase's control tower, and chuckled at the lead pilot's display of guise humor. No more than five minutes after announcing his first change of course, Major Weisman's lead jet had achieved the required cruising altitude of 45 thousand feet, and was about to leave the protected skies over central Israel. From this point on, until he reached his intended Iranian target, Major Weisman knew he had to carefully disguise every single word that was now being transmitted over the closely monitored Middle East airwaves.

"This is EZ Boy 1 speaking to all my extended family members, both at home and abroad. I am now leaving the protection of our fenced in yard and will be visiting several of my next-door neighbors for a period of time. To daddy back home, and all of my tag-a-long brothers and sisters, stay your present course and just remember this important fact; there are many dogs and cats in our neighbor's yard that will be watching you every move. Be ever alert and don't ever hesitate to contact me on station EZ 8:31."

To all those listening, both in the air and on the ground, Major Weisman's coded message was quite clear to The EZ 8:31 squadron leader that he was about to leave Israeli airspace and enter the unfriendly skies over neighboring Jordan. Traveling at a supersonic mach 2 speed of 1500 miles per hour, each of the eight Israeli fighter jets would be arriving at their assigned targets over central Iran in a little less than an hour.

From this moment on, enemies, both in the natural and supernatural realm would be on constant alert for their presence.

Monday, November 7th
8:56 p.m. Israel Standard Time
Jebel Atatia
Jordan

Ever since he started his four o'clock shift, every single blip appearing on Corporal Amal Jabari's radar screen was accounted for as recognized air traffic. Corporal Jabari, along with five other Jordanian Army communication specialists, was recently assigned to man the Jordanian Army's newly installed radar outpost, strategically located 50 kilometers within Jordan's western border with Israel. Employing the latest in high-tech radar capabilities, including being able to assess the far-reaching advantages of 12 fixed, multi-sensing mountaintop radar towers, Jordan could account for every single object larger than a kite flying over their airspace, from a range of mere inches off the ground to the highest levels of the atmosphere. This newly installed security system replaced the Jordanian military forces need to patrol its borders with Israel with thermal imagining binoculars and archaic radar surveillance systems mounted atop mobile traveling humvees.

"Bahir," motioned Amal Jabari to his fellow radar specialist, Corporal Abdullah Bahir, who was standing under the open radar facility door, smoking a cigarette, "can you take over for a second or two? I've had too much coffee to drink. I got to piss!"

Abdullah chuckled to himself at his comrade's request. Only a few minutes before, he too had to go outside and eliminate a pot full of coffee from his system. Frowning, he tossed his half-smoked cigarette onto the rock-covered mountaintop surface beyond the door. "You better make it fast," the annoyed Jordanian Army corporal commented, "I've only got ten more minutes left of my break."

Without hesitation, Jabari got up from his post and quickly exited the twenty-by-thirty foot metal-framed enclosure for the privacy of a nearby sandstone boulder.

Bahir Abdullah begrudgingly assumed his partner's assigned task, glancing only occasionally at Jabari's radar screen. But only moments before Corporal Jabari's return, Abdulla noticed a fuzzy spot along the far left margin of the radar screen that shouldn't have been there.

"Jabarai!" Abdullah turned toward the opened door and shouted, "Get your ass in here!"

Immediately, Amal Jabari appeared at the door, his pant's zipper still wide-open.

"What the hell's wrong?" a flustered Jabari cried out. "Are you that addicted to cigarettes that you can't wait until I finished?"

"No, no, it's not that!" Abdullah hastily replied. "You've got to see this. There's something strange on the screen!"

Without making further comment, Corporal Jabari immediately walked over to Abdullah. Bending low, Jabari's eyes opened wide as he too witnessed the presence of mysterious lights on his assigned radar screen.

"They aren't ours," Jabaria immediately confirmed after positioning the screen's movable cursor over the top of one of the eight moving objects."

"Then whose are they?"

"That's strange," an equally perplexed Jabari answered. "This new software program is supposed to instantly supply us with the type of aircraft we're dealing with. According to the message on the screen, whatever those eight objects are, they've not been programmed into the system."

"Did you see that?" a stunned Bahir Abdullah exclaimed, his right index finger pointing to a radar screen now devoid of any digital returns.

"I saw it, but I don't believe it! How do we report something that was once there, but isn't any more?"

"Jabari, man, what do we do?"

"The answer's quite simple. If there's nothing there, there's nothing for us to report!"

"This seat is all yours," Abdullah responded with a shrug. Standing once again, he removed a pack of cigarettes hidden in his inside jacket pocket. With cigarettes in hand, he walked toward the opened door. Before leaving, he turned one last time and said, "I'll be back in ten minutes. I really need a smoke!"

Monday, November 7th
9:04 p.m. Israel Standard Time
Over Western Iraqi Airspace

Even though U.S. combat operations had officially ended in this former Saddam Hussein stronghold, American Air Force pilots still continued to play a vital role, flying daily missions over the skies of Iraq, protecting U.S. military ground personel and bombing ISIS targets throughout Iraq.

Peering down through the protective shield of his cockpit window from a cruising altitude of 35,000 feet, U.S. Air Force Captain Brent Macmillan smiled as he entertained this singular thought. *Just three more days and I can kiss that godforsaken desert hellhole goodbye forever.*

The twenty-year veteran pilot had very good reason to celebrate. For almost an entire year, he and his partner, Captain Corry Stokes, had flown uneventful nightly surveillance missions over the skies of Western Iraq. But in less than three short days both U.S. Air Force pilots would be ending their eleven-month tour of duty in Iraq. At exactly 9:45 a.m. on Thursday morning, Captain Macmillan and Captain Stokes would be boarding an Air Force C-130 transport plane leaving Iraq's Balad Air Base for a two-day reintegration program in Germany before permanently ending their service careers as fighter pilots for the U.S. Air Force.

Before their deployment, these two F-15 fighter pilots were hoping to boast that at no time, in over 250 missions, had they encountered any form of hostility over Iraq's mostly uninhabed westersn wilderness. Little did these seasoned F-15 pilots realize, that in moments their perfect streak of uneventful evening patrols was about to come to an abrupt end.

Patrolling at their routine altitude of 35 thousand feet, Captain Stokes commented, "Mac, just two more nights and we can kiss this job goodbye."

"You must be reading my mind!

"I bet Skyler's really happy about that.

"She better be! I told her yesterday that I was actually contemplating settling down and getting a real job flying for some top commercial airline."

"That's not you, Mac! You're more the type to be flying daily tours over Grand Canyon, or joining NASA to fly missions to Mars."

"You are so right, my friend! Anything is more exciting than flying these boring patrols night-after-night over this desert wasteland."

No sooner had Brent Macmillan finished his last radio transmission to Captain Stokes, than his eyes focused on a strange flashing image on his cockpit instrumental panel almost too incomprehensible to accept.

"I don't believe it! I think we have company directly above us at 5 o'clock."

"I see them," an equally shaken Captain Stokes said as he stared in disbelief at two additional flashes on his screen, also. "Whatever, or whomever they are, they're flying about 5,000 feet directly above."

"Let's go!" Macmillan, throttling his F-15 jet to the necessary speed and altitude needed to intercept the intruders entering American guarded Iraqi airspace.

In a matter of seconds, Corry Stokes made visual contact with one of the mysterious objects.

"My God, Mac!" he declared, astonished beyond belief by the blue symbol displayed on the object's main fuselage. "They're Israeli F-16s!"

"And they're armed to the teeth!" Macmillan stated.

"What do we do?" Corry Stokes asked in a panic. "We didn't receive any notice that Israeli fighters would be heading our way."

"We do exactly what we've been trained to do," replied his is cool-headed partner. "Until we're told otherwise, we engage; so he closed in on the lead trespassing aircraft.

Nothing more needed to be said. The highly trained American fighter pilots closed in on their target, simultaneously engaging the tactical electronic-warfare systems on their forward instrument panel. With each jet's onboard computer locked in on their target with an accompanying pair of Sidewinder missiles, Captain Macmillan attempted to contact the lead Israeli fighter jet.

"This is United States Air Force Captain Brent Macmillan contacting the lead pilot of the Israeli F-16 aircraft now flying illegally over protected Iraqi airspace. I am ordering you and your pilots to cease your present advance over Iraqi airspace. By the authority given to me by the United States Air Force, I am now ordering you to immediately change course and leave Iraqi airspace or I will have no other choice, but to shoot you down. How do you respond?"

Perspiration was streaming down Captain Macmillan's brow. He knew that the Israelis were the American's staunchest military allies in this volatile land of Muslim instability, but he had his specific orders to shoot down any unauthorized plane flying over his assigned territory. While his partner, Captain Corry Stokes, desperately attempted to contact his home base of Balad Air Base located 60 miles north of Baghdad, Captain Macmillan issued his final command to the silent pilot behind the controls of the lead Israel F-16 fighter jet. "This is United States Air Force Captain Brent Macmillan contacting the lead pilot of the Israeli F-16 aircraft. This is your last chance to turn around and go back to your home base before I am forced to fire upon you."

To Captain Macmillan's surprise, the pilot commanding the lead Israeli jet responded. "This is Israel Defense Force Major Dani Weisman contacting U. S Air Force Captain Brent Macmillan. Unfortunately Captain Macmillan, I, too, am on an ordered mission from my superiors and I must fulfill my assigned duties, no matter what."

Now Captain Macmillan was really desperate. If what the Israeli pilot was saying was true, why hadn't the American pilots received notice in advance to allow the Israeli pilots free airspace over Iraq?"

"Major Weisman, I have not received any orders to allow you to proceed." You must change course now, or I will be forced to fire upon you!"

"Do what you must, Captain Macmillan," responded the Israeli pilot. "I must also fulfill my mission."

"Dear God, what shall do I do?" Macmillan cried. With his right index finger posed on the throttle's integrated trigger, he makes a conscious decision, "Do it!"

Having no other option, he squeezed the throttle's trigger, releasing a blazingly fast high-speed projectile into the inky black darkness beyond his advancing aircraft. In an instant, the entire sky ahead of the American F-15 pilot brightened, indicating to Major Macmillan that his intended target was destroyed. In a moment later, the now devastated F-15 pilot received the worst untimely message of his entire military career.

"Mac!" declared the excited voice of his partner, Corry Stokes. "I just received confirmation from Balad. We're to stand down! The Israelis are free to proceed."

"My God, what have I done!"

"Rest assured, Captain Macmillan, I am still alive!"

"I don't believe this!" the stunned American pilot declared. "You're dead! I just witnessed your jet being destroyed by a Sidewinder missile."

"On the contrary, Captain," the transmitted voice of the EZ 8:31 squadron leader stated calmly. "What you just witnessed was Israeli technology destroying your missile, leaving my aircraft completely unscathed."

"Major Weisman, how is that possible?"

"Maybe one day we'll sit down and talk about how it works, but right now, Captain Macmillan, you must excuse me. As I said before, I have an important mission I must fulfill."

Monday, November 7th
10:17 p.m. Israel Standard Time
Natanz Nuclear Power Plant
Natanz, Iran

As the two expected vehicles arrived at their destination, a deafening applause radiated in all directions from this Iranian desert outpost. So powerful was its intensity that even the mortals assigned to guard the Natanz Power Plant's main entrance gate had to cover their ears in order to prevent the high-frequency vibrations from damaging their ear drums. Once inside the highly secured compound, a parade of cheering demonic apparitions closely followed directly behind the flatbed trucks. The bizarre procession came to an abrupt end near the back entrance to the plant's administrative building. Once again, the demonic hordes cheered as human workers, dressed from head to toe in protective radiation suits, drove up to the bed of each truck and began immediately removing their cargo with motorized hydraulic lifts. Once the final metal container marked "Iranian melons" was removed from the truck bed and placed somewhere safely inside the Natanz Power Plant's administrative building, a massive demon, his muscular shoulders adorned in a royal blue cloak stood on the edge of a now empty truck bed and addressed his cheering subordinates.

"Every one of you, shut up and listen carefully to me," the scathing voice of their commander, the arch demon, Apollon, thundered.

Where moments prior, mind-deafening hoots and hollers resonated throughout this arid desert complex, now a dead silence prevailed.

"Let there be absolutely no misunderstanding! In order for this elaborate plan to work, every one must diligently follow through with his specific assigned task."

Thousands of surrounding yellow eyes were now intently focused on the massive winged demon standing on the edge of an empty flatbed truck.

"In less than an hour from now, these same trucks that transported the four melon containers all the way from the Shahid Rajai loading docks will receive their new cargo."

Displaying a prideful smirk, the arch demon continued. "This time, each truck bed will receive two metal containers filled to capacity with Iranian melons. Carefully concealed at the bottom of each container will be a single nuclear weapon capable of destroying a populated city the size of Tel Aviv."

Amazingly, the demons remained standing in a rare state of obedient silence, fearful of being singled out for harsh discipline by the commander. Still displaying a prideful grin, Apollon completed his speech. "Sometime early tomorrow morning, these same two trucks will arrive at the Shahid Rajai loading docks with their cargo of "Iranian melons." The metal containers will once again be hoisted onto the deck of the Iran Deyanat. This time, our melon containers are scheduled to arrive on the 24th of November at the Egyptian city of Port Suez. From there, they will be transported by truck overland to fruit markets in downtown Cairo. Before the trucks arrive at the Egyptian Capitol, I've arranged for some of our very good friends working inside the Muslim Brotherhood to remove the hidden melon container's hidden contents. Our Muslim comrades will then repackage each of the nuclear weapons in a smaller, less conspicuous container, that is fully equipped to shield against any form of leaking radiation, and can be easily transported across the loosely guarded Sinai Peninsula. From there, they will be carefully smuggled into the Gaza Strip where I have also personally arranged to have my own handpicked Hamas militants receive and store the atomic weapons for safekeeping. On some future date, known only to our Lord Satan and myself, these same weapons will be detonated in specific locations throughout Israel."

Raising his clawed left fist high above his head, Apollon culminated his speech.

"At that time, the land of Palestine will be governed forevermore by the rightful heirs of Abraham's first-born son, Ishmael. There will no longer be a covenant land named Israel."

411

With evil sneer, the arch demon Apollon looked skyward, stretching his clenched left fist high above his head. "Too bad, Jesus!" he brazenly mocked the King of the Universe. "Without an Israel in the Middle East, you're going have to put your Second Coming plans on hold.

With a clenched left fist held high and a defiant sneer, Apollon declared his pledge of loyalty to his lord and master, "Praise be to Satan!"

Even before Apollon's demonic subordinates had their chance to raise thousands of clenched fists skyward saluting the adversary of God, it happened. A brilliant flash of indescribable searing heat consumed every single minute molecule as far as their yellow eyes could see. At the same moment, an escalating tower of fiery gases rose high into the atmosphere directly above their scaly heads. A moment ago the Natanz Power Plant's sprawling administrative building stood in the background. In its place, a massive kilometer wide cavity had formed in the desert floor, literally swallowing up all traces of any former human existence.

In less than a minute or two following the first atomic blast over the Natanz Nuclear Power Plant, three separate detonations took place, illuminating the darkened starlit skies over central Iran to near daytime brilliance. The combined hellish effects of mankind's ultimate display of self-imposed destruction all but erased any visible signs of the Iranian nuclear power facilities that once existed at Qom, Isfahan, and Arak.

With an indescribable scene of hellish destruction all about, a dazed, but unharmed Apollon sat on the irradiated scorched ground attempting to remove the numerous traces of burning embers that presently smoldered through his once elegant royal blue cloak. In every direction he turned, Apollon watched in sheer horror as thousands of his fellow demonic subordinates, including his associate Allahzad, the Prince of Persia, wandered aimlessly about in a state of total confusion.

"This is all Michael's doing!" Apollon cried out, his strained voice seething with intense hatred toward his angelic counterpart. "I swear Michael will pay for this! I will personally see to it that all of his beloved Israel will be set ablaze!"

Standing, Apollon belted out an ear-piercing command to his mystified masses. "Get off your rear ends!" he thundered. "Those bastardly Israelis have done this! Find and destroy their planes, now!"

Acting immediately on Apollon's explicit command, thousands of winged demonic apparitions took flight into the sulfurous reddish-black skies above the smoldering cavernous pit where the Natanz Nuclear Power Plant once stood.

Chapter Twenty

"For He shall give His angels charge over you, to keep you in all your ways." –Psalm 91:11

Monday, November 7th, 2016
3:17 p.m. EST
Monongahela Valley Hospital
1163 Country Club Road
Monongahela, Pennsylvania

It is as large as a football, weighs just under 3 pounds, and you cannot live without it. Even though this pinkish-brown boomerang shaped organ, located mostly in the upper right-side of the abdomen, performs over 500 vital bodily functions, one of the most overlooked facts about the liver is its unique ability to regenerate its damaged parts. With as little as 25 percent of healthy liver tissue still remaining, this amazing internal organ can totally restore itself into a whole functioning liver again. For the millions of innocent victims stricken each year with the advanced stages of liver cancer, the knowledge of this incredible truth holds little value. With so many intricate blood vessels involved, even the world's most highly skilled oncology surgeons would never consider surgically removing more than half of a patient's liver at one time—at least not until today.

Peering down into his patient's exposed body cavity, Dr. Jerome Canady paused before proceeding. Never in his twenty-three years of removing cancerous tumors that have entwined themselves around internal organs had he witnessed anything quite like this. The massive tumor wrapped itself around every conceivable major blood vessel leading into and out of the liver. Before continuing, Dr. Canady took in a deep breath and turned to the person standing to his immediate right. "Anita, please send somebody upstairs to the ICU waiting room," he quietly petitioned his personal physician's assistant. "Have them tell Dr. Graham that we need prayer down here, right now!"

Monday, November 7th, 2016
3:24 p.m. EST
Monongahela Valley Hospital
1163 Country Club Road
Monongahela, Pennsylvania

In all her many years working as a nurse in Mon Valley Hospital's ICU unit, Nurse Hilda Graves had never seen anything quite like this. As far as she could see, there were scores of people lined up and down both sides of the long corridor just beyond the locked double-doors of the hospital's second floor intensive care unit. The scene was not any better inside the ICU's waiting room. Looking much like sardines packed in a tight can, people of all shapes and sizes occupied every available space in this modest twelve-by-twenty-five foot room. Those individuals not lucky enough to find an available chair or couch to sit on had to stand shoulder to shoulder along the room's limited wall space. Appearing somewhat apprehensive when she first entered the capacity filled room, her nervous fears were quickly set to ease by the calming voice of a middle-aged man holding out a slice of pizza in her direction.

"Nurse Graves, could you kindly do me a big Texas favor and help finish off this big pepperoni and mushroom pizza we ordered?"

"That's a very tempting offer, Mr. Graham," the nurse replied with a nodding smile, recognizing Eliot Graham by his numerous appearances on television. "I'm afraid I have to pass on your generosity, but I've been asked to come up here with an important request from the downstairs O.R."

By now, everyone within listening was silent, waiting anxiously to hear the purpose of the nurse's mission.

"Mr. Graham," Nurse Graves stated in a calm professional voice, "the O. R. is requesting that all of you pray specifically that Dr Canady is able to remove all of Mrs. Graham's tumor."

Pastor Mel Hileman, who was standing right behind Eliot, lifted his right hand high above his head in an attempt to attract the attention of everyone gathered in the room. In a clear, forceful voice, Hileman announced, "Everyone listening, quickly step out into the hall and take hold of the hand of the person standing next to you."

Nothing else needed to be said. Acting promptly on Pastor Hileman's request, the occupants of the second floor ICU waiting room quietly exited, joining hands with friends and relatives already assembled in the outside corridor.

"Folks," Pastor Hileman announced as he gripped his wife's hand on the right and Eliot Graham's hand on the left. "We are now going to pray."

Standing shoulder-to-shoulder, over one hundred heads bowed before God. "Dear Heavenly Father," Hileman humbly acknowledged, "we gather here in one accord. In Jesus' name, we ask that it will be Your Divine Hand guiding Dr. Canady as he attempts to remove every vestige of cancer inside Rosemary Graham's body. We also stand in total agreement, according to Your Word found in 1st Peter 2:24, that the very moment Dr. Canady makes his final suture, that by Jesus' 39 strips alone, Rosemary Graham will have a brand-new liver, completely free of cancer, forevermore. We ask this in Jesus' precious name. Amen!"

"Amen," echoed a resounding chorus of over one hundred voices.

Monday, November 7th, 2016
10:24 p.m. Israeli Standard Time
In the Skies over Southern Iraq

With the first part of their perilous mission accomplished, the last of the Israeli F-16 fighter jets exited Iranian airspace. Some day each would realize that this return trip to the safe borders of Israel would prove to be the most challenging venture of his life.

"This is EZ Bird 8 contacting EZ Bird 1 flock leader, over," IDF pilot Major Roni Zuckerman tranmitted.

"Greetings, EZ Bird 8!" the mission commander responded.

"What is your present heading, EZ Bird 8?"

"My present coordinates are 30.2875N–48.339 E!"

"Welcome to the friendly skies over southern Iraq, EZ Bird 8," Major Dani Weisman responded. "This is EZ Bird 5 contacting EZ Bird 1."

"Yes EZ Bird 5, this is EZ Bird 1."

"Flock leader, EZ Bird 1, this is EZ Bird 5 flying at 31.544, 47.962," Captain Arie Herzog responded. "Dani Boy, not only do I have the possibility of uninvited guests rapidly approaching on my rear, according to my fuel gauge, I am presently flying this bird on fumes."

"You're not alone, EZ Bird 5!" Captain Abram Yitzel, transmitted. He was piloting the F-16 falcon jet less than a kilometer away. "I can count at least ten aircraft, possibly Iranian Saeqeh-80s, rapidly approaching from the south!"

"EZ Bird 1, this is EZ Bird 6. I'm also flying on fumes!"

"This is EZ Bird 1 speaking to my entire flock," Major Dani Weisman transmitted to each of his seven trailing F-16 pilots. "Ever since entering Iraqi airspace, I have been attempting to contact our friends on the ground, requesting their permission to set each of our birds down at Balad Air Base. I will keep on trying until I get a response. Until then, we have no other choice but to continue to follow our designated flight path home. May the G-d of our Fathers Abraham, Isaac, and Jacob be with each of us!"

Major Dani Weisman was fully determined to complete his assigned mission, no matter what the final outcome would be. "Adoni, no matter what happens," he silently prayed to the G-d of his nation, Israel, "I now place my life and complete trust into Your hands. Watch over my fellow pilots and bring us all safely home."

Even before he had the opportunity to close his short prayer with a traditional amen, two dire warning signals flashed across his control panel screen. With his left fuel gauge flashing empty, a more ominous sign appeared on his radar screen to the right.

"Two incoming missiles," Major Weisman calmly affirmed to himself. Seemingly unfazed by the sight of two deadly projectiles rapidly approaching his aircraft from the rear, the EZ 8:31 group leader made one final comment before closing his eyes. "Well, G-d, I guess now I know the answer to my prayer."

Monday, November 7th, 2016
3:26 p.m. EST
Monongahela Valley Hospital
1163 Country Club Road
Monongahela, Pennsylvania

Thoracic surgeon Gene Manzetti stood opposite Jerome Canady, working with him to prepare Rosemary Graham's abdomen for tumor extraction. With his initial role completed, Dr. Manzetti stepped aside, allowing the oncology surgeon full access to his patient's exposed internal organs. At this point there was no turning back. The only question Canady asked himself was, *where do I start?*

"Remove the tumors wrapped around the hepatic artery and the portal vein first before attempting to remove the main tumor," Rosemary Graham's assigned angel, Joveniel, spoke into Canady's right ear.

Odd, Canady silently thought to himself. *That thought never entered my mind before.*

An unexplained sense of confidence seemed to permeate Canady's entire being. From that moment until the final suture was tied, ending what would eventually turn out to be an extremely tedious, eleven-hour long operation, Rosemary Graham's assigned angel, Joveniel, would direct the gifted mortal's thoughts and hands to making medical history.

Monday, November 7th, 2016
10:24 p.m. Israeli Standard Time
In the Skies over Southern Iraq

In all his years of intensified training, nothing could prepare this seasoned IDF fighter pilot for a moment like this. Seconds before the projectiles made impact with his aircraft, Major Weisman closed his eyes. What happened next would prove to be the most incredible moment of his life.

"What just happened?" Weisman blurted out in a mental state of shock. There was no blast or explosion. To the veteran pilot's total amazement, he opened his eyes to a completely intact cockpit with fully functioning instrumentation. "This can't be!" he laughed out loud. I should be dead!"

"I second that motion!"

"Arie, is that you?" a totally awestruck Weisman asked.

"Dani, tell me if I'm wrong! Weren't we told that the Trophy defensive system is programmed to destroy only one incoming missile at a time? Well, I was just struck both broadside and behind by what I think were two Iranian Stinger missiles. There's absolutely no way I should be talking to you right now!"

"Dani," Major Roni Zuckerman interrupted, "right now, look at your fuel gauge and tell me what you see."

"My G-d! My mind can't accept what my eyes are telling me!"

"If your eyes are telling your mind that you have a completely filled fuel tank, then believe it, Major Weisman. Mine does!" Major Micah Cohen ecstatically affirmed.

"I third that motion!" Captain Moshe Ben Yuri replied.

"And I as well!" Captain Nathan Greenspan added.

"Guys, what in the world is going on here?" the euphoric voice of Captain Elon Kaufman exclaimed.

"It was G-d! Do you remember the story the Prime Minister told us about Ezra?"

"There's no other rational explanation," the somber voice of Major Micah Cohen agreed. "It had to be G-d! He has divinely protected us the same way He did over three thousand years ago when our ancestors returned home from ancient Babylon."

"My G-d!" declared the stunned voice of Captain Abram Yitzel. "There truly is a G-d!"

"Without a doubt!" an imperceptible response just beyond the human's protective cockpit windshield said.

The human pilots were correct in their assumption that they were somehow being divinely protected. Little did these mortals realize that from the very moment their eight aircraft left the protective borders of Israel, each of their jets were being accompanied by a team of two battle-ready warriors, charged by their commander, the Archangel Uriel, to keep their assigned pilot and aircraft safe from all harm during their journey over enemy territory.

"Nothing smells worse then the putrid stench left behind by the guts of a demon!" Brakiel declared. He was one of two angels assigned to accompany Captain Yitzel's aircraft.

Flying parallel to his angelic partner at supersonic speeds, Zohiel laughed as he watched Brakiel attempt to use the razor-sharp edge of his sword to scrap away the demonic entrails that had exploded all over his protective body armor.

"Sorry about that," chuckled his spotlessly clean, armor-clad partner. "It's too bad the aircraft's Trophy defense system doesn't have the capacity to destroy two demon missiles at one time."

"Laugh now," grumbled Brakiel, flinging the last vestiges of demon guts from the end of his sword into the surrounding darkness. "The very next demon sent hurling our way is all yours, Zohiel!"

"Brakiel, that may not be happening any time soon," said Zohiel with a confident stare.

"How can you be so sure of that?"

"Look behind you, my friend!"

Following Zohiel's simple instructions, Brakiel's lower jaw dropped as he turned to witness an astonishing sight in the darkened skies behind the aircraft.

"What are they doing?" the dumbfounded Brakiel asked as he stared in total disbelief at the unbelievable sight of millions of scaly-winged demons fleeing at supersonic speeds in the direction of the distant Iranian border.

"Zohiel, what do you make of that?"

"Praise be to God on High! Brakiel, look to the skies above and you will find your answer."

Once again, the angelic warrior's mouth opened wide as he gazed up at an awesome sight. As far as his highly perceptive eyes could see, from horizon to horizon, the darkened skies directly above his assigned aircraft were filled with countless numbers of his fellow warriors, pursuing the rapidly retreating demonic hordes with extended swords.

"Praise the Lord God Almighty!" Brakiel cheered, elated at the sight of the numerous puffs of orange-red sulfurous smoke exploding in the distance skies.

"Dani Boy, did you see that! There are explosions in back of us everywhere you look!"

"Someone out there is firing stinger missiles at the Iranian jets!" the transmitted voice of Captain Elon Kaufman exclaimed..

"Everyone, look at your radar screens!"

"My G-d, Dani!" Captain Nathan Greenspan declared. "Not only are the Iranian jets leaving Iraqi airspace, they are being pursued by hundreds of fighter jets."

"You guys seemed to have stirred up some kind of hornet's nest back there!"

"Captain Macmillan, is that you?"

"None other, Major Weisman! I hope you and your fellow Israeli pilots don't mind, but I've taken the liberty to invited a few of my American Air Force buddies stationed at Balad Air Base to come out here and assist you in clearing some very unwanted trespassers from the skies over southern Iraq."

A euphoric combined cheer from the voices of eight grateful Israeli F-16 pilots echoed throughout the cockpits of the more than four-dozen American fighter jets, presently pursuing the hostile aerial invaders back to their Iranian borders.

"Major Weisman, you may be happy to know we have also received a Pentagon directive straight from the desk of the president giving you and your pilots landing and refueling privileges at Balad Air Force Base."

"Captain Macmillan, I believe I can speak for my fellow pilots. Under any other circumstance, I wouldn't think twice about turning down such a generous offer, but more than anything else right now, we all want to go home."

"Major Weisman, correct me if I'm wrong, but according to my calculations, you guys should be flying on fumes right now."

"Rest assured, Captain Macmillan, not to discount your math, but we presently have more than enough fuel to get us all safely back home."

"How's that possible, Major?" Corrie Stokes asked. "An F-16 Falcon only has enough fuel capacity to fly no more than 1200 miles, and you guys have already surpassed that and more!"

"Captain, I can only answer your rational question with this irrational response – "With G-d, all things are possible!"

"Amen!" seven other Israeli voices shouted in humble unison.

"Amen!" an approving chorus composed of 16 angelic voices agreed.

Chapter Twenty-one

"For we know that all things work together for good to those who love God, to those who are called according to His purpose."

~Romans 8:28 NKJV

Tuesday, November 8th, 2016
12:56 a.m. Israeli Standard Time
Tel Nof Airbase
Rehovot, Israel

From the hills of Galilee to the north, Jerusalem to the east, and Tel Aviv along the coast, tonight of all nights, fear and anxiety ran rampant throughout all Israel. For the nearly eight million citizens who called the Jewish state their home, the inevitable had finally happened. Less than two hours ago, Prime Minister Yacov Ben Yizri, announced to the entire world that his nation had unilaterally carried out a daring mission deep inside enemy territory. Eight Israeli F-16 aircraft, each armed with a single bunker-busting bomb, had successfully targeted and destroyed four Iranian nuclear power plants scattered at various locations throughout the Islamic country. According to the prime minister's brief press release, his decision to order the bombings was based solely on Israeli intelligence reports presenting conclusive evidence that these four underground nuclear facilities had created enough weapon's grade nuclear material to produce at least a dozen nuclear bombs—more than enough needed to totally destroy Israel.

Tonight especially, anxiety ran exceedingly high for all those situated inside Tel Nof Airbase's control tower. With his nation on total lockdown, and his military on full standby alert, a nervous Yacov Ben Yizri paced back and forth across the control tower's floor, driven that moment by one singular concern—the fate of eight brave pilots.

"Eliana," Captain Eli Levitt whispered as he knelt at the side of his air traffic control specialist, "it's been over four hours. Shouldn't we have heard something from Major Weisman by now?"

Not wanting to bring any undue attention to her supervisor's concern, Lieutenant Greenfield leaned forward at her control station desk, making another attempt to contact the EZ 8:31 mission's lead pilot.

"EZ Bird 1, this is EZ Bird 8:31, do you copy?"

After making several more attempts to contact Major Weisman, Eliana Greenfield looked up to her boss and shook her head in frustration. With a solemn expression on his face, Captain Levitt turned his attention now to the middle-aged man, dressed in a dark business suit, staring in quiet solitude through the plate glass window at the darkened runway below.

"This is EZ Bird 1 contacting EZ Bird 8:31, do you copy EZ Bird 8:31, over?"

Completely astonished by what she just heard through her headsets, Eliana Greenfield immediately switched on the control tower's surround sound speaker system for all ears to hear.

"Come again, EZ Bird 1, what is your present location?"

"EZ Bird 8:31, my friends and I decided to scrub our original flight plan and follow the northern path taken three thousand years ago when the Prophet Ezra lead our people safely back home to Israel. Do you copy that, EZ Bird 8:31?"

Not a single dry eye could be found in the circular room filled from one end to the other with high-tech equipment. Except for

First Lieutenant Eliana Greenfield, everyone present inside the elevated glassed-in enclosure—other air traffic control personnel, high-ranking government officials and military brass—were now celebrating what they just heard with dancing, emotional hugs and hand slapping high-fives. Only one person present was recognizing the true source of today's modern miracle.

All eyes focused on this one man, his hands raised high above his head toward the ceiling. As the man started to pray, a strange silence returned to the glass-enclosed room.

"Adoni," he began, "my words are totally inadequate to express the gratitude that my heart wants to say to You. Thank you, Adoni, for this great victory that You alone have brought against your people's enemies. Thank you, Adoni, for bringing our eight pilots back home safe and unharmed. Adoni, please forgive me and Your people, Israel, for not trusting in You and honoring Your Holy Name."

With tears of humility streaming down his face, Yacov Ben Yizri ended his short, but powerful prayer with a simple, "Amen."

"Amen!" a chorus of agreeing voices shouted throughout the circular room.

"Amen!" said the Archangel Michael.

"Amen and Amen!" the Archangel Uriel reiterated.

Tuesday, November 6ᵗʰ
10:32 p.m. EST
Intensive Care Unit
Monongahela Valley Hospital
1163 Country Club Road
Monongahela, Pennsylvania

A broken man, who only weeks ago appeared destined to be elected President of the United States, stared aimlessly at an array of plastic tubing leading in and out of his wife's torn body.

Glancing at his wristwatch, his weary mind struggled hard to recall the last time he had any sleep. All he could remember was that it had been very early in the morning when a team of hospital nurses wheeled his unconscious wife into the same ICU room where he was now reclining on a very uncomfortable chair. From the moment the ICU nurses left Eliot Graham and his wife, Rosemary, alone in their semi-darkened room, Graham's eyes remained fixed on a metal box suspended from a pole to the right of his wife's hospital bed where illuminated rows of changing numbers displayed his wife's vital signs. From time-to-time, his thoroughly exhausted mind would entertain this one singular thought. *"Lord, search my heart. Let me know if there is anything found there that is not pleasing to you. Lord, I am willing to surrender everything I have, all of my worldly possessions. I am willing to to do anything you ask of me, just to have my wife, Rosemary, returned to me in complete health."*

Finally, the very moment sleep was about to overtake the vigilant Graham, a beaconing voice brought his wondering mind back to reality.

"Mr. Graham."

From his reclined position, Eliot Graham opened his eyes to the greeting smile of Hilda Graves, the nightshift ICU nurse assigned to care for the needs of his anesthetized wife.

"I'm so sorry to bother you, Mr. Graham, but Dr. Canady has ordered some more blood work on Mrs. Graham," she said with an expression of compassion. "Mr. Graham, why don't you take a break and visit your family in the waiting room? I'll stay with Mrs. Graham until you return."

Without saying word, Eliot rose, accepting the nurse's sincere offer with an affirming nod of appreciation. Before exiting the restricted confines of the small room, he bent low and affectionately kissed the cheek of his most precious earthly possession.

"I love you so much, Honey," he softly whispered into her ear. "Nurse Graves will take good care of you until I return."

Tuesday, November 6th
10:39 p.m. EST
Intensive Care Unit
Monongahela Valley Hospital
1163 Country Club Road
Monongahela, Pennsylvania

"Daddy!"

The silence was broken. Sleepy eyes opened and heads immediately turned in the direction of a screaming teary-eyed teenager whose arms were locked around her father. "How's Mommy? Is she going to be okay?

"Has she tried to open her eyes, Daddy?" his oldest daughter, Mary Elizabeth, questioned.

By now, the Graham family patriarch was completely surrounded on all sides by his seven children, all anxious to find out their mother's present condition.

"No," Graham calmly answered Mary Elizabeth. "Your mom's still sleeping."

"Dad, what are the doctors saying?"

Before Graham could respond to Nikki's question, an odd visual diverted his attention in the direction of a large, wall-mounted television located in the far back corner of the room. "What's going on, guys?" their highly intuitive father asked, his eyes totally captivated by the incredible images on the muted screen.

"Dad, we all decided not to alarm you," his eldest son, Eliot responded.

"That's right, Dad," William, his middle son, explained. "We figured you had more than enough to worry about just dealing with mom."

"What else should I be worrying about?"

"This is it," Eliot Jr. said as he stared intently into his father's puzzled eyes. "Sometime late last night, eight Israeli F-16 jets, armed with bunker-busting bombs, flew into Iran and took out four of their nuclear underground facilities."

"What? Have the Iranians retaliated against Israel?"

"Not as of yet!"

"What about Hezbollah or Hamas? Have they launched a missile attack against Israel?"

"There were some reports late last night about missiles fired across the Lebanese and Syrian border, and from the Gaza Strip," Graham Jr. replied, "but so far, Dad, I haven't heard of one single missile striking the ground anywhere in Israel."

"Praise God!"

"There's more good news, Dad! President Harris has ordered all branches of our American military, presently serving in the Middle East, to protect Israel from retaliation not only from Iran, but any Islamic regime in the area."

"Nikki, this is wonderful, almost too good to be true!"

"Are you all ready for some more good news?"

Everyone turned their full attention to an African-American man, dressed in green hospital scrubs, standing alone in the hallway just beyond the entrance to the IUC waiting room.

"As I said," Dr. Jerome Canady smiled, "are you ready for more good news? I want to give a good report to the family of Rosemary Graham."

"Did I hear the word, good news, just being mentioned?" a familiar voice from hallway just beyond the ICU waiting room, asked.

"Is that who I think it is?" a jubilant Jerry Banks questioned as he stepped out into the hallway to greet the smiling faces of his two pastors. "Mel, Ocie, your timing couldn't be more perfect!"

Once Ocie and Mel Hileman joined the ranks of the more than two-dozen members of Rosemary Graham's family in the 12 by 25 foot room, Dr. Canady proceeded with his big announcement. "Only moments ago, I received the results of Mrs. Graham's latest blood tests." Canady paused briefly, smiling broadly as everyone present took in a big breath of air. "I am both honored and extremely happy to tell you that every reading on Mrs. Graham's blood tests indicates absolutely no sign of cancer, and more importantly, Mrs. Graham, has once again, a perfectly functioning liver."

Instead of screams of elation and cheers of jubilation that accompanies hearing such wonderful news, the gifted oncology surgeon humbly stood in awe as he witnessed a room full of grateful Christians, their hands raised high above their heads, uttering heartfelt thanks and praises to the God who orchestrated this entire miraculous event. After allowing a few minutes for each person to give honor and glory to God, Pastor Mel felt led to say, "I feel the Lord's leading for everyone to join hands to pray and thank God corporately for this miracle."

The three formerly sleeping grandchildren were now wide-awake, joining their tiny hands in humble solidarity with their mommies and daddies as Pastor Hileman began to pray.

"Dear Heavenly Father,

Thank you…Thank you…Thank you! You are always faithful in hearing and answering the prayers of your children. You always stand by Your Word. In Romans 8:28, Your Word says, "*That all things work together for good to those who love God, to those who are called according to His purpose.*" Father, those of us gathered in this room are fully aware of who caused all of this to happen, but what the devil meant for evil, you meant for good. Thank you for selecting Dr. Jerome Canady for the awesome task of completely removing that hellish tumor from Rosemary's liver. Thank you, Jesus, for assisting this gifted doctor during the entire operation, guiding his hand the entire time as he removed every vestige of cancer from Rosemary Graham's body. Thank you for Rosemary Graham's speedy recovery. Again, dear Heavenly Father, all glory goes to You alone. We ask this all in the Name of Your Son and our Lord, Jesus Christ. Amen."

"Amen," everyone responded, including two imperceptible *angelic beings standing in the hall beyond the ICU waiting room.*

"I love watching happy endings," Muriel commented as he turned to his fellow Archangel companion.

"There are still a few more surprises awaiting Eliot Graham tonight," Yahriel said. "Just watch!"

"Look over here everybody! Holding the television remote, Graham's excited son-in-law, Cotty Ketterman, directed everyone's attention to the wall-mounted television. "Everybody listen! Keenan McShea's about to make a really big announcement."

Once again, the entire room became silent as the popular television personality stood center stage in the Fox Newsroom, ready to address millions of viewers with the second most talked about news item of the day. "Folks, throughout America today, the people have spoken." Looking down at a slip of paper just handed to him, Keenan McShea looked into the camera and smiled. "This is close, very close," he declared with raised eyebrows. "Here it is, folks! I have just received the unofficial results of today's presidential elections."

Everyone in the room held their breath as Keenan McShea announced the name of the third runner up. In third place, with 32% of the popular vote, the Republican Party's candidate for President of the United States, Robert Berry."

Eyes widened and jaws dropped. Everyone in the ICU waiting room was thinking the same thought: *Could it be possible? Even though Eliot Graham officially dropped out of the presidential race three weeks ago, was there still a chance that Eliot Graham could be elected president?*

"Folks, I have to admit," smiled the savvy reporter, "in all of my years of announcing election results, I have never seen anything like this.

Once again, everyone took a deep breath as McShea announced the name of America's next president and the second-place runner up. "In second place, with 32.5% of the popular vote, the American Value Party's candidate, Eliot Graham."

At least for one person in the room, a sense of true relief permeated every fiber of his being. "Thank you, Lord!" Eliot Graham declared out loud.

"And now," announced a more solemn faced Keenan McShea, "receiving 33% of the popular vote, not only elected as the next President of the United States, but also, more importantly as America' first elected woman president, Analise Devoe!"

With reality sinking in, everyone in this room filled with staunch conservatives stood in shock by the startling news that, at least for four more years, a devotedly progressive Democratic *president would once again be governing America.*

"I see that one person in the room was happy with the results," the Archangel Muriel commented. "What other surprise do you have in store for Mr. Eliot Graham?"

"The Lord has honored me with supplying the answer to his prayers," Yahriel announced with a beaming smile. "Here she comes now with the good news."

"Mr. Graham."

Turning in the direction of the beaconing call, Eliot Graham's face brightened at the appearance of Nurse Hilda Graves.

"Your lovely wife, Rosemary, awaits your presence."

"She's up?"

"More than that, Mr. Graham, she's asking for you."

Nothing more needed to be said. Without saying another word, Eliot Graham left his family and quickly exited the waiting room.

"Where did Daddy go?" Sydni asked, realizing that he had seemingly vanished out of thin air.

"I don't know! her stymied older sister, Nikki, replied. "He was just here a second ago!"

"The Lord is well pleased with you, Joveniel." the Archangel, Muriel commended.

"A job truly well done!" the Archangel, Yahriel said.

Bowing to his knees as a submissive act of loyalty to his commander, Muriel, Rosemary Graham's assigned guardian angel, received his recognition with a simple *"Thank you, Sir. I am honored serving under your command."*

"Arise, my friend," his commander ordered in a more serious tone. *"I have one last comment to give your before we part company."*

"Yes, Commander, I will be more than happy to receive your comment."

Winking in the direction of his angelic co-equal, Muriel smiled. *"Joveniel, you make an excellent female human nurse."*

"Yes, Commander," said the blushing angel. *"I receive that as a compliment."*

Epilogue

The wiles of devil have not only blinded the eyes of the world's lost masses, but most of Christendom as well. In light of the recent rise of worldwide terrorist attacks against the innocent, it's easy to blame Islam as the source of today's evil. It is also easy to place the blame for the world's countless woes on politics and politicians. Unless we, who call ourselves Christians, recognize and call out the true source of all evil, Satan's grip on America and the world will grow even stronger. In the end, our silence will be our nation's downfall.

Christians, wake up! Satan and his multitude of minions are your real enemies. The time for living his deceptive lifestyle of complacency and comfort is over. We are called by our Lord and Savior Jesus Christ to be the salt and light of this world. We are called to "Love the Lord your God with all your heart, with all your soul, and with all your mind and to love your neighbor as yourself." Now is the time for the true followers of Christ to rise up and lead this nation back to God and His Truth...our only hope...our only answer!

"Choose you this day whom ye will serve; ... but as for me and my house, we will serve the Lord" (Josh. 24:2, 15)

Neill G. Russell